3 4028 09215 8121
HARRIS COUNTY PUBLIC LIBRARY

Mystery Ross X
Ross, Kat
The Daemoniac

$12.99
ocn964953375

First edition.

DAEMONIAC

Kat Ross

FBI Anti-Piracy Warning: The unauthorized reproduction or distribution of a copyrighted work is illegal. Criminal copyright infringement, including infringement without monetary gain, is investigated by the FBI and is punishable by up to five years in federal prison and a fine of $250,000.

Advertencia Antipirateria del FBI: La reproducción o distribución no autorizada de una obra protegida por derechos de autor es ilegal. La infracción criminal de los derechos de autor, incluyendo la infracción sin lucro monetario, es investigada por el FBI y es castigable con pena de hasta cinco años en prisión federal y una multa de $250,000.

The Daemoniac
First Edition
Copyright © 2016 Kat Ross

All rights reserved. No part of this book may be used or reproduced in any manner whatsoever, including Internet usage, without written permission from the author.

This story is a work of fiction. References to real people, events, establishments, organizations, or locales are intended only to provide a sense of authenticity and are used fictitiously. All other characters, and all incidents and dialogue are drawn from the author's imagination and are not to be construed as real.

Cover design by Damonza

ISBN-13: 978-0-9972362-4-8

New York is a great secret, not only to those who have never seen it, but to the majority of its own citizens.

—James D. McCabe Jr., 1868

CHAPTER ONE

WHEN I THINK back on the grisly events of that summer, the first thing I remember is the heat. Spring was late and short, following on the heels of the worst blizzard New York City had ever seen. What began as a blustery March thunderstorm turned overnight to two feet of snow. The papers called it the Great White Hurricane. By the time we dug out, more than two hundred souls had perished, some with their frozen fingers sticking up pathetically from the mountainous drifts.

In typical New York fashion, just a few months later, we did nothing but complain of the humidity. By mid-June, the mercury had soared up to the nineties and lingered there, like a fat dowager in her favorite armchair. It was an evil sort of heat, driving men to beat their children and carriage horses to drop dead in their traces. We kept waiting for a rip-roaring thunderstorm that never arrived. The wealthy fled to mansions in Newport or Long Island's North Shore, while the thousands of wretchedly poor tenement dwellers resorted to sleeping on rooftops or even in the filthy streets in hopes of catching a stray breeze.

Being somewhere in the middle of those two extremes, I opted for an iced tea and open window. Which is how, on

Thursday the ninth of August, 1888, just three weeks before the Ripper began his reign of terror in London, I came to see a young couple walking slowly down West Tenth Street, eyeing the house numbers as they went. The woman looked wilted in a long-sleeved striped gown over petticoat, knickers, chemise and bustle. Her husband was blonde and clean-shaven, with hair neatly parted on the side and the erect bearing of a military man.

"New clients," I said.

"Really… "

"You're not listening, John."

"Sorry!" He looked up from a thick medical textbook and grinned. "Clients. New ones. Too bad Myrtle isn't home. You'll have to send them on their way."

"It was the wife's idea to come," I said, following their progress with interest. They had paused in front of number fifty-one, better known as the Tenth Street Studios, a sprawling work and exhibition space that had helped turn once sleepy Greenwich Village into a mecca of the city's art world. "He's reluctant. In fact, he's very close to scrapping the whole idea. They're arguing about it now. Let's see… He was definitely in the army at some point, but he's in civilian clothing with a respectable paunch so most likely discharged. Far too young to have been in the war. Aha! They're crossing the street now."

The townhouse where I lived with my sister Myrtle was situated at 40 West Tenth Street, between Fifth and Sixth Avenues. Myrtle was seven years my senior, and our parents had left her in charge while they gallivanted around Europe on an extended tour. Their trust was well-intentioned, if misplaced. Within a fortnight, Myrtle had gone haring off on a mysterious assignment for the Pinkerton detective agency, and life since then had been very dull.

Normally, I relied on John Weston, my closest friend since we were both children, to keep me company. But he had just enrolled at Columbia's College of Physicians and Surgeons, and now his nose was stuck in a book more often than not. Frankly, I was bored silly.

"Let's just hear them out," I suggested.

John looked up, a lock of straight brown hair falling across his forehead in a way that certain girls of our acquaintance seemed to find irresistible. Not that the attention went to John's head. Overly.

"What do you mean?" he said, eyes glinting with mischief. "Why, Harry, are you suggesting we *lie*—"

"Of course not," I replied primly. "It's probably some trifling matter anyhow. But I can at least do them the courtesy of relaying the facts of the case to Myrtle when she returns." I sighed. "Whenever that is."

John shrugged his heavy shoulders. "Alright," he said, laying aside a well-thumbed copy of *Gray's Anatomy*. "I suppose I could use a break. It's like learning a foreign language." He squinted at me. "Now you, Harry, have a lovely skull. Phenomenal supraorbital development—"

"And there's the front doorbell."

I jumped to my feet, pulse quickening. Moments later, a knock came on the parlor door. I hastily arranged myself in an armchair near the cold hearth and rested my chin on one hand.

"Come in!"

The door flew open, revealing Mrs. Rivers, our housekeeper, and just behind her, the man and woman from the street. He looked flushed and uncertain, she grim and determined.

"Are you Miss Fearing Pell?" the man asked doubtfully.

"Oh yes, she most certainly is," Mrs. Rivers said, beaming.

It's one of the reasons I loved the dear, dotty old creature. She never seemed to realize that when callers asked for Miss Pell, it was *never, ever* me they wanted.

"Please make yourselves comfortable," I said, gesturing to the sofa. John gathered up his textbooks and piled them on an end table as Mrs. Rivers retreated back downstairs, shutting the door discreetly behind her. "This is my associate, Mr. Weston. I can assure you, anything you say will be held in the strictest confidence. Although I should explain that—"

"Yes, yes, I know, your services are in great demand. But we have nowhere else to turn." An edge of desperation crept into the man's voice. "Nowhere."

"You misunderstand," I said firmly. "What I mean is that—"

"Your fee is not an issue," he cut in, taking a handkerchief out of his waistcoat pocket and mopping his forehead. He had pale blue eyes and prominent ears that made him look boyish, though I placed his age somewhere in the late twenties. "But I must be assured of complete discretion. Miss Pell, the story I wish to tell you could destroy a man's reputation if it ever got out. Two men, since I ought to include myself."

This was the point at which I should have stated plainly that I was not, in fact, Myrtle Fearing Pell, the Great Detective, but her nineteen-year-old sister. I'm still not sure what possessed me. But I was intrigued. And they seemed like good people in dire need of aid. I didn't have the heart to send them away empty-handed. What happened next was impulsive and foolish, but then I've never been lacking in either of those qualities.

"You have my word," I said, looking at John.

"Mine as well," my friend added, and he had such an open

and honest face that I could see our visitors relax their guard a little. "And actually, it's *Doctor* Weston."

He flashed a bland smile that dared me to contradict this claim. Well, if I was getting a promotion, I guess John deserved one too.

I walked to the sideboard and started pouring glasses of iced tea. "Doctor?" I inquired sweetly, holding one up.

John demurred.

"Please," I said, pressing refreshments into the hands of our guests. "The heat's enough to drive one mad."

The wife looked at me sharply at this, but she accepted and took a tiny sip. "Tell them, Leland," she murmured.

Her husband seemed to gird himself for a very unpleasant task. He drew in a deep breath, eyes darting around the room as if searching for some kind of deliverance. He opened his mouth, then closed it again without speaking.

"Just start from the beginning," I said gently.

He nodded once. Cleared his throat and placed the tea on the table. "My name is Leland Brady. For the last two years, I've worked as a real estate agent at the firm of Harding & White on Maiden Lane. My wife Elizabeth and I live in Hastings-on-Hudson."

"The village in Westchester?"

"Yes. We grew up there." He glanced at Elizabeth. "Along with our dear friend, Robert Aaron Straker." He paused. "It is Robert that brings me here, you see. He has vanished."

"Please go on," I said, steepling my fingers the way I'd seen Myrtle do it.

"Pardon me," Brady suddenly exclaimed, "but you look awfully young! Are you really twenty-six years old? They say you've solved cases the police deemed hopeless. The mad chemist who poisoned those schoolchildren... the Bowery bank robberies… I'd never fathom such a thing, a little girl—" He seemed to catch himself and had the decency to look slightly abashed.

I swallowed and dropped my eyelids to half-mast. I supposed there was no turning back now. "Indeed, Mr. Brady. I have consulted with the police force on occasion when they were hard-pressed to cope with crimes beyond the scope of mundane experience. But I remain an independent consultant, at liberty to pick and choose those cases that offer unique or outré features that interest me." I could do Myrtle in my sleep. "Perhaps you would best be served by filing a report at the Bureau for the Recovery of Lost Persons."

Located at Police Headquarters on Mulberry Street, the Bureau handled some seven hundred missing persons cases a year. Each day, the descriptions of the lost would be checked against the returns of the morgue. It was a sad catalogue of suicides, murder victims and, in even greater numbers, those whose fates would forever remain a mystery.

But Brady shook his head vehemently at this suggestion. "No, I don't wish to involve the authorities, not yet. That is absolutely essential. Not until all other avenues are exhausted. And if it is outré that you seek, then what occurred four days ago will certainly fit the bill!"

"Pray continue then," I said.

He nodded. "First, I must tell you a bit about Robert. He's always been impetuous and headstrong, a dreamer who imagined that he would strike it rich someday. Robert was orphaned at a young age. My family took him in, and we became like brothers. We were country boys, Miss Pell, and keen for adventure. When we were both eighteen, Robert talked me into enlisting and we joined the Army on the Frontier." Brady rummaged through his pockets and produced a photograph, which he handed to me. It showed two federal soldiers, one of whom was clearly Brady, the other a darkly handsome young man with a mustache and thick black hair. They stood side by side against a dramatic backdrop of open prairie, with snow-capped mountains in the distance.

"This was taken three years ago in Wyoming. We had been called out to restore order in the town of Rock Springs after the rioting there."

"You refer to the massacre of twenty-eight Chinese miners by their white counterparts," I said.

The episode was one of the more shameful ones in the long history of simmering racial tensions in the Western states, where immigrant laborers—both Chinese and European—formed the backbone of the Union Pacific Railroad's operations.

"Yes. Our orders were to escort the survivors from Evanston back to their homes." Brady's expression grew troubled. "We arrived a week after the violence. There were still bodies lying in the streets. Some had been burned. Others appeared to have been literally torn apart. Many of our fellow soldiers didn't seem too bothered, but Robert was quite affected by it."

"A decent man, then," John said quietly, but with force. He despised bigots of all stripes.

"Yes, despite his failings, Robert was always kind-hearted. Which makes what occurred later even more inexplicable." Brady took Elizabeth's hand. An attractive woman with a strong jaw and piercing, intelligent hazel eyes, she nodded encouragingly. "Rock Springs soured us both on army life, and neither of us reenlisted when our tour was finished. We returned to Hastings, where I asked for Elizabeth's hand and she happily obliged." They exchanged a quick smile. "Robert served as the best man at our wedding. Thanks to a family connection, I managed to secure a position with my current employer. The future appeared bright. Robert's parents had left him a small but adequate sum with which to make his way in the world. As a single man with no pressing attachments, he decided to take lodgings in the city and seek his fortune here. I suppose it was inevitable that between the duties of domestic life and my new position, which entails long hours and frequent travel throughout Manhattan, we fell out of touch. A year or so passed, in which I scarcely heard a word from my old friend. Until two weeks ago, when he arrived unannounced at my office on Maiden Lane.

"I'll be honest, Miss Pell, I was shocked at Robert's appearance. He had lost a good deal of weight, and his clothes were ill-fitting and shabby. His cheeks had become as hollow and sunken as an old man's. There was a pathetic tremor in his hands that spoke of heavy drinking. I didn't wish to embarrass him by drawing attention to the fact that he had fallen on hard times, for Robert was prideful. But I insisted on taking him out to lunch, and he finally relented. At first we spoke of small, inconsequential matters, as old friends do. He inquired after Elizabeth, of whom he was always quite fond. But after a while, I steered the conversation around to what he had been up to since leaving Hastings. Robert was cagey, but I persisted in my questioning and eventually got it all out of him." Brady picked up the glass of iced tea, turning it round and round in his hands without taking a sip. "It seems that within just a few months of his arrival, Robert had managed to squander his modest inheritance on a series of failed business ventures. He was forced to abandon lodgings in a respectable part of town and move to a flat on Leonard Street in the Five Points, that squalid little patch of earth where it seems even the Almighty has turned away His face in shame."

I looked over at John, who had a soft streak and was clearly moved by the story. Mr. Straker had indeed fallen far. It was no exaggeration to say that the Five Points, bounded by Anthony, Cross and Orange Streets on the Lower East Side, was the most notorious slum in America, and possibly the world. It had even managed to thoroughly shock Mr. Charles Dickens, that hardened chronicler of social ills, when he visited in 1842 accompanied by two policemen, and the place had scarcely improved since. It was claimed that a single tenement, the Old Brewery, saw a murder a night for fifteen years running.

"You might wonder why Robert didn't simply concede that his gamble had fallen flat and return to his hometown, where my wife and I would have been more than happy to take him in until he got back on his feet," Brady continued. "His was a story all too typical of this city, where vast fortunes are won and lost on an hourly basis. There was no shame in it."

"New York is most effective at taking the conceit out of a man," John agreed wryly.

"But as I mentioned before, Robert was prideful, excessively so. He couldn't bear the thought of others knowing his defeat. And so he had clung on to what seemed barely a life, hoping for some miracle to occur that would provide his salvation." Brady sighed.

"And did he find it?" I asked.

Brady gave me an even look. "He found something, but it was not salvation. Quite the opposite, Miss Pell."

At this point, Brady turned his palms up beseechingly, looking in turn from John to me as though seeking absolution himself. "You must understand, all that I did, I did at Robert's request. For it seems that his visit to my office that day had an ulterior motive. It is not my habit to drink spirits during working hours, but Robert ordered brandy after the meal and I could hardly refuse to join him. To be honest, I felt in need of a stiff jolt myself. When he asked for a favor, I assumed he wanted a loan. I told him I would be happy to give him as much as my modest income allowed. Robert appeared offended at this. He said he didn't need my money, but rather my assistance with a delicate business matter. I must admit, I groaned inwardly at this, imagining that he wished me to invest in yet another hare-brained scheme, or worse, take advantage of my employer in some way. I expressed my reservations and Robert laughed long and hard, as though he found it terribly funny. It was quite irritating. I was on the verge of paying the check and leaving when his demeanor became quite serious again. There was a wild, desperate light in his eyes. He insisted that what he asked of me would in no way compromise my honor, nor would it strain my purse. I had only to meet him at a certain address the following evening at eleven o'clock. He said an opportunity had presented itself to turn his ill-fortune around."

"The salvation he had been waiting for," I murmured.

"Precisely. I could see he was extremely excited and attempting to suppress it. What could I do but agree? Of course, when he gave me the address, I almost changed my mind. It was near to Robert's rooms, an infamous alley of brothels and disorderly houses." Brady suddenly seized a chunk of his own hair in a paroxysm of guilt and regret. "Would that I had followed my own instincts and turned him down then! None of it might have happened!"

Elizabeth made a small noise and took her husband's hand in her own delicate, small-boned ones. John and I waited awkwardly while Brady composed himself.

"I asked Robert what sort of legitimate business

transaction he could possibly conduct in such a place, at such an hour. Why, we'd be lucky if we weren't both murdered for the boots on our feet! Robert responded that he was aware of the dangers and that is why he did not wish to go alone, but he would if he had to. He was very composed and resolute as he told me that he understood perfectly if I declined and would not hold it against our friendship. Oh, he had me over a barrel, Miss Pell. As I said, I have no other siblings, and Robert occupied the place of a brother to me, despite our recent estrangement. As long as it would not impinge on my own honor, I could hardly see my way to refuse him anything. I told him I would be there, along with a pistol I often carried when passing through less savory portions of the city.

"Once I acquiesced, he seemed to relax and his demeanor changed yet again. He became quite chatty, almost grandiose, and confessed that he had by chance made the acquaintance of a medium who hinted that she was privy to some occult ritual which would bring untold wealth to those who performed it to the letter. He pretended to find the whole thing amusing, but I could see he had fallen entirely under her spell. I reminded him that such women were famous for luring the unwary into traps whereby their confederates would first rob and then slit the throat of their victim, discarding the body in the nearest river. He responded that that was why he preferred not to go alone. I could see that it was hopeless to dissuade him, so we agreed to meet the following evening and parted ways. I must say, I felt my own good fortune most keenly that night," Brady added, looking with quiet but profound adoration at his wife. "Seeing Robert penniless and alone… Well, it made me view my own circumstances with fresh eyes."

Elizabeth spoke up for the first time. She had a pleasant contralto and firm, confident manner that I admired. "Leland confided in me what had occurred that day. Perhaps another woman would have begged her husband not to keep such a sordid appointment, but Robert is like a brother to me also." Her eyes flashed. "And I have the utmost confidence in my husband's abilities. I bade him to go, and to keep both of them safe."

I sensed that we were approaching the crux of the matter and said nothing, waiting patiently for Brady to resume his narrative.

"At the appointed hour, I found my way to the address Robert gave me," he said. "It was a grim dwelling, even by the low standards of the neighborhood. A gang of vile-looking youths lounged on the corner, but I gave them a glimpse of my pistol and they turned their attentions elsewhere. Robert was waiting for me in the doorway. He led me down a flight of narrow, pitch-black stairs to the lowest level of the tenement, a dungeon with only thin slits at street level to admit fresh air from the outside, if the air in that pestilential place could be called fresh." Brady's mouth twisted in distaste. "I'd heard tell of such hells, but to actually stand in one, amid the damp and the stench… It had rained heavily the night before, and there was a stagnant pool of water on the floor. It soaked right through my shoes. Well, I came close to turning tail and running, and I'm not ashamed to admit it. Robert must have sensed me quail, for he laid a steadying hand on my sleeve. And then a candle flickered to life. It was the medium."

"Did you catch her name?" I asked.

"Santi, she called herself. Madame Catarina Santi. A battered wooden table and three chairs had been placed in the center of the room. She told us to sit down. I just wanted to get the whole thing over with, so I obliged. I suppose I expected some knocking about of the table, moaning noises, the usual chicanery of her profession. The woman, Santi, took out a book and began reading from it. I can hardly remember a word now, but it seemed perfect nonsense at the time. I nearly laughed, for she was so drunk, she could hardly form a coherent sentence." Brady swallowed. "My amusement soon turned to disgust when she suddenly produced a rooster, I know not from where, and proceeded to tear it apart with her bare hands. The table was awash with blood and feathers. I looked at Robert and saw that he was as shocked as I at this savage turn of events. I was rising from my chair to leave when a foul wind extinguished the candles." Brady paused and gave John and me a level look. "You may decide for yourselves whether to believe the final part of my story. All I can say, and my wife will attest to it, is that I have never been a man of vivid imagination. I always thought the Spiritualist rage to be a load of bunkum."

"And you've revised your opinion?" John asked eagerly.

Brady didn't answer right away. Finally, he sighed. "I don't know. I can only tell you what I saw and heard that night. Robert was to my right. He cried out once and then went still. I cannot explain the wind since as I said, the only air came through mere slits in the wall, but I would swear to it on my life. It had a faint smell of sulphur or creosote." He stopped talking abruptly and placed the glass of iced tea back on the table.

"What happened next?" I asked.

"I felt a… presence in the room. A subtle displacement of the atmosphere. Santi screamed for us to close our eyes. She was quite hysterical."

"I thought the room was dark," I said.

"It was. I didn't understand what she meant. But I did it anyway. Some small voice inside told me that as pointless as it seemed, it would be wise to listen."

John was fairly falling off the edge of his seat at this point. He believed in *everything,* the more mystical and macabre, the better.

"What do you mean by a presence?" he asked.

"I mean that we were not alone in that room," Brady snapped. "I don't know who it was, *what* it was. But the hair on the back of my neck stood straight up, and every primal instinct screamed *run, you fool, run.*" He visibly collected himself. "It seemed to go on for hours, but I think it was only a few minutes. Finally, the wind died and I heard Santi fumbling around for the matches. I realized that I had my hands pressed tightly against my face and let them go. I had not even been aware of it. She relit the candles. All appeared to be the same. I won't say normal, as she was stained with gore down the front of her dress, but I could detect no difference in the room. *Please leave now,* she told us, and I was more than happy to comply. Robert was staring into space with a vacant look on his face so I shook him until he came back to his senses. I put an arm around his shoulders and led him out of that loathsome place, up the stairs and onto the street. Oh, to see the stars again! It was like emerging from a tomb. I looked at my pocket watch and was surprised to see it was only just past midnight. Of course, it was too late to catch a train home to Westchester, so I escorted Robert to his flat and then I returned to Maiden Lane, where I spent the night on a couch in my office."

"Did you discuss what had happened?" I asked.

"Not then. Robert barely spoke a word, except to thank me for accompanying him. He was quite subdued. My mind was still reeling from the strange things I had experienced, and I had no wish to speak of them either. I kept thinking that it must have been a hoax, albeit a rather frightening one. By the next day, as I ventured into the sunshine for a strong cup of coffee, the whole thing seemed like a bad dream. However, I feared for Robert's state of mind. I knew he had put all his hopes in it, and those hopes would now be dashed. So I went back to call on him."

"And found him gone?" John interjected.

"No, he was at home. But he was very agitated. Robert was normally a man of calm, level-headed disposition, except for his poor judgment in business matters. We had been through a good deal together, in the army and as young men with a thirst for adventure. He was just the sort of fellow you would wish to have at your side when the seas got rough. But that morning... I scarcely recognized him. All the blinds were drawn tight and there was an unpleasant, close odor to the room. When I tried to open a window, he stopped me, almost violently. He was ranting."

"About something in particular?" I asked.

"Yes. He kept saying that 'it is loosed' and seemed to be under the delusion that something was stalking him. He blamed Santi. I tried to persuade him to come home with me, but he declined. He said he didn't want to put Elizabeth in jeopardy. I could hardly make heads or tails of his tirade."

"Are you certain he said *it?*" I said. "That he wasn't referring to a person?"

"I'm certain. It struck me at the time as odd. He also said, 'It comes through the eyes.' He was looking at himself in a shaving mirror as he said this. I came forward and laid a hand on his shoulder but he shook it off. I asked him what he meant, but he refused to elaborate. I was anxious to get home and reassure my wife that I was fine, so when it became clear that Robert would not come with me, I left. That was the last time I saw him." Brady put a hand to his forehead and rubbed it wearily. "I returned the following day, determined to make him see reason. Clearly, he was unwell. I knocked, but he failed to answer. I have returned thrice more, to no avail."

Brady trailed off, as though reluctant to continue. Elizabeth's hands were clasped so tightly, the knuckles had turned white.

"John," I said quietly. "Would you fetch Tuesday's papers?"

He gave me a confused sort of look but complied. Brady and his wife sat on the sofa, stone-faced, while I picked the *World* off the pile and opened it to page four.

"I believe I know why you're here," I said. "Madame Santi's real name was Becky Rickard, was it not?"

Brady didn't respond, but the look he gave me was an answer in itself.

"It seems she was a well-known spiritualist who had suffered public humiliation when her tricks were revealed," I said, scanning the brief article. "Her clientele abandoned her and she disappeared. This was about six months ago. We know where she ended up. She was like your friend, Mr. Straker. One may ascend to great heights in this city, but lose your grip on the rungs and the fall will be steep and swift."

John tentatively raised a finger. "Pardon, but did you say *was?*"

I tossed the paper on the table so he could see the headline. "Yes. Someone stabbed her to death three days ago."

CHAPTER TWO

J OHN SNATCHED UP the paper and began devouring the gory details, at least, those few the reporter had managed to coax out of the police. The murder was described as "savage" and "brutal," although the article glossed over the specifics. Most of it was devoted to breathlessly recalling Becky Rickard's earlier career as a darling of New York Society and her plunge into destitute anonymity when two of the Fox sisters of Rochester in upstate New York—virtual founders of the Spiritualism movement—had admitted that the mysterious rapping sounds they had long claimed were messages from beyond the grave were actually Margaret cracking her toe joints. As their protégé, Becky, who then called herself Valentina von Linden, was equally tarred with the brush of fraud and disgrace.

The article was accompanied by a sketched portrait of a blonde woman with very large eyes and a small, petulant mouth. It claimed the "fiend" had "mutilated her beauty" in some way. The police had no suspects.

Myrtle always said that a good detective ought to familiarize herself with the criminal mind, for there is nothing new under the sun that hasn't been done already. For this reason, she had all the papers delivered every day. She would lounge around in her dressing gown and scan their pages for potentially intriguing cases, filing it all away in her photographic memory. I did my best to imitate this habit, and recalled the Rickard murder well, as it was only a few days past.

The *World* reported that she had been discovered in her flat on Baxter Street above the Bottle Alley Saloon, after a neighbor reported a foul odor. Apparently, the windows of the single room had been sealed and the extreme heat had hastened decomposition. Robbery was ruled out as a motive, since a gold locket was found with the body, along with two hundred dollars in a purse on the bed.

"Ms. Rickard was killed on Sunday, or more accurately the early hours of Monday, sometime after your encounter with her," I said. "The large sum of money is certainly worth noting. Did you or Mr. Straker pay for her services?"

"Absolutely not!" Brady rejoined. "And Robert barely had two cents to rub together."

"She must have just come into it then. It could be a coincidence. Or not."

Brady stood and paced to the window, where he stood with his back to us, arms rigidly clasped behind him. That left me and Elizabeth, who leaned forward entreatingly.

"Please, Miss Pell, I beg you: reserve judgment until all the facts have been gathered. You don't know Robert like I do. Lord knows he has his faults, but he is incapable of such a crime. It is simply not within his character, even if he has become... unhinged. And I worry that if the killer is still out there, Robert's own life could be in danger!" She lowered her voice a notch. "It is I who talked Leland into coming here. He has been in an agony of indecision. If we go to the police and wind of my husband's involvement reaches his employers, he would almost certainly lose his position. Robert's name would be dragged through the mud however it turns out. And there's not a shred of real evidence linking him to the murder."

"That you know of," I said.

She shrugged this off. "I'm aware of your reputation. That you take cases which seem on their face to be… bizarre… and unravel the truth. Perhaps it is women's intuition—"

"I prefer the term logical deduction," I said.

Elizabeth gave me a small smile. "Indeed, I apologize. But I think what you do is *wonderful*. Please, Miss Pell. Robert is an orphan, without family to aid him. There is, quite literally, no one else we can turn to."

"Do you believe your husband's story?" I asked.

"I believe *he* believes it," she responded.

Privately, I agreed. When Brady had rubbed his forehead, it caused his coat sleeve to brush against his hair, picking up a small amount of pomade. In fact, the sleeve had a significant stain, only slightly darker than the fabric's regular color but visible to a keen observer, indicating that he had performed this anxious gesture numerous times in recent days. He had also neglected to clean his boots, and a small white chicken feather adhered to the left sole.

Elizabeth and I looked at each other for a long moment. A rush of nervous excitement coursed through me. I could say no and send them on their way. It would certainly be the wiser course of action. The truth is I *wasn't* Myrtle. I lacked her contacts, in both the police force and criminal underworld. I was still quite young and frankly, I looked it. It was a measure of the Bradys' desperation that they believed otherwise. I supposed they wanted to believe.

I'd have to be mad to even consider taking on this case.

"My fee is payable only upon a successful conclusion, but

I may require reimbursement of expenses during the investigation," I heard myself say.

"Oh yes, that is perfectly acceptable," Elizabeth said, eyes shining. "Thank you, Miss Pell!"

"You won't thank me if I find your friend is indeed a murderer. And we must be clear on the terms. If I uncover evidence proving his guilt, I will take it to the police."

"Agreed," she said. "I only ask that you look into the matter for one week. After that, if it remains unresolved, we will break our silence to the authorities, for what it's worth."

"I think that's fair," I said. "Can I keep the photograph of Mr. Straker? I may need to show it around."

"Of course. I'll get it from Leland right now."

Elizabeth ran over to the window to inform her husband they were now officially my clients, as John finished the article and started sifting through the papers to see if he could glean any additional details from the coverage.

"So they hired you," he said under his breath. "Are you sure you know what you're doing, Harry?"

"No," I said. "Quite the opposite."

John shook his head. He'd willingly gone along with more than one hare-brained scheme—if he wasn't the one who'd hatched it himself. Still, this was another league entirely. I wondered, not for the last time, what I'd gotten myself into. If Myrtle found out…

Brady strode over and shook my hand and then John's hand, expressing his gratitude, and I thought I'd better buckle down and think about how to start.

"I'll need to see Mr. Straker's rooms immediately," I said. "Who knows? He could have returned."

"I already hunted down his landlord," Brady said. "A sour, pinch-faced man, he wouldn't give me the time of day until

I said I would pay all of Robert's back rent plus two weeks ahead. The greedy fellow quite lit up at that." He frowned. "It's an outrage what they charge for such squalid lodgings. In any event, I insisted that he give me a key." He patted his pocket. "I'll admit, I haven't gone yet. I was hoping you'd accompany me, Miss Pell. And you too, Dr. Weston. I suppose I'm more than a little afraid of what we might find."

John agreed immediately. He had boxed and wrestled through high school and was physically fearless. I had seen him best men twice his age at the club where he trained.

"Would an hour from now suit you?" I said. "We can meet there, if you'll give me the address."

Brady scribbled it on a scrap of paper, and John escorted him and Elizabeth to the front door. He returned a few moments later with a thoughtful look on his face.

"What do you make of it, Harry?" he asked.

I should mention that my Christian name is actually Harrison, after a paternal grandfather, although no one calls me that except for my mother, and then only when she is very cross.

"It's too early to form an opinion," I said. "We must see his rooms, and then we must learn everything about the Rickard killing, including those facts that have not been published in the papers."

"And how are we going to do that?"

"I'm working on it." I returned to the window seat and flopped down, hoping vainly for a breeze. "I suppose you believe Straker was possessed by some sort of demonic entity that turned him into a homicidal maniac."

"Well, it did cross my mind," John replied. "If you want to work for the S.P.R., you'd better open yours a little."

The S.P.R., or Society for Psychical Research, had been

founded in 1882 to investigate paranormal phenomena. Its stated mission was "to approach these varied problems without prejudice or prepossession of any kind, and in the same spirit of exact and unimpassioned enquiry which has enabled science to solve so many problems, once not less obscure nor less hotly debated."

In other words, its membership was comprised of both adamant skeptics, like myself, and fervent believers, like John. My Uncle Arthur had just joined the year before. He tended toward the latter, and was also a member of the venerable Ghost Club, which, unlike the S.P.R., subscribed wholeheartedly to the occult.

Both entities were based in London, but the Society had agents across the Atlantic. They investigated apparitions, clairvoyance, precognitive dreams, thought-reading, hauntings, mesmerism and more or less anything that seemed to defy the laws of known science. Much of it involved exposing clever fakes. The job required wit, subtlety, nerves of steel, and a firm grip on sanity. John knew I wanted nothing more in life than to work for them someday. But first I would have to prove I had what it takes.

And this case could be just the way to do it.

"I'm not jumping to any conclusions," I said, reciting Myrtle's mantra. "One must never make the facts fit the theory but rather vice versa. Clearly, Straker had been under a great deal of pressure for a long time. It's hardly unthinkable that he snapped. He could easily have gone back to Rickard's flat that night. But why?"

John shrugged. "Revenge? Brady said he seemed to blame her for his predicament."

"Maybe. The violent nature of the attack does seem personal. Whoever the killer was, they were full of rage." I picked up the *World* and scanned its pages. "Oh, Edward's in the society column again for some stunt at Saratoga Springs. They crowned him King of the Dudes."

"Again?" John asked, rolling his eyes.

"Again." The first occasion had been during the height of the March blizzard, when he strolled into a bar wearing patent leather boots that went up to his hips. "Apparently, he changed clothes forty times in a single day at the racetrack. That's got to be a new record, even for Edward."

I tossed the article to John and quickly sorted through the rest of the papers. *The New York Times* complained of "filthy Europeans" taking the garment factory jobs of "American working girls" (who themselves earned about three dollars a week), while on the same page it reported that a tenement fire had killed a family of eight.

The Herald devoted half a page to a grocer who had murdered his partner and chopped the body up, stuffed the pieces into a set of luggage, and dumped them at Grand Central Depot.

I returned to the *New York World*, which seemed to have the heaviest coverage of the Rickard killing, when my eye caught on a familiar byline and inspiration struck. "Paper and ink, John! I need to send a message."

I dashed off a note and left it for Connor, a street urchin in my sister's employ. A boy of somewhere between eight and eleven (I think even he was unsure), Connor was the nominal leader of the fearsome-sounding Bank Street Butchers, although in reality they were far tamer than the other gangs that roamed the city's streets, limiting their activities mainly to pickpocketing the elderly and infirm.

Connor would be an invaluable ally, I decided. He was

a perfect mercenary, and I doubted he would care about my impersonation as long as I paid him more than Myrtle did.

"Who's that to?" John said, trying to read over my shoulder.

"You'll see," I said, swatting him away. "Now, I think it's time we went to 91 Leonard Street. Our client will be waiting."

We hailed a hansom cab on Fifth Avenue and proceeded three blocks downtown to Washington Square Park, where we turned east toward Broadway, passing the elegant marble-fronted St. Nicholas Hotel and Theatre Comique. It was still morning, so the great mass of streetcars and wagons and horses and omnibuses was mostly flowing south. Every now and then, the whole thing would become hopelessly tangled up, and police would rush in to redirect traffic around whatever obstacle had presented itself. If you wished to cross the avenue on foot during rush hour, that was your chance to do it. Otherwise, it was a certain suicide mission.

At the intersection of Broadway and White, just a few short blocks from City Hall, we turned left towards Baxter Street. It is a true cliché that only in New York can one go from opulence and bustle to pure, undiluted misery in a matter of seconds. The buildings seemed to sag and lean against each other in weariness, as though moments away from collapsing completely. In the August heat, the stench was indescribable. This was the heart of the Five Points, whose gloomy, crooked streets housed thousands of families, mostly blacks and Irish immigrants. I asked the driver to slow as we passed the former dwelling place of Becky Rickard. It was above a hole-in-the-wall "distillery" that was already open for business at this early hour. The building was a two-story wooden shanty, and a "room to let" sign had already been placed in the upstairs window.

"We should find out if someone requested the body, or if she was sent to Potter's Field," John said.

Those whose families couldn't afford a burial were sent to the paupers' cemetery on Ward's Island, separated from nearby Randall's Island by a treacherous channel aptly called Little Hell's Gate. Its forty-five acres contained hundreds of thousands of corpses. Those who could be identified were packed into mass graves, while nameless souls got their own bit of dirt, so they could be dug up if anyone ever came forward to claim them.

"We need to interview any relatives we can find," I agreed. "They might know where the money came from. And if she had any enemies."

Straker's Leonard Street digs were just around the corner. Number ninety-one was a faded red-brick building in marginally better shape than its neighbors. A trio of grubby, barefoot boys played on a pile of rubble out front, while a woman with a youthful body and hard, wizened face hung washing up to dry. Flies buzzed around a dead horse that lay ignored in the gutter a few feet away, its body little more than skin and bones.

John paid the hansom driver, who cracked his whip and headed back in the direction of Broadway as fast as he could go. The children gawked at us as we entered the building but no one made a move to block our way. The heyday of truly vicious gangs like the Dead Rabbits had ended a decade before, although even the police still hesitated to enter certain parts of the Five Points, like the notorious Bandit's Roost.

We ascended a set of rickety stairs to the third floor and found Brady waiting on the landing. He was sweating profusely in the airless shaft and looked relieved to see us.

"The family across the hall hasn't seen Robert since

Monday morning," he said by way of greeting. "I gave them a few dollars for their cooperation. You wouldn't believe how many people are living over there." He produced a key and took in a shaky breath. "I don't suppose I can put this off any longer. I just pray that Robert hasn't... " Brady trailed off.

I shared a look with John. We both understood there was a good possibility that Straker had taken his own life in a fit of remorse, or fear of the gallows (the electric chair at New York's Auburn Prison would get its first customer, a hatchet-murderer, almost exactly one year later). As a medical student at Columbia, John had seen his share of bodies. Myrtle, no stranger to the morgue, delighted in lecturing me on the various aspects of death by fire or water or the hand of one's fellow man. But I'd never seen it up close before. I just hoped I wouldn't faint or otherwise embarrass myself.

Brady turned the key in the lock and pushed the door open. We all stood there silently for a moment taking in the scene. John, for whom action came as naturally as breathing, was the first to enter.

The room was small, illuminated only by a single shaft of light that filtered in through a smudged window looking onto the tenement next door. To the left was a cracked shaving basin, half-filled with murky liquid. An unmade bed occupied the far corner, while a battered dresser and chair made up the rest of the furnishings. The drawers of the former had been yanked out, their contents strewn across the floor. Next to me, Brady let out a long, pent-up breath.

"He appears to have fled," John said, taking in everything but touching nothing.

The few belongings that remained confirmed Brady's account of a one-time country gentleman fallen on hard times. A pair of boots stood upright at the foot of the bed. They were expensive and finely made, but the soles had been patched a dozen times and the left toe had a gaping hole. The same was true of the clothing that lay scattered about. It was tailor-made but worn nearly threadbare.

I slowly walked the perimeter of the room. Brady stayed in the doorway, pale-faced and anxious. When I reached the bed, I slid my hand between the thin mattress and the frame. My fingers brushed a hard edge.

"Would you call your friend a sentimental man?" I asked, holding up an oval cameo photograph. It depicted a woman with the same striking, dark good looks as Straker. "His mother, I presume?"

Brady took the cameo and nodded. "Yes, to both counts. That was the only picture he had of her."

"Curious that he would leave it behind, don't you think?"

"More than curious," Brady said thoughtfully. "It's unthinkable."

"Even if he was in a great hurry?" I pressed. "Could he have forgotten it?"

"When we were growing up and shared a room together, Robert looked at that picture every day," Brady said. "More than once, I even overheard him talking to it." He laughed at John's expression. "Not in a morbid or disturbing way. Just a son who missed his mother. They were very close."

"How did his parents die?" I asked.

"They drowned in an accident on Easter Sunday. Their rowboat capsized on a nearby pond and neither knew how to swim. It was a terrible tragedy. Robert was only seven."

"May I keep this for now?" I asked, examining the cameo. The woman's full lips were curved in a smile, but her eyes had a cool, detached quality.

"If you wish," Brady said, handing it back. "Just keep it safe so we may return it to Robert when he is found."

I continued my circuit of the room, taking care to note every detail, as Myrtle had trained me to do. When I reached the window, I dropped to hands and knees and took out a small magnifying glass.

"Was Mr. Straker a smoker?"

"He took the occasional pipe," Brady replied.

"But not cigarettes?"

"No, never. He very much disliked the smell."

I removed an envelope from a hidden pocket in my dress and brushed a small amount of ash into it. "Well, someone was here smoking Turkish Elegantes. He—or she—stood at the window, probably for at least eight minutes. It's clear from the indentation in the mattress that Mr. Straker was in the habit of sleeping on the right side of the bed, with his feet toward the door. The ash is in an area he would naturally walk through when he awoke, and yet it is undisturbed. Therefore, it was deposited recently."

Brady clapped his hands. "Brilliant, Miss Pell! So someone else was here."

"Indeed."

"But are you really able to pinpoint the exact brand that was smoked?" he asked incredulously.

"She has made a study of tobacco ash," John replied, grinning. "Miss Pell can distinguish thirty-seven different types, isn't that so?"

I caught his eye and smiled back. "Thirty-nine, John. But who's counting?"

"Perhaps this stranger also cut himself shaving?" Brady said faintly.

He had finally ventured into the room and was standing

before the basin. He was looking down and I could see his forehead and bat-like ears reflected in a mirror mounted on the wall, no doubt the same that Straker had gazed into when he ranted that *it comes through the eyes*.

John and I crowded around the basin. What I had initially taken for dirty water was in fact a distinctly pinkish color. John bent down and sniffed it. He said nothing but nodded when I looked at him questioningly.

Someone had washed blood from their hands in this very room.

CHAPTER THREE

M Y NERVES THRUMMED at this discovery and I was forced to stifle a small scream when at that exact moment the door banged open and Connor came bounding up to us.

"I delivered yer message," he said, his bright copper hair curling at the ends from the damp heat. He was at the gangly stage, all knees and elbows, but he carried himself with the self-possessed air of a kid for whom adult supervision had been all but non-existent. "What's in there?"

John moved hastily to block the basin from view.

I'd given him the address in the note I'd left with Mrs. Rivers. Now I was having second thoughts about the wisdom of this decision.

Connor surveyed the room with exaggerated disdain. "Boy, this place is a dump!" he muttered under his breath. Then his sharp eyes fixed on a small blue disc that must have spilled from one of the dresser drawers and rolled half under the bedclothes. Before I could stop him, Connor had snatched it up. He gave a low whistle. "Chamberlain's," he said with reverence. "He's a real class act. Wonder what one of his checks is doing in a joint like this?"

John held out a hand and Connor reluctantly handed it over.

"Mr. Chamberlain's establishment is one of the finest in the city, even if it is entirely illegal," John remarked dryly. "Did you know Mr. Straker was a gambler?"

Brady shook his head. "Robert was never a betting man, not even for a friendly card game."

There was silence for a moment.

"Circumstances may have led him to change his mind," I said. "And if he had racked up debts, he would have been under a great deal of pressure. Even more than we know of."

"I don't see as how he'd even get in the door," Connor said, scratching his head. "Like I said, Chamberlain's is a class act. Judges and senators and bankers and what have you. Not no Five Points riff-raff. They'd laugh him right down the front stairs."

Brady gave the boy a once-over, and didn't appear impressed at what he saw. Although Connor prided himself on keeping up appearances (his shoes were remarkably clean), he drew the line at soap and water and I had to stop myself from reaching out and swiping at the sooty smudges on his face and ears. In his world, I think that would have been a hanging offense.

"Who is this lad?" Brady demanded coolly.

I groped for an appropriate response. All I knew of Connor's background is that his mother had died of yellow fever. Myrtle caught him in the act of stealing her billfold two years back, and now paid him quite handsomely to relay the gossip on the streets and find people who didn't want to be found.

Connor had been sleeping in the gutter or, if he was lucky, flophouses far worse than this one. Now he stayed at Tenth Street most nights. I didn't know what happened to his father.

He never spoke of it and I didn't press him. There was darkness in Connor's past, but children can be remarkably resilient, and he was a cheerful kid, even if he did love to play the devil for poor Mrs. Rivers.

"He's a... free-lance consultant," I said at last.

"Oh, I like that!" the little cutthroat exclaimed. "Very swank. Think I'll use it myself."

"Did you receive an answer to my message?" I asked, hoping to change the subject.

"Yeah. Miss Bly will meet you at noon. Atlantic Garden."

"Excellent," I said. "I'm starving. You'll join us, won't you, John?"

He nodded, as Brady's whole countenance altered from anxiety at our discovery to one of awe.

"Nellie Bly?" he asked. "The reporter?"

"Yes, she's a dear friend of my... " I caught myself just in time. "Of mine."

Thankfully, Brady didn't seem to notice the slip.

"I admire her stories very much," he exclaimed. "Very much indeed! Such a courageous young lady. Elizabeth simply adores her. *Ten Days in a Madhouse*... Absolutely shocking." He fiddled with the key to Straker's flat. "Do you think I might... come along and meet her?"

I smiled regretfully. "I'm sure she would be delighted, but I think it best if we exercise the utmost discretion. Our appointment is related to the case." I cast a significant look at the basin. "Which has acquired a particular urgency, as I'm sure you'll agree. Perhaps another time?"

"Oh yes. Certainly." Brady swallowed his disappointment. "I should be getting back to the office anyway." His eyes landed on Connor with no small measure of distaste. "May we speak? In private?"

"Of course." I gave my messenger fifty cents, which cheered him up considerably, and sent him back to his usual haunts in Greenwich Village with the task of putting the word out to the Bank Street Butchers that there was a considerable reward for the first boy who found Mr. Straker. Then I turned to my client. "You're wondering if I'm going to go to the police now."

He nodded.

"I agree that things appear to be more complicated than I first imagined. But I remain unconvinced of your friend's guilt. So the answer is no. Not yet."

Brady's shoulders sagged a little. "Thank you, Miss Pell. I know it looks bad. But the picture… He would have taken it if he'd been able, I just know it! There's someone else involved, some enemy of Robert's, and by God, when I find him!" Brady clenched his fists.

"I have to ask for the purposes of elimination, so please don't take offense," I said. "But are you by any chance a smoking man?"

"Absolutely not! You can ask anyone."

"Alright then," I said. "There are several threads I plan to follow. I will pay you a visit tomorrow morning with an update on what I have found."

And so we all departed Straker's sad and rather ominous lodgings, Brady heading downtown for Maiden Lane, and John and I for our luncheon appointment on the Bowery.

"Nellie!" John said as we emerged onto Canal Street, its energetic hubbub and bright sunlight seeming like another world entirely. "Good thinking, Harry. She must be pals with all the police reporters in the city."

"Yes, and since they'll never give us the time of day—the police, I mean—we'll just have to go around them. Oh, I'd give my eyeteeth for five minutes at the crime scene when it was still fresh! What clues did those fools overlook? But it's too late now. We'll just have to hope someone took decent notes."

"And the ash?" John said. "Do you really think there was another person there?"

"I'm sure of it," I answered. "Turkish Elegantes is a specialty brand. You can visit the Bedrossian Brothers and see if they recall any recent customers. Their shop is at 23 Wall Street. Think of it as a nice after-lunch walk."

"And what will *you* be doing?" John demanded.

"That depends on what Nellie says," I replied, slipping my arm through his. "Come on, I'll buy you a bratwurst."

The Third Avenue Elevated, which ran from South Ferry to Harlem, clattered overhead as we entered the cavernous, block-long space of the Atlantic Garden. Had it been a Sunday, nearly a thousand revellers would have packed the two-tier hall, mostly German families with all their children, brothers and sisters, cousins and neighbors. To the dismay of New York's Puritans, beer drinking was the principal pursuit. But the place had none of the dissolute atmosphere of the city's dance halls and concert saloons. It was clean and neat, with an ornately frescoed ceiling and lifelike mural that at first glance appeared to depict a tranquil rural scene, but which on closer inspection revealed itself to be a cemetery—an apt motif for our meeting, I thought.

Groups of men played cards and dominoes as they enjoyed a leisurely lunch. One could usually hear live music, anything from a quartet to a full orchestra, but as it was a Thursday afternoon, the place was quieter than usual. John and I bought sausages and sauerkraut at a counter near the door and pushed past the teenaged serving girls (all in extremely short skirts and red-topped boots with tinkling bells) until we spotted a familiar figure waiting at a quiet table near the rear stage.

"Harry! John! It's good to see you both again," Nellie called out, a smile lighting up her face, which never failed to strike me with its youth and prettiness. At the ripe old age of twenty-three, Nellie had gained notoriety as Joe Pulitzer's new star reporter when she got herself committed to the lunatic asylum on Blackwell's Island. The resulting articles she wrote for *The New York World* described it as a "human rat-trap," with dozens of women bathing in the same ice-cold tub until the water turned black, rancid food, and some fourteen hours of the day spent sitting on hard benches, with inmates not permitted to speak or move.

This bit of so-called stunt reporting led to a grand jury investigation and sealed her reputation as the foremost woman journalist in the country—a profession that was still very much a boys' club. She and Myrtle had that in common, both refusing to be bound by convention and pushing the limits of what women could accomplish. It solidified their friendship, which I had imposed upon by asking Nellie to meet us here. It was a risk, but one I had to take.

"So you're interested in the von Linden murder," she said, her wide brown eyes sparkling with curiosity. "Is Myrtle on the case?"

"You could say that," I replied cagily, tearing into my sausage with a vengeance.

"I asked Fred for his notes. He wrote up the story and got a copy of the full police report." She pulled a notebook out and began riffling through the pages. "What do you want to know?"

"Everything."

"Well then, let's start with the official cause of death:

exsanguination. She bled to death. Not surprising since she had thirty-one stab wounds."

"Did they find the murder weapon?" John asked.

"A kitchen knife belonging to the victim. So perhaps a crime of impulse?" Nellie speculated.

"Perhaps," I said. "What else?"

Nellie read for a moment. When she finally spoke, her voice was subdued. "It also says she was... bitten. About the face and neck. Incisal biting—that's the front teeth." Nellie looked up at us. "We're not talking about teeth *marks*. We're talking actual removal of the flesh. He took pieces out of her."

"How do you know it's a he?" John asked, laying his fork down. Both of us were rapidly losing our appetites.

"With crimes like this, it's always a he," Nellie responded flatly. "Here's something... the police found a good quantity of chloral hydrate in the room. It seems she was an addict."

I glanced at John. "Brady said she was slurring her words. He thought she was drunk."

"It's a powerful sedative," John confirmed.

"Who's Brady?" Nellie asked.

"Myrtle's client," I said. "He has a personal interest in discovering the murderer. Have the detectives got any leads?"

"Not yet."

"Does it say if they found a book?"

"A book?" She scanned the notes. "What's the title?"

"I'm afraid I don't know."

She looked at me strangely. "No, that's not mentioned. But here's something bizarre. The killer appeared to have an attack of conscience. He wrote on the wall, *ignosce mihi deus*. Seems the police had quite a time figuring it out at first."

"Because it was Latin?" I asked.

"No, because it was written backwards."

I could see John struggling to conjugate the verb and took pity on him. Latin was never his best subject. "It means, *God forgive me*," I said.

"He probably did it after he covered the face, since there were blood drips from his fingers on the pillowcase," Nellie murmured, scanning the notes.

I leaned forward. "What do you mean?"

Nellie looked up. "Oh, he covered her up. I suppose he didn't like looking at his own handiwork. Her features had been nearly obliterated."

John frowned. "Doesn't that strike you as more than a bit contradictory? On the one hand, the killing is frenzied, vicious. But then he takes the time to cover her up. It's almost a twisted act of kindness."

"Or remorse," Nellie said.

"What is it, Harry?" John prompted. "You know something."

I looked up from my reverie. A tall blonde serving girl approached the table but Nellie waved her away.

"Today's *Herald* has a small item on page six. An organ grinder, fourteen years old. He was strangled Tuesday night." I looked down the length of the hall, at all the people eating and drinking, and thought of the teeming crowds in the streets outside, nearly a million and a half strong, oblivious to the fact that among them walked a killer. "The boy's death only merited a few paragraphs. He wasn't famous, like Becky Rickard, a.k.a. Valentina von Linden. But I remember one detail: a rag was placed over his face."

John and Nellie were silent.

"Male. And asphyxiated rather than stabbed. You've got to admit, the crimes are different," John said at last.

"I know. But we can't ignore it," I responded. "There could be other similarities we don't know about."

"I'm heading over to the *World* right now to meet with my editor," Nellie said. "You can come along if you like. See if any of the crime beat boys are around."

"And I'll run down to the Bedrossian Brothers," John said, adding wryly, "Who knows? Maybe we'll get lucky and they'll remember a sinister fellow buying Turkish Elegantes who considerately left his calling card."

We made plans to meet later at Tenth Street and I accompanied Nellie to her offices at 32 Park Row. Mr. Pulitzer had grand plans to build a new headquarters that would be the world's tallest building at twenty-six stories, but this dream wouldn't be realized until the following year. For now, the popular newspaper occupied a nondescript five stories across from City Hall Park, in what was called Printing House Square because it was home to nearly all the city's presses.

Nellie led me through the bustling newsroom to a desk occupied by a young man with ginger hair and an easy-going grin. This was the same "Fred" she had poached the notebook from and, once she'd dropped the name of the illustrious Myrtle Fearing Pell, he was happy to share the few facts he had gleaned about the latest murder.

"I'd been called to cover a fire in the Tenderloin or I would've written something," he explained. "Still might, if I can get some quotes from the family. It's a bit of a shocker. Probably a mugging gone bad, poor kid, though I don't know who'd want to rob an organ grinder, most of 'em rent their instruments because they can't even afford to own them. It's not much of a living, and this one was no exception."

"Where did it happen?" I asked.

"Broadway and Fourteenth Street. The body was found at the base of the George Washington statue, by the slave market."

Union Square was the city's theater district, and the phrase was jokingly used to describe the south end of the park, where out-of-work actors would hang around hoping to catch a break from managers and agents who often cast their plays from the throngs of hopefuls.

"It must have been after midnight, as the area is crowded until quite late in the evening," Fred said. "The sick bastard killed the kid's monkey too, can you believe it?" He shook his head at the seemingly limitless depravity of New York City—depravity that was helping *The World's* circulation grow by leaps and bounds. "There's your headline."

"What about the state of the body? I read that the face had been covered."

Fred nodded. "I heard it was a handkerchief."

"The *Herald* said a rag."

Fred shrugged. "Does it really matter? Oh yeah, my friend at the *Times* said there was a weird symbol burned into the grass at the base of the statue. No way of telling if it's related. His editor passed on the story, so he gave me his sketch." Fred dug through the mountain of loose paper on his desk and pulled out a scrap with a bunch of squiggly lines that I copied into my own notebook. "Anyway, I can't tell you much more. No witnesses have come forward with anything useful. The kid's name was Raffaele Forsizi, family fresh off the boat from Italy. Seems he was on his way home from Central Park. He'd been playing there all day." He lowered his voice. "I did get one piece of information they haven't published yet."

He told us, and then jumped to his feet in a sudden burst of energy. "Sorry, ladies, but I've got to run. I'm on deadline, and my editor will have my hide if I'm late. Hey, if your sister solves it, do I get an exclusive interview?"

"If my sister solves it, I swear she won't talk to anyone

else," I said with a smile. "Do you happen to have the family's address?"

Fred gave me a building number in the West Forties and I thanked him again, but he was already jamming a hat on his head and blowing us a kiss as he fairly levitated out the door. Nellie walked me back out to Park Row and made me swear to keep her apprised of any new developments. I could see her journalistic instincts told her there was a lot more to the story than I was letting on, but she didn't press too hard.

"Myrtle always plays her cards close to the vest," Nellie said. "But I expect the *World* to get a scoop when she's ready to lay them on the table!"

The competition among New York's five major dailies was intense and somehow heightened by their close proximity to each other (I could see four of them, *The Sun, The Times, The World* and *The Tribune*, from where I was standing). Mr. Pulitzer may have been a crusader but he loved scandal and sensation just as much, if not more.

And I had a feeling there would be plenty of both before this case was over.

I said goodbye to Nellie, promising to keep in touch. It was now late afternoon and heavy, dark clouds had rolled in. The temperature was dropping quickly, providing relief from the oppressive heat but hardly lightening my grim mood. Pedestrians scattered as the first drops began to fall. I picked up my pace, wishing I'd thought to bring an umbrella.

As much as I was dying to share what I'd learned with John, I didn't go straight home. Instead, I ducked around the corner to the Western Union office at 195 Broadway.

Here I will tell you quickly about my Uncle Arthur.

First off, he's not actually my uncle. More of an unofficial godfather. But I've been calling him that since I was a child and although we may not be blood relations, he is and always will be family to me.

Second, he is a doctor but his passion is writing adventure stories, and I think he will be famous for them someday. Uncle Arthur's latest novella *A Study in Scarlet*, featuring the brilliant and mercurial detective Sherlock Holmes, had just been published in *Beeton's Christmas Annual* a year before, and though not many have yet read it, I thought it was brilliant. He says Holmes was modelled on a former professor, which I don't deny, but I also think there's more than a little of Myrtle in there, and maybe even myself, although that's probably wishful thinking.

In any event, he followed my sister's exploits with keen interest. At twenty-seven, Arthur was only a year older than Myrtle and they'd always been close. I'll confess, it wasn't easy growing up in her shadow. Besides having a dazzling intellect and vast storehouse of forensic knowledge, Myrtle was born with an aptitude for unravelling the most convoluted and devious criminal minds. Her record was unblemished, except for one man, but we shall come to him later. What I'm trying to say is that I couldn't resist bragging a little. All my life, I'd been the *other* Miss Pell. The drab little planet orbiting Myrtle's star. Now, I had a case of my own between my teeth, and I was running with it.

As I composed the cable, I told myself that there were prominent occult elements which would be of interest to Uncle Arthur, who, as I mentioned before, was an ardent Spiritualist. He might even have contacts here that would be essential for the investigation. There was little danger that he would communicate with Myrtle herself, since no one had any idea where she'd gone off to.

Plus, Uncle Arthur was a member of the S.P.R. It could be

the very introduction I'd been yearning for. They didn't hire kids, but if I managed to solve this case, they might rethink their position.

I told myself all these perfectly reasonable things, but in the end, I was just hoping to impress him.

I summarized the case as succinctly as possible and paid the exorbitant transatlantic fee to send it to Southsea. Then I dashed into the rain and caught a jam-packed streetcar on Church Street that brought me uptown to Sixth Avenue and Tenth Street.

"Oh dear, you're soaked to the bone!" Mrs. Rivers exclaimed as I made my way upstairs, leaving large, squelchy footprints on the rose-patterned carpet. "I'll brew up a pot of tea."

She headed toward the kitchen, still sprightly and dark-haired despite her advanced years. Not much seemed to surprise our housekeeper anymore. She'd practically raised Myrtle (which couldn't have been very pleasant) and seemed resigned to the fact that her charges had little interest in men, fashion or parties—the Holy Trinity of upper class femininity.

"It's a monsoon out there," I told John, who lounged in his usual place on the parlor sofa. Annoyingly, he was bone dry, his errand having been much briefer than mine.

Connor was there too, curled up in an armchair with one of the penny dreadfuls John had taught him to read when he wasn't busy mugging old ladies. This one was titled *Feast of Blood*, and featured a skeleton looming over an unconscious maiden in a clinging white gown. When she was in a crusading mood, Mrs. Rivers would confiscate them, but he seemed to have an endless supply.

"At least you got clean the natural way," Connor complained, looking me over with a jaundiced eye. "*She* made me take a bath. Said I couldn't come in for supper otherwise. With soap!" His voice took on a tone of profound outrage. "The lads'll think I've gone soft."

Mrs. Rivers sniffed. "I'm sure you'll manage to get filthy again before bedtime, Master Connor. You always do."

He smiled in quiet satisfaction and went back to reading.

My housekeeper handed me a fluffy towel and I dried myself off as John related his visit to the exclusive hand-rolled tobacco shop.

"Dead end," he said ruefully. "No one remembered any particular customer and they don't keep lists. How did you make out?"

Mrs. River had gone back downstairs, so I told them everything I'd learned from Fred about the killing of the Forsizi boy. Connor gave a low whistle.

"The monkey too? That seems… what's the word?"

"Gratuitous," John offered. "It means over the top."

"Yeah, gratuitous," Connor repeated, rolling the word around in his mouth like a gumball.

"So is stabbing someone thirty-one times." I peeled off a wet stocking and flexed my toes, which had shrivelled into little white prunes. "And the face was covered. Again, it's almost as if two different people were there. One who was full of rage, another who felt guilt or pity for the victim."

"Or a single person who is terribly conflicted," John pointed out. "You're familiar with the case of Louis Vivet?"

I was, but Connor wasn't, so John summarized his peculiar history. A Frenchman, Vivet suffered from what doctors called multiple personality disorder, a rare condition where a traumatic event causes a person's psyche to split into distinct identities, some of whom may be entirely unaware of the others. In Vivet's case, the proximal event was a terrifying encounter with a viper that wrapped itself around his left arm when he was thirteen years old (although it should be noted that he also had a wretched childhood, which certainly played a large factor in his illness).

"Lost time," I said.

"What?"

"It's one of the principal symptoms. The sufferer experiences lost time. They may find themselves places with no recollection of how they got there, or simply awaken from a fugue state with hours having passed."

"That happened to me just the other day," Connor said. "Course it was after a few of the lads nicked a bottle of the old Rattle-Skull from a drunk on the Bowery... "

I opened my mouth to lecture the boy on the evils of liquor in general, and Rattle-Skull (whatever that was) in particular, but John rode right over me.

"*If* the two murders are related, and I'm still not sure they are, it's conceivable that he doesn't know he's doing it," he said. "Or he wakes up after the deed is done and feels compelled to metaphorically hide his actions by covering the face. We should ask Brady if Straker had any history of lost time."

"Yes. And I have another question for my client." I tried, unsuccessfully, to suppress the glee in my voice. I'd been saving the best for last.

John's eyes narrowed. "What is it, Harry?"

"I'm just wondering what happened to Straker's things from the army," I said, as Mrs. Rivers bustled in with a steaming mug that she pressed into my hands. "Thank you."

"Of course, dear."

I took a sip and waited for her to leave.

"Because what? Oh, do get on with it!" John exclaimed.

"Because," I said, "what Fred told me, but that hasn't been reported yet, is that something was found just next to the body, as if it had fallen from the boy's hand: the button from a soldier's uniform!"

CHAPTER FOUR

J OHN WAS INTRIGUED when I told him this, but it didn't have quite the dramatic effect I was hoping for. As much as he enjoyed tales of the supernatural, he had a strong pragmatic side as well and insisted that it really didn't prove a thing. In fact, in his view, it made it *less likely* that Straker was involved, in the Union Square killing at least. Should we not consider the simplest explanation: that it was someone actively serving in the military? Multiple personality disorder was certainly a sensational explanation, John argued, but it was also extremely rare, with less than a hundred reported cases in the world. And while a few patients, including Vivet, had alter egos that were impulsive and even criminal, none had committed murder.

There was also the ash to consider. Without doubt, a second person had been in Straker's flat. And the strange symbol burned into the grass, which resembled a capital X alongside a number four, with a short line drawn through the slanting part of the four. I showed it to John and Connor, but it meant nothing to them either.

We ate supper and batted some ideas around for a while, most of them pure speculation. As I'd hoped, Connor was more than willing to offer his assistance. He seemed happy to have a new case to puzzle over, and it dawned on me that he had been just as bored as I was with Myrtle gone. He'd gotten used to a life of adventure and intrigue, and thought it hilarious that I was pretending to be the Great Detective.

A little too hilarious.

"Alright," I said crossly, as he rolled on the floor, clutching his sides. "It's not that funny."

"No offense, Harry," he groaned, catching his breath. "But if Myrtle catches you… I hear there's a ship leaving for Brazil from Pier Twenty-Nine next week. You might want to start packing your—"

Connor let out a whoosh of air as I whacked him in the head with a pillow. John, who had loyally kept a straight face until this point, finally crumbled, and I was forced to threaten him with the pillow as well, which only made them both worse.

Then Mrs. Rivers burst in demanding to know what all the racket was about, and even I succumbed to a fit of the giggles.

"You're daft, the lot of you!" she exclaimed. "And it's nine o'clock. Time for John to go home, and young Connor to brush his teeth."

This brought a chorus of hisses and boos from "Young Connor," mostly under his breath. As much as he complained about Mrs. Rivers, he didn't dare to openly defy her.

The two of them acted like mortal enemies, but it was thanks to her that he was fed and clothed and had a place to sleep at night (the spare bedroom in the attic). I doubt it would even have occurred to Myrtle to do more than give him a few coins for his services, but once Mrs. Rivers had ascertained that Connor quite literally had no one and nowhere to go, she insisted that we take him in. My mother was hesitant.

"*Isn't the boy a professional thief?*" she'd asked diffidently. But Mrs. Rivers had been adamant and Connor was wise enough to recognize a good thing when he found one. Four months later, the silverware was still intact, although I'd caught him eyeing it longingly on a few occasions and from his mutterings I gathered that he'd already priced the contents of the entire house down to the penny.

"Sorry, Harry, force of habit," he'd responded when I'd found him in the dining room one day, admiring a gold-fili-greed serving tray. "A man's got to keep in practice or his skills get rusty!"

So in theory, Connor was reformed. But I had a feeling his extracurricular activities remained unsavoury, to put it mildly.

We walked John to the door. His assignment for the next day was to visit the Hell's Kitchen address Fred had given me for the Forsizi family and find out all he could about Raffaele's habits and his final hours. Connor would keep combing the streets for Straker. He seemed confident that if the man was lying low in a cheap boarding house or fleabag hotel, the Bank Street Butchers would cross his path eventually. As for myself, I would go to see Brady, and then pop over to the Astor Library to ask if anyone there was familiar with the symbol.

We said goodnight and Connor succumbed to the gruff mothering of our housekeeper, which I don't think he minded half as much as he claimed. It was a lovely night, warm and with a faint glow lingering in the sky over the Hudson. I stood in the doorway as John walked away backwards, giving me a final wave before turning east for home.

He lived on Gramercy Park with so many brothers that he claimed the only peace he ever got was at my house. As the youngest, he'd led a rough and tumble childhood, and I think his brothers were the chief reason he'd so enthusiastically embraced boxing. In lieu of bare knuckles, the boys some-times wore ladies' lace gloves, which I thought ridiculous and told him so. I also told him that I'd inform his parents (his father was a district court judge) if he didn't teach me the pugilistic arts.

"That's blackmail, plain and simple!" he'd objected. "Plus you're a lady."

This was when we were both fifteen.

I'd promptly punched him in the nose, which silenced his objections.

So John taught me to box, although he insisted we wear the padded gloves mandated by the Queensberry Rules and, despite my vocal complaints, refused to hit me in the face.

Anyway, since he'd gained early admission to medical college the previous fall, John was spending more and more time at Tenth Street. I think it was the only place he could get any studying done. Fortunately, it was summer and classes didn't begin for another month. With any luck, the case would be wrapped up well before then.

Because the truth was, I needed his help. Badly.

Oh, I was clever. In fact, in any other family, I'd be considered the brainy one. And thanks to my persistent nagging, Myrtle had taught me some of her craft. But I lacked practical experience and I knew it. If I failed, I'd have more than my new clients to answer to. I very much doubted that my sister would take kindly to my impersonation. Our parents, despite their thoroughly modern view of women's place in the world, might do something rash like refuse to leave me at home again. My mother thought I should enroll in Vassar or Wellesley, but I chafed at the thought of spending all day in a stuffy classroom listening to the droning of an elderly professor. I wanted to be in the thick of things, pitting my wits against an adversary, as Myrtle did. So I had followed her lead and set a course of self-study that focused exclusively on subjects relevant to forensic science, such as chemistry, anatomy, and the rich and bountiful history of crime in the city. I had a decent store of theoretical knowledge, although it had never been put to the test until now.

All of these things worried me. But they weren't what kept me awake that night.

I lay in bed for a long time studying the photograph of Leland Brady and Robert Aaron Straker in Wyoming. They seemed so young, more boys than men. Brady was looking directly at the camera, but Straker stared off into the middle distance, as though his mind were elsewhere. Perhaps it was my imagination, but his gaze had a certain hollow, empty quality. I wondered if it was taken before or after the Rock Springs massacre.

They both wore dark single-breasted uniforms with five brass buttons down the front and colored piping on each cuff. I couldn't help staring at Straker's buttons in morbid fascination. Had one of them been seized by the Forsizi boy in his final death throes?

As I tossed and turned, visions of Becky Rickard morphing into the strangled corpse of the child organ grinder, I feared that one thing was certain. If we didn't stop it, there would be more to come.

Straight after breakfast, I took a trolley downtown to Brady's office at 90-94 Maiden Lane, two blocks from the controlled frenzy of the New York Stock Exchange. Harding & White occupied the top two floors of a handsome cast-iron building built for an investment banking firm. The rest of the narrow, curving street was devoted to retail stores advertising watches, chains and engagement rings. As one of the first streets to be illuminated with gas lamps, Maiden Lane had become popular with evening shoppers, and was now the center of the city's jewellery district.

A young secretary escorted me into Brady's small but tastefully furnished office, where my client was sorting through a stack of documents. Several large maps of Manhattan and Brooklyn were pinned to the wall behind him, next to a gleaming wooden telephone. I admired it with envy; my parents' modern sensibilities didn't extend to what they considered frivolous inventions whose sole purpose was to promote idle rumor and gossip.

"Miss Pell!" Brady looked up with a strained smile. He wore a light linen suit that was already hopelessly wrinkled from the humidity, and dark half-circles shadowed his light blue eyes. "Do you have news to report?" He gestured to a couch near the window. "Please, sit down."

I placed my hat on the couch but remained standing. "I won't be long, Mr. Brady. There have been some developments that you might be able to shed further light on."

I gave him a summary of what we'd learned from Nellie and Fred, except for certain details, like the bit about the button. At the mention of a second body, Brady paled.

"Do you really think it's connected?" he asked.

"Yes, I do. This symbol was found burned into the grass near the body." I showed him the paper. "Do you recognize it?"

Brady examined it closely and shook his head. "I'm sorry, no."

"You didn't see it anywhere at the séance? On the floor, perhaps? Or the table?"

"I don't think so."

"That's all right. Now I know we went over this yesterday,

but I'd like you to think back once more. Are there any more details you can recall about the ceremony itself? Words or phrases the medium used? I'm hoping to track down the book she had."

Brady shuffled his papers into a neat pile, then laid them down with a sigh. "I've thought about that night many times since, wondering if I really heard and saw what I did, and if so, what it all means. It hardly seems real, and yet part of me is certain it was." He gave an embarrassed chuckle. "I was never much of a church-going man, but recently—well, our little village chapel is the only place I truly feel at peace. I prayed for Robert there, prayed for his eternal soul… " Brady trailed off, then shook himself and picked up a fountain pen. "I'm sorry. You were asking if I remember any details, other than the wind and… what came after. I'm afraid the answer is no. The whole thing was in Latin, and while I studied it a bit in school, that was many years ago."

He said this casually, unaware of the significance of his words.

"Could it have been *backwards* Latin?" I asked, thinking of the message in blood left by Becky Rickard's killer.

Brady frowned. "I really don't know. It sounded like Latin, but as I said, she was clearly intoxicated. It struck me as unintelligible. So… yes. I suppose it's possible."

I decided to try a new tack. "Did your friend ever suffer from episodes of lost time?"

"I'm not sure I understand."

"Did he complain of finding himself places with no memory of going there? Did he ever seem to forget conversations or experiences? Or simply behave in a manner that was markedly different from his usual personality?"

Brady didn't need to consider question this long. "No, never. Not that I can recall."

"You said you hadn't seen Mr. Straker in more than a year before he approached you last week, is that correct?"

"Yes."

"So you have no idea what other friends and acquaintances he may have made since moving to the city?"

"None."

"Places he went regularly?"

"I'll be honest. Since we parted ways, Robert's life is a perfect blank to me. He spoke in vague generalities about his finances, and referred to a business deal gone sour, but he provided no details and I didn't press him. I'm sorry I can't be of more help." Brady glanced at his watch. "I hate to be abrupt, Miss Pell, but I have a business meeting in just a few minutes. And it's best if, er, I don't introduce you."

"I understand perfectly." I retrieved my hat, a confection of black silk with a daring spray of glossy ebony feathers that I'd bought for myself on the Ladies' Mile, and set it on my head. "You've been more helpful than you might imagine."

I turned toward the door, then stopped as if I'd just thought of something. "Oh, one last question. Do you happen to recollect what Mr. Straker did with his uniform after he left the army?"

Brady perked up at this, his oversized ears making him look like a kid hoping to please a favorite teacher. "Well, that's one I can answer with certainty!" He scribbled on a document with great flourish and tossed it to the side. "Robert kept it. I believe he thought it would impress the ladies."

"Have you seen it recently?"

"Oh, not recently. Not since we lost touch." Brady looked

up with a musing expression. "Now that I think of it, we didn't see it among his effects, did we?"

"No, we didn't," I replied with a smile. "Good day, Mr. Brady."

As I stepped out into the late morning sunshine, I briefly wondered if my client realized that the noose was tightening around his friend's neck. I also wondered if he was being entirely forthcoming in his assertion that he knew nothing about Straker's activities in the past year, and what had led his friend down such a dark path. I wasn't quite ready to break my promise about going to the police, not yet, but my conscience was starting to whisper that it might not be such a bad idea. Deep down, I found the prospect of Straker's guilt disappointing. I'd hoped my first case would present more of a challenge.

Perhaps it was a technicality, but I'd told Elizabeth that I would wait for proof and in my view, there were still loose threads to follow. The book, for example. I wanted to know where Rickard had gotten it, and why she had the princely sum of $200 in her miserable flat. So while I waited to hear about John's trip to the Forsizis' apartment, I headed over to the best place in the city to conduct research: The Astor Library.

Built at Lafayette Place by the immensely rich fur trader turned real estate magnate John Jacob Astor, the library contained more than two hundred thousand volumes on history, art, science and literature. I passed through the elegant entrance hall, with its Italian marble pedestals supporting busts of ancient sages, and found a librarian. A young man with a bushy mustache that turned up at the ends like the grin of the Cheshire Cat, he seemed slightly taken aback at my request, but dove into the stacks and returned a short while later with three books.

"I don't know about that symbol you showed me, but you can try these. It's all we have on grimoires," he said, as I filled out the required slips.

"Grimoires?"

"Yes, I presumed that's what you wanted when you said it was used at a séance." He lowered his voice a fraction and leaned across the counter. "You know, books of magic. How to communicate with angels, devils, spirits, that sort of thing. I'm afraid we don't have much on the occult, but perhaps these will be of some use."

I thanked him and settled into a chair in the main reading room, which had large rectangular tables arranged in the middle of a double-height gallery topped with a glass skylight. Not surprisingly, none of the books were grimoires themselves. Two were tomes of history, with a few paragraphs devoted to folklore and witchcraft, and one was a biography of the eccentric English metaphysician Francis Barrett. But I managed to learn a few things.

Most grimoires promised spells or incantations to make the user wealthy, or to construct items of black magic such as a Hand of Glory (the dried and pickled paw of a criminal who had died on the gallows). They often, but not always, involved a pact with the devil or his chief minister, Lucifuge Rofocale. And the most popular grimoires, at least in the last century, were the Key of Solomon, the Dragon Rouge, and the Black Pullet.

Could the book Becky Rickard read from have been one of those three? And what exactly was she trying to accomplish? Did she think the ceremony would lead to a great treasure? Or was she attempting to raise a demon? Perhaps it was both. And what of the wind Brady described? Did Rickard have a confederate whose job was to create the impression of a supernatural presence? And if so, to what end? Brady insisted they hadn't paid her any money for the performance. She was already disgraced, with no hope of returning to her former life. What was the point of it all? And why had she chosen Straker?

I closed the dusty cover on *A History of Medieval Europe* and realized that more than two hours had gone by and I was absolutely famished. Right on cue, my stomach rumbled and a stout man to my left—most of the patrons were men—glanced over disapprovingly. I gave him a bright smile, set my hat at a jaunty angle, and lugged the books back to the desk. Astor was a research library so I couldn't borrow them, but I'd picked every bit of meat from *those* bones anyway. If I wanted to learn more, I'd need to consult a specialist.

It was only a few blocks home with a shortcut through Washington Square Park, but I still felt thoroughly cooked by the time I got there. The midday heat was thick enough that pedestrians jostled for space on the shady side of the street, and the poor horses looked as though they'd rather be anywhere else. New York City in August may have its charms, but I'd be hard-pressed to name them. If it weren't for the investigation, I would have been sorely tempted to catch a hansom to the Cunard pier at Forty-Eighth Street and take the next ship across the Atlantic.

But I felt that the threads of the case, which had seemed so hopelessly tangled just a day ago, were slowly beginning to unravel. I still didn't know what pattern they would ultimately form, but at least I had the satisfaction of catching hold of the ends. So when I found John lying prostrate on the hall carpet, I gave him an impatient poke with the pointy toe of my boot.

"Go away," he groaned. "It's too hot."

"I take it your sojourn to Hell's Kitchen wasn't pleasant," I said.

John stared up at the ceiling, his brown eyes glassy and unfocused. "Another waste of time. The boy's father barely spoke any English. He managed to tell me that Raffaele was pretty much the family's sole means of support. The man was… broken. In every way. I gave him some money but it won't last long. There were a bunch of little kids too." John sighed. "He said his son had no enemies. He didn't understand how such a thing could happen. Then he handed me over to a sister who seems to be the family's official translator. She told me as much as she could about Raffaele's routine, but I don't think it matters. The killer was a stranger."

I knelt beside him, my upbeat mood deflating. "We'll find him," I said quietly. "If it's Straker or someone else, we'll find him."

John turned his face away and that's when I noticed the dried blood. I laid a hand on his cheek, gently turning him to face me. "What happened?"

He blinked. "Oh. Right. Then I got in a fight."

Fortunately, Mrs. Rivers was out for the afternoon. I settled John into a chair at the kitchen table and cleaned him up with a damp cloth. He had a nasty cut just below his left ear where he'd taken a glancing blow from a cane, but his other wounds appeared to be superficial. All things considered, I'd seen him in worse shape after a match with his friends at the club. Then I made us both turkey sandwiches on thick slabs of Mrs. Rivers' homemade rye bread. The food perked him up some, and John told me how he'd been jumped by a couple of neighborhood thugs on his way back to the Ninth Avenue El.

"Guess they figured I'd be easy pickings," he said. "Some swell from uptown slumming it for the thrills."

"Moran's boys?" I asked.

James Moran was a paradox: outwardly respectable,

diabolically clever, and at the age of twenty, the brains behind an ugly bunch of Irish lads who specialized in extortion, robbery and murder for hire. Myrtle had been trying to catch him for two years with no success, which told you quite a bit about James Moran. He was a different breed of criminal entirely from the likes of Danny Driscoll of the Whyos, who had just been hanged in January in the Tombs prison yard at the age of thirty-three. Like most other New York gang leaders, Driscoll was a loose cannon who spent half his short life in a jail cell, and the other half either assaulting people or getting arrested for it.

Moran had committed one infamous crime. He'd served his time and now gave every appearance of being a model citizen. A gifted student of mathematics, he could be seen roaming the campus of Columbia College on 49th and Madison, dressed in an immaculate dark suit and pearl grey silk hat. Moran moved seamlessly between society and the streets, laughing off the dark rumors that swirled around him and simultaneously exuding just enough danger and intrigue that New York's Knickerbocker matrons couldn't resist putting him at the top of their guest lists.

John shrugged in answer to my question. "Moran's? I don't think so. They never move in less than packs of five, and these two struck me as minnows hoping to swim with the sharks— but more likely to be swallowed whole."

It wasn't John's style to boast and add that he left them lying in the street, but I'd seen him box and knew that whatever injuries he had, he'd inflicted tenfold on his opponents.

"Well, *doctor*, I found out a few things too," I said, and filled him in on my visits to Brady's office and the Astor Library.

"Myrtle would say the uniform is interesting, but not

conclusive," he commented. "Straker could have thrown it out, or given it away."

"Agreed. We'll move on for now. No evidence of prior mental instability either, according to Brady. I've been thinking about the book."

"A grimoire," John said. "I've heard of those. Magical textbooks."

"With a dark side. We're talking pacts with the devil, John. Rather heavy stuff for a medium, don't you think? We need to learn more about Becky Rickard, a.k.a., Valentina von Linden, a.k.a. Madame Catarina Santi. What she was like, who her other clients were. Someone came to her flat in the middle of the night, and if it wasn't Straker, it could very well be someone who'd used her services before. Maybe the same who gave her the money."

"What about other mediums?" John said. "At least a few must have known her."

I should explain that Spiritualism, the idea that one could speak with the dead, wasn't nearly as popular as it had been twenty years before, when Mary Todd Lincoln was holding séances in the White House (which her husband reportedly attended). The Seybert Commission had investigated dozens of claims of "rappings," so-called automatic writing and spirit photography, concluding in 1887 that not a single case was genuine. Personally, I shared their scepticism, although I admired some of the Spiritualist organizations for their embrace of women's rights and staunch opposition to slavery.

But while the mystical frenzy that followed the great blood-letting of the War for the Union had ebbed, it never vanished altogether. If you decided that you simply had to speak with dear Aunt Eunice, even though she'd been gone for twenty years, there were any number of ladies and gentlemen more than happy to assist you—for a small sum, of course.

I was just praising John for his excellent idea when a knock came on the front door.

Our caller was a young man, pleasant-looking and dressed in a stiff collar, checkered coat, lavender pants and high-heeled shoes with captoe buttons up the side. He removed his top hat and peered at us through rose-tinted spectacles.

"Nellie says Myrtle's on a new murder case, but I happen to know she's out of town," he said with an evil smile. "So you either invite me in and tell me everything or I'll have no choice but to—"

Before he could finish, John seized one arm and I seized the other, and we hauled Edward Dewey Dovington upstairs into the parlor, where we deposited him in an armchair and stood guard to either side.

Edward blinked once and adjusted his cravat. "No choice but to cable your parents, Harry. Not that I know where they are either. Is that iced tea?"

He made to rise and John placed a firm hand on his lapel.

"I'll only give you some if you swear to take what I'm about to tell you to the grave," I intoned.

"Sure," Edward said cheerfully.

"Swear on Dirty Laundry," John ordered, which was Edward's favorite racehorse.

"Well, that's serious! I'll have to think about it."

"Edward… "

"Oh, all right then," he grumbled. "I swear! But this had better be good."

So we told him everything, from the moment I saw the Bradys walking up Tenth Street to John's encounter with the Hell's Kitchen hoodlums. Edward asked questions here and there, but mostly he just listened, twirling a gold pocket watch with long, elegant fingers.

"So you're pretending to be Myrtle," he said at last. "I hate to say it, Harry, but you'd need to grow at least four inches and color your hair black to make that remotely plausible."

I drew myself up to my full height, which just reached John's shoulder, and scowled. "That's not the point," I said. "What do you think? Will you help us?"

Edward gave a lopsided grin. "Well, there's no point in going back to Saratoga this season. I couldn't possibly top myself."

Our friend owned no less than five thousand custom-made ties and several hundred pairs of pants, most of them in hues that would make a sunset blush. While some used the term "dude"—meaning a fop or dandy—as an insult, Edward embraced it.

He and John had attended school together at the elite St. Andrew's Academy. When some of the other boys bullied Edward about his taste in clothing, John had laid them out flat (and gotten punished for it). They'd been fast friends ever since.

"I've never hunted a murderous fiend before, mortal or otherwise, but it sounds like you have a real dickens of a case on your hands," Edward said. "So you can count me in. Although if Myrtle catches us, I'm denying everything." He removed his spectacles and tucked them into a breast pocket. "May I have my iced tea now?"

I poured glasses all around while we plotted our next course of action. We needed to follow up on the gambling angle, which was really the only lead we had on what Straker had been up to in the last year. Edward volunteered that he'd been to Chamberlain's many times and was on friendly terms with the man, so we added a visit to that opulent den of iniquity to our schedule for the following evening. Edward and I would start canvassing mediums the next morning to see what they knew about Becky Rickard. But it was still late afternoon, with hours yet of daylight, so when John proposed we examine the cellar where the séance had taken place, we all agreed it was certainly worth a look around.

The address, which I'd obtained from Brady the day before, was just around the corner from Rickard's flat, on Worth Street. I donned my hat and changed into an old pair of shoes that I wore when I boxed with John in the garden. I didn't know quite what to expect, but from the way Brady had described the cellar, it was a grim destination that awaited us. Mrs. Rivers had not yet returned, so we left a note saying we'd gone for a walk in Washington Square Park to look at the new bronze statue of Giuseppe Garibaldi (denounced by *The New York Times* as "monstrous" after the poor man's legs had been yanked apart and strangely contorted to fit a cheaper pedestal when the project ran out of money).

I felt bad deceiving the old girl, but I could hardly tell her the truth. She didn't understand why I needed to prove myself, why having a sister like Myrtle—who was everything I wanted to be, except better at all of it—had become so intolerable.

"Don't worry, dear," Mrs. Rivers had told me not long ago, when she saw I was in a brown study. "Myrtle may be famous, but you're the pretty one. I imagine the young men will be lining up to ask for your hand."

I knew she meant well, but it turned my depression into cold fury. That night, I'd cut all my hair off. I informed my bewildered parents that I'd rather be sent to the lunatic asylum on Blackwell's Island than be married off at eighteen. Six months later, it had finally grown back some and just brushed my chin. Loyal friend that he was, John insisted that it suited me perfectly, although he grew quiet when I declared that I would never be any man's wife.

"Tell me about this séance, Harry," Edward said as we stepped out onto Tenth Street. "I've been to a few myself, and I thought them no better or worse than a two-penny magic show. However, some girls of my acquaintance take these otherworldly communications so seriously, they will not make any major decision without consulting a medium first."

"I'd be delighted to," I said, "but unfortunately, of the three people who were there, one is dead, one missing, and the last unable to recall much beyond some mumbo-jumbo in Latin, followed by what he called a foul wind."

Edward had inherited a fortune from his grandfather three years ago, when he was just fifteen, and his shiny black barouche and driver waited at the curb.

"Harry's client said he felt a presence in the room," John chimed in. "Something malignant."

"He never actually said the word *malignant*," I protested as we climbed into the carriage, which had two facing benches— John and I taking one, Edward the other.

"Oh, fine, but the clear implication was evil." John stretched the word out into about six syllables. "She was reading from a grimoire, so she could have been trying to summon anything."

"It seems—" Edward began.

"Don't tell me you believe any of that eye-wash," I cut in, addressing John to my right. "I think you'll find our killer is a man of flesh and blood, as much as you are." I gave his chest a little poke for emphasis. "Becky Rickard didn't spontaneously combust, or die of some mysterious fright. She was stabbed with a perfectly ordinary kitchen knife."

John paid me no mind, speaking to Edward, whose head swivelled between us as though he were watching a match of lawn tennis.

"Imagine," John said as we headed east on Eighth Street toward Broadway, "just for the sake of argument, that this Madame Santi believes she has instructions to summon a demon which will make her and Straker rich beyond their wildest dreams. Both of them are in dire straits. They'd once been respectable, and if not exactly wealthy, at least comfortable. Now they've hit rock bottom. Santi is a fraud, Straker a bankrupt pauper. She obtains a grimoire, perhaps from a former client. Somehow, she crosses paths with Straker and entices him to join her. She didn't count on Brady being there, but it doesn't really matter as long as he doesn't interfere with her plans. So she finds a place where they won't be disturbed and starts the incantation, but she's a chloral hydrate fiend and can't keep it straight. Let's say she took an extra-large dose before the ceremony to soothe her nerves. She makes a fatal mistake and *unleashes* something." John paused as we entered the flow of traffic on Broadway, most of it heading uptown as the city disgorged thousands of commuters to satellite towns in Brooklyn, Queens, the Bronx and Westchester.

"Something?" Edward asked, arching an eyebrow.

"Something," John affirmed. "It enters Straker and possesses him. Forces him to commit unspeakable crimes, for which he is then overcome with remorse."

"Oh, *that's* scientific," I muttered.

"Arthur Conan Doyle would take my side," he said. "Which is simply to keep an open mind to all possibilities. Don't forget, Straker spoke of it 'entering through the eyes.' What else could he have meant?"

"Alright," I said. "So where is he now?"

"I don't know," John conceded. "Hiding out somewhere, I suppose."

I fanned myself with my hat as we jounced over a set of horse car tracks at Broadway and Canal Street. "Here's an alternative theory. Someone kills Ms. Rickard, goes to Straker's flat and washes up—hence, the bloody water in the shaving basin—and leaves with his uniform. Now, this person could be Straker himself or someone else entirely, I'm not sure yet. If the former, then I agree with you, John, that he has gone into hiding. Assuming he is still in the city, which, considering his limited means and lack of family, is quite likely, we must try to imagine where he might go. If it is the latter, then poor Straker is either abducted or dead himself."

"But what of the organ grinder?" Edward asked, with a puzzled frown. "How does he fit into either of those theories?"

John and I looked at each other ruefully.

"Not a clue," he said, and for once, I couldn't disagree.

We turned off Broadway into the twilit world of the Five Points, where Edward's fancy carriage drew more attention from the local denizens than seemed salutary.

"Let's make this quick," I said, as John offered up his hand and I climbed down into the overflowing muck of Worth Street.

The building where Rickard, Straker and Brady had convened that fateful night looked ordinary, if the decrepit skeletons that lined that block could be called so. Four stories of rotting wood towered over us, but our eyes were drawn to that portion below the level of the sidewalk where our investigation had led us. I could make out a tiny ventilation space perhaps two inches high and three wide in the outer wall, but the rest of the cellar was entirely hidden from view. I tried to imagine living in such a place, as I knew tens of thousands of the city's

most unfortunate were forced to do. It suddenly occurred to
me that it might not be empty. Such cellars were widely used
as nightly lodging houses, a small step up from the cold com-
fort of the streets.

Luckily, it didn't take long to locate the proprietress, a
tall, raw-boned woman with bluish veins tracing a map across
her cheeks and the strong aroma of cheap whiskey about her.
I noted smallpox scars on her neck and forehead, which she
had taken care to cover with a cosmetic paste. America's last
serious smallpox outbreak erupted between 1865 and 1873.
It hit four cities—Philadelphia, Boston, New York and New
Orleans—so she could have been from any one of those, but
her broad accent placed her as a native-born resident of the
Lower East Side.

At first she was suspicious, though her attitude changed
when Edward pressed money into her hand.

"Oh, I knew Becky," she said, tucking the bills into a hidden fold of her grey dress. "She used my place sometimes,
when she needed privacy. Always paid up front."

"So you rented it to her last Monday night?" I asked.

"Yeah. But I can promise you, she was still alive when
she left."

"How can you be sure?" John asked.

"'Cause she came up to see me." The woman jerked a
thumb toward her second-floor flat. "Said she'd left a bit of
a mess and gave me a couple of extra bucks to clean it. Most
wouldn't of, but she did. Becky was honest like that."

"What kind of mess?"

She scratched her hair, which was pulled into a loose bun.
"There were a strange smell, like rotten eggs. She'd butchered
a rooster, though not any way I'd seen before. Its neck weren't
wrung. Feathers were scattered about. That's all."

"Were there gentlemen with her?" John asked.

"I saw two. One looked like a real swell. I've seen the other around here before. They left first."

"Can we see it?"

She squinted at us and sucked her yellowed teeth. "That'll be another buck."

John produced the bribe this time, and she led us inside and down a narrow, rickety set of stairs just as Brady had described. It grew very dark at the bottom and the proprietress took a kerosene lantern down from a hook on the wall and lit it. I could still detect the faint aroma of sulphur in the dank air.

"Just through here," she said, pushing open a wooden door. "It's a funny thing. The whole building used to be crawling with roaches. But since that night, I ain't seen a one of 'em."

The space that lay beyond was perhaps sixteen feet square and eight feet high. The table and chairs used in the séance were gone, replaced by a filthy straw mattress that had been pushed up against one wall. The floor was hard-packed dirt, and though I could see a single shaft of daylight through that tiny slit, the overall impression was of standing at the bottom of a grave.

We clustered in the doorway for a moment, reluctant to enter any further into the room. Then Edward surprised me by striding forward and bending down.

"Would you be kind enough to bring the light over here, madam?" he said politely, and the landlady was so flattered at being called madam that she fairly skipped over to him.

"What have you found?" John asked, as we gathered round a spot on the floor.

"I'm not sure," Edward said. "What do you think, Harry?"

I peered in the dim light, then crouched down, heedless of my green silk dress. "It looks like a… scorch mark," I said.

I took out one of the same envelopes I had used to scrape up the ash from Straker's flat and swept a small amount of the blackened dirt inside. Then, behind me, John gave a soft cry. He'd found another mark. We fanned out and discovered no less than five of them, equidistant from each other in a rough circle. I gathered a bit from each and was tucking the packets away when John seized my wrist, bringing it to his nose.

"The smell, Harry, it's coming from the dirt."

I frowned. I'd almost stopped noticing it. "The sulphur, you mean?"

"Yes. And there's another word for it." He released my hand and, for the first time in all the years I'd known him, John looked genuinely disturbed. "Brimstone."

CHAPTER FIVE

FOR THE NEXT fifteen minutes, we examined the cellar thoroughly, but there was little more to discover there. I noted some dark reddish stains in the center of the room that could have been dried blood, but that simply corroborated both the landlady and Brady's account of a rooster being slaughtered. I knew I wasn't alone in craving some fresh air. The place had such an oppressive atmosphere that it seemed time stood still. We could have been down there for minutes or hours.

Our hostess had beat a retreat back to her second floor flat as soon as it became clear that no more money would be forthcoming. John kept glancing with undisguised longing at the stairs, but he gamely helped Edward and me to examine every inch of the walls, floor and ceiling before gathering up the lantern and following in her footsteps.

"Revelation," John said as we piled into the barouche and the driver cracked his whip, urging the horses onward towards the relative safety of Broadway. "I don't know the exact quote, but it's the bit about the lake of fire and the mark of the beast. Sulphur and brimstone."

"She probably set it up as some kind of effect," I said.

"Rickard, I mean. That could have been the foul wind Brady spoke of."

"Perhaps," John said. He still looked troubled.

"At least we know he was telling the truth, about some of it, at least," I said. "John, don't you know a few of the fellows who work at the morgue?"

Dusk was settling over the city streets, the gaslights flickering on with a warm yellow glow. On that fine summer evening, the dense forest of telegraph and electrical poles that had crippled the city during the Great Blizzard was enjoying its final lease on life. In less than a year, they would all be felled as the lines moved underground.

John nodded absently. "Yes, I've gone to observe autopsies there on several occasions."

"Why don't you go down tomorrow and see if anyone's claimed Becky's body?"

"It's Paul's birthday, but I can go in the afternoon." Paul was one of his brothers. "It also might be worth another trip to Leonard Street to talk with Straker's neighbors. See if they remember any visitors. I feel as though the man is a cipher."

"Excellent idea," I said. "Just be careful. We've been lucky so far, but outsiders asking too many questions can get into serious trouble down there. Now, Edward. Do you think any of the girls you know subscribes to the *Banner of Light*?" This was the most popular weekly publication of the Spiritualist movement. "We need a listing of local mediums."

"I can certainly ask around," he replied.

"If you could do it this evening, we'll get cracking first thing. Why don't you come by around ten o'clock tomorrow and pick me up?"

Edward promised to do so, and took me home first, as John's Gramercy Park address was on the way to his own townhouse on East Thirty-Seventh Street. Mrs. Rivers was bustling about the kitchen and humming to herself when I entered. The mouth-watering aroma of blueberry pie emanated from the coal oven.

"Did you have a nice walk in the park, dear?" she asked as I pulled a chair up to the kitchen table. "I see you made yourself lunch."

"Yes, lovely," I lied. "How was your afternoon?"

"Oh, I popped by Fulton Market for some fresh berries and cream and then I met a friend for tea. Why, what on earth happened to your dress?"

I looked down and noticed for the first time that I was absolutely filthy from the waist down.

"I tripped and fell in the street. But I'm perfectly fine." The strangeness of the day, combined with the heat in the kitchen, made me suddenly very sleepy. "Tell me, Mrs. Rivers. Do you believe in hell?"

She gave me a squinty look, like she was wondering if perhaps I might have struck my head after all, but our housekeeper was used to strange questions by now. "Hmmm. That's a tickler. I'm a good Christian woman, of course, and I do believe in Judgment Day. Those who are virtuous and do right by others shall go to their everlasting reward."

"But what about the bad ones?" I said. "The sinners? What happens to them?"

Her eyes narrowed. "Have you been reading Connor's abominable stories? I don't know how the boy sleeps at night. There was one about a man who got eaten by cats. Cats!"

"I haven't, but it sounds like you have," I said, grinning.

"Oh, I'd never!" she exclaimed, but the flush in her cheeks said otherwise. "Now, as for sinners. Well, the Bible says they will go away to face eternal punishment. You know that from Sunday school, Harry."

"I know what it says. But do you believe it? The stuff about… fire and brimstone? Demons?"

Mrs. Rivers hesitated, her dark, clever eyes searching mine, and for a brief moment, I wondered if I'd misjudged her all these years and she wasn't the doddering old lady she appeared to be. Then she stood up and used hot pads to lift the pie out of the cast iron stove. She set it to cool on the windowsill, softly humming *Lift High the Cross*.

Mrs. Rivers poured us both glasses of iced tea and sat back down.

"In my seventy-two years in this world, I've seen many things. Extremes of both good and evil. Take the Kelly family of Kansas. I read all about them in the papers last year. On the surface, perfectly respectable ranchers. They often welcomed travellers for a meal at their farmhouse in that desolate region called No-Man's-Land. The mother would cook while the 18-year-old daughter Kit would chat with the visitor. Soon, the father and son would appear, and all would gather round the dinner table."

I vaguely recalled hearing the name Kelly, but I had been sick with a bad fever for several weeks just before Christmas of 1887 and missed out on much of the news at that time.

"What do you think happened next?" Mrs. Rivers said, primly sipping her tea.

"I suppose they were murdered horribly?" I guessed.

"Indeed. But in a most ingenious fashion. You see, the poor man's chair would be placed above a carefully concealed trap door, and at the signal, a switch would be thrown and they would plunge into the Kellys' pitch-black basement. The lucky ones died in the fall. The others… " She trailed off and shook her head. "Well, when the family fled one day, some of their neighbors came poking around. They soon discovered the remains of three people in the cellar, so decomposed that they could not be identified. Four more bodies, including a woman, were found buried beneath the stable, and three more near the barn."

I imagined suddenly falling into a lightless hole filled with rotting corpses and felt a shudder of revulsion pass through me.

"And they were hardly the first," Mrs. Rivers chattered on. "The Benders—surely, you've heard of *them*? Kansas, as well. What *is it* about Kansas? In any event, ordinary churchgoing people. Except that they lured visitors to sit in front of a curtain placed so that the back of the poor soul's head made a slight indentation, at which cue John Bender Sr., who was standing *behind* the curtain, would bash them on the back of the skull with a sledgehammer, toss them down into a hidden pit, and then slit their throats. Just to be sure, you know. Nine in all! Including an infant and an eight-year-old girl. And they got away with it. A posse went after the Benders, but they were never found."

Mrs. Rivers let this unnerving fact hang in the air for a moment. "What can we call such creatures as the Kellys and the Benders? They look like us, speak like us, but their hearts are as black as the anonymous graves of their victims. Are such beings born or created? I don't know. But you asked me before if I believe in the devil." She smiled. "The answer is yes, dear, I do. And so, I think, should you."

We both turned as Connor entered the kitchen in his usual style, not unlike a small, scabby tornado.

"I smell pie," he said, collapsing into a chair.

"It's cooling," Mrs. Rivers said sternly. "And it's for *after* supper."

He scowled and took something out of his pocket. It was about eight inches long and pinkish-grey and tapered to a point at one end. He began coiling it around his index finger as Mrs. Rivers looked on in mounting horror.

"What is that?" she asked faintly.

"This?" Connor dangled it so the end brushed his bare knees.

"Yes, that. Is it... ?

"The tail of a Norwegian rat?" He admired his prize with the intense gratification of a prospector who just stumbled over a vein of pure gold. "Yes, it is. And a right beastly rat it was too. Me and the lads found it in an alley by the waterfront. Course it was dead a'ready. But Billy had his knife so... "

"Out!" Mrs. Rivers bellowed.

"But—"

"Now! Harry, take him to the garden and hose him down! See that *thing* is disposed of."

"Yes, ma'am," I said. "Come on, Connor."

Mrs. Rivers was muttering something about the Black Plague as I hauled him out of the kitchen. The moment we were out of earshot, he grabbed my arm and started pulling me up the stairs.

"I knew that would do her," he whispered. "I got news. We need to talk."

I followed Connor up to his attic room, where I found a grubby kid sitting on the single bed.

"This is Billy Finn," Connor said. "Billy, this is Myrtle's sister, Harry. Tell her what you told me."

From the gaps in his front teeth, I guessed that Billy

Finn was about eight years old. He had a pug nose and curly brown hair.

"Pleased to meetcha," Billy said, putting away the pen-knife he'd been using to clean his big toenail, which stuck through a gaping hole in his shoe.

"Did you find Straker?" I asked.

"Maybe tho," Billy said, the missing teeth giving him a faint lisp. "There's a feller around matching that description." He eyed me cagily. "But I understand yer offering a reward?"

"Indeed," I said impatiently. "Where did you see him?"

"Can't be sure it's him," Billy said. "How much did you say it wath?"

I made up a number on the spot. "Fifty dollars, if it really is Mr. Straker."

Billy tried to keep a poker face but I could see he was struggling. Fifty dollars was a small fortune.

"That's before my commission," Connor interjected smoothly. "Ten percent."

"Aw, Connor," Billy protested. "Five percent."

"Take it or leave it," Connor said, crossing his arms.

"But I gave you that rattail! Don't it count for nothin'?"

"Ten percent."

"Yer worse than a diddle cove, I thought we was friends!"

"We *is* friends," Connor said regretfully. "But business is business."

Billy mumbled something that sounded like "gripe-fist," but he finally nodded.

"Alright," he said, spitting in his palm and shaking hands with Connor, who did the same. "Ten percent."

The negotiation concluded, Billy turned to me. "I'll need to see a pitcher, if you got one. Make sure it's the right feller."

"Hold on." I ran to my room and brought back the

photograph of Brady and Straker in Wyoming. Billy examined it closely.

"The one with dark hair. Is it him?" I asked.

"Dunno. I'll let you know later. After I go down there."

"Where's *there*?" I demanded impatiently.

"That's confidential," Billy said. "A feller's gotta his keep his professional sources to himthelf."

"Well, this man could be very dangerous," I said. "Do not approach him under any circumstances. All I want is an address."

"Got it."

I stared at him hard. "Be careful, Mr. Finn."

"Don't worry, I ain't no noddle." Billy stood up and put his cap on, a checkered thing about two sizes too large. "I can thee mythelf out."

"Wait." I gave him two quarters. "A feller's got to eat supper," I said with a smile.

Billy grinned. "That he doth, Mith Pell, that he doth."

He slipped out the front door, whistling a cheerful tune. I watched through the window as his small form disappeared into the night.

"Be careful, Mr. Finn," I whispered again, praying that I hadn't just made a terrible mistake.

And then Mrs. Rivers called us for supper and I forgot all about Billy as we laughed and talked and stuffed ourselves with lamb stew and blueberry pie.

It was the last time I would do so for many days.

By ten-thirty the next morning, I stood with Edward outside a brownstone at 418 West Twentieth Street. The mighty Hudson shimmered less than a quarter mile distant, its waters bristling with the tall masts of sailing ships and the great steam funnels of the Rotterdam and Atlas Lines. It was a stately street of shade trees and Greek Revival, Italianate and Georgian townhouses, although just a block or so west, the residential neighborhood dissolved into a dodgy patchwork of warehouses, lumber yards and distilleries bounded by the Hudson River Railroad.

Number 418 had been divided into flats, and a small hand-lettered sign indicated that Mr. Charles Dawbarn lived on the top—and thus, the cheapest—floor.

"Ready?" Edward asked me, nervously smoothing his buff waistcoat. He was wearing Hessian boots with tassels over robin's egg blue trousers and a yellow paisley cravat. The points of his collar were so high and stiff that Edward was forced to lean his head back slightly to accommodate them, but he didn't seem to mind this at all.

"I'm ready," I said. "Let's go."

We ascended the stairs and knocked on the door of number four. It was opened by a man who looked strikingly like my Uncle Arthur, except that he was older by several decades. He had short dark hair parted on the side and a large, walrusy mustache. He must have been well over six feet tall, with an athletic build just starting to soften into the paunch of late middle age.

"May I help you?" he inquired.

"I certainly hope so," Edward said heartily. "I read about your talents in the *Banner of Light*. We were hoping you might be willing to assist us in communicating with someone on the *other side*." Edward took my hand tenderly in his own. "My sister, Katie, is to be married, you see. But she desires to confirm that the prospective groom has the complete blessing of our mother, who passed away three years ago."

Mr. Dawbarn nodded and stood aside. "Of course. Please come in."

He led us into a small parlor, where a ginger cat perched in the center of a round wooden table. Mr. Dawbarn shooed the cat away and pulled shut the curtains.

"What we embark upon is no less than a journey beyond the physical realm to higher dimensions," he intoned, lighting several candles and arranging them on the table. "A piercing of the veil between life and death. I myself have personally communed with hundreds of spirits, and each has been a unique experience. I prefer to work with groups of five or more, as the collective energy to summon the desired spirit is greater. But I am willing to attempt it for your sister's sake, as such a potent connection as parent and child makes such manifestations easier."

"Yes, we were very close," I said, pinching the tender flesh inside my elbow so that tears sprung to my eyes. "Now, as to your fee… "

Mr. Dawbarn sighed gently, as though such earthly matters were well beneath him, and gestured to a small plaque that featured the full menu of his services, ranging from written communications transcribed while in a trance to an hour-long communion with "discarnate entities." Edward and I opted for the last one, which cost $5.

As Mr. Dawbarn prepared for the séance, I took a quick look around. The parlor contained a single bookcase with titles like *The Spirits' Book* by Allan Kardec, *The Night Side of Nature* by Catherine Crowe, and *Mysteries* by Charles Elliott. A heart-shaped planchette with a pencil attached sat on a shelf, but the layer of dust on top signalled that it had not been called into service for so-called automatic writing in several months at least. A sad vase of wilted flowers and rather threadbare rug completed the furnishings.

"Let us sit and join hands." Mr. Dawbarn took a deep breath and closed his eyes. "We must ask each question only one time. And once it begins, I must request that you not leave the table for any reason. We must maintain the circle."

I cast a sidelong glance at Edward, trying hard not to giggle.

"Certainly, Mr. Dawbarn," I said, hoping he took the quaver in my voice for fear rather than amusement. "I've only been to one other séance before. Madame Valentina von Linden. She helped us talk to dear Uncle Albert. He seemed very happy."

The medium's eyes opened. He cast a wary look my way. "Von Linden?"

"Oh yes. She was marvellous! Wasn't she, Frank?" I nudged Edward with my foot.

"Quite," he said faintly.

Mr. Dawbarn seemed to relax when he realized that we were unaware of "Valentina von Linden's" fall from grace. "I am pleased you have some prior experience," he said.

"Do you know her?" I persisted. "I mean, you're both so well-respected."

His chest puffed out a bit at this. "We have met. But we moved in different circles. She charged such lofty fees that only the rich could afford her services. I prefer a sliding scale that's more democratic." He gave us an oily smile. "All classes should have the opportunity to communicate with their dearly departed, should they so desire."

Which I took to mean, *I'm willing to fleece even the poorest citizens if they're desperate enough.*

"So she catered mainly to society?" I asked.

"One might say that." And now it seemed I was starting to arouse his suspicions, because he frowned. "Shall we proceed? Or do you wish to spend all morning discussing Madame von Linden? Because I'm afraid I have other clients arriving… "

We assured him that we did indeed wish to continue, and spent the next half hour listening to rapping sounds that Mr. Dawbarn assured me was my mother spelling out a message of congratulations on my impending nuptials, with the proviso that I wear a single white rose in my hair. When the table bucked up and down (at the behest of Mr. Dawbarn's knee-cap), I remarked that mother must have taken up weight-lifting as she was always a skinny little thing, and he swiftly concluded the séance.

"I hope your mind is set at ease," Mr. Dawbarn said as we forked over a $5 bill.

"Utterly," I assured him. "Would you care to see a picture of her?"

I'm not sure what came over me. But I had a sudden urge to prove conclusively that this man was a fraud. Would not a true psychic be able to tell whether a photograph was truly of the spirit he had just been allegedly communicating with?

I reached into my bag and pulled out the cameo I'd taken from Straker's flat, and thrust it into Mr. Dawbarn's hands.

"This is your mother?" he asked uncertainly.

"Yes," I replied, shooting Edward a warning look, as he was peering over Mr. Dawbarn's shoulder with unconcealed curiosity.

There was no doubt that Straker's mother was a beautiful woman. She had thick raven hair, styled loosely on top of her head so that wisps fell across her bare shoulders. Her eyes were such a dark brown that they appeared black, which complemented her olive skin perfectly. She wore a simple gown with a hint of lace at the bosom. But again, it was her expression that riveted the viewer's gaze. A certain narrowness to the heavy-lidded, almond-shaped eyes, a slight upturn to the lips that spoke of cunning, even cruelty…

Mr. Dawbarn gazed upon Straker's mother for a long moment and then a curious thing happened. He gave a shudder; not an ostentatious shudder, but one that seemed to emanate from some primal part of his being.

"She died by violence, did she not?" he asked, pushing the cameo back at me.

"Drowning," I said. "It was an accident."

"Something unclean has touched this," Mr. Dawbarn muttered, wiping his hands on his waistcoat. "There is a… taint."

"Taint?" Edward asked. "What does *that* mean?"

For the first time, our host seemed at a loss for words. If it was part of his act, he was better than I'd thought.

"I'm not entirely sure. But I've never felt its like." Mr. Dawbarn suddenly seemed anxious to be rid of us. "Congratulations on your marriage, Miss White." He herded us toward the foyer like a pair of sheep. "Best of luck to you both."

"Thank you," Edward said. "I—"

And with that, the door shut firmly in our faces.

"Well, he could work on his goodbyes," Edward said as we made our way down the stairs. "Who was that in the picture, anyway?"

"Straker's mother," I responded. "We found the cameo hidden under his mattress. Brady seemed to think it proved that Straker had been the victim of foul play, as he would never leave such a treasured item behind. He was an orphan, you know."

"Did she really drown?"

"That's what Brady said. Straker's parents died together in a boating accident."

"What do you make of all that talk about *something unclean?*" Edward lowered his voice an octave in a fair imitation of Mr. Dawbarn.

"He's probably trying to get us to come back and pay him more money to find out," I said, as we reached the street and Edward called for his carriage, which waited on the corner.

"But he didn't seem like he wanted us there a second longer," Edward pointed out. "I think it's a bit spooky, Harry. There's something off about that lady."

"Now you sound like John," I grumped.

We reprised our act six more times that day, in six different but somehow depressingly alike parlors, with little to show for it but aching backs from sitting in hard wooden chairs for hours on end. None of the mediums we consulted knew Becky Rickard by any of her various names, or wouldn't admit to it if they did. By the last séance, at a house up in Harlem, Edward actually fell asleep midway through and began snoring, which the medium—a stern old bat with an iron-grey bun and black dress whose style had its heyday thirty years ago—didn't take well.

I was just starting to despair that the two central figures in the case—Robert Straker and Becky Rickard—would forever remain enigmas when Edward had the idea of calling on the Fox sisters directly. Thanks to his friends who dabbled in Spiritualism, he knew which church they attended on Sundays and suggested that we join the congregation in the morning. I wasn't at all sure they would talk to us considering the bad publicity they'd been getting, but it was worth a try.

The other encouraging development was that John's run of poor luck finally broke. He found out that Becky's body had indeed been claimed from the Morgue at Bellevue by a sister named Rose, and managed to secure her address, which was a town in western New York called Cassadaga Lake. Afterwards, he canvassed Straker's neighbors, who confirmed that he drank heavily in the last few months, most often at the dive on Baxter Street below Becky Rickard's flat. They had never seen him in the company of anyone else, and couldn't recall any visitors. Apparently, Straker was a solitary fellow who spent most of his time at home alone and rarely spoke to his neighbors, which they interpreted as snootiness. Straker was not well-liked, but he never gave anyone trouble either, even when he was dead drunk, which they impressed upon John was an extremely rare quality in the Five Points.

To me, all of this pointed to some catastrophe befalling the man: either he was the victim of foul play, or his already fragile mind had snapped and sent him on a homicidal rampage. I told John about Billy Finn, who should be reporting back to us any moment now. I wish I'd pressed him harder to tell me where he'd gone. The Bowery and Lower East Side were jam-packed with anonymous lodging houses and fifth-rate hotels. Straker could be holed up in any of them, just one of a thousand lost souls in that miscreant's paradise. If Billy had indeed found him, I hoped he wouldn't be foolish enough to tip the man off that he'd been discovered. Connor assured me that Billy was the very soul of discretion, but I wasn't so sure. A full day had now passed, and I couldn't help worrying that something had gone wrong.

John, meanwhile, was leaning toward the supernatural explanation: that Mr. Straker was possessed by one of the minions of Hell. His conviction was starting to infect Edward, who I could see was still troubled by both what we had found in the cellar and Mr. Dawbarn's strange reaction to the picture of Straker's mother.

So when a cable arrived from Uncle Arthur that evening expressing interest in the case and offering the name of an expert in demonology and the occult at St. John's College, I handed that task over to them. At the very least, the man might be able to identify the symbol burned into the grass near Raffaele Forsizi's body. And while I doubted that we were dealing with otherworldly forces, it was possible that the killer was under the *delusion* that they were possessed, which made it necessary to understand precisely what such a fantasy might entail.

I'll admit, I was thrilled that Uncle Arthur had written back so quickly. It put the wind back in my sails, which were starting to sag. Myrtle's system was to gather as much information as possible before drawing any conclusions. She spent days or even weeks in this phase, refusing to discuss the case except in the vaguest generalities. But her brilliance lay in her ability to sort through the haystack of clues and unerringly single out the needle—the one or two pieces of evidence that pointed conclusively to the solution. This was Myrtle's true gift.

She had once inferred the guilt of a wife-murdering banker based on a bent hatpin and glass of milk. Another memorable case hinged entirely on the *absence* of cat hair on a vicar's socks.

I had tried to mimic Myrtle's discipline, but instead of the picture becoming clearer, the lines were bleeding into each other like the watercolors of that rebellious French impressionist Claude Monet. Why was the killer remorseful? And why, then, did he kill again? Was it even a single person? Some gut instinct told me it was, but Myrtle would scoff at such a notion. Hard facts—that's what solved a case. The problem was, I didn't have any.

As I waited in my room that night for Mrs. Rivers to fall asleep, I resolved to make a trip upstate to Cassadaga Lake and see if Rose Rickard could shed any light on her sister's final days. For if it wasn't Straker, Becky's murderer was someone she knew, and knew well. That I felt sure of.

The clock finally struck eleven and I crept down the stairs, taking care to avoid the creaky floorboard on the second-floor landing. I had dressed formally for the occasion, as Edward suggested: a sea green sheath with a tight-fitting cuirasse bodice and lacy hem that just brushed the floor. My arms were bare, save for a pair of embroidered gloves.

John wasn't happy to be left out of our little excursion, but his parents would die if he set foot in a gambling establishment, even if it *was* the finest in New York, and his brothers had snuck out of the house so many times in their younger, hell-raising years that Judge Weston had paid to have bars installed in the windows of their Gramercy Park mansion. Fortunately, my own parents were more trusting, and it was no difficult matter to make good my escape.

The night air was deliciously cool as I tripped down the front steps. I gave a little wave to Edward, who waited at the curb in his gleaming barouche. "You look radiant, Harry," he said as I nodded to his driver, who handed me up into the carriage. "We'll need every ounce of persuasion we can muster since ladies are frowned upon at Chamberlain's, if not banned outright. It's gentlemen only, and when I say gentlemen, I mean the ones who are so wealthy, they don't even carry cash." He grinned. "Like me."

"Well, I'm not going there to dine on lobster or lose at

faro," I said tartly. "I'm going to find out if he knew Mr. Robert Straker."

We turned up Sixth Avenue, passing the turreted brick and sandstone pile of the old Jefferson Market Prison, and followed the elevated Metropolitan Railroad tracks north. Starting at Fourteenth Street, elegant department stores like R.H. Macy's, Hugh O'Neill's and the Stern Brothers sat cheek-by-jowl, their windows dark at this late hour.

Edward lit a cigarette and blew a curl of smoke out the window. "What do you know about John Chamberlain?"

"Not much," I said. "Only that he makes a very good living taking money from rich swine." I smiled. "Like you."

Edward laughed. "Yes, that about sums it up. He's a careful man, Mr. Chamberlain. It's said that he refuses admittance to men of limited means, men who can't afford to lose, especially if they have families."

"How chivalrous."

"Actually, I think it's genuine. He doesn't need to squeeze the last pound of flesh from his customers. There are plenty of others willing to do that. No, he's elevated gambling to a kind of art, and he doesn't skimp on the amenities. His chef is superb, his wine cellar rivals Delmonico's, and you'll be offered the finest cigar afterwards—all free of charge, of course. John understands that he'll earn it all back tenfold at the card table."

"It doesn't add up, does it?" I mused. "Not exactly Straker's level. Of course, we don't even know when he was there. It could have been a long time ago, when he still had some of his inheritance. Maybe he kept the check as a souvenir of better days."

"We'll soon find out," Edward said, tossing his cigarette into the gutter as the carriage turned onto Twenty-Fifth Street and headed east toward Broadway. "Now listen, Harry. I need you to stay quiet and look pretty."

I glowered at him, and Edward shrugged helplessly. "You're the one who insisted on coming," he reminded me. "Don't expect a warm welcome. John will be perfectly polite, he always is, but the others won't like it. Not one bit. This is their sanctuary, and not even, er, ladies of the evening are permitted."

"The whole world is their sanctuary," I responded with some exasperation, "but I do see your point. The goal is to leave with some information, not annoy the most powerful and arrogant men in New York. I'll do my best."

We stopped in front of a large brownstone that looked the same as its neighbors to either side, except that all the blinds were shut tight. I gave Edward the photograph of Straker as a sign of goodwill that I intended to follow his lead and, shoulders squared like soldiers heading off to battle, we ascended the broad steps to the front door. Our knock was answered by a reserved black man in a butler's uniform. He appeared to know Edward by sight and ushered us inside without speaking. I smiled at him and received a tiny one back, but he gave no outward hint of surprise or displeasure at my presence.

If I thought this was a sign that Chamberlain's clientele would be similarly at ease, I was sorely mistaken.

The butler took Edward's overcoat and top hat and opened the door to a front parlor, where he asked us to wait while he summoned the master of the place. It was a lavishly decorated room. Clearly, no expense had been spared to make visitors feel like royalty. My feet sank into velvet carpeting several inches thick as I gazed around in wonder at the ornate furnishings and lavender walls.

The real action, however, lay beyond the door the butler had disappeared through, and we were the only people there.

"I always thought this an appropriate motif," Edward said in amusement, as he stood before a large reproduction of Gustave Doré's ghoulish *Dante and Virgil in the Frozen Regions of Hell*. "Don't ever say John Chamberlain lacks a sense of humor."

"And that one?" I asked, checking my reflection in the mirror hanging above a black-veined marble mantelpiece. I could see the painting behind me, a beautiful woman in white with mournful eyes and her hands raised in supplication.

"That one is *Jephthah's Daughter*," Edward said. "Aren't you familiar with the Bible story?"

I stood up on my toes but I was still too short to see more than the top half of my face. Unlike Myrtle, whose coloring was closer to that of our mother, Louise, I took after the paternal Harrison side of the family, whose ancestors were Scots with fair skin, blue eyes and an abundance of freckles. I didn't have it quite as bad as our poor cousin, Alec, whose *freckles* had freckles, but the summer sun had brought out a spray across my nose.

"Jephthah? I don't know, all those Old Testament names sound the same to me."

"That's because you spend most of your time in church with a chemistry book jammed into the hymnal," Edward teased.

"True." I adjusted my hat to cover my still unfashionably short hair. "So who is he?"

"A pleasant chap who fought the Ammonites and promised God that if he won, he'd sacrifice the first person who came out of his house when he returned. Unfortunately for his daughter... "

We stared at the painting for a long moment.

"Have you ever noticed that women always get the short end of the—"

I trailed off as the door opened and John Chamberlain entered the room.

He wasn't a tall man, but he exuded charisma and sheer *presence*. He wore an impeccably tailored dark suit that contrasted with Edward's flamboyant costume like a raven next to a flamingo. He had black hair and eyes, and although he was much older than I was, it didn't take me long to decide that he was one of the most attractive men I had ever seen.

"Miss Pell," he said, taking my hand and offering up a little bow. "I know your sister by reputation. It's truly a pleasure." He turned to Edward. "And Mr. Dovington. We're always delighted to have your patronage." His voice was soft and cultured, a voice that guaranteed discretion and promised to satisfy any whim, no matter how small. "Won't you join me in one of the private dining rooms?"

John Chamberlain seemed to instinctively understand that we weren't there to gamble. I took his proffered arm and we went through a second door that led to a dining room with a long table at which several dozen men in evening wear were eating, drinking and talking. It groaned under the weight of enough food to feed a regiment. I saw platters of roast pork, roast beef, rack of lamb, broiled trout, jellied eel and goose liver pâté. Mounds of creamy potatoes and buttery asparagus and bowls of aspic salad, that revolting gelatinous concoction that Mrs. Rivers so adored. There were loaves of steaming bread and silver tureens of savory soup. Most of the men were already red-faced from the wine that flowed freely from waiters bearing crystal decanters.

In that first moment that we walked through the door,

before the din of conversation died abruptly, I spotted the salt-and-pepper beard of Boss Croker, head of the well-oiled political machine known as Tammany Hall, alongside the balding pate of Mayor Hewitt and fiery red hair of the industrialist George Kane, Sr. The three men were laughing at some joke when Croker's eye landed on me and his face suddenly collapsed in on itself, as though he had sucked on a lemon.

One by one, every single man at that long table turned and stared at us. Their hostility was palpable, almost animal in its intensity. Edward stepped up to flank me on the left as we walked down the length of the enormous table toward another door on the far side of the room, which seemed to recede with every step I took.

"Gentlemen," Mr. Chamberlain said, smiling pleasantly as if nothing was amiss.

I kept my head high but couldn't help the flush in my cheeks, which burned hot with embarrassment. To this day, I'm still not sure what a bunch of grown men, most of them rich and powerful, found so threatening about a teenage girl, but I swear you could have heard a pin drop in Chamberlain's that night. I realized how brave Edward had been to bring me here, what a good friend he was, because I had no doubt that he would pay a steep social price for violating the sanctity of their boys' treehouse.

About halfway down the whispers began. My corset felt horribly tight by the time we made the door, and it wasn't until we were through and it was shut firmly behind us that I felt I could breathe again.

"I apologize if that was awkward for you," Mr. Chamberlain said as we ascended a flight of stairs, and he appeared to actually mean it. "I've been intending to make alterations, but it's an old house and I'm afraid there's no other way through."

"I'm the one who should apologize, sir," I said. "I knew what to expect, and I wouldn't have come if my mission wasn't one of the utmost urgency."

I had a brief, glorious image of myself solving the case that had stumped the police and what that sea of pinched old faces would look like *then*, but Mr. Chamberlain's smooth voice brought me back to reality.

"Of course. No one will disturb us in here," he said, entering a small private dining room with a cold hearth. Snowy white linen covered the table, although no places had yet been set. "May I offer either of you refreshments?"

"I—" Edward began.

"No thank you," I said firmly. "We won't take up more of your time than is strictly necessary. The question is a straightforward one." I nodded at Edward, who sighed and took out the photograph.

"We're looking for this man," he said. "Have you seen him?"

Mr. Chamberlain took the picture and examined it, but his expression gave nothing away.

"We found one of your checks in his flat," Edward added.

Our host smiled, but it didn't reach his black eyes. "You understand that complete discretion is the cornerstone of my business?" he asked. "The men who come here expect their identities to be protected. Betting on games of chance is still technically illegal in the State of New York." He handed back the photograph. "Of course, the police are paid a fortune to look the other way. But it would still be considered very bad form for me to divulge the names or activities of my patrons."

"We already know his name," I said. "It's Robert Aaron Straker. The problem, Mr. Chamberlain, is that he has vanished, and may well be the victim of foul play." I decided I'd better not play up the homicidal maniac angle as we hadn't yet gone to the police. "A friend has asked us to look into the matter. All I wish to know is if he was here."

Chamberlain considered this. "I have no desire to get involved in any official investigation," he said. "That would be exceedingly bad for business." He gave me a hard look. "Is there currently such an investigation?"

"No," I said. "And if you help us, there may never be."

He nodded. "Alright. I don't see the harm in answering a few simple questions. Yes, he was here. Only once."

"Was he alone?" Edward ventured.

"No, he was with another man. No one I knew personally. As you know, I'm quite selective about who passes through the front door. But both appeared to be gentlemen of adequate means, so I let them in."

I shared an excited look with Edward. Finally, we were getting somewhere.

"May I ask what this other man looked like?"

"There was nothing remarkable about him. I'd say he was about Mr. Dovington's height, light brown hair. I can't recall his eye color."

"What happened next?"

"His companion retired to the faro tables, while Mr. Straker chose roulette. He quickly proceeded to lose a large sum of money. They began to squabble." Mr. Chamberlain adjusted the cuffs of his jacket. "I'm not in the habit of eavesdropping on my patrons, but when their argument became disruptive to my other clientele, I was forced to intervene. From the little I heard, my impression was that the other gentleman was a stockbroker who had invested money for Mr. Straker and lost it when the Exchange was closed down during the blizzard. He had advanced him a sum to gamble with, and Mr. Straker wished for another advance which the man refused to give him. It all became rather ugly."

"What did you do?" I asked.

"I requested that they leave, which they did."

"When did this happen?"

"Several months ago. Not long after order was restored following the storm."

"Oh." I bit my lip in disappointment. It seemed too long ago to be connected to the Rickard killing and all the rest.

"I thought I'd seen the last of them," Mr. Chamberlain said. "Until Straker returned. Two weeks ago."

I leaned forward. "Indeed?"

"Yes. I almost didn't recognize him, so much had he changed in just a few short months. I'll put it this way: he was not a man I would welcome to my table, simply because he clearly couldn't afford to lose a single cent."

Somewhere in the house, a clock struck midnight. I imagined all those paragons of business and politics had finished stuffing themselves and were now well occupied with being fleeced by the house dealers. It was a satisfying thought.

"Mr. Straker was much the worse for drink," Chamberlain went on. "He demanded entry and said he was looking for the gentleman he had been here with before. He seemed quite angry and upset. I told him that I'd never seen the man before or since, which was the truth. Finally, he left. That's all."

"So he never mentioned the man's name?" Edward asked.

"Never."

"Was either of them by chance a smoker?"

"Not Mr. Straker. But the other one, yes."

"Did you happen to notice which brand?"

"I'm sorry, no. It's just a vague recollection."

"I see. Well, thank you, Mr. Chamberlain. You have been more forthcoming than I could have expected."

Chamberlain graciously inclined his head. "It's my pleasure to assist a lady, Miss Pell. And if I ever have need for you or your sister's services, I won't hesitate to call. Unlike certain others of my sex, I have no objection to women in any sphere of life. I believe change is coming, and we can either get out of the way, or be knocked down flat." He smiled. "I'll escort you out."

As I had guessed, the dining room was empty when we passed through it a second time except for several black servants bearing the wreckage of the banquet into the kitchens. They studiously avoided eye contact as we walked by. I knew that many of the black people hired in the finer establishments, like Chamberlain's, had come originally from the plantation houses of the South, where simply looking a white person in the face could be a lynching offence. Not that the North was a great deal better. We just pretended to be.

Mr. Chamberlain kissed my gloved hand at the front door and wished us a good evening. Since we were in the Tenderloin, there were plenty of revellers still out and about. Morrissey's, Chamberlain's only real rival in high-class gambling, was just a block away on Twenty-Fourth Street, and the rest of the neighborhood was a profusion of nightclubs, saloons, bordellos and dance halls.

"Nice job staying quiet, Harry," Edward said with a laugh as we climbed into the barouche and headed downtown toward Greenwich Village. "Actually, you handled him perfectly. John's a decent man, underneath. And the implicit threat of bad publicity did loosen his tongue."

"If only he could have given us a name," I said. "Now we have two mystery men instead of one. But it does seem as though Straker had an enemy. And a smoker, too, although that describes half the men in New York."

"So he lost his money during the blizzard, poor fellow," Edward said. "Rotten luck."

"That seems to be Mr. Straker's curse," I replied, angling the photograph in my lap so it caught the light of a passing street lamp.

Was it possible that a series of unfortunate circumstances had caused his mind, even his entire personality, to fracture? We knew now at what point things had taken a sharp turn for the worse. The blizzard had struck on March 11th and lasted for three days. It engulfed the entire Eastern Seaboard, leaving death and ruin in its wake from New Jersey to Rhode Island. Commerce ground to a standstill, and it was during this time that Straker lost his inheritance. I imagined him lying that first night in the room on Leonard Street, listening to the drunken screams and shouts drifting from the cheap whiskey bars, and wondered what sort of dark thoughts ran through his head.

It was now five months later. According to Chamberlain, he had come in just two weeks ago, apparently still seeking to settle the score with the nameless broker who squandered his money. What else had befallen Straker during that time we could only guess at.

As I looked at those dark, slightly dreamy eyes, I couldn't help but wonder: were they the eyes of a martyr, or a madman?

CHAPTER SIX

I WOKE LATE the next morning to bright sunshine streaming through my bedroom window. I lay there for a moment, still pleasantly half asleep, when I remembered that Edward, John and I were supposed to attend the eleven o'clock service at Holy Trinity Episcopal Church.

Sundays in New York are less of a religious observance than an opportunity for the gentry to parade in their Sabbath finery. Except for the Bowery, which can't be bothered to put a lid on sinning for even a single day, the whole town shuts down and a social, festive atmosphere takes over.

I jumped out of bed and threw on a high-necked dress suitable for church. Holy Trinity sat at the intersection of Madison Avenue and Forty-Second Street. I recalled it as having a large, handsome steeple, and being a bit swamped by the tidal flood of passengers heading to and from Grand Central Depot on Lexington.

Mrs. Rivers raised an eyebrow when I told her where I was headed, as she knew well how restless I became when sentenced for an hour to a hard pew, but I guess she thought a little of the Holy Spirit might leak into me for she raised no objection. She seemed unaware of my trip to Chamberlain's the night before, and I'd taken great care not to make a sound as I crept back to my bed. If she noticed a slight puffiness around my eyes at breakfast that morning, Mrs. Rivers didn't remark on it.

I found Connor in his room and learned that none of the Bank Street Butchers had seen or heard from Billy since Friday evening, when he'd come to the house.

"I want them all looking for him straightaway," I said, my stomach twisting with guilt. "Do nothing else. If he's not found by this evening, we'll need to report him missing. And see if anyone knows where he went the day before he came to you. It might give us some clue as to where he thought he saw Straker."

Connor nodded in a businesslike fashion. "We're on it, Harry. But Billy goes off sometimes. To clear his head, he says."

"When there's $50 to collect?" I asked grimly.

"Minus my—"

"Yes, yes, your ten percent commission. Just find him!"

I grabbed a hansom cab on Fifth Avenue, but as it was nearly 10:45, the traffic was already heavy. An overturned cart at Thirty-Second Street provoked further yelling and cursing and general mayhem. My driver did his best to gallop the last few blocks (ignoring the outraged fist-shaking of a group of old ladies attempting to cross), but it was no use. I was still late to the start of the service.

Disapproving faces turned my way as I scurried to a rear pew, trying not to step on too many toes in the process, although after running the gauntlet at Chamberlain's, I figured it would take more than a few scowls to faze me.

I scanned the congregation for John and Edward and finally spotted the backs of their heads about halfway toward the pulpit, where the minister was holding forth about The

Gospel of Matthew. My eyes instantly glazed over. There was something about the soft creaking of people shifting in the pews, the dim light and the echoing, sonorous sermon that always made me want to curl up and go to sleep.

So I spent the next few minutes trying to find the Fox sisters. It wasn't easy since I was in the very back of the church, but when we stood up to sing *Come, Thou Almighty King*, I got a quick glimpse of two women who seemed to fit the description. They were middle-aged, with dark hair and a close enough resemblance to each other to be related. Neither was exactly pretty, and you might even say that Margaret was downright plain, but they had a charismatic quality that drew the eye.

There were actually three of them—Kate, Margaret and Leah—but from what I'd read in the papers, Kate and Margaret were feuding with their elder sister. This had led them to publicly confess that their decades of supposed communication with the spirits had all been an elaborate hoax. According to Margaret, they had started at a very young age (Margaret was fifteen, Kate was twelve) by using an apple on a string to make bumping sounds that their mother believed was a ghost. Encouraged by the success of this deception, the girls then claimed they had made contact with a murdered peddler named Charles B. Rosna. When shards of human bone were discovered buried in the cellar, their reputation as psychics began to grow.

It was now some forty years later, and the very same women who had ignited the Spiritualist movement had just brought it crashing to its knees. Would they be willing to talk about Becky Rickard, whose terrible end could be traced back, at least in part, to the Fox sisters' confession?

I waited impatiently for the service to conclude, leaping

out of my seat before the final "amens" had faded away, and met John and Edward at the door.

John broke into a wide grin when he saw me. "Late to church again, Harry? What was it this time? Broken clock? Lame horse? Overturned cart blocking the road?"

"As a matter of fact, yes," I said. "The last one. Listen, I think I saw Kate and Margaret before." I craned my neck to see over the crowd surging through the front doors. "But they've disappeared."

We hurried outside, where the parishioners were milling around, the ladies sporting their fanciest hats, the gentlemen brandishing silver-headed walking sticks. It was a pleasant day, with a fresh breeze coming off the East River. I searched the chattering crowd in vain. Evidently, the Fox sisters didn't socialize much anymore.

"Over there," John said.

Two figures in black were walking arm in arm toward Fifth Avenue, not exactly rushing along, but not dallying either. We caught up with them at the corner of Bryant Park.

"Excuse me," I said, stepping in front of them. "I'm awfully sorry to bother you, but my name is… Miss Pell. Am I correct in presuming that you are Margaret and Kate Fox?"

The sisters' faces instantly became guarded.

"Are you a reporter?" Kate asked.

"Not at all. I'm a consulting detective. I've been hired to look into the murder of Becky Rickard."

The women shared a quick look. "What do you want with us?" Margaret asked. "We had nothing to do with it."

"I know that," I said. "I'm just trying to learn a little more about her and who her clients might have been."

"And who are they?" Kate pointed to John and Edward,

her dark eyes wary. She was thinner than her sister, with a pointy nose and long, almost mournful face.

I gave my friends' names, making sure to introduce John as "Doctor Weston."

"Well, I'm sorry, but we can't help you," Kate said, turning away.

"Please!" I called after them. "Just a few minutes of your time. Becky's killer deserves to be caught and punished, but the police aren't getting anywhere. It's not even in the papers anymore. No one cares." I swept up my skirts and ran after them. "She was only twenty-five!"

Margaret stopped. She whispered a few words to Kate, who shook her head in vehement disagreement, then stalked off alone.

"I'll talk to you for Becky's sake," Margaret said at my approach. "Come, let's walk in the park."

I waved over John and Edward and we found a shady spot near the imposing fifty-foot-high wall of the Croton Distributing Reservoir. Perhaps it was my morbid streak, but whenever I passed by this place, I always thought of the thousands of bodies that used to lie in a potter's field beneath our feet, and whose eternal rest was cut short in 1840 when they were all dug up and relocated to Ward's Island.

If ghosts were real, one would think they'd be haunting every square foot of this city.

Margaret Fox turned out to be a kind woman, who seemed truly sorry at what had befallen her one-time protégé. She explained that Becky had travelled to Rochester to see them when she was just nineteen. Becky had an ethereal quality that fascinated audiences, especially men. She was well-spoken and passionate about Spiritualism and soon became a sought-after public speaker.

"We conducted many séances together," Margaret said, "but then Becky began to call herself Valentina von Linden and got herself invited to a few society parties. She was convinced she'd find a rich man to marry her, the poor fool. She didn't understand that while any of those so-called gentlemen would be happy to carry on a dalliance and whisper promises in her ear, she was too far beneath them to be taken seriously."

"Were there any men in particular?" I asked.

"Yes, one who she seemed head over heels for, but she wouldn't tell me his name."

"Did you get any impressions about him?"

Margaret thought for a moment. "Very rich. One of the older New York families. She said he was terrified his mother would find out. I think he was afraid of being disinherited."

"Did she ever say what he looked like?"

"I'm afraid not. She was very secretive. I think he insisted on it."

"What about her clientele?" John asked. "Can you give us any names?"

"I could." She gave us a sharp look. "But I'm not sure I should. What's the use in dragging more people through the mud?"

"Because one of them might be Becky's killer," I said. "Two hundred dollars was found near her body. She must have gotten it from somewhere. You know she was living in abject poverty?"

"I didn't before I read what happened in the newspapers," Margaret said wearily. "We would have tried to help her. But she never asked."

It reminded me of what Brady had said about Straker, that he was too proud to admit defeat.

"The money rules out robbery," I said. "And it was such an

exact amount, as though she'd just gotten it and hadn't spent any yet. We need to know who gave it to her."

Margaret Fox sighed. "Alright, I'll tell you some names. But if anyone asks, they didn't come from me, understood?"

We all nodded. John took out a notepad and started writing as Margaret began her recital.

"… Miss Lucy Gould, Mrs. H. R. Pendleton, Mr. and Mrs. March, the Kanes, Mrs. Robert Mortimer, Lord Balthazar, the Whittiers… "

By the time Margaret Fox finally wound down, John had filled six pages with his illegible scrawl. So much for narrowing the field of suspects, I thought glumly.

"Did she ever express any interest in black magic or grimoires?" I asked.

Margaret looked scandalized. "Absolutely not! Such things are antithetical to all that Spiritualism stands for."

If I told her about the séance, I'd have to explain my client's involvement, which would inevitably lead to the fact that I was withholding all this information from the police. So I tried to hedge a bit.

"Have you ever seen this symbol?"

I showed her the piece of paper Fred had given me, but I wasn't surprised when she answered in the negative. *No one* seemed to know what it was.

"Did she ever mention the name Robert Straker? Or Leland Brady?"

Again, Margaret shook her head. It appeared the well was running dry.

"You'll have to excuse my sister," she said, as we walked together toward Sixth Avenue. "She's had a hard time of it in the last year. Leah has been trying to take her children away. It's a terrible mess." She was silent for a long moment.

"I taught Becky how to use her ankle joints to make rapping noises. She had a real talent for it. She didn't seem bothered when she found out that we were frauds. The funny part is that despite everything, I think she really believed it."

"Believed what?" Edward ventured, taking Margaret's hand and assisting her into a hansom headed downtown.

"In the spirit world. In ghosts. In all of it." Margaret Fox sat back and nodded to us. "I wish you luck with your investigation, Miss Pell. Becky deserved better than she got. And if it is one of those society boys... well, I hope he hangs."

And with that, she was gone.

I spent the afternoon in Myrtle's chemistry laboratory on the top floor of our home, testing the scorched earth from the cellar. I placed it in a test tube and added a few hundredths of a gram of benzoin, stirring the mixture with a glass rod. I then covered the open end of the test tube with a disc of moist lead acetate paper. I heated a glycerol bath to 130 degrees and plunged the test tube inside, quickly raising the temperature to 150 degrees.

Within seconds, a deep black stain appeared on the reagent paper, confirming the presence of sulphur. Or brimstone, as John melodramatically put it. As I could think of no reason such an element would naturally appear, and the traces had been undisturbed by recent footprints, we could safely assume that it was placed there during the séance. But why, and how?

As often happens in New York in the summertime, the cool morning proved deceptive. By late afternoon, it was sweltering again, and I found myself overcome by a kind of stupor. John had gone home to enjoy a Sunday dinner with his boisterous family, and Edward had headed out to the Coney Island Jockey Club to bet on the races at Sheepshead Bay.

His enthusiasm for the investigation had been powerfully rejuvenated by the possibility that one of his friends or acquaintances might be a cold-blooded killer. Edward promised to wrangle us invitations to a ball the following week hosted by the Kanes at their mansion on Central Park West. As much as I disliked such events, I agreed that since nearly everyone on John's list would be there, it gave us a chance to survey Becky's former clients in the flesh.

I ate lunch with Mrs. Rivers (pushing the dreaded aspic salad to the side of my plate, where it quivered malevolently), and retired to my room to think about the case. Margaret Fox's revelations gave us a whole new avenue to explore. If Becky did have a rich paramour, he had treated her badly. Perhaps a broken heart had also caused her chloral hydrate addiction.

I changed into a lighter shift and curled up on my big canopy bed, which had a view of the rooftops looking south. What if Becky had truly loved him, as Margaret seemed to believe? What if she had waited for him to come to his senses, even as her life fell apart around her?

What if, I thought, she finally grew tired of waiting, and love turned to fury?

It seemed as though this man was in a position to lose everything if it came out that he was having an affair with a girl like Becky. What if she had tried to blackmail him?

That could certainly account for the indications that the killer was struck with remorse after the crime, since he'd once cared for her. But there were problems with this theory. First, the money. He should have taken it with him, unless he was too dazed at what had just occurred and forgot to. Second, the backwards Latin. Third, the Forsizi boy.

And fourth: Straker. It would mean he had nothing to do with it, that the séance that same night was just a coincidence. But we still had the problem of the blood in his flat, and the fact that the man was missing.

I couldn't shake the unpleasant feeling that I was missing something critical, some clue that Myrtle would recognize in an instant as the key to the entire case. That I couldn't see the forest for the trees.

As far as suspects, we had Straker, of course, and the man who had accompanied him to Chamberlain's. Then there was Becky's paramour.

And there was also Brady. He was there that night. He said he hadn't returned home, but had gone to his office to sleep because it was so late. He too had served in the Army. He could have gotten access to Straker's flat somehow. It wouldn't have been difficult.

But it made no sense. Where was his motive? After all, Straker had approached *him*, not the other way around. We had only Brady's word for this, but the story rang true. Myrtle had taught me seventeen signs to watch for when a person lied, from subtle eye movements to speech patterns and hand gestures, and Brady had displayed none of them. Either he was a spectacular, pathological liar, or he wasn't lying at all.

I must have drifted off because the light was fading from the sky in a blaze of orange and red when my eyes opened again. Sweat had glued the shift to my body. I threw off the sheet and sat up. Groggy as I was, I felt as though I'd awakened suddenly. That some noise had pulled me up from the depths of sleep.

Like the creaky floorboard on the second-floor landing.

"Mrs. Rivers?" I called out. "Connor?"

There was no answer.

My nerves began to tingle, although I couldn't say precisely why. The house was quiet. But I was certain that just before I woke, someone had been climbing the stairs.

I'd left my door ajar about an inch. Now, my eyes locked on the doorknob. Every sense seemed to heighten, the details of the room snapping into sharp focus. I thought I heard a tiny sound in the hall. A *stealthy* sound. My heart hammered in my chest as I placed one bare foot on the floor, then the other.

Myrtle kept guns in the house, but they were all locked up in her study on the second floor.

If it was a burglar, the best thing would be to make a loud noise so he knew someone was home. Most house-breakers just wanted the silver. They weren't in it for assault. Or murder. Those were capital offenses.

I opened my mouth to scream but something stopped me. A powerful feeling that whoever was out there was not, in fact, a burglar.

That they were here for me.

And if I gave myself away, the game would be over.

With one eye on the door, I searched the room for something I could use as a weapon. My vanity had only a silver comb and hairbrush, a button hook, a bottle of Crosby's Brain Food with vitalized phosphates, and a tin of powder that mother encouraged me to dust my freckles with (and which itself had gathered dust since she'd been gone). A messy stack of books and journals sat on the table next to my bed. The top one, which lay open, was an article by the Scottish surgeon Henry Faulds in *Nature* titled "On the skin-furrows of the hand," in which he proposed a method for recording fingerprints with ink. It was fascinating stuff, but I doubted I could do much damage with it.

I took a step towards the door, goosebumps rising under

my thin shift despite the heat. Because now I was sure I heard something, just outside.

Soft breathing.

I scanned the room, the first wings of panic fluttering in my throat. My gaze landed on the dresser. It held a vase of fresh flowers, bright yellow marigolds from the garden. Mrs. Rivers must have placed them there while I napped. The distance, perhaps fifteen feet, took forever to cross. I placed each foot with exquisite care, the blood rushing in my ears. It made no sense, but I was seized by the absolute certainty that the moment I made a single sound, that door would burst open.

And then I smelled it. The faintest waft of tobacco smoke.

A minute later I gripped the vase in my hand. It wasn't much, but better than nothing. A blow to the head might slow him down at least.

Whoever he was.

I raised it high as the door began to slowly swing open. Two inches.

Three.

"Harry? Are you up there?"

Mrs. Rivers' tremulous voice sounded miles away. The kitchen, maybe.

Oh no. *Mrs. Rivers.*

"Run!" I screamed, slamming into the door and pressing my back against it. "Get out of the house!"

I listened for the sound of pounding footsteps, for the creak of the landing signifying that the hunter now sought other, easier prey.

All was quiet outside for an endless minute.

"Oh drat," I muttered. "Alright, Harry, here goes."

I stepped to the side of the door and yanked it open, vase poised to crash down. The hall was empty.

"Mrs. Rivers?" I called, peering down the stairs.

I started to make my way toward the first floor, two long flights. The hair on the back of my neck twitched at every shift in the air, and I'm not sure I took a breath until my feet were planted firmly on the hall carpet.

"Mrs. Rivers?" I whispered.

The only reply was the monotonous tick of a grandfather clock.

I realized that I'd gone right past Myrtle's study and kicked myself for a fool. But there wasn't time to go back upstairs. I had to warn my housekeeper and get us both out of the house.

To my right was the formal parlor (less cozy than the one John and I used as our unofficial headquarters), to my left a corridor that led to the dining room and kitchen. None of the lamps were lit yet, and all was shrouded in the half-light of dusk. Connor was probably out looking for Billy. I tightened my sweaty grip on the vase. Full darkness would have been better, if only to hide in. As it was, every shadow, every hump of furniture, looked vaguely man-shaped.

I took a deep breath and turned the corner toward the kitchens, running smack into a faceless form. I shrieked and wielded the vase like a battle axe, but the blow landed wide of its mark, shattering against a bookcase instead of my assailant's skull.

Which actually turned out for the best, since my shriek was answered by one of even higher pitch.

"Harrison Fearing Pell!" Mrs. Rivers bleated, clutching her chest, and I knew I was in big trouble.

"I thought you were a burglar," I protested, helping her to an armchair.

"Where are you going?" Mrs. Rivers demanded as I dashed down the hall. "Have you lost your mind completely?"

"Just wait!" I called over my shoulder, as I swung wide the front door and leapt barefoot onto the stoop.

Tenth Street was deserted in both directions.

"Come back this instant!" Mrs. Rivers sounded scandalized. "You're wearing a nightdress!"

It couldn't be.

Maybe I *was* losing my mind.

I was just turning to go back in when a sharp pain flared in my right foot, like a bee sting. I hopped back and examined the sole, where a reddish blister was already rising. I bent down and scanned the doorstep. When I saw what lay there, my breath caught in my throat, filling me with a strange combination of relief and fear.

Half of a Turkish Elegante cigarette.

Smoke curled lazily from the glowing tip, which I had stepped on.

"Harry!" Mrs. Rivers called again, more insistently.

"Coming!"

I gave the street once last survey, locked the front door, and carried the cigarette into the kitchen, where I extinguished it in the sink. Then I went into the parlor to try to explain why I had just attacked my housekeeper with a vase.

It seems that Mrs. Rivers had been working in the garden all afternoon. When it started to grow dark, she came inside to call me for supper but suddenly remembered that she had left the water running outside. She went to shut it off and therefore didn't hear any of the warnings I'd screamed from upstairs, which may have saved her life. Because I think that at the very moment she was returning to the garden, our man was descending the stairs.

Perhaps he hadn't realized anyone else was home, and got

spooked when she called my name. But if he'd met her face to face, he might have decided that he couldn't leave her alive.

I didn't tell Mrs. Rivers any of this, of course. I said I'd had a nightmare and blamed it on nerves, a catch-all disorder that everyone seemed to accept could strike women for no real reason. Mrs. Rivers could see I was genuinely shaken up, if not the true cause of it. She offered me a dose of Dr. Beeton's Soothing Remedy, a dreadful concoction she used to pour into me and Myrtle when we were little that tasted like licorice and contained enough morphine to tranquilize a horse. I politely declined. So Mrs. Rivers settled for feeding me soup and ordering me back to bed. While she was in the kitchen, I locked all the downstairs windows and shut the blinds. Full dark had fallen. To my overheated imagination, the night seemed to press against the house like a shroud. I was glad that although our street was a quiet one, the neighborhood would remain lively for many hours yet.

My gut told me that the intruder wouldn't return that same night, but I didn't care to take foolish chances. So before returning to my room, I stopped in Myrtle's study and took a Russian model Smith & Wesson revolver from her gun cabinet. I'd fired it before, though never at another human being. I thought I could manage to do so if it came down to it.

When Connor returned home at around seven, I told him in whispers all that had transpired. His young face hardened and he dashed out while Mrs. Rivers was in her bath, returning minutes later to say that the Bank Street Butchers were now watching the house and would sound the alarm if any suspicious men so much as glanced at the front door.

As disturbed as I felt, I also knew that the investigation must be getting close to something uncomfortable for our killer, something that had flushed him out and provoked him into taking such a risk. But was it the trip to Chamberlain's? The revelations of Margaret Fox? Or something else entirely?

And then there was Mrs. Rivers. It was one thing to keep her in the dark that I was playing at being a detective, quite another to put her at risk. Twice that evening, I started towards my bedroom door, intent on telling her everything, and twice I changed my mind at the last moment.

As it turned out, the decision would shortly be taken out of my hands.

At the hour just before dawn, a loud pounding came on the front door. Mrs. Rivers and I reached it more or less simultaneously. A sleeping cap covered her hair, and her eyes grew wide when she saw the gun in my hand.

"Who is it?" I shouted.

"Nellie! Open up!"

I let out a long breath and unlocked the door. Nellie Bly stood alone on the doorstep, her short bangs plastered to her forehead in damp curls that looked like question marks. She eyed the gun in my hand and I quickly set it on a side table we used for mail.

"Is Myrtle back yet?" she asked, and I could tell from the urgency in her voice that something serious had happened.

I had a sinking feeling I knew what that thing was, and her next words confirmed it.

"There's been another, just tonight. The face is covered, Harry, just like the Rickard and Forsizi murders."

"My sister's not here," I said, pulse racing with both dread and excitement. "But please, come in."

Pounding feet on the stairs signified the arrival of Connor, his copper curls and long white nightshirt giving him the look of one of Botticelli's angels, except dirtier.

"Ah, it's you Miss Bly," he said. "I thought… "

"What's going on?" Mrs. Rivers demanded, as Nellie strode into the parlor. "What murders?"

"I'm helping Myrtle with an investigation," I said, aiming for a casual tone. "Nothing to worry about."

"Nothing to worry about? You're running about brandishing a gun after nearly braining me with a vase, and now Miss Bly shows up in the middle of the night and says there's been *another one*? I think you haven't been exactly truthful with me, Harry!"

"But—"

"Is John mixed up in this too?" She looked at my guilty face and sniffed. "Of course he is. You two are always partners in crime. Well, if you think that just because your parents are away—"

"I hate to interrupt," Nellie said with a tight smile. "But there's no time. I know the detective who was called to the scene. He's one of the smart ones. A friend of Myrtle's, and of mine. He might give us limited access. But we have to leave right away. Before the body's carted off to the morgue."

I nodded to Nellie. "Give me one minute."

I dashed up the stairs, ignoring Mrs. Rivers continued diatribe, and changed out of my nightclothes into a plain dress of navy blue. Adrenaline made my fingers clumsy, and it took three tries to get my boots laced up. Then I was racing back down and apologizing to my housekeeper, even as I hurried Nellie out the door with Connor on our heels.

"The cat's out of the bag," I told him. "May as well bring the boys inside until we get back."

Connor stood on the steps and gave a loud whistle. Six small, ragged forms emerged from the shadows across the street and rushed over, pouring into the parlor as Mrs. Rivers clutched her robe more tightly across her bosom. They were all armed to teeth with an assortment of crude weapons.

"Oh my," Mrs. Rivers muttered faintly.

"I'll explain everything when I get back!" I shouted over my shoulder.

Nellie had engaged a hackney for the trip and we climbed in. A light rain was falling. The city slumbered around us, its last revellers having stumbled off to bed and the early risers not yet stirring.

"Where are we going?" I asked as we pulled away, the plump form of Mrs. Rivers still silhouetted in the doorway.

"The waterfront. Sixty-Third Street. The victim is a young woman, no identification yet."

"How was she killed?" I asked.

"I don't know. Only that it was definitely murder. Who were those kids?"

"The Bank Street Butchers. They're on Myrtle's payroll."

Nellie laughed. "I've heard of them. The police in the Ninth Ward call them the Bank Street Bedbugs, since they're a pest that's proven impossible to get rid of."

We turned north on Fifth Avenue and I leaned forward. "Listen, Nellie, we need to make a quick stop for John Weston. He's training to be a doctor. His observations could be invaluable."

She hesitated, raising an eyebrow. "Your partner in crime?"

"I know how that sounded," I said. "But please trust me. It's on the way. He lives at Gramercy Park. Two minutes, that's all I ask."

"Alright then. But only if you tell me why you answered the door with a revolver in your hand."

"Fair enough," I said.

So I told her all that happened since last we met,

concluding with the fact that someone had stalked me in my own house just hours before.

"Has it occurred to you," Nellie said slowly, "that it should have been *you* tonight? That this person is driven to kill, and his needs were left unmet? That he was forced to find another victim?"

"Yes," I said. "That has occurred to me."

"Because it seems like a mighty coincidence. Did you go to the police?" She stared at me. "You didn't, did you? For God's sake, Harry, why not? This isn't a game. There's a violent lunatic out there. Does Myrtle know? I can't believe she'd put you at such risk." Nellie paused. "Well, actually I can. But that doesn't mean you have to go along with it!"

"Half a block further," I told the driver as we reached the west side of Gramercy Park. "Nellie, the client doesn't want to go to the police. Not yet."

"Mr. Brady?" She never forgot a single scrap of information.

"Yes. We assured him of discretion. Just for a week. His reputation is at stake, as is that of a dear friend of his."

"Is it really worth it?"

"I hope so." I swung down from the carriage before it came to a full stop. "Wait here, I'll be right back."

John's house was a four-story brick building with a chest-high wrought-iron gate around the outside. His bedroom was on the top floor, but his brother Andrew's faced the street on the second floor. I scooped a handful of gravel from their front walk and tossed it up towards his window, where the tiny stones rattled like hail on a tin roof. It took two more throws but finally the sash slid upward and a head with tousled brown hair thrust itself through the frame.

"Who's down there?" Andy whispered through the bars. "Julie?"

"It's Harry," I whispered back. "I need John. It's an emergency!"

"Hey there, Harry. Hang on a minute." The head disappeared.

I stood in the thin drizzle, stamping my feet impatiently. I could see Nellie was getting anxious too. With every minute that passed, we jeopardized our access to the crime scene. But I did need John with me. Not just for his medical expertise, though it would certainly be useful. The truth is, I was scared. It's one thing to theorize about death in an abstract way. I knew that Becky Rickard's end was a brutal, terrifying one, and the poor Forsizi boy must have suffered as the life was choked out of him. But I hadn't actually laid eyes on either one of them.

In the next few minutes, I'd be standing before the still-warm body of a young woman whose life had been cut short. I'd be seeing what might have been done to *me*, if fate hadn't intervened. And to face that, I needed the steadying presence of my best friend.

Maybe we weren't so different from Leland Brady and Robert Straker. I thought back to that morning, only three days ago but seeming somehow much longer, when my client and his wife first knocked on the door of 40 West Tenth Street. What was it Brady had said?

He was just the sort of fellow you would wish to have at your side when the seas got rough.

That was John. We both had tempers, and we'd had our share of heated arguments. But I also knew that if I was in trouble, John would take my side without hesitation. He would always speak his mind if he thought I was wrong. And he would always try to protect me from the judgment of others.

I stared into the thick foliage of Gramercy Park, listening to the steady drip of the rain. Had I inadvertently attracted danger that even John couldn't shield me from? Was it already too late?

My nerves were drawn so taut that I jumped a little when the tumblers gave a loud click and the front door opened. The Westons' bull pup Angus pushed past John's legs and started energetically sniffing my boot. I gave him a scratch behind the ears. Then John emerged. His hair stood up in stiff bits and pieces, and he was still tucking his shirt into a pair of wool trousers. He usually greeted me with a lazy grin, but John was no fool. As I did when Nellie banged down my door, he'd guessed what had brought me here in the middle of the night.

"You've either found Straker or there's another body," he said without preamble. "And if it was Straker, I'd still think it could wait until morning. That means a body."

I nodded once. "The face is covered, it's got to be our man. We must hurry, John. Nellie's waiting. She knows the detective but once word gets out, it'll be a mob scene and we'll lose our chance."

"Don't worry." Andy stood behind him, stifling a yawn. "I'll let you back in. Just make sure you're here before five-thirty. Dad's an early bird, and he'll tar and feather both of us if he catches you out. Nice hair, Harry."

I'd already stuck my tongue out before I realized that a consulting detective should probably display more dignity. If John was closer to me than a sibling, then Andy was like an irritating older brother, eternally trying to get a rise. He was twenty-two and about to graduate from Columbia with a degree in law, although given his appetite for mischief, I'd always expected him to be on the wrong side of the dock.

"I won't keep him more than an hour," I promised. "And don't tell anyone where we've gone."

Andy snorted. "Paul's dead to the world 'til nine at least, and Bill snuck out to go dancing two hours ago." He laid a hand across his heart. "So your secret's safe with me, Harry. See you in a bit."

"Thanks, Andy."

He smirked. "You can thank me with a ki—"

Andy's last words were muffled as John firmly shut the front door in his brother's face.

"Come on, then," he said. "Before the other fools wake up. He forgot about Rupert, and we know he's the worst of all!"

The streets were virtually empty except for a handful of idle cabs around Grand Central, so we made the four miles northeast to Sixty-Third Street in less than half an hour. As we sped through the dark, wet night, I filled John in on my afternoon. When I told him about the Turkish Elegante-smoking intruder, his eyes darkened. Like Nellie, he thought I should go to the police, Brady be damned. He also thought I should leave the house. When I refused to do either of these things, he went on a brief rant about "excessive confidence" and "overweening ambition," then subsided into tense silence.

I could see that Nellie thought he was right, but she also wasn't the type to tell another woman what to do. So the only sounds as we neared the waterfront were the hiss of mud under the wheels and blowing snorts of the horses. When we turned onto Avenue A at its southern terminus on Fifty-Fifth Street, the brackish smell of the East River filled our lungs. I spotted the glimmering beacon of the Blackwell Island Lighthouse a half mile to the north. The island itself was a catalogue of human misery, housing a lunatic asylum, prison, workhouse and charity hospital once devoted exclusively to smallpox patients but now ministering to inmates and New York's poor.

"Almost there," Nellie said. "According to Fred, it's a malt-house called Neidlinger, Schmidt & Co., right on the water. They use a grain elevator to raise and store the malt once it's unloaded from the ships. The body was found at the base of the elevator by a night watchman."

"When was that?" I asked.

"Just over an hour ago, sometime after three."

I could see why the killer would find this an attractive location to carry out his grisly work. The brief stretch of Avenue A dubbed Sutton Place had recently been developed as a residential area of brownstones, but once we passed Fifty-Ninth Street, the waterfront reverted to its shabby, industrial origins. My stomach tightened as we rounded the corner of Sixty-Third Street and saw the harsh glare of electric arc-lights set up in front of a block-long building with a tower girded by a spiral iron staircase. Connected to the tower by a passageway overlooking the river was a huge grain elevator built of corrugated iron and wood.

The elevator stood some fifty feet from the main building, right on the edge of the wharf. It looked to be about ninety feet tall and forty square at the base, though it tapered toward the top like a medieval battlement. The lights were aimed at something at the bottom.

Our driver stopped the carriage as a patrolman materialized out of the darkness, wearing the blue frock coat and domed felt helmet that I always thought made New York's municipal force look like English bobbies.

"Hold up," he said gruffly, seizing the bridle. "You can't go any further. This area's closed off. Police investigation."

Nellie showed him her credentials from *The World* and his

face changed from suspicion to grudging respect, as so often happened with our famous friend. It was probably the only reason we weren't thrown straight out on our ears.

"Wait here," he told us. "Maybe you're known to Sergeant Mallory, and maybe you're not. But no one gets through without his personal say-so."

The patrolman returned a minute later and signalled that we should get out of the carriage. "You can walk from here," he said. "Stay to the middle of the street, and go straight to the sergeant. He says he'll talk to you." He looked hard first at Nellie, then at me, ignoring John completely. "Though it's not a sight for a lady."

Nellie was clearly used to these kinds of idiotic remarks. "Thank you," is all she said, as we started off towards the river, and what our quarry had left there.

"Not a sight for anyone," the officer muttered under his breath, "save perhaps the Devil himself."

CHAPTER SEVEN

THE RAIN EASED up some as we made our way toward the arc-lights arrayed around the base of the grain elevator. The ground here was rough and uneven, with chunks of loose paving stone alternating with soggy patches of earth. Twice I tripped, and twice John's strong hand kept me from falling. It broke the ice between us a bit, although I knew he hadn't forgotten our argument.

Tattered clouds raced past overhead. A sliver of moon appeared, then vanished just as quickly. The smell of the river grew stronger, and I could see white and yellow lanterns bobbing on the masts of anchored ships to the south. Long Island City lay across the expanse of black water, on the far side of Blackwell's Island. It was still night, but I could see from the faint bluish line on the horizon that dawn was not far off.

None of us spoke as we approached the small group of uniformed officers. We had no urge to speculate as to the state of the body. We'd know for certain soon enough.

As we came into the periphery of the light, one of the figures detached from the others and greeted us. Sergeant Mallory was a short, broad-shouldered man with an air of world-weary competence. He was young to have earned the rank of detective, early thirties, which meant he was either very smart or very well-connected. As his leather shoes showed signs of wear, I deduced the former, since a well-connected man would almost certainly be a wealthy man. It also implied honesty, which was a rare enough trait in any civil servant, but especially in law enforcement.

"Miss Bly," he said, looking John and me over with shrewd brown eyes. "I thought you were alone. Sometimes I doubt Officer Beane would remember his own mother's name if it weren't tattooed on his backside. Pardon, ladies. But he neglected to mention two *additional civilians* walking around my crime scene."

"They're here for Myrtle," Nellie said quickly. "This is Harrison Fearing Pell and her associate, John Weston. Myrtle's on the case." She crossed her arms and stuck her chin out, as if daring him to cross the great detective.

Mallory frowned. "*What* case? And how did you get here so quickly? I only got the call an hour or so ago."

"My sister noticed a certain pattern emerging," I said carefully. "Killings where the victim's face has been covered. All in the last week."

"All?"

"Two others. Becky Rickard and Raffaele Forsizi."

"I know the cases," Mallory said warily.

"We wondered if they were connected so we've been waiting to see if it happened again," I said, trying not to fidget under his intense gaze. "Myrtle would have come herself but she's been hired by the Pinkertons. I'm here on her behalf."

"I know the whole department is leaky as a sieve, but this is ridiculous," Mallory muttered through his mustache. "You've beaten the morgue boys!" He thought hard for a moment and seemed to reach a decision. "Alright, listen. I may regret this, but Myrtle did me a good turn once, when I was fresh to the force, and I owe her one. However," and he held up a wagging finger, "that doesn't mean you get something for nothing. I'll let you have a look, tell me what you think, but I want to know what Myrtle knows and why she thinks these cases are tied together." He blew out a long breath. "Which I pray they aren't, because the good people of New York have been through enough this year."

I decided right then that I liked Sergeant Mallory. He wasn't arrogant and inflexible, like some of the detectives Myrtle complained about. And he seemed like he wanted to catch the killer badly enough that he'd take advice from a woman—and risk the ridicule of his colleagues.

I also knew I was navigating some tricky waters. I didn't want to out-and-out lie to a police officer, which was obstruction of justice and who knew what else, but I wasn't ready to break a promise to my client yet either. So I danced around the truth, keeping Brady's and Straker's names more or less out of it, and sticking to the similarities in the crimes. I mentioned the impression of remorse or ambiguity, and the possibility that more than one person could be involved. When I described the Rickard scene, and the writing that was found there, Mallory nodded in grim resignation.

"Miss Bly, I'll determine which details can be published and which will be held back, agreed?"

"Agreed," Nellie said.

"We managed to identify her fairly quickly," Mallory said. "She had a note from her dentist in her pocket recommending cocaine toothache drops. As it happens, one of my men recognized the name—Anne Marlowe. She was an actress, performing down at Niblo's. He saw the show with his wife last week. We checked and the description seems to match, although to be honest, it's hard to know for sure. What's left of her is… well, you'll see in a minute. Come on."

The whole time we'd been talking, my eyes kept drifting towards the center of that spotlight. But my view of what lay there was blocked by two patrolmen and the corner of the grain elevator. Now, we followed Mallory a dozen steps to the open space at the very edge of the East River where what remained of Anne Marlowe lay face-up in the thin rain.

"She was covered with a burlap sack," Mallory explained. "The watchman actually tripped over the body. He thought it was a bag of grain at first."

The sack now lay to the side, carefully folded. Beside me, I heard Nellie take in a sharp breath. John was perfectly still, but I could somehow feel his heart racing. I knew he was picturing someone else lying there.

"Cause of death was strangulation?" I heard myself say in a calm voice that seemed like another person entirely.

"Yes," Mallory said. "The chain was ripped from a longer length we found in the kiln building. We're still working out how he managed to do that. But the links match perfectly."

"Not a cutting tool?"

"No. They were torn apart with brute force."

I studied the body, trying to blot out the horror of what had been done to another human being and focus only on what it told me about her killer. The chain had been wrapped three times around her neck, so tightly that her lower jaw had been pushed up at an unnatural angle. From the regularity of her features, I guessed that she had been attractive in life, perhaps even heart-breakingly lovely. But the ghastly bloating and discoloration made it impossible to tell.

She was fully dressed, lying on her back with her arms arranged at her sides as though she were sleeping. Her gown was beige with thin pink stripes and a broad lace collar that fell over the shoulders. Only her shoes were missing, but it seemed not unlikely that they had fallen off in the struggle.

Anne Marlowe's left wrist had been slashed open but there was only a small amount of blood, indicating the wound was inflicted post-mortem.

"The writing is over here," Mallory said, pointing to an area of wall about fifteen feet north of the body. "It seemed like gibberish until you mentioned the backwards Latin. What do you think, Miss Pell?"

It took only a moment to translate what I saw, which was this:

Erebihorp tsetop mulos em srom

A strange chill went through me as I spoke the words:

"Mors me solum potest prohibere."

"Which means?"

"Only death can stop me."

Mallory growled. "If it's death he wants, I'm sure a jury would be delighted to arrange it. Well, we know we're dealing with an educated man at least. You don't learn Latin in the free schools."

"Yes," I agreed. "John, would you be good enough to stand over there, just to the right of it? Now raise your hand up as though you were going to write something. Excellent! How tall are you, John? About five foot ten? I think we can safely say our man is of similar build, perhaps an inch or so taller. So just shy of six feet."

Mallory nodded. "That seems a safe deduction."

"What about footprints? The ground is soft from the rain."

"Yes, we found several sets. One is clearly the watchman's. There are at least three others, I've already taken precise measurements and noted the pattern of the soles. I'd say that two are large enough to fit the man we're looking for. So if we ever find his boots, we may get a match."

"I'd like to examine the body, if you don't mind," John ventured. "I have some medical expertise."

"Certainly, just be quick about it," Mallory said, glancing toward the alley that led back to Sixty-Third Street. "I've learned about all I can here. She needs to go to the Morgue for formal identification. And before you ask, the watchman saw and heard nothing. He says he passes by about every half hour, so I figure death occurred sometime between three and three-thirty a.m."

"Any signs of a carriage?" I asked.

"None, and I looked first thing."

"Then how did he get her here?"

Mallory just shook his head.

"I already sent some men to rouse Niblo's owner and find out what time she left, and whether or not she was alone. But I don't think we'll know much until tomorrow."

Niblo's Garden was one of New York's grandest and most popular theaters, especially in the summertime. It had burned to the ground twice over the years, and each time been rebuilt, most recently by the department store magnate A.T. Stewart. I'd passed by it a few days before, on the way to Straker's flat, and had a vague sense of seeing an advertisement for a Jules Verne epic.

"Wasn't the Forsizi kid found by the Union Square slave market?" Nellie pointed out. "Maybe there's a connection to the theatre. I know Niblo's is on lower Broadway, but... "

We all turned at a soft exclamation from John. He was crouched down next to Anne Marlowe's head, which was angled slightly to the side.

"There's something here," he said. "It appears to be burn marks."

"I thought those were lacerations from the chain," Mallory said, bracing hands on knees and shifting to stay out of John's light.

"No, they're definitely burns. Here, here and here." He indicated one dark spot to the left of the jaw and two to the right. "You see, it looks quite similar to the characteristics of a cigarette burn. Whatever touched her was at least four hundred degrees. The blister hasn't even formed yet, which is consistent with a third-degree burn." John carefully turned her head as far as the brutally cinched chain would allow. "You see how the edges are sharply defined?"

"So you're telling me he's a smoker?" Mallory asked. "That he tortured her first?"

I thought of the Turkish Elegante stub sitting in an envelope inside my vanity. But John's next words surprised me.

"No. I said they *look* like cigarette burns. But they're not." He sat back on his heels. "You're not going to like this."

Mallory sighed, took off his hat and ran a hand through thinning brown hair. "I don't like anything about this day so far. How much worse could it get?"

"Worse," John said. "I'm ninety-nine percent certain they're fingerprints."

Perfect silence greeted this bizarre statement.

"Fingerprints," Mallory echoed flatly. "Burned into her flesh."

"The ridges are quite visible. I'm just telling you what I'm seeing."

Mallory leaned in until his face hovered just inches from Anne Marlow's. He swore under his breath.

"You see them?" John asked softly.

"I see them."

"The positioning seems to indicate a right-handed individual gripping the throat just so." John mimed holding Anne the way you might if you were pinning someone down, or if you were large and powerful enough to lift her off her feet. "The thumb here, and the pointer and middle fingers here."

"But it's impossible," Mallory objected. "Even if a man's flesh could get that hot, which it can't, the defining patterns of the skin would be burned away. So it must be something of wood or metal. There's no other explanation."

John didn't respond.

"Could a person forge a device made to resemble a fingerprint?" Mallory demanded.

"It's possible," John said, although his tone implied that he found the likelihood of such a scenario to be vanishingly small.

"Something like a... a brand." Mallory nodded to himself. "Yes, it must be. *Why* is another matter. But this killer is clearly a lunatic. We may never know *why*. All I want to know is *who*." His head snapped around. "Miss Bly! I don't object to your publishing a story. It might even bring some witnesses out of the woodwork. But you are to keep these burns to yourself. Also the writing. If the public learns we have a murderer taunting the police in Latin—and penned in blood no less— we'll have a panic on our hands. Half the city is sleeping with windows open due to the heat, and the other half is on the rooftops. I agree that the Rickard killing seems to be linked, but I'm not sure about the Italian kid. I'll need to speak with the detective who handled that one." Mallory seemed almost to be talking to himself at this point. I knew it was time to leave. But I needed to be sure he understood what we were dealing with. For I was now fairly certain about one thing.

"Sergeant?" I laid a hand on his sleeve.

"Miss Pell?" Mallory replied distractedly, as the clatter of hooves signified the arrival of the morgue wagon.

"There will be more, unless you catch him," I said. "Probably very soon."

The detective held my gaze for a moment. He wasn't a handsome man, but he had nice eyes. Hazel, with flecks of gold. In the instant before he looked away, I saw a flash of... not fear, exactly. Not yet. But worry.

Sergeant Mallory knew.

"Keep in touch, Miss Pell!" he called after us, as we made our way back to the carriage.

Dawn was fast approaching now, casting a tired, grey light over the proceedings. The ramshackle buildings that had seemed so ominous when we arrived in the dark of night now struck me as simply seedy and more than a little pitiful. It was a lonely place to die.

"I'm going to Niblo's tomorrow," I told Nellie and John. "If Mrs. Rivers doesn't follow your father's lead and put bars on the windows."

"Maybe she should," he said. "I might be less worried about you."

"John's right," Nellie said. "You're mad to stay there, Harry."

"Maybe I won't then," I declared, reaching a sudden decision.

"You won't?"

"How would you fancy a trip upstate?" I asked John, as we turned south onto First Avenue and some semblance of civilization again. "To Cassadaga Lake?"

"Becky Rickard's sister," he said, interest sparking in his tired eyes.

"I can't quite explain it, but I still feel she's the key to this

case. She was the first victim, and the most savagely killed."
Nellie shot me a dubious look. "Not that Anne Marlowe's
death wasn't savage. But Becky was *stabbed*. Thirty-one times."

"And bitten," John quietly reminded us.

"Exactly," I said. "It feels different. More personal."

"The ones after... it's almost as if Becky gave him a taste
for it, so he kept going. But she's the one he really wanted.
And to know why, we need to know who she was. If her sister
will speak with us... "

"I'll cable her ahead tomorrow while you're at Niblo's,"
John said.

"And I'll join you in interviewing the other cast members," Nellie offered. "I'll need to for the story anyway."

We arranged the details of the following day's plans as the
carriage carried us downtown. Traffic was still thin, but morning rush hour in New York starts early and wagons and ped-
dlers' carts and all manner of two- and four-wheeled convey-
ances were gradually filling the streets. I agreed to meet Nellie at the theatre at noon. John would buy our train tickets
(including one for Mrs. Rivers, whom I would need to coax
into the trip), and inform Edward of the latest developments. We hashed over what we had learned and made lists
of questions.

But by unspoken agreement, there was one topic we
avoided. The most inexplicable and disturbing thing of all.

No one mentioned the fingerprints that had been seared
into Anne Marlow's throat.

When I returned home, I found the Bank Street Butchers
sleeping peacefully on the carpet. I woke them with gentle
shakes and they slipped into the early morning, leaving only

six mugs with traces of hot chocolate around the rims and grimy smudges on the parlor sofa. Billy was not among them.

Mrs. Rivers dozed in an easy chair. I covered her with a blanket and stood there for a moment, swaying a bit on my feet. Exhaustion and despair washed over me in a wave. Another young woman was dead. Billy had vanished, and I could no longer make myself believe that he would turn up anytime soon. *I* had sent him to some terrible fate. I'd drawn the attention of a savage killer, and put us all at risk. When Mrs. Rivers woke up, she would be furious. And rightfully so. I'd made a mess of things so far.

Then Connor sat up, rubbing his eyes, and I pulled myself together enough to update him on Anne Marlowe, leaving out the more lurid details. I think he sensed my black mood, for he awkwardly put an arm around my shoulder and gave me a little pat.

"It's all right, Harry," he said.

"No, it's not."

"Myrtle—"

"That's the problem!" I burst out. "I'm *not* Myrtle. Myrtle would have solved it already. She would have solved it *days* ago. I'm just… I'm just not as good as she is, and I never will be."

There. I'd said it. And in my heart, I believed it for truth.

Connor gave me an even look. "I was about to say, Myrtle wouldn't have done anything differently than you have. You've worked every angle there is to work. It's just a tough nut. This Straker. Is it him? Do you think he… he took Billy?"

I just shook my head and tried not to cry. "I don't know. I honestly don't know."

"I'll report him missing today if you like," Connor offered.

"Yes," I said. "Please do that. Does he have any family?"

But of course he didn't.

When Mrs. Rivers finally woke up, I made a half-hearted attempt at feigning illness, which the old bird saw through instantly.

"Sit down, Harry," she said, not unkindly. "I'll make you some eggs and toast."

I slumped into a chair at the kitchen table. "Any coffee?"

"There's a fresh pot on the stove."

I poured a cup and wrapped my hands around the warmth. "I'm sorry," I said, keeping my eyes on the wide-beamed wood floor, immaculate as always and faded nearly white from years of scrubbing.

I felt a powerful urge to unburden myself, to confess to all the lies I had told this good woman over the last five days, and a simultaneous impulse to somehow salvage the situation by telling yet *more* lies. The problem is I couldn't think of any decent ones.

Mrs. Rivers cracked two eggs into a bowl and began to whisk them with practiced efficiency. "Care to tell me what's going on?"

I'd expected her to yell at me, or at the very least to deliver a lecture on the behavior expected of young ladies, and how I'd failed miserably to meet those expectations. But she seemed calm. Reasonable, even. So I decided to make a clean breast of it.

"I'm investigating a murder," I said, the coffee perking me up some. "Three murders, actually. They're probably connected. John and Nellie and Edward are helping me. Connor too. Except Nellie thinks it's Myrtle's case." I took another sip. "And the client thinks I *am* Myrtle."

"I see." Mrs. Rivers set a frying pan on the stove and placed two pieces of bread into the toaster, which always reminded me of a medieval torture rack.

"I know what you're thinking," I said, still feeling half like an utter fraud. "But Myrtle was only sixteen when she solved her first case. I've told Uncle Arthur, and I think I can get him to talk to the Society for Psychical Research, if I have a good result. That's what I want to do with my life, work for them. I think I'd be good at it. I just need a chance to prove myself."

"Did someone come after you yesterday?" Mrs. Rivers asked, swirling the eggs around in the pan.

"Yes. And it scared me, but not enough to quit. What are you going to do?"

Mrs. Rivers didn't answer right away. She finished cooking breakfast, buttered the toast, and set it on a plate. Then she poured herself a cup of coffee and joined me at the table.

"Myrtle's not easy to have for a sister, is she?"

I shrugged and took a bite of toast. "She's all right."

"I remember once when you were five, and she was twelve. Your parents had gone to Wallingford after the terrible tornado there. Aunt Marny lived not far from the path of the whirlwind, and she'd begged your father to offer his aid as a medical doctor. They'd left at once, of course, and were gone for several days. Your sister spent the afternoon locked in her room, which was hardly unusual for Myrtle. You kept trying to get her to come out and play with you. You did worship her so."

I scowled and shook salt on my eggs.

"Anyway, at about four o'clock she came downstairs with a sticky sweet smile on her face that should have tipped me off right away. In hindsight, Myrtle was up to something. But you'd been a perfect terror all morning and I suppose I just hoped that Myrtle was finally behaving as a sister to you."

"Me, a perfect terror?" I objected. "But I was always a docile child."

"Don't talk with your mouth full, Harry," Mrs. Rivers said absently. "And *docile* is not the word I would choose. You just wanted a bit of attention from her, but the only time Myrtle noticed your existence is when she needed a subject for one of her atrocious experiments."

"Experiments?"

"It's all right, dear, you've clearly blotted it out of your memory. Probably for the best. In any event, I was in the midst of preparing a roast for dinner. Myrtle said she had something she wanted to show you upstairs. Well, the next thing I knew, you came tearing into the kitchen, white as a sheet. When I asked what had happened, you started to cry and babbled about the house being haunted. I marched up to Myrtle's room and there she was, cool as a cucumber. She didn't deny it. Myrtle never did. She usually seemed faintly surprised that we thought she'd done something wrong. She explained that she was merely trying to teach you a lesson about observation. So she'd turned down the lights and orchestrated a series of cheap parlor tricks, which naturally were terrifying to a five-year-old child. She had you convinced that spirits had moved the furniture around and made Myrtle levitate. I believe there was also something about ectoplasm coming out of her mouth."

An unpleasant memory surfaced from the depths. Not the whole thing, just fragments. Myrtle peering down at me, like an entomologist examining some interesting species of spider.

"*You look but you don't see*," I said. "That's what she told me. I had no idea then what she was talking about."

Mrs. Rivers shook her head in a long-suffering way. "I tried to explain to her how inappropriate, even cruel, her lessons were. She just looked at me with those pale eyes. Then she said, 'You don't care if Harrison grows up to be a blind fool, but I do. She's not as smart as me, but she's not hopeless. There's potential. I won't see it wasted.'"

"Well, that sounds like Myrtle," I said. "Even her compliments manage to somehow be insulting."

"I tried to keep a closer eye on her after that. It took you weeks before you could sleep in your own bed again, even after she'd shown you how the tricks were accomplished. Of course, you followed her around more than ever. You seemed grimly determined to please her. And I'll give her one thing. She never lied, not even when she should have. Myrtle didn't understand social niceties."

"Or didn't care," I said. "Well, I'm not doing this to gain her approval, if that's what you mean. Once, I would have. But like Myrtle, I don't care, not anymore." The lie came easily. "I'm doing it because I want to."

And that was also the truth.

"Do you think you can solve it?" Mrs. Rivers asked.

The question surprised me. "Yes. Yes, I do. Given enough time. We've made progress in the last day. Something's going to break, I can feel it."

"Well, I'm afraid time is the one commodity you're running short of, Harry," Mrs. Rivers said. "More toast?"

"No, thank you. What does that mean?"

"I received a cable from your sister this morning."

"Really? What did she say?" I rinsed my plate and tried to ignore the sinking feeling in the pit of my stomach.

"She concluded her work for the Pinkertons. There was a counterfeiting ring operating out of western Illinois and eastern Missouri. The Secret Service has known about it for years but they were very careful. No one could catch them at it."

"But Myrtle did," I said.

Of course she did. The poor things didn't stand a chance.

"It's in *The New York Times*. Front page, Saturday. She's still seeing to a number of final details, but she expects to be home within four days."

This was bad news indeed. I had no idea what she'd do if—*when*—she caught me impersonating her. There was a possibility she would find it funny. Myrtle was often amused by the most inexplicable things.

But there was a good chance she wouldn't.

And frankly, Myrtle scared me.

"Four days?" I echoed, the plate forgotten in my hand.

"*Within* four days. So perhaps sooner. Do turn off the tap, Harry, you're wasting water."

"Right, sorry." I obeyed, my hand moving like a mechanical claw.

"We'd better get busy then," Mrs. Rivers said. "What's the next step?"

I stared at her. "You're not going to try to stop me?"

"Not in the least. I'm going to *help* you. I've been waiting years for someone to bring Myrtle down a notch or two. It'll be good for the girl." She rubbed her hands together in something very close to glee. "Don't get me wrong. I love her. But... "

"I know," I said. "I know exactly."

Mrs. Rivers was very excited when I told her we were all going upstate to Cassadaga Lake to interview the dead medium's sister. She said she would commence packing for both of us immediately, leaving me free to meet Nellie at Niblo's Theatre. Connor would stay with Mrs. Rivers' sister, Alice, who had a flat on Forty-Third Street. I didn't want him sleeping in our house alone, and we needed him close by in case Billy turned up. Connor did tell me that some of Billy's few possessions were discovered missing from the Butchers' lair, implying that the boy had rabbited for some reason. It gave me hope that he was still alive, but I wondered what could have frightened him so much that he'd forgo the chance to earn $50.

In any event, things were looking up. Four days would be plenty of time, I told myself. Why, Myrtle had once solved the poisoning death of a zookeeper in sixteen minutes.

And yet it was with a quickened step that I made my way to Western Union to send a cable to Uncle Arthur. I told him about the third body and the possible society connection. I made sure to include the taunting message and strange fingerprints, as I knew it was the occult aspects of the case that most appealed to him, and which would pique the interest of the S.P.R.

That accomplished, and with an hour yet before I had to meet Nellie, I settled myself in the parlor and began to methodically go through the newspapers in search of any crimes that could be related to the case. I'd neglected this duty for several days, but it seems I hadn't missed much. There was no mention at all of Raffaele Forsizi. Becky Rickard merited three quick updates, none more than a paragraph. All said essentially the same thing: the police were baffled. Anne Marlowe's murder had occurred too late to make the presses, but I imagined it would be everywhere by tomorrow. An actress found strangled, even if she wasn't a star, was the type of story that sold newspapers, and even the less sensational ones like the *Times* could hardly resist splashing it on the front page.

Then there was the usual array of garden variety crimes and human interest stories. A guest was robbed of his luggage at the Fifth Avenue Hotel. A woman killed her husband and sister after they ran off together to Jersey City. A fisherman caught a man-eating shark in the Hudson River at Cornwall, and some ten thousand people turned out for the final performance of Buffalo Bill's Wild West Show at Erastina in Staten Island.

In more serious news, Susan B. Anthony and Elizabeth Cady Stanton had electrified a large audience at Jamestown's Allen Opera House on the topic of women's right to vote, a volcano erupted in Japan, and General Sheridan was laid to rest at Arlington Cemetery.

I rubbed my eyes, still a bit bleary from lack of sleep.

Mors me solum potest prohibere.

Only death can stop me.

A far cry from *God forgive me.*

He was getting worse.

A tap at the window gave me a start.

My hand twitched towards the revolver on the table. I kept it always within reach now. But it was just a crow. A quite large one. It perched on the sill, its shiny doll's eyes fixed on me. Then it pecked the window again.

"Hungry, are you?" I said. "No crumbs left from breakfast, I'm afraid."

The crow just watched, still as a stone.

I liked birds. I thought they were beautiful, and despised people who kept them in cages. This one was a deep, glossy back, with a long, sharply pointed beak.

"Wait here," I said.

I ran downstairs to the kitchen, where I found a crust in the garbage. I carried it up to the parlor, half expecting the crow to be gone. I'd never seen one around here before. Pigeons and sparrows by the boatload, and the occasional seagull, but never a crow.

It was still there. And it was still staring through the glass, at exactly the spot in the doorway where I'd appear.

I took a step into the room and stopped.

I knew I was being foolish. But there was something strange about it. About the way it sat there, so still. As though it had come here just for me.

It's only a bird.

Myrtle would die of laughter if she could see me now, I thought. The great detective, jumping at her own shadow. Afraid to give a crust of bread to a starving crow. I forced my feet to move. Maybe it was someone's pet that escaped. That's why it's not spooked by the fact that I'm walking towards it. That's why it's stepped *closer* to the window.

I reached for the sash and again, I hesitated, my fingers brushing the glass just inches from that curved beak. It was utterly irrational. But I had the sudden conviction that it would be a very bad mistake to open the window.

"Miss Pell?"

I nearly jumped out of my skin as a female voice called through the parlor door, accompanied by a light knock.

"Yes?"

"It's Elizabeth Brady. I'm sorry to call without warning. But we must speak!"

My guilty conscience perked up immediately, wondering if my ruse had been discovered. But it wasn't anger or accusation I heard in her voice. It was fear.

"Of course, do come in," I said, quickly slipping the revolver into a drawer.

I was walking to the door when I remembered the crust in my hand. I turned back to the window.

The crow had vanished.

CHAPTER EIGHT

I SETTLED ELIZABETH into the armchair that John always favored to study his medical books, an overstuffed mountain of green plush that made its occupant look like Alice after she drank from the mysterious bottle. Or was it the cake? I could never remember. In any event, I was glad to see her, as I'd been wanting to speak with her myself.

Mrs. Brady was a handsome woman, with a wide, well-formed mouth and prominent cheekbones. She wore a rather austere dress of navy blue silk and her auburn hair was caught up in a small matching hat trimmed in maroon velvet. Her posture was composed, but the paleness of her skin and ragged fingernails told a different story. They had been chewed to the quick, a fact she tried to conceal by folding her hands in her lap.

"I'll be frank, Miss Pell," she said calmly. "My husband has no idea that I am here."

"I understand," I said. "I'll hold this meeting in the strictest confidence."

"Thank you. I would have come sooner but it was impossible to get away. Then, yesterday, Leland happened to mention what you found at Robert's apartment—the ash. I knew I couldn't wait any longer."

"What is it?" I schooled my face to stillness, but my heart gave a little *thump*.

"About four months ago, I ran into Robert, purely by chance. I had gone shopping with some friends in the city. We went out to lunch afterwards, a place not far from here called Selari's."

"Yes, I know it." Selari's was a bohemian café at University Place and Tenth Street that Edward and his pals often frequented after the races.

"It was just a few weeks after the storm. We were sitting near the window when I saw Robert pass by. He looked like a ghost. I hadn't seen him since the wedding, and he appeared much changed, but I knew it was him. I made some excuse to step outside and caught him a block away." She took a deep breath. "Leland doesn't know of our encounter, but only because Robert made me swear not to tell him. He was very distraught. I asked him what the matter was and he told me he had been wronged by a business partner."

"I can't say if he was intentionally wronged, but we did learn that he lost a good deal of money on the Exchange when it was shut down," I said.

"Poor Robert." Elizabeth picked at the seam of the chair's arm. It was an unconscious compulsion, an outlet for her anxiety. I wondered what other destructive habits she had acquired.

"The ash?" I prompted.

"Yes, he was talking about this man and he complained that when they would meet at his office, he could hardly stand the stench. I asked what he meant, and he said the man reeked of cigarette smoke, which Robert could never abide."

"I don't suppose he mentioned what brand of cigarettes it was," I said.

"No, he didn't. And before you ask, he didn't tell me his full name. But he did refer to him as Gerald. Does that help?"

"Very much," I said, although I wasn't so sure. "I suppose half a name is better than none. We'll certainly pursue it. Did he tell you anything else?"

"Not really. The whole thing lasted less than five minutes. I told him I had to get back to the table before my friends wondered where I had gone, and that's when he asked that I not tell Leland I had seen him. He was clearly ashamed. I replied that it's not my habit to lie to my husband, but he begged so piteously... I finally relented. I couldn't really see the harm in keeping it to myself." Her hazel eyes grew sad. "Until a week ago. I knew I had to tell you, but I couldn't, not with Leland there. Tell me, Miss Pell. Do you think Robert is still alive?"

"I don't know. But we haven't found his body, so there's a good chance. I wish I could be more encouraging but I think you're the sort of woman who prefers the truth."

"I am, and I appreciate your honesty," she said stiffly.

I then proceeded to ask Elizabeth the same questions I had put to her husband: whether Straker had suffered from lost time, if he ever seemed confused or volatile, and who else he might have known in the city. I even showed her the symbol from the Forsizi killing. But she had nothing more to offer on any of it.

"You should know that there's been another killing," I told her, glancing at the clock. It was 11:45. I needed to leave to meet Nellie, but I had to warn Elizabeth first. Hastings-on-Hudson was just a short train ride from the city. Clearly, she wouldn't even consider the idea that Straker was our man, but

I could. And it was hardly outside the realm of possibility that he would return at some point to his childhood home.

"Oh God." Elizabeth shuddered as I summarized the details. "I'll tell Leland. But he's already asked that I stay at my mother's house. He worries that this maniac might go after him and find me at home instead. He's been so busy at work lately, even sleeping in his office when he has to show a property late. He frets endlessly over my safety. We both decided that it's easiest if I go to Connecticut for a few days. I won't tell my parents what's happened. Just that I thought I'd visit for a bit."

"That would be for the best," I agreed. "And just as a matter of form, do you know where your husband was last night?"

Elizabeth seemed puzzled at this question. "Why?"

"I have to ask."

"I see." Elizabeth inclined her head coolly. "Well, yes, of course I know where he was last night. I'm not in the habit of losing my spouse, Miss Pell."

"I apologize if I've offended you."

"It's just that I really can't imagine why you'd suspect Leland, of all people. But I don't mind telling you. He was home, with me. And he couldn't possibly have gone out, so you can just cross him off your list."

"How can you be sure he couldn't possibly have gone out?" I asked. "Just for the sake of argument. Did you stay up all night?"

"No." She seemed annoyed. "But our dog has taken to sleeping directly in front of the bedroom door, which is on the third floor of the house. She's quite protective. If she's disturbed in any way, she barks. Leland's always shushing her."

"And I take it she didn't stir last night?"

"Not a whit. And our window looks down on a sheer

drop. But this is all ridiculous, Miss Pell. You don't seriously suspect either of us, I hope?"

"No," I said with a sigh. "I don't. What's your dog's name?"

"Osa. It means she-bear in Spanish. Leland picked up a few words during his time out west. She's a husky, quite a lovely dog. I feel much safer having her around when Leland is at work."

"I can imagine," I said. "Well, if you remember anything else, even if it seems unimportant, anything Robert told you or some impression you had, please send a cable. I'll do the same, if I can think of any more questions."

Elizabeth gave me her parents' address in Danbury and I walked her to the door.

"Find him, Miss Pell," she said, and I wasn't sure if she meant Robert or the mysterious smoker. "If anyone can, it's you. I fear Robert has gotten involved in something very dark. Oh, how I wish they had never gone that night! But it's too late now." Her reserve seemed to melt and she seized my hands in hers. "Thank God we have you on our side. If it were anyone else, I would despair of ever knowing the truth. But Myrtle Fearing Pell has never failed to cut to the heart of the matter."

I gave a sickly smile. "That's not exactly—"

"Oh, don't be modest." She released me but her eyes searched my face for a long moment that, to me at least, felt horribly awkward. "And I apologize for what my husband said, but he can hardly be blamed. You do look quite young. I imagine it's hard to get people—men—to take you seriously, despite your reputation."

"Er, yes," I said. "Comes with the territory, I suppose."

"Yes. I suppose so. Well, good day, Miss Pell." She turned for the stairs. "Be safe."

"Good day, Mrs. Brady."

Four days.

I didn't know whether to laugh or cry.

Before she was brutally murdered, Anne Marlowe was beautiful. The photograph in my hand showed a woman who looked
strikingly like Lord Leighton's muse Dorothy Dene, with faint
shadows beneath her dark brown eyes that lent her an aura of
tragic glamour. Her face was a perfect oval, capped by a mop
of chestnut curls. She had flawless skin and a small but expres-
sive mouth. It was hard to reconcile this person with the horror that had been left at Neidlinger, Schmidt & Co.

I handed the photograph to Nellie and turned back to
the young lady who had given it to us. Her name was Mary
Fletcher. She was twenty years old and one of the ballet girls.
Mary lived on East Forty-Eighth Street, while Anne lived on
East Fifty-Ninth, so they would usually go home together after
the performance on the Third Avenue Elevated.

We were in the dancers' dressing room of Niblo's Theater.
I'd remembered rightly; the current show was *Mathias Sandorf* by Jules Verne, whose plot resembled *The Count of Monte
Cristo*. Sandorf is a Hungarian patriot who is betrayed and
condemned to death by the Austrian government. He escapes,
and spends the next fifteen years plotting his revenge. Anne
played his daughter. Her big scene was at the very end, when
the two are reunited.

This particular performance had soldiers and Indians and
cowboys and acrobats, and an actual waterfall on stage. It
was produced by Bolossy Kiralfy, that impresario of musical
extravaganzas. Like most of the cast, he had an iron-clad alibi
for the previous night: a party to celebrate the play's glowing

reviews. Mary was tired and Anne had a toothache, so they had left early.

"She might still be alive if we'd stayed," Mary said, wiping her nose with a damp handkerchief. She was a slender, waif-like girl, with pale eyes and pale hair that seemed the exact same color.

"Did Anne have any boyfriends?" Nellie asked.

"No. Not that she talked about."

"Special fans? Men who sent her flowers, or came back night after night?"

Mary frowned. "I don't think so. Lilla Vane gets most of that kind of thing."

"Can you tell us everything you remember when you went home last night?" I asked, wondering if this was going to be another waste of time.

"I already told the police," Mary said wearily.

"Just once more? Sometimes we recall details that we'd forgotten when we retell a story."

"I suppose, if you think it might help. We left the party at about half past ten. It was drizzling. Anne and I discussed taking a hansom cab as there were several waiting at the curb, but that would've been expensive. In the end, we decided to take the El, like always."

"Did you see anyone outside the theatre?"

"Not really. I mean, there's always people on Broadway. I recall a couple, walking arm in arm. They were laughing loud. I figured they'd been drinking."

Nellie gave her an encouraging smile. "You have an excellent memory, Miss Fletcher. Do go on."

"We caught the uptown train at Houston Street. It was fairly deserted at that hour, which was usual. It's one of the reasons I was so glad to ride home with Anne."

"How long did the trip normally take?"

"About twenty-five minutes."

"What did you talk about?"

"I don't know. Nothing special. Other cast members, mostly. Anne was a bit of a gossip. Not malicious or anything. She just liked to talk. She was really happy to finally have a speaking part."

"Did she seem worried or anxious about anything? Excited?"

"Not at all. She was a little quieter than usual, but I think it's just because her tooth hurt."

"Who else was on the train with you?" Nellie ventured.

Mary closed her eyes. "Give me a moment. There was a mother and child. The child was pretty, no more than five years old, and I remember thinking she should be in bed. Two or three men. Not together, separate. I'm afraid I can't remember much about them, except that one was a soldier."

"A soldier?" I leaned forward. "Are you sure?"

Mary nodded. "I'm sure. I don't remember when he got on. He might have been there already, I just don't remember. But the uniform stood out."

"Where was he?"

"The other end of the car, I think. Across from us. Now that you ask, I do have a vague sensation that he might have been watching us. But I wasn't really paying attention." She smiled and tears welled in her eyes again. "Anne was so lovely, you know? Men always stared at her. You just got used to it."

I exchanged a look with Nellie.

"Can you remember anything about what he looked like? Anything at all? Height, hair color, whether he had whiskers, that sort of thing."

Mary thought hard for a minute, then shook her head. "I'm really sorry," she said. "He was sitting down, of course,

so I can't tell you how tall he was. And I barely looked at him.
I'm fairly sure he was clean-shaven. And young, although
that's just an impression. The uniform is the only thing I'm
really certain about."

"When did you get off?"

"Forty-Seventh Street. That's where we said goodbye.
Anne stayed on for two more stops." She swallowed. "Do you
think it was someone from the train? The soldier?"

"I don't know," I said.

But I did know. It was him.

I couldn't say if he was a real soldier, or if he just dressed
up like one. But there was no doubt in my mind that Mary
Fletcher had seen Anne Marlowe's killer. And we now had
independent confirmation that Raffaele's murder was connected. The button found near his hand had indeed been
ripped from his assailant's uniform. I couldn't wait to tell John.

"Do you think I'm in danger?" Mary asked.

"You could be," I said. "You're a witness. And he doesn't
know how much you remember. The best thing would be to
leave the city for a little while. Can you do that?"

"Leave the city? But I can't quit the show! It just opened!"

"Do you live alone?"

"No, I share a flat with three other girls."

"Well, that sounds relatively safe," Nellie said. "Can you
take another route home? Stay away from the Third Avenue El?"

"Certainly. I wouldn't take it alone anyhow. Not after
what's happened."

"Why don't I speak with Mr. Kirafly and see if he can't pay
for a cab for the next week or so, just until the case is resolved?
It's the least he can do."

When Nellie decided she wanted something from somebody, she was relentless. It's how she landed her job at the

World. Still in her early twenties, she was already an accomplished reporter. She'd written a series of investigative stories on the plight of women factory workers, and later travelled to Mexico, where she was nearly arrested after denouncing the dictatorship of General Porfirio Díaz.

But when Nellie had first arrived in New York from Pittsburgh last year, no one would give her the time of day. She scraped by for a bit sending features to her old editor at the *Dispatch*, until she had the clever idea of getting a foot in the door by interviewing the editors of the top newspapers in town on their opinions about women journalists. Then she finagled an appointment with John Cockerill, Pulitzer's managing editor, and talked her way into the undercover assignment at Blackwell's notorious asylum. It was a risky gambit, but it worked. Nellie Bly became an instant sensation.

I had no doubt that Mr. Bolossy Kiralfy would be wet clay in her hands.

"You think he'd do that?" Mary asked, her pale eyes wandering restlessly across the pots of face paint and glittery costumes for the Automaton Dance and Fête of the Storks.

"I'm certain of it." Nellie smiled. "And if he won't, my readers will hear about it."

Mary didn't smile back, but she cast Nellie a grateful look. "Thank you, Miss Bly."

Nellie gave her a card in case she remembered anything else and we exited through the main auditorium, where the French daredevil Charles Blondin was dangling from a tightrope strung across the stage. He shouted at us in annoyance but I barely heard. My pulse was racing. We were closing in on our quarry.

All the talk about the Devil and dark forces had me half believing we were facing a monster, a wraith who materialized and vanished like a wisp of smoke. But he was real. Mary Fletcher had seen him. He was young, and clean-shaven. He dressed as a soldier when he stalked his victims. It wasn't much to go on, but it was more than we had a few days ago.

What we needed to figure out is *why* them. Why those particular people? What did they have in common? A medium, a street musician and an actress. Nearly everything about them was different.

Becky Rickard is stabbed early in the morning of Monday, August 6th, a message of apparent remorse written on the wall. Raffaele Forsizi is strangled the following evening, August 7th. No message, just a symbol that so far we had been unable to identify. Five days go by. Then Anne Marlowe is killed on Sunday night. There's a message, but it's more boastful than guilty.

There seemed to be no common thread.

And yet there had to be. I just wasn't seeing it.

"Isn't he the chap who walked across Niagara Falls?" Nellie asked, as we made our way down the center aisle, the three tiers of box seats looming on either side like a great honeycomb.

"Yes," I said, still distracted. "Blindfolded, on stilts, pushing a wheelbarrow. I think he even sat down halfway once and cooked an omelette."

Nellie arched her eyebrows. "A lunatic, then?"

I grinned at her. "A kindred spirit."

"I'll have to do a feature on him," she said. "Now, about Miss Fletcher. What's all this about a soldier? You know something, Harry."

I reminded her about Raffaele Forsizi's button.

"There's more," Nellie said, looking at me in that thoughtful, penetrating way she had. "You're holding back. Out with it."

I waged a brief debate with myself. But in the end,

expediency won out. Nellie couldn't help if she didn't know about Brady and Straker and all of it. And there was no time to waste. So as we stood on the corner of Broadway and Prince Street next to the busy main entrance of the fashionable Metropolitan Hotel, I laid it out as coherently as I could. Everything except the fact that Myrtle had no idea what I was up to. And that (God help me) she could be on a train home as we spoke.

"So this Straker fellow used to serve in the army?" she asked. "And he's vanished?"

"Yes. One of the Bank Street Butchers, a kid named Billy Finn, thought he found him, and now he's disappeared too. But we shouldn't jump to conclusions."

Nellie gave me her skeptical look. "He sounds pretty guilty to me."

"This morning, Elizabeth Brady came to the house. She said she ran into Straker a few months ago. Her story jibed with what Chamberlain told me and Edward, that Straker seemed to be holding a grudge against the man who lost his money. A stockbroker, first name Gerald."

"That's all you know?"

"He's a heavy smoker. Like whoever broke in yesterday evening."

"And I suppose you want me to find this man?"

"If you can. It might be a wild goose chase, or not, so be careful. John and I leave for Cassadaga Lake this afternoon. I don't expect to spend more than a night there, but if you can follow up… "

"Yes, yes, I'll have your undying gratitude." Nellie waved a hand. "How about you buy me dinner at the Hotel Windsor? I'm quite partial to their strip steak."

"It's a deal," I said, thinking I'd try to wheedle some money

from Mrs. Rivers when we returned. I had a small allowance
that she doled out each week, but it wasn't even enough to
cover the tip at the Windsor's elegant restaurant.

"Good luck upstate," she said. "I'm off to strong-arm Mr.
Kirafly. And then I have to write my story on Anne's murder.
The others may not realize yet that we have a repeat killer on
our hands, but it won't take them long. This is going to be
big, Harry."

"I know. Maybe it's better. At least people will be on
their guard."

Nellie snorted. "And panicking. There'll be heavy pressure
on the police to catch the killer. Croker and Hewitt are aller-
gic to bad publicity. They might need a scapegoat." She smiled
grimly. "So let's both be careful."

We parted ways with a quick hug, and two hours later, I
boarded a train at Grand Central Depot with John and Mrs.
Rivers. Cassadaga Lake was situated in Chautauqua County,
in the far southwestern corner of New York State. We planned
to take the Hudson River line north to Albany, where we
would switch to the New York Central, which passed by the
west side of the lake.

Late afternoon sun poured through the cavernous glass-
and-iron space of the train shed, whose ceiling, unbroken by
pillar, column or wall, arched more than a hundred feet over
our heads. The dozen tracks were serviced by modern raised
platforms, which were bustling with tourists, commuters
and porters. Grand Central was the pet project of Cornelius
Vanderbilt, who had snatched up thirty-three acres of land—
some of which he outright seized from reluctant owners who'd
refused to sell—between Forty-Second and Forty-Eighth

Streets, and Lexington and Madison Avenue. One of the buildings in the way was a new Hospital for the Ruptured and Crippled, which barely escaped demolition.

It was said, only half jokingly, that if the law was not on the Commodore's side, he would simply go to the Legislature and have a new law put in place.

But I had to admit, the station was impressive. It was like standing inside the airframe of a zeppelin, and I felt a thrill of excitement as we stepped aboard and the steam locomotive gave a great belching whistle, slowly gathering speed as the tracks veered northwest toward the Hudson River.

We deposited the luggage in adjoining first-class compartments and then settled ourselves in the dining car. John had spent the morning doing basic research on our destination, and over lunch he told us about the curious community called the Cassadaga Lake Free Association.

"It was founded forty-odd years ago by a group of people interested in mesmerism," John said, diving into a plate of roast chicken.

"Mesmerism?" Mrs. Rivers asked. "What on earth is that?"

"A rather cock-eyed theory that there's an invisible force surrounding the body which can be manipulated to heal sickness. The fellow who invented it would wave magnets around and induce his subjects to do very silly things. It was all the power of suggestion, really. It's largely discredited now, but had a strong following for decades."

Mrs. Rivers gave a sniff, but I could see she was intrigued. This was a woman who embraced quackery with open arms. When Myrtle and I were little, she would dose us with vile concoctions on a daily basis. She owned no less than three of Dr. Scott's Electric Belts, swore by Dr. Scott's Electric Foot Salve, and regularly chugged the contents of a brown bottle with the ominous label *Microbe Killer*. It claimed to "cure all diseases," and she refused to renounce it even after Myrtle took it into her chemistry laboratory and discovered that *Microbe Killer* was in fact diluted sulfuric acid, colored and made palatable with a healthy measure of red wine.

"Anyway, in 1873, a bunch of them got together and bought twenty acres of land, calling it the Cassadaga Lake Free Association," John went on. "It became a hub for Spiritualists and Freethinkers. They hold regular séances and claim to communicate with the dead. Rose Rickard is a medium there. I received a cable back just before we left. She's willing to speak with us about her sister."

"I wonder if they were very close," I said, nibbling on some tasty fried oysters. "And why she didn't go to Cassadaga after the whole Fox sisters fiasco."

"Maybe they wouldn't welcome her there," John mused. "Not after her reputation was destroyed."

"Poor child," Mrs. Rivers murmured.

"I also received a response from that professor at St. John's College, the one recommended by Arthur. His name is Father Bruno Alighieri. I have an appointment to meet with him on Thursday afternoon. He may be able to shed some light on the grimoire."

"And that symbol," I said. "It has to mean something, to the killer at least."

"I did some reading on demonology while I was at the Lenox Library looking into Cassadaga," John said. "I know you refuse to credit it, Harry, but there have been cases of possession that appear to go far beyond the bounds of simple abnormal psychiatry. Take the case of Jeanne Fery, a twenty-five-year-old Dominican nun. She claimed her father made a pact with the Devil, and that she was inhabited by a demon called Namon. She injured others and herself, and spoke in different regional dialects that she wouldn't have known. Two exorcisms were conducted, and she got better."

"When was this?" I asked.

"The 1580s."

"Yes, they were very enlightened back then. I'm sure we can take their word for it."

John threw his hands up. "Just because Myrtle traumatized you as a child—"

"You told him about that?" I shot an accusing look at Mrs. Rivers, who shrugged.

"—you refuse to even consider the possibility that what we're facing is something... more than a man. Look, when that wind came, Becky screamed at them to close their eyes. Brady obeyed. But what if Straker didn't? What if he opened himself somehow?"

"To what?" I stared out the window. We'd left the city behind, and the view now was of thick forest and rolling farmland. The barracks of the West Point Military Academy rose up on the far shore. In the middle of the river, a southbound steamboat trailed a perfect v-shaped wake, its bright blue flag snapping in the breeze.

John pushed a lock of hair from his eyes. He had such long lashes. I'd never really noticed them before.

"To a fallen angel," he said.

CHAPTER NINE

THE CONVERSATION QUIETED for a moment as a waiter came and cleared the plates away. The moment he left, Mrs. Rivers leaned forward.

"You really should listen to him, Harry," she said in a stage whisper that was probably audible to the cooks in the next car. "I've always thought it quite likely that there are demons walking among us. Remember the Benders!"

"Not you too." I crossed my arms defensively and tried not to think about the crow. "I believe you've both gone mad."

"What about the brimstone?" John persisted. "The backwards Latin, which is a hallmark of diabolical pacts? When they burned Urbain Grandier at the stake for witchcraft in 1634, it was one of the chief pieces of evidence against him."

I stared at John. "Are you actually siding with the Inquisition?" I asked.

"That's not the point. Alright then, how about the chain? And the fingerprints? They were burned into her throat, Harry! I saw it."

"Oh my," Mrs. Rivers said faintly, raising a hand to her neck.

"Well, I can't explain those—"

"Aha!"

"—yet. But I will."

We glared at each other for a moment. Some of the other diners had turned to look at us.

Mrs. Rivers made a soothing noise. "I have an idea!" she said with forced cheer. "How about a lovely game of whist?"

"Fine," I said through gritted teeth.

"Fine," John said, beaming his brightest, fakest smile at me.

So we played cards until Albany, and both got trounced by the ruthless card sharp that lurked beneath Mrs. Rivers' benign old lady façade.

The New York Central train pulled into the tiny station at Cassadaga early the next morning. John coaxed a farmer into giving us a ride into town on his wagon, and I think half my teeth were loose by the time we finally arrived at the Grand Hotel. Its name was a bit of an exaggeration as the hotel looked like nothing so much as a large, whitewashed barn. But it was situated near the shore of the lake and surrounded by tall elm trees that cast welcome shade across the front porch.

It was such a pleasure to be out of the city, breathing clean, cool air that I soon shook off the weariness of our long trip. John had booked three rooms on the second floor, each with a small balcony. We split up to bathe and change our clothes, and met on the veranda feeling much refreshed an hour or so later. Mrs. Rivers had donned her "country bonnet," an enormous thing of black lace that made her seem as if she was speaking out of the mouth of a cave. I opted for a simple cotton shift and left my head bare, provoking John to twirl a bit of hair around his finger and pretend to wear it as a mustache. I slapped his hand away but couldn't help grinning. When he played the fool, it was quite impossible to stay annoyed at him.

At first glance, the village was like any other quaint rural community, with Victorian gingerbread houses laid out in neat rows. But as we strolled to the address John had obtained for Rose Rickard, I began to notice certain singular features. The first was a clearing with rows of benches facing a sort of pagoda bearing the words *Forest Temple*. This was empty. But a quarter mile later, we came across a large auditorium, whose crowd overflowed out the open doors. The speaker was an attractive middle-aged woman, and she seemed to be criticizing Darwin's theory of evolution.

As we passed, I slowed down to catch a few words of her speech.

"—but atoms are not intelligent! Molecules are not intelligent! When the physical scientist declares that he has discovered the process of creation, he omits the one power of creation that alone is capable of solving the mystery!"

"Who is that?" I whispered to a man in a bowler hat, who seemed mesmerized.

"Cora Scott," he whispered back. "Isn't she marvellous?"

I made a noncommittal noise and we continued on our way.

"It's an odd place, Harry," John said.

"Yes, it is. Did I tell you Myrtle is on her way home?"

His eyes grew wide. "No, you neglected to mention that."

"She solved her case. We have three days to do the same with ours."

Neither of us spoke for a minute. Mrs. Rivers had gone ahead to admire some primroses in the garden of a clapboard house.

"And if we don't?" he said finally.

I sighed. "We're probably mincemeat either way. But at least we'd have the satisfaction of catching a murderer." An image of Anne Marlowe, her face purple and bulging, flashed before my eyes. "To be honest, I don't care about myself anymore. I just want him stopped. And I'm not confident the police can do it."

"Maybe Myrtle can help," John ventured cautiously.

"I'm sure she could. But would she? I know my sister better than anyone, but I still haven't a real clue what makes her tick. She can be almost human sometimes. And then she'll turn around and say or do something that makes me wonder if she has any empathy at all. But don't worry your pretty head about it." I chucked him under the chin. "I can handle Myrtle."

"It's all right, Harry," John said solemnly. "I'm a little scared of her too."

"I am not scared of her."

"Yes, you are."

"No, I'm not!"

"Oh look, here we are." He steered me over to the house where Mrs. Rivers had stopped. The garden was indeed lush and beautiful, a riot of flowers and fragrant herbs. "This is it. Number Seven, Library Street."

A curtain twitched as walked up the path to the front door. It opened before we had a chance to knock.

A blonde woman stood there. I scanned her features and saw no resemblance to Becky. But the signs of a powerful grief were writ large in her red-rimmed eyes.

"I've been expecting you," she said.

"Miss Rickard?" I asked.

"It's Mason now. I'm married. Won't you come in?"

"I'm Miss Pell, and this is Dr. Weston and Mrs. Rivers. Yes, thank you. We've come a long way."

We entered a small parlor with a round table in the center covered with a cloth. The curtains were of a heavy, dark velvet, but they had been pulled wide to admit the daylight. A cold fireplace occupied the far wall, next to a sideboard topped with what I guessed was a mirror, but this too had been covered in a black mourning cloth.

Four cups of coffee had been laid out on the table, alongside a tempting array of sandwiches.

Rose Mason bade us to sit and began pouring the coffee.

"Your first time at Cassadaga?" she asked.

"Yes," I replied. "Have you lived here long?"

"About three years. My husband Samuel and I met here. He's a teacher."

"At the school in town?" John asked, methodically ploughing his way through the plate of sandwiches. It's a good thing his father was wealthy, I thought, because between John and his brothers, the Westons must have spent a fortune just keeping them all fed.

"Yes, the Lyceum."

"How lovely!" Mrs. Rivers said.

"He should be home any minute," Rose said, examining us, and something in her face seemed guarded, wary even. "In fact, I believe I hear him now."

The garden gate rattled and a moment later the door was opened by a handsome black man, tall and slender in a white shirt with suspenders and the sleeves rolled up to his elbows. His short, curly hair was greying at the temples, although he couldn't have been more than thirty-five. He stopped when he saw us and then broke into a smile, revealing a set of even white teeth.

"Hello," he said to me. "You must be Miss Pell."

"And I'm John Weston," John said, jumping up to shake his hand. "A pleasure, sir."

The rest of us followed suit with a warm greeting, and Rose's tense expression relaxed a bit.

"They've just arrived," she said, standing next to her husband, who wrapped an arm around her waist.

"You must come to the picnic by the lake later," he said. "The whole camp turns out for it. It's a summertime tradition after we host a speaker."

"Oh, that sounds nice," Mrs. Rivers said.

"Thank you, we'd love to," I said.

There was an awkward silence. The spectre of Becky's death, and why the three of us were here, hadn't yet been touched upon, but we all knew it couldn't be put off much longer.

"Shall I stay?" Mr. Mason asked his wife quietly.

"It's all right, I know you have work to do. I'll be fine."

He gave her a searching look and she nodded firmly.

"I'll be in the study," he said, giving her a quick peck on the cheek. "See you all at the picnic."

Samuel Mason retired upstairs and we sat down again.

"Perhaps I should explain our role so there's no misunderstanding," I said. "We're not part of any official investigation. Have you heard of my sister, Myrtle Fearing Pell?"

"Of course. Her reputation is known even in the hinterlands." Rose gave a small smile.

"Myrtle's client attended a séance with Becky shortly before her death. It's rather complicated, but a friend of his has also disappeared and he fears that it could be connected." I'd already decided I just couldn't pretend to be Myrtle to this poor woman. It felt wrong to lie any more than I had to. "I'm terribly sorry about what happened. I'm just hoping you can tell me something about Becky's life."

Rose nodded. "I begged her to leave the city. There was nothing for her there. But she refused." Rose paused and her expression darkened. "There was a man involved."

"What about your parents?" John asked. "Couldn't they have intervened?"

"I don't even know if they're still alive," she said shortly. "We've been estranged since… well, for several years now."

I got the impression this had more than a little to do with her marriage.

"As far as I know, Becky didn't speak with them either. But here, I have something to show you. I sent a copy to the police in New York, but I never heard anything back."

Rose went to the sideboard and fetched a letter from a drawer. "It's postmarked the very day she was killed." Her lips tightened. "I had no idea as I read it that she was already lying in the morgue."

She spread the letter flat on the table and we all leaned over to read it.

Dearest Sister, it said in a looping script. *I pray that you and Samuel are well. The heat here has been dreadful, but I am happy to say that I have come into a sum of money which will allow me to come see you for a visit in the countryside soon. It is long overdue! I miss you very much, and the Spirits tell me that I may soon be an aunt. I pray this is indeed true, as I plan to spoil him (or her!) terribly.*

Now, I have a confession to make and I hope you will

*not hold it too much against me, but as you are my only
sister, and more than that, my closest friend, I wish you
to know everything and ask only that you withhold judgment until we are again reunited.*

*Two nights ago, I was approached by a man in the
Bottle Alley Saloon beneath my flat. He is known to
me, and he made me a proposition that I was hard-
pressed to refuse. You see, I have not been so well lately,
Rose. I don't wish to worry you overly, as things are
brighter now, but this city is not a kind place to a single
girl without means of support. I tried a job in the garment factories, but the work is very hard and the hours
long, for so little recompense it is a bitter joke. So when
he offered me two-hundred dollars for a night's work, I
leapt at the chance. He gave me a book of great Power,
and asked only that I find someone willing to join me
in carrying out a mystical ceremony described within
its pages.*

*He assured me that the intent was not to bring harm
upon anyone, only to bring wealth to the user. I was very
firm on this point, as the magic seemed dark to me and
I would never willingly go along with a ritual that went
against our Religion. But I consulted the Spirits and
they told me that all would be well, so I am reassured
that this is the correct path. As it happens, I know such
a man as would be willing, a fellow who lives nearby
and who is a gentleman through and through, although
fallen on hard times by no fault of his own. He stood
up for me once when some rough boys were bothering
me, and I thought I would do him a good turn by asking
him to join me this evening, which he has agreed to do.*

He is a fine-looking fellow, Rose, and did my poor heart not already belong to another (the Spirits curse him!) I might look on him with some favor. But that is another story, which I shall fully relate when I come to see you.

Please send my regards to Samuel, and be consoled that things are looking up for me and I shall soon quit this wretched city.

Your loving sister, Becky

The pathos of the letter left everyone quiet. We knew now how Becky had come by the book, but not who had given it to her, or why. Rose folded the letter up again, very gently, and returned it to the sideboard. Her gown hung loose, and just before she turned back to the table, she laid a hand across her belly.

"The man Becky refers to is named Robert Aaron Straker," I said after a minute. "I mean the one who agreed to join the ritual, not the one from the bar. He lived near to Becky and was a close friend of Myrtle's client. We're trying to find him."

"Do you think he had something to do with Becky's murder?" Rose asked.

"Inadvertently, yes," I said. "But I don't think he did it."

"Who do you think did then?"

"We're still working on that," I said, rather lamely. "But I'm curious about the book. We believe it's a grimoire. Did she ever talk about things like that? The darker aspects of the occult?"

Rose shook her head. "Becky was a sweet, simple girl. I still find it hard to believe she was involved in black magic."

"How about this man who broke her heart?"

"She wouldn't tell me his name." Rose's expression hardened. "The scoundrel. He promised Becky all sorts of things, including marriage, but of course as soon as he had what he wanted, he lost interest and tossed her aside. I warned her but she wouldn't listen."

"Margaret Fox thought he was rich," John said.

Rose sniffed at the mention of Margaret. "Those women... it's shameful the way they dragged Becky down with them, just to get back at Leah. Like a bunch of squabbling hens, without a thought of who they'd hurt in the process. It's amazing how many people in this community still hold them in high regard. As if none of it ever happened." She shook her head in disgust.

"But yes, Becky's lover had money, lots of it. He bought her all sorts of things when they first met. She came up for a visit last Christmas and I couldn't help but notice all the new dresses and expensive jewellery. That's when she admitted she had a gentleman. She referred to him as her 'fiancé,' but I didn't see any ring on her finger. She became annoyed when I pressed her about it."

I shared a look with John.

"She never told you anything specific, anything at all we can follow up on?"

"No." Rose poured herself a cup of coffee but didn't drink it. "I've gone over our time together in my mind so many times. Every word she said. She was just so careful. His warnings—or threats—had clearly made an impression."

I tried to suppress my frustration but I felt like kicking something. Hard. We would never find this man, I thought. There was no one left to interview. He'd covered his tracks too perfectly.

And then Mrs. Rivers spoke up for the first time.

"Why don't we ask Becky?" she said.

CHAPTER TEN

WE ALL TURNED to look at my housekeeper, who looked blandly back.

"Well, Mrs. Mason *is* a medium," she said, toying with the strings on her bonnet. "She's also Miss Rickard's sister. That's a powerful connection. And we may not have known Becky personally, but we care very much what happened to her. Why not hold a séance and ask her ourselves what happened?"

I opened my mouth to politely object but John cut in before I had a chance.

"I think that's an excellent idea," he said. "If Mrs. Mason is willing, of course."

Rose looked at each of us in turn, although I can't say what she was searching for.

"I've considered it," she said. "Of course I have. But there are dangers in reaching out to spirits that died by violence. They're unpredictable. Angry. And if they've failed to go on to the other side, if they linger in the twilight plane between our world and the next... Suffice to say that the restless dead are not the only ones who dwell in that place. There are other entities, far more dangerous. We run the risk that they too will answer the call."

I didn't trust myself to say anything, so I kept quiet. The poor woman had been through a great deal and I had no wish to insult her beliefs.

I also had had enough of séances. Just the memory of that day with Edward made my back ache.

But John was determined, and he had a staunch ally in Mrs. Rivers.

"We have to try, don't you think?" he said. "I know it's unorthodox"—this comment was aimed at me—"but we might actually find something out. Open mind, Harry."

"I'll confess, the idea does make me a tad nervous, but I'm willing," Mrs. Rivers said.

"Are you certain?" Rose asked. "As I said, the risks are real. Most of the mediums here wouldn't even attempt it. Not so soon."

Privately, I felt the biggest "risk" was to my self-respect, but with the others staring at me, I finally nodded assent. It couldn't do any harm, at least. And maybe John would be forced to admit that the whole thing was a load of eye-wash.

"We'll hold it tonight," Rose said decisively. "After the picnic. It's only been a week since she died. Her spirit won't have gone far from the first gate yet." She stood. "I'll begin the preparations."

We made our goodbyes and walked back to the Grand Hotel. My feet felt heavy as lead. The more I considered it, the more reluctant I was to take part in the séance. It was ridiculous. The other séances hadn't bothered me in the least. I'd found them by turns silly and boring.

The difference, I realized as we climbed the steps to the shaded veranda, is that we hadn't been trying to summon a real person. A person who had been viciously stabbed and bitten. Who had died in just about the worse way it's possible to die.

"Are you all right?" John asked, concern in his eyes. "You look awfully pale."

"I'm fine," I said. "I think I'll just rest for a bit."

We had two hours before the picnic, so I sat down at the writing table in my simple but comfortably furnished room. I added what Rose had told us to my notes and copied down Becky's letter, which I'd memorized.

Rose was clearly pregnant, just as her sister had predicted. Her sorrow couldn't dim the glow in her cheeks, and her dress had recently been let out to accommodate a swelling belly.

A lucky guess, I supposed, although it gave me an uneasy feeling.

Becky was without doubt a fraud. Margaret Fox had confirmed it.

But she was also a true believer.

Human beings are complicated creatures, I thought, looking out over the still, dark waters of the lake. We have the ability to hold two perfectly contradictory ideas at the same time, with untroubled consciences. Take the slave owners and their accomplices. They inflicted unimaginable horrors on their fellow man, and blithely went to church on Sunday like good, pious men. Those same slaves had been freed by the North's victory in the war, and yet the highest court in the land refused to enforce the Civil Rights Act, explicitly placing its stamp of approval on racial discrimination.

The way I figured it, the people of Cassadaga Lake might be eccentric, but if they allowed Rose and Samuel Mason to live in peace, they were all right by me.

I reviewed my notes again, searching for something I may have missed, some connection I'd failed to make. Maybe it was just imagination, but I could feel it. A niggling sense that the break I sought lay right in front of me, written in my own hand.

The afternoon passed in this frustrating way, and I was no closer to a revelation when four o'clock arrived. I *was* hungry though, and the repast that the Masons had laid out on a blanket near the shore made my heart—and stomach—leap with joy. There was fried chicken and potato salad, corn on the cob and strawberry rhubarb pie. The kitchen staff at the Grand Hotel had also given us a dinner basket, which included iced tea, fresh-baked bread, and cold sausages with sage and apple.

We sprawled on the gently sloping grass, puffy white clouds sailing overhead, and I listened with half an ear as John and Samuel talked about baseball (they were both Giants fans) and their mutual disgust with the decision the previous year to ban black players from the national league.

John told a few amusing stories about his professors at Columbia College, leading Samuel to relate how he'd been one of the first students to enroll at Alabama's Tuskegee Institute. The school had opened on Independence Day, 1881. At the time, it consisted of little more than a rickety one-room shack.

"I remember that in those first months, if it rained while Mr. Washington was teaching, I would have to go stand over him with an umbrella," Samuel said ruefully.

But Booker T. Washington, who had been born into slavery and was still just twenty-five years old, was a man of considerable energy and resourcefulness. He soon moved the school to an abandoned plantation nearby. The mansion house had been burned down in the war, but Samuel told us that the students set to work renovating the property, building a kiln in which they forged bricks for classrooms, a dining hall, dormitories and a chapel. Over the years, enrolment grew from about thirty to more than five hundred, right in the heart of the former Confederacy.

"We planted our own crops," Samuel said, biting into an apple. "We had to, if we wanted to eat. Clearing that land was not a pleasant task, but when some of the students complained, I remember that Mr. Washington would pick up his axe and lead the way into the woods." He laughed. "No one felt equal to arguing with that."

One of his classmates had told him about the Cassadaga Lake Free Association. Samuel was intrigued. After he graduated, he heard that the great orator Frederick Douglass would be appearing here so he hopped on a train north. Douglass spoke passionately about women's suffrage, a cause he had championed for forty years since the Seneca Falls Convention. Rose Rickard was also in attendance, and the two had hit it off immediately. They courted for a year and married in the auditorium, with the blessing of their neighbors if not Rose or Samuel's families.

As we sat on the grass together, I noticed a few curious and even hostile stares from whites, but most either paid us no mind or came over to greet the Masons with smiles and local gossip. It truly was an enlightened village. Interracial marriage was officially illegal in many states, and not tolerated in the rest, including New York.

I thought they must love each other very much to have risked so much.

I lay back, stuffed to the gills, and watched as darker clouds began to mound over the western edge of the lake. As they advanced, bringing a cool breeze that smelled of rain, everyone scrambled to pack up their picnic things before the arrival of the storm. Whitecaps churned the surface of the water, sending a pair of swans gliding for the safety of a sheltered cove.

The first drops were just beginning to fall as we reached the Masons' house.

It was black as night outside as we put the food away. Distant thunder rumbled and my apprehension returned. In fact, I was starting to feel downright ill. As though a fever was coming on.

"Is something the matter, Harry?" John asked. "You look flushed."

"I feel a little odd, but I'll be all right," I said, summoning a wan smile. "I think I ate too many sausages. Let's just get this over with."

John helped Samuel light candles in the parlor. Then John, Mrs. Rivers, Rose and I sat around the table in the center of the room. Samuel, who was trained in shorthand, took a chair near the hearth. We placed our hands on a planchette set atop a "talking board." It was made of wood, and painted with the letters of the alphabet. Rose explained to us that this was a fairly new device in the Spiritualist community, which allowed for swifter communication with the dead than the previous system of rapping out each word. We were not to guide the planchette ourselves, merely to allow it to move where the spirits wished.

In the center of the table, she placed a framed picture of Becky, taken when she was a child. It showed a solemn, unsmiling little girl of about ten, in a dark frock with a white ribbon around her neck. For a split second, the ribbon seemed to become a chain, its links cinched cruelly around her throat. I blinked and the image was gone.

I don't trust myself to describe what followed accurately, as some of it invoked intense memories of the séance Myrtle staged for me as a child. Instead, I shall present to you the exact transcript of the proceedings as it was taken down by Samuel Mason. It has not been altered in any way. I will note that I also saw things which he makes no mention of, such as the black fog I witnessed rolling out of Mrs. Rivers' mouth.

Here it is then, unredacted, and you may judge it as you see fit.

DATE: August 14th, 1888

SITTERS: Miss Harrison Fearing Pell, Mr. John W. Weston, Mrs. Ernestine Rivers

MEDIUM: Mrs. Rose Rickard Mason

COMMUNICATORS: Becky Rickard and Unknown

ROSE MASON: I begin this séance by asking the kind Spirits to protect us from evil. I beg their aid and shelter from the dark. Now I call to the Spirit of my sister, Becky, who passed to the other side a week ago. I wish to speak with her. Can you hear me, Becky?

[no response]

ROSE MASON: Are you there, Becky?

[no response]

ROSE MASON: I call on the spirit of Becky Rickard.

HARRISON PELL: Excuse me, but I don't think this is—

c-o-l-d

ROSE MASON: Becky? It's me, Rose.

[no response]

ROSE MASON: We want to help you.

h-e-l

ROSE MASON: Yes, is that you, Becky?

[no response]

JOHN WESTON: Is she saying hell?

ROSE MASON: We want to find out who killed you, Becky. Can you tell us that?

h-e-l-p-m-e-h-e-l-p-m-e-h-e-l-p-m-e-h-e-l-p

JOHN WESTON: [unintelligible]

ROSE MASON: Where are you, Becky?

c-o-l-d

ROSE MASON: Tell me who killed you. Do you know his name?

[no response]

ROSE MASON: Are you still with us?

h-e-i-s-h-e-r-e

ROSE MASON: In this room?

n-o-t-h-e-h-u-n-t-e-r

ROSE MASON: The hunter is with you?

h-e-w-a-l-k-s-i-n-t-h-e-d-a-r-k-t-h-e-c-o-l-d

ROSE MASON: Becky?

[no response]

ROSE MASON: Is he preventing you from speaking to us?

[no response]

ROSE MASON: Becky, is he with you now?

[no response]

ROSE MASON: I can help you, Becky, I promise. Tell us

who he is. Who the hunter is. We'll stop him. We'll find him and stop him. Who did this to you, sister?

[planchette moves violently]

dgshflksieldjhssksidrfarrumohrrr

HARRISON PELL: Please, I can't—

JOHN WESTON: I think it stopped.

ROSE MASON: Becky?

[no response]

ROSE MASON: Are you still there, Becky?

[no response]

ROSE MASON: Please answer me. If you're there, give us a sign.

JOHN WESTON: She's gone.

ROSE MASON: Wait, there's something—

JOHN WESTON: Harry, I can see your breath.

HARRISON PELL: What's happening?

ROSE MASON: I think we should stop now.

JOHN WESTON: Yes, I think so too.

HARRISON PELL: Let go.

JOHN WESTON: Harry?

HARRISON PELL: She won't let go. It hurts—

ERNESTINE RIVERS: Burn them all.

ROSE MASON: What?

ERNESTINE RIVERS: I'll eat them and then I'll burn what's left. BURN THEM ALL.

JOHN WESTON: [unintelligible]... Oh God.

HARRISON PELL: What is—

ROSE MASON: Who speaks to us? Are you the hunter?

ERNESTINE RIVERS: We are dust and shadow.
[laughs] Abyssus abyssum invocat. Do you miss your
sweet sister?

ROSE MASON: I command you to leave. I wish to speak
to Becky.

ERNESTINE RIVERS: Your baby is dead. It rots in
your womb.

HARRISON PELL: Do you see it, John? What is that?
What is that?

JOHN WESTON: For God's sake, help her!

ERNESTINE RIVERS: [unintelligible]

The séance ended at this point because Mrs. Rivers fainted dead away. I was screaming, and Samuel had jumped up to aid his wife, who was also hysterical. John is the only one who maintained any semblance of self-control, and even that was put to the test when the mirror over the sideboard fell to the floor and shattered.

He yanked open the heavy drapes and threw the talking board into the garden. It was still raining outside, but not hard. Greyish daylight flooded the room. The smell of wet roses followed it, and whatever had been among us fled.

A doctor was summoned and examined Rose in her bed-room. Ever helpful, Mrs. Rivers (whom John had revived with a glass of sherry) swept up the broken glass. The rest of us sat there, not speaking, and though I hardly knew Rose, I wept with relief when he came downstairs and said that the child she had carried for five months was perfectly fine. Samuel rushed to be with his wife and we let ourselves out.

My hands had stopped shaking, but I felt curiously disembodied, as though it had all happened to someone else. Mrs. Rivers remembered nothing after the start of the séance. John and I didn't tell her. We couldn't.

All the rest, the part with Becky, I could attribute to Rose pushing the planchette. Why she would do so, I didn't know. But it was possible.

I could even believe that my housekeeper had suffered a bout of temporary insanity. It wouldn't be much of a stretch, actually.

What I couldn't explain was that when Mrs. Rivers spoke, her voice had sounded like... well, like several people speaking at once. An overlapping, echoing quality that is beyond the capability of human vocal cords to produce.

And then there was the black fog.

No one saw it but me.

"Do you believe now?" John asked as we reached the hotel, and though he didn't say it in a gloating way, all my fear and confusion fused together in one hard, hot lump of anger. And aimed itself like a stone hurled from a slingshot at my friend.

"I don't know what I heard," I said, pushing past him. "It happened too fast."

"You've got to be joking!" He followed me up the stairs. "For God's sake, Harry. Mrs. Rivers—"

"Lower your voice, she's just ahead."

"Mrs. Rivers was... possessed by something. You saw it!"

"She could have known about the baby. I figured it out in two seconds flat."

"That's hardly the point!"

"Then what *is* the point? I'm tired and I want to go to bed."

"What about the mirror?"

I didn't answer. A wave of dizziness passed through me. I steadied myself on the bannister. "This is so typical," John muttered.

"Excuse me?"

"If something doesn't fit your tiny view of the world, it doesn't exist."

"*My tiny view?*"

"Yes. Your capacity for denial is boundless, Harry." A heat came into his eyes that made me uncomfortable. "Something can be right in front of you and you just… you just don't see it."

"I don't know what you're talking about," I said coldly, furious at myself and him both without being entirely sure why.

He stared at me for a moment without speaking. Then he sighed. "Goodnight, Harry."

"John," I said.

But he was already walking away.

CHAPTER ELEVEN

I KEPT ALL the lamps burning that night and still didn't sleep a wink. Contrary to what I had told John, I remembered quite a lot of what had happened in Rose Mason's parlor.

I wished I didn't.

Becky (if that's really who was speaking through the board, an idea I was still struggling mightily to accept) called him The Hunter.

In my mind, it was definitely a capital H.

I'd been thinking of him as the soldier, but Hunter suited him better. I suddenly knew with cold certainty that he took great pleasure in stalking his victims before he killed them. He had come within inches of my bedroom door and never gave himself away. If I hadn't heard the soft whisper of his breath, I wouldn't have known he was there. If the landing hadn't creaked, I might never have woken up. Or woken to hands already tightening around my throat.

Abyssus abyssum invocat.

Deep calls to deep.

Or hell calls to hell.

Well, that one was fairly self-explanatory.

We are dust and shadow.

The line was from Horace, if I wasn't mistaken. I laughed and it felt strange, but good too. I hadn't realized demonic entities from the twilight plane liked to quote poetry.

I threw off the sheet and hugged a pillow to my chest. There had to be a rational explanation for what had happened. There *had* to be. Otherwise, the case was hopeless.

More than ever, I knew we needed to see this professor at St. John's. If Uncle Arthur recommended him, he must know an awful lot—more than I did, at any rate, which was next to nothing. The appointment was for Thursday afternoon, the day after tomorrow. I'd planned to let John handle it, but now I had my own questions for the man. And if we left on the first train out, we could still get home in time for me to pay a visit to the Bottle Alley Saloon. It was the last chance to find out who had given Becky the grimoire.

I felt calmer as I made a plan. Because even if John had been right all along, even if the man we sought was no man at all, that didn't change the fact that maybe, just maybe, I could still catch him on *my* terms. He might walk in the dark and cold, but I believed in my heart that he walked in this world, too.

I rose at dawn. High cirrus clouds formed a herringbone pattern in the sky, their undersides gilded pink by the rising sun. The lake was like a sheet of glass, its surface unbroken except for the splashing of a gang of rowdy ducks. I washed my face in a ceramic basin nearly identical to the one we'd found in Straker's flat. A quick inspection in the mirror revealed bloodshot eyes and tangled hair. The latter was improved by a vigorous brushing, although pieces of it kept drifting up toward the ceiling in a nebula of static electricity. That problem, in turn, was solved by a hat. I donned my last clean dress, a pinstriped silk fit for travel, and ventured downstairs.

Nothing stirred as I made my way to Library Street save a fat tortoiseshell cat that watched with slitted eyes from a porch swing as I passed. The greenery between houses drooped heavy with dew. Although the sun had barely broken the horizon, my dress felt too warm, and I guessed the damp would burn off by breakfast. All in all, it held the promise of a lovely morning. I felt almost sorry that we had to leave.

But The Hunter could already be choosing his next victim. And I hadn't forgotten that Myrtle would be home in three days now. Time was running short indeed.

It took Samuel Mason more than a minute to answer my knock. He too was bleary-eyed, but he smiled politely when he opened the door, which is more than a lot of people would have done under the circumstances.

"I won't bother you long, Mr. Mason," I said. "I only wanted to make sure Rose is all right."

"Thank you for asking. She's on bed rest for the next week or so. But we're both fine."

"I also wondered if I might have a copy of the transcript from the séance. There's an expert I'd like to show it to."

"Just a moment." He disappeared and came back with a sheaf of notes, which he thrust through the door. "Here, take it."

"I can make a copy—"

"That's all right. I don't want it."

"I understand."

"Is there anything else?" He said this mildly, but I got the feeling my welcome was wearing thin.

"No. Thank you for all your hospitality."

He nodded. "Good luck, Miss Pell."

It was a subdued trio that boarded the eight o'clock train to Albany. I slept most of the way, the monotony of the landscape and the gentle click of Mrs. Rivers' knitting needles lulling me into a restless slumber. The connection to the Hudson River Line was waiting upon our arrival, and we steamed into the platform in New York just as full dark was setting in.

A blood-red late summer moon rose above the buildings outside the station.

A Hunter's Moon.

We took separate hansoms from Grand Central Depot, John to his home on Gramercy Park, and ours to West Tenth Street. As he handed Mrs. Rivers into the cab, he reminded me that we were attending a ball the following night at the Kane mansion on Central Park West.

"There's no getting around it, Harry," he warned. "You'll have to wear something nice. Temple is quite strict when it comes to evening attire. And by that, I mean no boots."

I swatted at him with my hat.

"Well, possibly boots, but be sure to scrape the mud off first!" John called as he swung up into his own hansom.

I made a face at him, and all was right with the world again, for the moment at least.

"Did you two have a row?" Mrs. Rivers asked, as we inched through heavy traffic down Fifth Avenue. "You've been awfully quiet."

"Not really," I said. "Well, maybe a small one."

"You're lucky he's the forgiving sort," she said airily.

"How do you know it was *my* fault?" I demanded.

Mrs. Rivers smiled. "Because it usually is, dear."

"Well, that's not... fair."

"At least one of you knows how to forgive. You might do well to follow John's example."

I scowled.

"So what is this grand party you're going to?"

"Edward got us invitations. He thinks Becky's mysterious paramour might be there."

"And how will you know if he is?"

"Not a clue."

Mrs. Rivers patted my hand. "You'll figure it out, dear. You always do."

Somewhat mollified, I rested my head on her shoulder. She smelled of lavender and Microbe Killer, which was actually rather pleasant.

When we got home, Connor was waiting for us on the front steps. He'd charmed Alice into buying him a bag of sweet rolls, which he handed round in the kitchen while Mrs. Rivers made a pot of tea. I watched the clock with mounting impatience. Finally, I managed to get Connor alone and borrowed an old set of his clothes, short britches and a loose button-up shirt with stains that smelled suspiciously like beer.

"Whatcha want those fer, Harry?" he asked suspiciously.

I'd considered bringing him along, but finally decided it was too dangerous. Besides, the people I needed to talk to would be more likely to open up if I was alone.

"Just something I have planned for tomorrow," I said, tucking my hair into a newsboy cap and surveying the results in the mirror. "What do you think?"

I figured I could pass for a boy if the lighting wasn't too good, which you could pretty much count on in a dive like the Bottle Alley Saloon.

"You could be one of the Butchers, if you wasn't so old."

"I'll take that as a compliment!" I said, kissing him on the cheek. "Goodnight, Connor. Thanks."

He squinted at me. "Night, Harry. And bring those back when yer done."

I was becoming an expert at sneaking out of the house undetected, a feat that was aided by Mrs. Rivers fondness for dry gin at bedtime. She referred to it as a "tot," although a tumbler would have been more accurate. In any event, she was snoring gently when I tiptoed past her room and out the front door.

Nightfall had done little to ease the searing heat of August. Still, as I walked east to catch a streetcar on Broadway, a feeling of exuberant freedom stole over me. Bare legs! On the street! I almost laughed aloud at the subtle (and sometimes not so subtle) looks of distaste on the faces of the ladies and gentlemen I passed, sweating in their long sleeves and multiple layers of clinging fabric.

When I stopped to pat the flank of a beautiful chestnut gelding at the curb and had to nimbly dodge a swipe from the driver's whip, I knew my disguise was working.

"Keep yer filthy hands to yerself!" he shouted at me as I danced out of range.

This was Connor's life, the good and the bad. I had a sudden amusing image of dressing him up as a rich girl and letting him be *me* for a day. All things considered, I doubted he'd care to make a switch.

It was the first time I'd ever gone out at night alone. I realized that there was the New York of the daytime, the one I knew. And then there was New York after dark, when a very different city awoke. The air hummed with its usual energy, but it had a wilder quality. Like anything was possible.

I hopped on a streetcar headed downtown. We passed Harry Hill's Dance Hall at Houston and Broadway, where it was rumored that Mr. Hill kept a private room in which his patrons could sober up before they went home, since a well-dressed man reeling down the street was practically an engraved invitation for robbery. Concert saloons like the nearby Gaiety seemed to draw a wider clientele, and though it was early yet, a boisterous crowd overflowed into the street.

Everywhere, *everywhere*, were people, louder, looser and yes, happier than I was used to. Handsome and ugly, young and old, rich and poor. Dressed by Saville Row tailors, and sporting rags that made my own outfit seem like finery. New York after nightfall belonged to the whores and the gamblers, the lovers and the brawlers, the pickpockets and their drunken marks. It was a true democracy in action.

A pair of showgirls in bright red garters and ruffled drawers ran giggling into a waiting carriage at Canal Street, their ascent aided by a white gloved man whose face was shadowed by a gleaming top hat. And in that brief instant, my buoyant mood deflated.

Because I knew that *he* was out there tonight too.

It had been three days since Anne Marlowe was killed. He would be feeling the urge by now. I wondered if he fought it, or if he had stopped even trying.

I kept my head down as I hopped off the streetcar at White Street and walked east to Baxter. If the Five Points seemed depressing by day, the lack of gas lamps made it downright frightening at night. It was too dim to see where to put my feet, but from the squelching sounds my boots made, I figured I'd walked through enough horse manure to fertilize the Polo Grounds baseball diamond.

There were noticeably fewer people on the streets here. I supposed it was safer to stay indoors. And for the ones who sought excitement—or prey—the action lay elsewhere. I felt eyes on me as I passed, but they were mostly indifferent. I was so busy being invisible that I nearly went right past the Bottle Alley Saloon.

It was easy to miss. There was no sign, just a little piece of plywood that said "distillery." The door was at the bottom of a flight of stairs, across which a man lay sprawled. He seemed in a stupor, so after a moment's hesitation, I took one step over his prone body, placing my right foot in the crook of his arm. I was just lifting my left foot to reach the second step when his eyes flew open and a hand with a surprisingly strong grip closed around my ankle.

"Where yer going, boy?" he slurred.

I kicked in a panic, but he didn't let go. I'd thought him to be elderly, but I could see in the yellow light spilling from the bar that he was young, and cheap alcohol had ravaged his features into a puffy, veiny mask.

"Get off!"

"No one goes in without my say-so," he said, pulling himself half upright as I hopped on one foot and struggled not to fall in his lap. "I'm the bouncer. Fat Kitty pays me to keep order, and by God, I'll know yer business boy or I'll cut out your liver and feed it to Kitty's dogs." He laughed. "They're always hungry, the poor bastards."

"I'm Becky's brother!" I said, giving another futile yank. "Sir, I'm Becky's brother."

He frowned. "Didn't know Becky had a brother."

"I came from the country, sir, upstate." I lowered my voice and hoped I sounded more like a boy. "Our mother sent me to claim the body."

His death grip slowly relaxed. "I liked Becky," he said. "Everyone did. She bought me a drink once."

"Did you know her well?" I asked, thinking that I might

not even have to go inside, the prospect of which was less appealing by the second.

"Nah. Kitty did though."

"Is she here?"

"Nah. She took the night off to see a show."

"Oh." I tried to hide my disappointment. "Can you let go of me now?"

He looked down at his hand as though he'd forgotten it was there. "I guess so. Charlie knew her too."

"Is Charlie inside?"

"What?" his eyes were already at half-mast again.

"Charlie. Is Charlie inside?"

"Dunno. Go on and find out if you want."

And with that he resumed his position on the stairs and went back to sleep.

"Thank you," I said, to no one, and continued my journey down the steps into the Bottle Alley Saloon without further interruption.

My first impression was of a root cellar. The floor was bare earth, just like the one where Becky had held the séance. But Fat Kitty had apparently decided that her customers deserved a touch of class, because she'd covered the walls with splashy posters advertising the "British Blonde Burlesque Troop" and "The Hurly Burly Extravaganza."

I counted four people in the place, all in various stages of inebriation. Gender was indeterminate, likewise age. But after my experience with the bouncer, I took nothing for granted and it was with extreme caution that I approached the bar, which was a board laid across two sawhorses.

The bartender sat on a stool in front of a poster of "The Beautiful Indian Maidens," whose feathered headdresses seemed to be the only "Indian" thing about them.

"Let's see your money first, kid," he said wearily.

The lighting wasn't great, but I guessed the bartender was about eleven years old.

"I'm looking for Charlie," I said. "Is he around?"

"She's over there," he said, pointing to one of the figures nursing a drink in the far corner. And then, warningly: "She ain't workin'."

"Oh." I tried not to blush. "I'm not here for that. I just want to talk to her."

He gave me a last hard look and nodded. "Go on then. But this place is for paying customers."

I threw a nickel on the bar and he seemed satisfied.

"Slow tonight. Maybe it's them killings in the papers. They're calling him Jekyll and Hyde." The boy spat in the dirt. "Let 'im come in here. I'll give 'im a taste of the old enforcer." He flexed his skinny arms and glanced meaningfully at a bat studded with rusty nails that was propped behind the bar.

"Jekyll and Hyde?" I repeated. Of course, it would be all over the news by now. We'd missed it up in Cassadaga.

He shrugged.

The Strange Case of Dr. Jekyll and Mr Hyde had just been published two years before, and was an instant best-seller. It told the story of a man who became a monster, who had two distinct personalities. One good, one evil. But how could they know?

"Nellie," I muttered.

"What?"

"Never mind."

I wandered over to the corner. Two women sat there, laughing quietly with each other. They looked up as I approached.

"I'm not working," the older one said immediately.

"I know. I'm not... My name is Harry. I'm Becky's brother. Are you Charlie?"

There was a long silence.

"What do you want?" the same woman asked. She had thick black hair and might once have been beautiful, but her front teeth were missing. The others looked white and strong. Someone had knocked them out.

"I'm trying to find a man who gave her something. A book. It was about a week before she died. He gave it to her here, so I thought maybe someone... " I trailed off.

"Poor Becky," she said. "You're her brother?" She scrutinized me. "You don't look nothin' like her."

"We had different mothers," I said. "But she's my only sister. Please."

Charlie glanced around the bar. The kid was busy paring his nails with a huge knife, and the two other patrons were face down on a plank.

"I don't know his name," she whispered. "But yeah, I was here that night. Becky bought a round for the whole place after. She was the happiest I'd ever seen her."

"Do you remember what he looked like?" I asked in a low voice.

Charlie laughed. "It would be hard to forget."

"Why's that?"

"He had a scar across his face. But not just any scar. It was dead white and shaped like a fishhook." She drew an invisible line from her right eye down her cheek to the corner of her mouth. "He scared me. Didn't stay long. He handed her a package and took off."

I nodded, but I barely heard the rest of what Charlie said. The hair on the back of my neck was standing up like the fur of a cat that's just been goosed. My mind raced, pieces of the puzzle falling into place, one after the other.

Because I knew this man.

His name was Thomas Sweet, and he was the bodyguard of George Xavier Kane, the wastrel son of George Kane, Sr., our host tomorrow night.

I thanked Charlie and stumbled out into Baxter Street. I should have noticed that the bouncer had disappeared, but my thoughts were spinning, rearranging everything I knew in the new light of what I'd just discovered. He was Becky's lover. Of course he was. George Kane, Jr. had a reputation as being a cad. And Margaret Fox had named the Kanes when she reeled off the list of society people who had used Becky's services. That's probably how they met. And Temple Kane... she was feared even by her closest friends. I couldn't imagine her reaction when she learned that her son, her *only* son, was sneaking around with her favorite medium. There would be hell to pay.

And Becky had paid it.

But why did he give her a *grimoire*?

I was just pondering this when a shadow detached itself from the alleyway ahead and began gliding toward me.

CHAPTER TWELVE

I SPUN AROUND to run in the other direction, but that way too was now blocked by three men. No, boys. The oldest, who seemed to be their leader from the way he swaggered a few feet in front of the others, couldn't have been more than sixteen. But he looked strong and vicious.

They spread out across the narrow street. I glanced over my shoulder. The shadow I had seen split into three more, blackjacks swinging from clenched fists. I felt like a fool. Their trap had closed before I'd even realized what was happening.

My pulse set off at a gallop as I considered my options. At least I was dressed as a boy. I prayed they'd be satisfied with roughing me up a little. I was a stranger, and this was their turf. Maybe assaulting interlopers was their usual evening entertainment.

Those hopes were dashed when I caught a blur of movement out of the corner of my eye. I braced for a blow, but instead, the thug yanked my cap off. They all laughed as my hair tumbled free. It wasn't long, but I guess it was long enough.

That's when sheer terror set in.

"Let me by!" I yelled. "Help! Somebody help me!"

This just provoked more laughter.

"I'm sure the Filth is on the way," the leader said, using a slang term for the police. "What do you think, Danny? When's the last time you saw a cop around here?"

Danny scratched his head. "Dunno." Then he grinned and pointed to a garbage heap. "Hey, ain't he buried over there?"

"Help!" I screamed again, even louder.

The windows on all sides remained dark. Somewhere, a dog barked frantically.

The leader crossed his arms and gazed skyward in feigned annoyance. He had flaming red hair and a nose that had been broken so many times it was just a flat knob of flesh. The other two had to be brothers, with identical dark hair and eyes, and the lean, hungry look of kids that had never had enough to eat in their lives.

I couldn't say what the ones behind me looked like because I was afraid to take my eyes off of Red Hair even for a second. I figured the others wouldn't attack until he did, or gave a signal.

The Bottle Alley Saloon lay just a block away. If I could somehow get past them, maybe Charlie or the bartender would intervene…

Red Hair seemed to read my mind, because he shook his head sadly.

"If you're lookin' fer Pickles, we told him to shove off. Pathetic excuse for a bouncer, if you ask me. Drinks more than the poor sots he tosses out. Now, we'd just like to have a little chat." He held his hands up. "We work for Mr. Moran. He's a gentleman, ain't he, boys?"

They all nodded.

"Why doesn't Mr. Moran ask me himself?" I demanded. "If he's such a gentleman."

"Shut your lip," Red Hair said coldly, walking towards me. "I know who you are. I know why you're here."

I retreated until my back was pressed against the crumbling brick wall behind me. For a split second, I saw a frightened face peek out the window opposite. But whoever it was clearly had second thoughts about the wisdom of witnessing what was about to happen, and the face disappeared just as quickly.

"And why's that?" I asked, silently berating myself for neglecting to bring Myrtle's revolver.

"Mr. Jekyll," said one of the dark haired boys, taking a menacing step forward.

"And Mr. Hyde," said his brother, following suit.

"What is it you want?"

The semicircle began to tighten around me. I looked for something, anything I could use as a weapon, but of course the few square feet I stood on was the *only* debris-free spot in the whole street. I was just weighing the merits of horse manure as a projectile when Red Hair closed the distance and stood in front of me.

"I want to know—" he began.

He didn't get any further because I suddenly decided that it was time to put John's boxing lessons to good use. In Red Hair's small mind, I was a girl. Girls didn't hit hard. Therefore, he had nothing to worry about. It was a mistake I doubted he'd ever make again.

I hauled off with a neat right hook that gave his poor abused nose yet another spectacular lump. Before he could recover, I followed it up with a knee to the groin. To my intense satisfaction, Red Hair deflated like a popped balloon.

I leaped over his body and rabbited between the two brothers, who looked utterly astonished that their leader had been felled by a wee lass. But within seconds, I heard hard footfalls in pursuit. They started to gain, and I poured on the steam. Tumble-down buildings flashed by in a blur as I ran, faster than I ever had before. But it wasn't enough. I could hear them getting closer. And to my growing dismay, I soon became lost in the maze of alleyways.

I'd thought I was headed west for the relative safety of Broadway, but the farther I went, the darker, gloomier and more deserted the area became. There were no street signs, but then I smelled the river and knew I'd gone in the exact opposite direction. I risked a glance over my shoulder. Only two of the boys were still pursuing. But I knew the others hadn't given up. They were probably circling around to trap me as they had before. I had no illusions that they knew the area far better than I did. It was only a matter of time before I was again hemmed in.

So I made for the water.

Shouts echoed from the adjacent alleyways. Once or twice I heard a strange, trilling whistle that must have been some secret communication. They were tracking me like hounds after a hare. Shuttered warehouses loomed on either side, reeking of fish and brine. The height of the buildings lowered, revealing the orange Hunter's Moon sailing high in the sky. And then I burst out into the open, near the edge of the wharf. Not far off, the Brooklyn Bridge straddled the river, its massive cables glowing with electric lights, appearing to my night-dazzled eyes like stars fallen to earth.

I could see a crowd of people, just a few blocks away, waiting to board one of the ferry lines. But as I veered toward them, two of the thugs tore around the corner and cut me off. They slowed as they saw me, evil grins widening on their faces.

I uttered an oath that would have made Mrs. Rivers' hair curl, and possibly John's as well.

Salvation was so close.

One of the thugs gave a high-pitched whistle, and my heart sank further when it was answered by a whistle to my right, and another just behind. I could see Red Hair coming now, and he didn't look happy. Dried blood crusted his lips, like a sinister circus clown.

I thought about screaming again, but the tiny figures milling around the pier would never hear me. Red Hair halted and slapped the business end of a blackjack into his open palm with a frightening *thwack*. The very same sound I imagined it would make when it shattered my skull.

Then he started coming.

He didn't say anything, or ask me any more questions. The time for that had passed. Now he just wanted revenge.

I spun in a circle. Every avenue of escape had been closed off.

I started to back toward the river. In my peripheral vision, I saw one of the thugs circling around to grab me from behind.

Then he gave a howl of pain and crumpled to the ground. I heard a hollow *crack*, like a wishbone snapping, and the thug—one of the dark-haired brothers—curled into a ball, clutching his kneecap. Standing over him, a stout cudgel in his fist, was Connor.

"You'll pay for that, boy-o," Red Hair snarled, as he and the four others tightened the circle.

Connor rushed over and grabbed my hand, his mouth tight.

"Did they hurt you?" he asked softly.

"Not yet," I said.

But as I watched them advance, my initial surge of hope melted like ice cream on a hot sidewalk.

It was still five against two. And they were all bigger, stronger and far meaner than us.

We inched backwards until our heels hung over the edge of the wharf.

Connor looked up at me. "Know how to swim, Harry?" he asked.

I nodded, heart pounding, and squeezed his sticky palm.

"Good," Connor said. "'Cause I don't."

And with that he whirled and we both leapt into the river. I felt a brief moment of sublime weightlessness, when the world tilts on its axis and time slows to a crawl, and then the black waters closed over our heads. It wasn't cold, but the current was strong, sweeping us out towards the middle where the shipping traffic was heaviest. If I'd been wearing my petticoats and corset and usual nonsense, I would probably have drowned. But Connor's clothing was lightweight cotton, and though it billowed out around me, I managed to keep afloat. What dragged me down was the boots, which were laced too tight to get off. But I found that if I kicked hard enough, they were manageable.

Connor had been yanked away from me when we went under. I frantically scanned the choppy surface, calling his name. It seemed an eternity, but then his head and arms broke the water about twenty feet away. He thrashed hard and I could see he was starting to panic.

Several adjacent splashes signified that our pursuers knew how to swim too.

"Hold on, I'm coming," I yelled, paddling against the current with all my strength.

Connor gave a choking cry and slipped beneath the waves.

The fear I'd felt on the pier was nothing compared to the sheer terror that seized me at that moment. I dove down into the foul murk, kicking and pulling with every ounce of strength I could muster. Aiming for the last spot I'd seen him.

It was pitch dark. My lungs screamed for air. But I knew that if I surfaced to draw a breath, Connor would be gone forever.

In the end, it was sheer luck that saved us. Spots danced in front of my eyes and I knew I couldn't last much longer. Then my boot kicked something soft. I spun, groping blindly, and my fingers closed around a piece of cloth. I hauled us to the surface, flipping Connor onto his back and holding him afloat with one arm. To my vast relief, he coughed up a few mouthfuls of water and fell limp.

I let the current carry us for a minute while I caught my breath, though I soon realized that the channel was not a desirable location. After a near miss with a square-rigged clipper ship, I stroked hard for the Clyde's Line pier, where a number of smaller boats bobbed at anchor. The wind rose. I thought I caught a glimpse of a dark head in the water, but the chop made it impossible to see far. Judging by the faint cries downriver, one of the thugs was floundering. Hopefully the others would heed his calls for help and give up their pursuit.

I reached one of the smallest boats and clung to it like a barnacle, but I didn't think I could hold us both for long.

I hissed Connor's name and shook him a little. His eyelids fluttered.

"Don't let go," I whispered, wrapping his thin arm around the gunwale. "Or we'll be swept out to sea."

Connor mumbled something too soft to hear, but he held tight. His red curls stuck to his forehead and his lips looked blue in the darkness. I locked my wrists together and we stayed like that for longer than I thought humanly possible. And then for a few minutes more.

Of course, I hadn't thought to save a little energy in reserve for when we let go and had to swim to the mossy green ladder of the pier, so I *did* almost drown us both on the way there. But my stiff fingers finally closed around the bottom rung and we dragged ourselves up out of the river, cold and tired but glad to be alive.

"How'd you find me?" I asked as we trudged east on Pike Street.

"Followed you," Connor said, wringing his shirt out. "Figgered you was up to something and I might have to save your bacon. I was about to jump in before when you dowsed that Jack Cove's mug with a fine right hook. It was lovely, Harry."

He gave me a happy smile. I shrugged as if it was nothing special for me to engage in fisticuffs with James Moran's henchmen, although I *was* feeling rather pleased with myself.

It was a long walk home.

The little money I'd brought had been sucked right out of my pockets. But this was New York, so we barely earned a second glance, wet, dirty and bedraggled as we appeared. On the bright side, no one chased us, or tried to brain us with a blackjack.

At least it was August.

My clothes had dried by the time we climbed the front steps at Tenth Street, where I found another unpleasant surprise. The only thing in the world I wanted was to get undressed and crawl under a set of clean, starched sheets. But all the lights were burning in the windows, even though it had to be nearly midnight.

You're in the soup again, Harry, I thought glumly. Mrs. Rivers woke up and found you out of your bed, and though she might be a mighty tolerant old lady, she'll be forced to take some kind of stand on unauthorized nocturnal escapes.

I opened the front door, steeling myself for a righteous dressing down. But it wasn't Mrs. Rivers we found in the formal parlor. Well, she was there too. But so were Nellie, Edward and John. They all turned and looked at me like I had two heads.

"Oh no," I said, slumping against the doorway. "Not another body."

Nellie shook her head. "Not a body," she said, downing a tot of Mrs. Rivers' dry gin.

"Thank God." I pulled a strand of seaweed from my hair.

Nellie gave me her tight smile. "It's two bodies this time."

Edward wrinkled his nose. "Do you smell something? It's like... sewage."

"I think that's Harry," John said. "Or maybe Connor. What happened to you? Where did you go? We've been worried sick. I was afraid... "

"George Xavier Kane was Becky's lover," I said. "I went down to the Bottle Alley Saloon. Now what's this about *two* bodies?"

We all talked at once for a confusing few minutes. I related my trip to the bar and run-in with Moran's thugs, and Nellie told me what she'd heard just two hours before through the police beat grapevine. Two more victims, only blocks apart, both strangled. Both faces were covered, one with a linen handkerchief, the other with her own bedsheet. It had happened inside the woman's flat.

I felt sick. While I was out playing dress-up, the Hunter had been conducting his grisly work. I stared into space, picturing their wide, terrified eyes as they realized what was about to happen.

I wondered if they had children.

I wondered what I could have done differently, if I could have prevented it somehow.

John must have sensed my feelings, for he came and stood next to me.

"It's not your fault," he said quietly.

"How do you know that?" I demanded. "How?"

"Because you're the smartest person I know."

"It's not enough," I said bitterly.

"Don't," John said. "Self-pity's not your style, Harry. Now, pull yourself together and let's get back to work."

I looked into his calm brown eyes and nodded.

"Right," I said. "Thank you."

He went to squeeze my shoulder, then thought better of it.

"You really are ripe, Harry," John said with a laugh.

I surveyed my companions on this strange, grim journey. Edward just kept repeating "*George Kane!*" in an amazed voice. They'd apparently just seen each other at the races that very afternoon. Our friend was impeccably dressed as usual, making me feel even more like the proverbial skunk at the garden party.

"There's no point in trying to get to the scenes now," Nellie sighed. "It's a full on mob scene. They've got the whole area closed off."

"Where did it happen?" I asked.

"Ninth Avenue and Seventeenth Street. Oh, and before I forget, no luck on that stockbroker named Gerald. I checked the employee records of the largest houses. There's only two, and they're both in their late sixties, highly respected. I can't imagine they'd be involved with this man Straker. As for the smaller houses… well, there are dozens. It would take months to check them all."

"Hold on a moment," I said. "I really have to change."

Even I could smell myself.

"That's a good idea, dear," Mrs. Rivers said.

She was acting suspiciously mellow, a state I attributed to the half-empty bottle of Hendricks gin at her elbow.

Not one to question divine good fortune, I dashed upstairs and washed as best I could, thinking hard as I donned a clean dress. John was right. We were at a pivotal moment in the case. We had a new suspect, a real one this time, and I felt a breakthrough was imminent.

"Let's review what we know so far," I told my friends when I returned to the parlor.

I rolled out a map of the city on the table and we all gathered round.

"The first victim, Becky Rickard, was killed at home." I used a fountain pen to mark Baxter Street with an X. "Raffaele Forsizi here at Union Square, and Anne Marlowe here, at Sixty-Third Street. The last two at Ninth Avenue." I made four more Xs. "What do you know about the latest victims, Nellie?"

"Not much. They were both women. He seems to be developing a preference. The one killed in her flat was a housewife whose husband worked nights. The other may have been a prostitute, I'm not sure."

"But he still took the time to cover the faces," John pointed out. "The ambivalence hasn't changed."

"Other than that they have nothing in common though," Edward said. "And he's escalating. The risk of getting caught in the act tonight was twice as high, but it didn't stop him."

"But they do have something in common," I said, feeling a surge of grim excitement. "Look at the map. We couldn't see it before, because there were only three, and Becky doesn't fit. But that's because her murder was different. She wasn't chosen randomly. The others were. Now if we take away Becky... " I covered Baxter Street with my hand.

John was the first to see it.

"The elevated trains," he breathed. "They were all killed within shouting distance of the elevated."

"Except for Anne Marlowe," I said triumphantly, "who was found on the waterfront, but her crime scene doesn't count because we know from Mary Fletcher that he first saw her on the train. *That's* where he stalked her. I'd thought it was just the one time, but it's *every* time. It's where he finds his victims, John. The perfect anonymous place to watch someone, to follow them when they get off. He dresses as a soldier because it makes them trust him."

Edward leaned over the map. "You're a genius, Harry. Union Square—the Third Avenue El. Then Anne Marlowe. Then two in the shadow of the Ninth Avenue El."

"John, do you still have your notes from the interview with Raffaele's family?" I asked.

If the organ grinder had taken a streetcar home, my grand theory would collapse like a house of cards.

"Yes, of course." He rummaged through his coat pockets. "Let's see... "

We all waited impatiently as he found it and flipped through his notes. When he looked up, I knew from his eyes that I had been right.

"His sister said Raffaele always took the El downtown after he played for the afternoon in Central Park," he said. "Trying to earn a few more pennies in the evening near the theaters."

We were all silent for a minute. I hated The Hunter more at that moment more than I ever had before.

"So who is he?" Nellie asked briskly. "Straker? George Kane?"

"Or Thomas Sweet," Connor ventured.

"Or Temple Kane," Edward said with a laugh. "I wouldn't put it past the woman."

"Or James Moran," Nellie added. "Why else would his thugs have hassled you? It sounds like they knew exactly who you are, Harry."

"It could be George Kane *and* Thomas Sweet," John said, as if the waters weren't muddy enough already. "Dr. Jekyll and Mr. Hyde."

"Perhaps we'll find out tomorrow night," I said, turning to Edward. "You obtained those invitations?"

"Engraved in gilt, on the finest paper," Edward said, twirling his pocket watch. "Seven o'clock sharp." He sniffed again. "You might want to take another bath beforehand, Harry."

"If it is George Kane, he's not going to admit to anything," John pointed out reasonably. "So what do we do then?"

I thought for a moment. "Then we turn the tables on him. We know where his stalking grounds are now. We hunt The Hunter."

CHAPTER THIRTEEN

IT WAS NEARLY two o'clock in the morning when my friends said their goodbyes. Mrs. Rivers had drifted off on the sofa, and Nellie helped me wake her up and settle her in bed before jumping in Edward's barouche with John.

It may have been the first time in his life that Connor didn't object to a hot bath.

I'd forgotten that we were supposed to meet with Uncle Arthur's demonologist the next day, but John hadn't. He was clearly looking forward to it more than I was.

As I finally snuggled under my covers, I decided that the somewhat inexplicable aspects of the case were useful insofar as they caught the interest of the powers that be at the S.P.R. In fact, it was fortunate, because the Society had no use for a straight-forward murder investigation. However, despite the strange things I had seen and heard over the last days, I remained firmly in the rationalist camp.

I knew in my heart that this man would be caught not through a bunch of psychic mumbo jumbo, but because he had made a mistake. He had revealed his pattern. And I vowed to myself that I would do all in my power to prevent any more innocents from falling prey to his blood lust.

Perhaps you think I should have gone to the police at this point. And perhaps you would be right.

I could defend myself by saying that we didn't really have anything concrete, but that wouldn't be the full truth. We had enough. Sergeant Mallory, at least, would have listened.

No, the full truth is that I still wanted to solve it myself. Despite what I had told Mrs. Rivers, I did care what Myrtle thought, very much. For once, just *once*, I wanted her to look at me with something approximating approval. I wanted to be the one coolly laying out my unimpeachable reasoning while my audience sat in quiet awe.

And it was nearly my undoing.

I spent the morning catching up with the papers. As I'd suspected, Nellie had coined the colorful moniker "Jekyll and Hyde" in her article on Anne Marlowe for *The New York World*, and her colleagues had leapt on it like a bunch of hyenas on the body of a dying wildebeest. The coverage was feverish: I counted the phrase "diabolical fiend" no less than nine times. That the killings were connected was no longer a secret, and *The Herald* declared that "no one was safe from his heinous depredations," pretty much guaranteeing widespread panic.

Two hours before my appointment at St. John's College, a knock came on the door. It was my client.

"Miss Pell," Brady said.

It was raining again, and he shook the water from his umbrella before stepping inside.

"A body has been found," he said as we entered the parlor and sat down.

"I know. Two actually," I said.

Brady looked at me in some confusion. "No, I mean

Robert. Well, I'm not sure it's him yet. But after much thought, I decided to do as you suggested and filed a report at the Bureau for the Recovery of Lost Persons yesterday. I didn't tell them everything, just that my friend had disappeared." He swallowed. "They contacted me this morning. A body was fished out of the Hudson. It fits Robert's description. But they said… they said it had been in the water for a while."

"I'm truly sorry," I said.

"I'll go to the morgue this afternoon to try to make an identification. I just wanted you to know."

I nodded.

"Do you have any leads? Frankly, Miss Pell, if it is him, I'm not sure I see the point in continuing. I appreciate all your efforts, but I hired you to find Robert."

"Do they think it was a suicide?" I asked.

"There was no mark of overt violence, if that's what you mean."

"I ask because the same person who killed Becky could have killed Robert as well."

"Yes, I see that. You mean this Jekyll and Hyde fellow?" He glanced at the pile of newspapers.

"The same."

Brady sighed. "Do as you see fit, Miss Pell. Of course, if Robert was murdered and there's a chance to bring his killer to justice, you have my full support. But I don't wish to speak of him as though he's dead. I still hold out hope, slim though it may be." He rose to leave and paused. "Do you smell that?"

I frowned. "What?"

"It's like… burning rubber."

I sniffed the air, wondering if the foul odor of the river still clung to my skin. "No, I don't."

He shook his head. "Never mind. Good day, Miss Pell. I'll let you know what I discover."

I showed him out and looked at the clock. John would be here at any moment.

I found Mrs. Rivers in the kitchen and explained to her where we were going. I reminded her to keep all the windows and doors locked, and not to let in any callers that she didn't know. Then I showed her how to fire Myrtle's gun and set it on top of the breadbasket.

"You just point it at them and pull the trigger," I said.

"Oh dear," she said faintly. "Perhaps I'll keep the rolling pin handy too. Just in case."

"Good idea," I said. "Any more word from Myrtle?"

"Not a peep."

I wasn't sure if that was good news or bad.

"Oh, and you received a cable from Mr. Doyle," she said. "It's on the table in the hall."

I dashed over and read the single sheet of paper with mounting excitement.

THE WESTERN UNION
TELEGRAPH COMPANY

THIS IS AN UNREPEATED MESSAGE,
AND IS DELIVERED BY REQUEST OF THE SENDER
UNDER THE CONDITIONS NAMED ABOVE.

THOS. T. ECKERT, General Manager

NORVIN GREEN, President

RECEIVED AT: 10:30 A.M.

SENT BY: ARTHUR CONAN DOYLE, SOUTHSEA, ENGLAND

RECEIVED BY: HARRISON FEARING PELL, 40 WEST TENTH STREET, NEW YORK, NY

DATED: AUGUST 16, 1888

CONTACTED SPR RE RICKARD CASE. OPINION DIVIDED BUT FURTHER DETAILS REQUESTED. PLEASE ADVISE LATEST DEVELOPMENTS SOONEST.

The boy had left a blank form, so I composed a brief response, focusing on the juicier aspects of the investigation. I had just finished when John arrived, as bright-eyed and bushy-tailed as if he'd actually slept more than four hours.

"It seems I have a toe in the door at the S.P.R.!" I told him gleefully, waving the telegram.

"Nice work, Harry. They'll have to hire you after this. But we'd better go, it'll take us at least an hour and it's a mess out there."

I left the message for Connor, who was running errands for Mrs. Rivers, and grabbed an umbrella from the stand. We slogged through the muddy streets to the elevated stop at Third Avenue and Ninth Street. As we waited for the train, water sheeting down from the lip of the platform roof, I thought I caught a glimpse of a soldier's uniform in the huddled crowd. My heart skipped a beat. But then the man turned, and I realized it was just one of the conductors, with bushy whiskers to boot.

We got off the train at City Hall, near the Brooklyn Bridge cable car terminus. The span itself had only been open for about five years now, but it was truly a marvel of modern engineering. It was the world's first steel-wire suspension bridge, and still the only land passage between Manhattan and Brooklyn, so traffic was always heavy.

As we crossed over the churning grey waters of the East River, I told John about my right hook and he crowed with delight.

"I might need to call on your services the next time Rupert puts fire ants in my bed," he said, grinning.

"Fire ants?" I asked, horrified. "One would think that's beyond even Rupert."

"He bought them at some exotic animal store in Chinatown." John pulled up the leg of his pants and showed me a series of nasty red welts. "And they're two weeks old now."

"That scoundrel," I said, suppressing a smile.

"Yeah. But you have to hand it to Rupert. He's dedicated to his craft."

It was a short walk on the other end to Myrtle Avenue (which John naturally found hilarious), where we caught yet another elevated line, a shiny new one that had just opened for service in April. We got off at Broadway, and two wet minutes later, we stood at the entrance of St. John's College on Lewis Avenue.

The college had been founded in 1868 to further the ideals of Saint Vincent de Paul, the patron saint of Christian charity. Its main hall was a stately, grey-brick building with a mansard roof that occupied the entire block. The humble wooden structure of St. John the Baptist Church sat next door, but Bishop John Loughlin had already laid the cornerstone for a grand new cathedral of blue granite modelled after Notre

Dame in Paris. Construction had just started that spring, and the site was still little more than a muddy hole in the ground as we climbed the front steps of the college and went inside.

It took a bit of hunting around to find Father Bruno's office, which was situated in the far recesses of the third floor. I'd expected an older, godly type, but he was an energetic man in his early thirties with a full head of curly brown hair and muscular forearms more typical of a longshoreman than a priest. We found him at his desk, grading papers. He'd pushed the sleeves of his black cassock up to his elbows, and the little square cap they called a biretta sat somewhat askew on his head.

"Come in!" he called through the open door when he saw us. "You must be Dr. Weston and Miss Pell."

"A pleasure, Father," John said, shaking his hand.

"You're late," Father Bruno said briskly. He wore little round spectacles, and his eyes were a watery blue. "I have to teach class in half an hour."

"We're very sorry," I said. "The trip from Manhattan took longer than we expected."

"Sit down then, we'd best get started." He gestured to a pair of chairs covered in books and went back to his grading. John set to work relocating the teetering stacks while I looked around.

The office was small, but it faced Lewis Avenue, so one could observe the progress of the new cathedral. On a sunny day, I imagined it would be quite bright and cheerful. This morning, however, thick rivulets of rainwater raced down the windows, giving the scene outside a distorted, underwater look.

Besides the windows, the walls were occupied with floor-to-ceiling bookshelves of polished maple. There were the usual volumes on Christian theology to be expected of a clergyman whose main purpose was to prepare boys to enter the ecclesiastical seminary. But Father Bruno's singular interests could be deduced in the collection of other, stranger titles: *Daemonologie. Iamblichus on the Mysteries of the Egyptians, Chaldeans, and Assyrians. Scot's Discovery of Witchcraft. Strange Newes, Out of Hartford-Shire and Kent. Demonology and Devil-Lore. The History of the Devils of Loudun: The Alleged Possession of the Ursuline Nuns, and the Trial and Execution of Urbain Grandier, Told by an Eye-Witness. The Foot-Prints of Satan: or, The Devil in History. The Dragon Rouge. The Clavicula Salomonis.*

"So you are friends of Arthur Conan Doyle?" Father Bruno asked as I sat down. "We've corresponded over one or two matters, but I've never met the man in person." He withdrew a slim volume and handed it me. *A Study in Scarlet.* "Arthur sent me this last month. His first published novel. I quite enjoyed it, despite its shortcomings. He's no great fan of the Mormons, is he? Well, nor am I. Though I don't think they are wicked as all that. In any event, do tell me what brings you here."

"We're trying to identify a grimoire," I said. "It was used in a black magic ritual that involved the sacrifice of a rooster."

Father Bruno nodded. "Animal and even human blood is a common feature in such rituals. For some practitioners, it represents a mockery of the Eucharist. Other simply believe that blood has a primal power. But there are many grimoires. What else can you tell me about this one?"

"Not much, except that its purpose was to bring the user great riches."

"That sounds like *The Black Pullet*," Father Bruno said, leaning back in his chair. "It claims to be written by an officer in Napoleon's army. He's wounded near to death, and rescued by a Turk who tutors him in the use of magical talismans.

The greatest of these is the Black Pullet. The hen that lays the golden egg."

"But that's just a children's tale," John said with a smile.

"So is the idea that sickness is caused by evil spirits," Father Bruno replied. "But people believe it nonetheless."

"Do you have a copy?" I asked.

"I'm afraid not." He took a book down from one of the shelves. "I have the *Dragon Rouge*, or *Red Dragon*, one of the texts that comprise *The Grand Grimoire*, which purports to have the power to summon Lucifer himself. But I've yet to run across a copy of *The Black Pullet*. Clever forgeries, yes. But not the real thing."

"So it wouldn't be a simple matter to obtain one?" I asked.

"I'd think not. These are very specialized items we're talking about." He laughed uneasily. "A hundred years ago, you could be burned at the stake merely for owning such a book."

"Like Urbain Grandier," I said.

"Precisely."

"Do you believe in possession, Father?" John asked suddenly.

"I think most cases of so-called demonic possession are in fact misdiagnosed cases of insanity," he said guardedly.

"Most probably are," John agreed. "What about the rest?"

"If you're asking whether or not I'm aware of any *authentic* cases in which a demon has assumed control of someone's body… " Father Bruno removed his glasses and began cleaning them on the sleeve of his robes. "There are one or two that appear persuasive. None for at least a century. I've certainly never witnessed such a thing myself, I'm only familiar with the phenomenon through the literature. The Church's official position is that insanity must be ruled out before an exorcism is authorized by the local bishop."

"What sort of things would they look for?" John asked.

"There are certain signs specified in the Roman Ritual. A sudden ability to speak a foreign language, often Latin or Spanish, of which the person had no prior knowledge. Extreme and repetitive blasphemy. Superhuman strength."

"But such cases are extremely rare?"

"Well, yes, of course. And even those are questionable. Take George Lukins, also known as the Yatton Daemoniac. It's a famous story in England. His exorcism was conducted on Friday the 13th, 1788. He claimed to be possessed by seven demons, and thus seven ministers were summoned to banish them. Lukins was illiterate, and yet he responded to questions in Latin in the same ancient language. The background is that he was a forty-four-year-old tailor from Somerset who had been exhibiting erratic behavior for years—barking like a dog, speaking in different voices, cursing and swearing, even walking on all fours like a beast. Doctors had declared him incurable."

"What happened after the exorcism?" John asked.

"Lukins appeared to be normal again."

"Do you think it's authentic?"

"It's impossible to say. The events occurred a hundred years ago."

"Suggestion is a powerful thing," I said. "An insane person could believe they've been cured so an exorcism might actually help them."

"I don't dispute it," Father Bruno said mildly. "That's why it's virtually impossible to say for certain whether any of these possession cases have canonical merit."

"Have you ever heard of a demon entering through a person's eyes?" John asked.

"The eyes?" Father Bruno tapped a pencil on the edge

of his desk. "Yes, I think there's one reference. Hand me the *Clavicula Salomonis*, would you? Just behind you, fifth shelf down. The black cover."

John obliged. Father Bruno leafed through the thin, yellowed pages.

"The concept of the Evil Eye goes back hundreds if not thousands of years, in nearly every culture," he said. "That a mere glance, with malevolent intent, can inflict a curse. But I suppose that's somewhat different. Let's see… Eyes are frequently described as portals. Oculi quas fenestrae animi."

"The eyes are the windows of the soul," I said.

"Very good." Father Bruno looked at me with approval, then continued his search. "Ah, here it is. A passage in one of the conjurations. *Let their eyes be darkened when the master comes. Let them see not, lest the demons of the abyss seek them out. For demons are animals of darkness*." His finger slid a few inches down the page. "It seems to imply that demons can exit the body in this way as well. Either to depart at the bidding of an exorcist, or to take possession of another soul."

"Have you ever seen this symbol before?" I handed him the scrap of paper I'd copied from Fred at *The New York World*.

Father Bruno studied the lines and angles. "It looks like it could be a diabolical signature."

"What's that?"

"The unique signature of a demon or similar spirit, designed to conceal their true name. They're usually used to seal an infernal pact for things like eternal youth or power."

"Would they be burned into a surface?"

"According to the books, they are signed in blood. But I suppose anything would do, as long as the signature itself is clear." Father Bruno traced the symbol with his fingertip. "*The Lesser Key of Solomon* asserts that there are seventy-two demons, each with their own mark, collectively called the seal of the demons. Most look like this, combinations of circles and lines and inverted crosses."

"How difficult would it be to find out about diabolical signatures?" I asked.

"Not very difficult, I imagine. They're mentioned in a number of prominent works on the subject."

"Have you ever run across someone who *believed* they were possessed?"

The priest smiled a little. "I think that describes the vast majority of cases. There is often an element of religious mania. It's no coincidence, I think, that many of the victims have been nuns." He hesitated. "I understand that the facts of your inquiry must remain confidential, but may I ask if the person involved is a member of the Church?"

"No," I said. "But his upbringing could have been quite strict, perhaps with the threat of going to hell or being tormented by demons. We're not sure."

"I see." Father Bruno shuffled his exam papers into a pile. "*Tempus fugit.* Is there anything else? My next class starts in five minutes."

"I think that's all," I said, standing as John did the same. "Thanks very much for your time."

"Say hello to Arthur next time you see him. Tell him I wish him luck with his detective novels!" Father Bruno laughed with genuine mirth. "Perhaps he'll get rich and famous someday. As it says in Chapter Seven, Book Two of Samuel, *The Lord sends poverty and wealth; he humbles and he exalts.*" He chuckled again.

We were walking to the door when I did think of one last thing.

"Might someone give a grimoire like *The Black Pullet* to a

person they wished to harm?" I asked. "If they truly believed it worked, and that it might summon a demon?"

The priest raised an eyebrow. "Are you asking whether such a book could be used as a murder weapon?"

"I suppose I'm asking if someone might *think* it could."

His shrewd blue eyes met mine, and now they didn't seem watery at all. "In my experience, Miss Pell, people can convince themselves of almost anything if they try hard enough."

It took nearly two hours to retrace our journey back to Manhattan. The rain didn't let up for a single minute, and neither did John, though I managed to mostly shut him out. If he'd harbored a single shred of doubt that we weren't hunting a daemoniac before, our visit with Father Bruno had obliterated it. I, on the other hand, was more than ever certain that while this case involved Spiritualism, diabolical pacts and murders that seemed both senseless and evil, its solution would be entirely earthly.

John finally tired of pestering me, and we parted ways with a promise to meet at ten o'clock. That left me five full hours to get ready for the ball. My nerves grew jagged thinking about what might happen that night, so I decided to just let the case simmer on the back burner for a bit.

Instead, I holed up in my room and took out all the notebooks I had compiled on the Society for Psychical Research.

I'd been working on them since the S.P.R. was founded six years before. I had just turned eleven, and Uncle Arthur came for a visit. I was supposed to be in bed, but I'd gotten in the habit of spying on the grownups from the second-floor landing. I liked listening to them talk. Arthur was a big bear of a man, with hands like ham hocks and an enchanting Scottish brogue. He was a natural storyteller.

Anyway, the subject of the S.P.R. came up, and something about it sparked my interest immediately. It was both mysterious and logical, orthodox and radical. Their work sounded dangerous. But exciting too. In imitation of my sister, I started writing down every scrap of information I could discover about them. I soon realized that while the chapter in London sought to engage the public, publishing its results in a scholarly journal, the Americans kept a very low profile. When I had filled ten notebooks, I put them in a box.

I kept the box hidden at the back of my closet, thinking that would keep Myrtle from finding out. Ha-ha. When you have a sister like Myrtle, you can just give up the idea of having any secrets. She laughed and said she'd turned down a job offer from the S.P.R. because she didn't like following other people's rules. I don't think she even meant to twist the knife, which somehow made it worse.

Once I'd stopped hating her, I vowed that I would work for them myself or die trying.

I knew the New York offices were downtown somewhere, but I'd never been able to find the exact address. Their president was a man named Benedict Wakefield. He seemed to be very rich, but exactly *how* and *why* was ambiguous. The only thing I knew for sure was that he was one of Edison's key investors in the Pearl Street Station, the first electrical power plant in New York.

The American S.P.R. kept the identities of its agents strictly confidential. But I'd learned that it had two distinct and warring factions. The leader of the skeptics was a man named Harland Kaylock. He was thirty-seven, unmarried, and lived in one of the new French-style flats on West Fifty-Seventh

Street. I'd followed him around town a couple of times, hoping he might lead me to the S.P.R. offices. He was very tall and thin, with sallow skin and a hooked nose. He dressed impeccably and never smiled, at least not that I saw. Mr. Kaylock's training was as a professional magician. I watched his hands, and his fingers were so quick and nimble they made me think of a capuchin monkey I'd seen at the Central Park menagerie.

Mr. Kaylock's arch-rival at the S.P.R. was Orpha Winter. She led the zealots and true believers, who saw the Society's mission not as debunking the occult, but elevating it to a par with other branches of natural science. I'd only seen her once, when we had both attended a lecture at Columbia by Frank Podmore, one of the authors of *Phantasms of the Living*, a sweeping study of psychic phenomena commissioned by the London S.P.R.

Orpha Winter sat in the front row of the hall. She had lush honey-blonde hair, which she wore in a complicated pile atop her head. Men stared at that hair, and I could see them wondering what it would look like unpinned and flowing down her back. She had tiny hands and feet, like a doll, and very red lips, and they were fixed in a small smile that never altered.

Mr. Winter was a banker, a stiff, prematurely grey fellow who rarely spoke and sat at his wife's side like a mouse next to a lion. Afterwards, they were surrounded by a circle of admirers. She made a pretense of asking his opinion and leaning on his arm, but it was no secret who was the dominant personality in *that* marriage.

I heard that the battles between Orpha Winter and Harland Kaylock were the stuff of legends.

Uncle Arthur was a new member of the London chapter, so I assumed that he was communicating with his contacts there about the Rickard case. However, it was those two I'd have to impress if I wanted employment on this side of the Atlantic. I wasn't sure it was even possible to make them both happy, but while my personal sympathies lay with Mr. Kaylock's faction, Mrs. Winter was far too powerful to ignore.

I was just contemplating this problem yet again when Mrs. River knocked on the door.

"It's eight o'clock, Harry!" she called. "You'd best start getting ready."

I glanced through the window at the lengthening shadows on Tenth Street, astonished that so many hours had passed. Indeed, it was growing dark outside. I jumped up and returned the box to its place under my bed. Then I took a hot bath and washed my hair in a lemon juice concoction my mother swore by. When I emerged from the tub, I found a new dress waiting, a simple yet lovely silk gown of the deepest blue with short sleeves and a tight bodice.

"It matches your eyes, dear," Mrs. Rivers said. "Go ahead, try it on."

I hugged her and tried not to wince as she laced me in.

"Now for your hair," Mrs. Rivers said. "Sit down, Harry, I have an idea."

"This thing isn't made for sitting," I grumbled, shifting the voluminous skirts around until I managed to perch on the edge of my vanity bench.

I watched in the mirror as she expertly set a series of lacquered Japanese combs in my hair, concealing its short length. Then she slid a choker of sapphires around my neck. They felt cool against my skin in the stuffy room.

"Your mother won't mind," Mrs. Rivers said, dabbing faintly tinted beeswax on my lips to give them a pink gloss. "She means you to have her jewellery anyway. Now, Edward says tonight's theme is 'The Splendors of Nature.' I thought you could go as The Night Sky."

I stared at the exotic creature in the vanity. It didn't look like me, but I supposed that was the point. It was as much a disguise as Connor's castoff clothing. Let them all be lulled and think I was an empty-headed, frivolous thing.

I smiled evilly. Perhaps there would finally be an advantage to no one taking me seriously.

Connor let out a low whistle when he saw me. He would be coming along as our driver tonight, to keep an eye on things from the outside. Mrs. Rivers had scrubbed him cleaner than I'd ever seen before, and forced him into an outfit that he complained made him look like Little Lord Fauntleroy. I told him he should try getting laced into a corset sometime, if he wanted to know what sheer misery really felt like.

Sitting down was uncomfortable and eating out of the question, so I paced the front hall until my escorts arrived in the barouche at ten o'clock on the dot. John's eyes bugged a little when I made my grand entrance down the staircase, but he recovered quickly and brushed his lips to my gloved hand.

"You look ravishing, Harry," he murmured. "The other girls will be green with envy, and the men will curse my good fortune."

John wore a conservative evening jacket with long tails and a starched white shirt. I could still detect faint bruising along his jaw from the fight in Hell's Kitchen nearly a week ago, but it was mostly covered by his high collar.

Edward, on the other hand, had a reputation to live up to. As it was a costume ball, he enjoyed more latitude than usual in his evening attire, and he used every inch of it. I counted at least six shades of rose in his cravat, contrasted by tight violet pants and lilac stockings. His handkerchief was a peculiar shade of purple he identified as "byzantine," and a pink carnation poked out of his lapel.

"I tried to convince Zenobia"—that was Edward's little sister—"to come back from Newport, but she's never been overly fond of the Kanes," he said. "She refused even when I told her I planned to go as The First Blush of Sunrise!"

John made a sympathetic noise. "She's certainly missing... something," he said.

"Do you think I might make the papers?" Edward asked, brightening a little. "If they're doing party portraits? Of course, black and white won't do me justice, but still."

"I'd say there's a very good chance," John replied with an admirably straight face.

Mrs. Hudson made a few minute adjustments to my hair and dress, pinched my cheeks for color, and declared me presentable, even to such a discriminating hostess as Temple Kane.

"Have her back by three, Mr. Weston!" she called down the steps as we climbed into the carriage.

"On my honor," John called back with a salute.

Despite myself, I felt a flutter of excitement as we headed uptown. I'd never been inside the Kane mansion before, but I'd heard plenty of stories about it. Situated just above the stretch of Fifth Avenue that was becoming known as Millionaire's Row, the Kanes rubbed elbows with such illustrious neighbors as the Astors and Vanderbilts. They were one of the first wealthy families to venture north of Fifty-Ninth Street (although others would soon follow suit), to what a quarter century before had been little more than a rutted dirt road cutting through a shantytown.

The Kane mansion faced Central Park, occupying most of the block between Sixty-Sixth and Sixty-Seventh Street. Designed by Stanford White, it was made of grey limestone and looked more like a museum than a private residence. All the windows were blazing with light as we joined the line of carriages pulled up in front.

"Ready for the lion's den, Harry?" Edward asked, as a liveried footman in a powdered wig approached the barouche.

I surveyed the crowd of extravagantly attired men and women presenting their invitations at the front doors. One appeared to be wearing an actual taxidermied cat's head as a hat.

"Oh, that's just Puss," Edward said, stroking the wispy fuzz of a new mustache he seemed very proud of.

"It's still wearing a collar," I said faintly.

Edward patted my shoulder. "Let's go find the punch."

"Sneak me some back, will ya?" Connor implored from the driver's seat. "It's thirsty work, sitting around watching rich people."

"I promise to bring you a pastry," I said, as John helped me down.

"How about the first dance?" he asked, fluttering his lashes.

I twined my arm in his and smiled. "That's the first sensible thing you've said all day."

And so we drifted into the current of partygoers as it swept slowly but inexorably towards the Kanes' ballroom, like a river to the sea.

CHAPTER FOURTEEN

"I'D FORGOTTEN WHAT a fine dancer you are," I said as John twirled me around the floor in an intricate mazurka, a dance they say was inspired by the Polish cavalry racing across the steppes of Central Europe. The tempo certainly was *fast*, and my cheeks were flushed by the time I spun to a stop and we started a more sedate waltz.

"True dancing can't be taught," he said absently, gazing over my shoulder. "It's improvised in the moment. It comes from the chemistry of the dancers, the space between them."

"Well, my toes thank you," I said. "It's terribly unfair that women must wear slippers at these things, while men are shod in tough leather soles. And the mazurka is especially treacherous. All those quick little stomps."

"Ah well, I've been practicing in secret," John laughed. He shook hair from his eyes and glanced meaningfully at my bodice. "I wouldn't want to get shot for any missteps."

Not much got past my best friend, I thought. "Is it that obvious?"

"Not really. I wouldn't have noticed if I hadn't seen you fooling with the… uh… placement just before we left." His teasing expression sobered. "Are you expecting trouble tonight, Harry?"

I shook my head. "Just preparing for anything, I suppose. That's one of Myrtle's maxims. She likes to quote General Washington: 'To be prepared for war is one of the most effective means of preserving peace'."

"I suppose we are at war, at that. But is it with the Kanes?"

He glanced over at George Jr., who stood in the midst of a group of friends near the punchbowl. Like John, he had skipped a costume and wore traditional evening attire. He had blonde hair, slicked back, and an arrogant laugh that was already too loud. As I watched, he threw his head back and roared at some joke, a glass of champagne tipping precariously in one hand. Temple looked over sharply from across the ballroom. She didn't seem pleased.

"I don't know," I said. "He's a cad, but is he a killer? It strikes me as more than a little odd that he would ride the elevated in search of victims. The trains are dirty, crowded, infested with vermin. Why not just stalk them from a carriage? It's more private, far fewer people would see his face, and it offers a quick escape route when the deed is done."

John slid his hand into the small of my back and expertly pulled me close, then spun me away again. "You're forgetting something, Harry. George likes slumming in downtown dives, like Billy McGlory's Armory Hall on Hester Street. Rich boys pay to sit up in the balcony and watch the thugs brawling down below. I heard he got too drunk once and ended up getting hauled outside and robbed." John grinned. "And left on the street without a stitch of clothing."

"Billy's a rough character," I said. "Maybe that's why George hired Thomas Sweet for protection."

Billy McGlory was one of the city's most prominent gangsters and club owners. Although Mayor Hewitt vowed during his campaign to shut down the seediest disorderly houses and red light districts, so far Billy had dodged the hammer. His bouncers were some of the most feared criminals of the Five Points, and the only edict they religiously enforced was that actual murder should not be committed inside the dance hall.

As we weaved through the other couples, I told John the famous story of how Billy once turned up at the offices of the *New York Sun* to complain about an article alleging a man had been stabbed at the Armory.

"He was stabbed just *outside* of McGlory's," Billy had objected to the editors. "I don't permit stabbing and shooting inside."

After re-interviewing the victim in the hospital, the newspaper ran a retraction the following day explaining that in fact, he had been stabbed on the street side of McGlory's threshold.

"The place is a cesspool of beastliness and depravity," John said earnestly, shaking his head in disapproval. Then he flashed white teeth in a wicked grin. "No wonder it's so popular."

"So you think riding the trains could be part of the thrill?" I wondered aloud.

"If we're dealing with someone who's a Jekyll and Hyde, like the papers say, he might adopt a totally different persona than the one he wears for the people around him," John pointed out.

Two teenage girls in identical harlequin costumes, except with the black and white reversed, flashed past as we spun along the edge of the dance floor. Parthena and Permelia Sloane-Sherman, twins and debutantes extraordinaire. Their matching blue eyes aimed daggers at me through gold-painted *colombinas* on sticks. They liked John. Therefore, they didn't like me.

"A mask of sanity," I said.

"Yes."

"And hunting in the streets would make him feel free, unencumbered by the expectations of society. Like a predator moving through the jungle."

"Let's say it is George," John said. "What's his connection to Straker?"

"What if Straker went back to Becky's flat for some reason? What if he witnessed her murder? George could hardly leave him alive."

"And yet we know that Straker *was* alive and at home the next day. At least, according to Brady."

"According to Brady," I repeated. "But there's something off about his story. Nothing fits."

My feet stumbled on the left box turn, but John caught me before I fell on my face in front of Mrs. Kane's entire ballroom.

"It fits if Straker did it," he said. "You may disagree with me on motive, but you must admit he's the only one the evidence really points to. Maybe Becky *was* blackmailing George. Maybe he gave her the money and the book to get rid of her. But it could be a coincidence."

We began the promenade.

"I don't believe in coincidences," I said.

"But what about Billy? He disappeared *going to find Straker*. How could George have known?"

"I don't know," I admitted.

"And back to Becky for a moment. Why would George want to kill her anyway?"

"So she wouldn't reveal their affair," I said. "It could ruin him if it came out."

"But you said yourself that he's a known cad. Becky wasn't the first, and I'm sure she won't be the last. George's parents may not like it, but they haven't disowned him yet."

We spun past Temple Kane, who was chatting with a

small circle of the most powerful women in the rigid hierarchy of New York Society. Mrs. Kane was in her late forties, but looked a decade younger. She wore a shimmering gown of gold leaf cunningly sewn to resemble fish scales. Her husband stood several paces away. His eyes passed over me, pausing for a moment, and I suddenly wondered if he recognized me from our brief encounter at Chamberlain's. But then a fat, red-faced man started speaking to him and he turned his back to us.

"Maybe he was afraid Becky would be the final straw," I mused.

The band struck up a new tune and John smoothly switched to a polka.

"Alright, I'll give you that one, even though I'm not entirely convinced. But that in turn brings us to Raffaele and Anne. Are you really certain it's the same killer?"

"I'm certain," I said.

"So if the motive was to stop a blackmailer, then why go after them? They had no connection to Becky."

"Because he's mad," I said. "Because he likes it. Stalking them, subduing them, watching them die. It makes him feel powerful. And he'll go to increasingly extreme lengths to recreate the rush he gets from killing."

John considered this. "There's been new research into a certain type of aberrant personality. Some call it mania without delirium, or moral insanity. It describes someone who engages in antisocial behaviour without regard for the consequences. They're often fluent liars and seem entirely lacking in empathy. But in other ways they're perfectly sane, capable of cool-headed planning and manipulation. The German psychiatrist Julius Koch has been doing preliminary work in this area."

"Thank you, Doctor Weston," I said, smiling. "I'd say that

description could fit George Kane, or his henchman, or both. Speaking of whom, he'd have to be in on it, don't you think?"

John didn't respond. I felt his shoulders stiffen beneath my fingertips.

"What is it? Thomas Sweet?"

I hadn't yet spotted George's bodyguard, the one who had given Becky the grimoire, but that didn't surprise me. Sweet was terrifying to look at, it was a large part of his effectiveness, and I somehow doubted that Temple Kane wanted her party guests in the presence of such a menacing man. He wouldn't be far, I imagined, but he'd keep well out of sight.

John didn't reply, just made a minute gesture with his chin toward the entrance foyer. I scanned the crowd. The Kane ballroom was immense, even by the standards of Mrs. Astor's 400, as the oldest and richest families were known. In the tradition of too-much-is-never-enough, the carved and gilded walls were covered in heavy oil paintings, frescoes and chandeliers decorated the ceiling, and there were enough flowers to sink a battleship.

Bewigged waiters in 18th century outfits that would have fit right in at Versailles dispensed buckets of champagne to the flushed, chattering guests. I caught a quick glimpse of Edward, like some rare Amazonian parrot, escorting Puss and her stuffed cat to the other end of the dance floor, where dancers were lining up for a quadrille.

And then I saw James Moran. He moved slowly through the crowd, his flat eyes taking everything in with a mixture of contempt and amusement. The women, young and old, whispered behind their fans. Some giggled. Others looked at him in frank appraisal. I suppose he was handsome enough, with his raven hair and lean, wolfish build. He was certainly rich, and the Moran name still held influence in New York politics.

But as his black eyes locked on mine, I knew I wouldn't care to be in a room alone with him for all the tea in China.

"Why do you think he's here?" John asked.

He'd stopped dancing, but his arm was still wrapped protectively around my waist. I gently disengaged it and took a step back.

"Oh, sorry Harry." He flushed a little. "I didn't mean… "

"I don't know why he's here," I said. "I've heard he hardly ever accepts party invitations. But he's coming this way."

Moran's eyes never left mine as he glided across the room, like a barracuda cutting through a school of bright tropical fish. Several men tried to approach him, and even one or two of the bolder women, but he brushed them off.

Suddenly, my bodice felt very tight. I'd stuffed one of Myrtle's smallest pistols in there, and had a momentary vision of myself shooting James Moran in the middle of the Kanes' ballroom, while three hundred party guests looked on in horror.

Then he was standing in front of us, his snowy white shirt immaculate under an open dress coat with silk lapels. John had a tight rein on himself, but his fists were clenched as though he were having fantasies of his own.

Moran allowed his gaze to linger on my bosom a fraction of a second too long for propriety, and then he seized my gloved hand and brushed it with his lips before I could snatch it back.

"Miss Pell," he said in a surprisingly soft voice. "I was hoping to see you here."

"Really?" I said. "Why so?"

"I was hoping we could talk."

"We *are* talking," I said with a thin smile.

"In private."

This was too much for John. "If you think she's going off somewhere with you after—"

I laid a restraining hand on John's arm. "You can say whatever it is you came to say right here," I said.

Moran looked around and arched a thick eyebrow. He looked as though he was trying not to laugh, and I decided that shooting him on the spot might not be such a bad idea after all.

"Well, we do seem to have everyone's rapt attention," he observed.

Indeed, the murmur of conversation had dropped several notches, and a few people were actually leaning towards us to listen better. Just at that moment, the band struck up Strauss's *Phenomene* waltz.

"I wish to apologize for last evening," Moran said. "It was not what I'd intended. I only want to speak with you. Say for the length of one dance?" He held out his hand.

John said nothing, but I could tell he was furious. He had every right to be.

"One dance," I said.

As distasteful as the prospect was, I needed answers too.

John looked at me with incredulity. "You can't be serious," he said.

"I'll be fine," I said. "I think it's worth it to hear why Mr. Moran has taken an interest in… certain matters."

"That doesn't mean you have to dance with him," John hissed.

"Unless we want everyone in this room to know our business, I don't see any choice," I said, reaching for his hand. John pulled it away.

"It's your decision, of course," he said stiffly.

"John… "

But he was already walking away. I watched as Parthena and Permelia Sloane-Sherman homed in on him, each one taking an arm and leaning in close as they led him to the punchbowl. He didn't look back.

"Shall we?" Moran asked.

I nodded curtly. He placed feather-light fingers on my back and we linked hands. A moment later, James Moran was whisking me into the fray. I could feel curious eyes on us, but between the music and our swift movement, I doubted anyone could eavesdrop on our conversation.

"So you're Myrtle's little sister," he murmured in my ear. "Does she know what you're up to, I wonder?"

I schooled my expression to perfect indifference. He hadn't a clue if he thought he could bait me so easily. "You're not as good a dancer as my last partner," I said.

"Dancing's not what I'm skilled at," Moran responded, a dark mirth in his eyes.

"Tell me something," I said. "Do you make it a habit to set your jackals on helpless young ladies?"

"I'd hardly call you helpless." Moran laughed. "By God, I thought Declan was ugly before, but you should see him now. And no, it's not my style. Things got out of hand."

"Out of hand? They tried to kill me."

The music rose and fell, the faces of the other dancers flashing before me. The barrel of the pistol pressed into my ribcage. I wondered if he knew it was there.

"Regrettable," Moran said, although he didn't look particularly sorry. "I shouldn't have sent Declan. He has an excitable disposition."

"Let's get to the point," I said. "What's your interest in the Jekyll and Hyde case?"

The tempo suddenly increased, and I realized that he'd

just been toying with me. He was every bit as good as John, perhaps even better. Moran's hand tightened around my waist and I had no choice but to let him guide me through the dizzyingly fast steps.

"The Forsizi boy," Moran whispered. "His brother works for me. I want this lunatic off the streets as much as you do, Miss Pell. Besides, it's bad for business."

"And what is it exactly that you want from me?"

"I want a truce between us until this man Straker is found. And I want to offer my assistance in accomplishing that."

I tried not to betray my shock that he knew Straker's name. From what Myrtle had told me, James Moran sat at the center of a vast criminal web, spinning its threads as it suited him. His family was an old one, and outwardly respectable. He had been a child prodigy in both music and mathematics. Then, at the age of sixteen, he had shot and killed his father and spent eight months in the Tombs. He had claimed self-defense, and his youth—along with the Moran fortune—had bought him an early release. Myrtle believed it was during this time that James Moran had made several key gangland connections.

There was a minor bloodbath when he got out of prison. None of it was traceable back to Moran, he was far too smart for that. But when the dust settled, he smoothly took control of New York's criminal underworld.

I believe I mentioned before that Myrtle's record was unblemished, except for one man.

Well, I was dancing with him now.

"What kind of assistance?" I asked.

"Whatever you require," he responded. "I've been watching you for some time, Miss Pell. You've made impressive strides. But it's not enough. You're at the stage where you need raw manpower. The kind the police could easily supply, but you haven't gone to them yet. I suppose you have your own reasons, and I've no desire to pry into those." He smiled like a lazy, sun-warmed cat, letting me know that *he* knew precisely what those reasons were. "But I can give you boys. As many as you want."

I suddenly realized where he could have learned Straker's name and my blood ran cold.

"Did you harm Billy Finn?" I demanded, trying to pull away.

Moran held me fast. "No, I didn't harm Billy. I know who he is, but I've nothing to do with his disappearance. In fact, I've had my own boys looking out for him. But he seems to have vanished."

I held his black eyes, trying to gauge whether or not he was telling the truth. It was impossible to tell.

"So you seek a truce," I said.

"Temporary, of course," he agreed.

Myrtle would be home in two days. Although Billy appeared to have run away, I couldn't shake the feeling that he was in terrible danger. And the Hunter. He wouldn't stop. He had a taste for it now.

"Tomorrow night," I said, reaching my decision. "We fan out and ride the elevated lines. That's where he finds his victims. He dresses as a soldier."

"I know."

The music died. Moran let go of me and stepped back.

"Tomorrow then, Miss Pell." He gave a deep bow. "Thank you for the pleasure of your company. I hope I may enjoy it again someday."

"Highly unlikely," I said. "And by the way, that leaky quill you've been using to solve problems is *still* leaky, though I see you've tried to repair it more than once. And you really should hire a professional piano tuner. You may be a brilliant player, but you're hopeless at adjusting the strings. Good evening, Mr. Moran."

I smiled in satisfaction and left him standing in the middle of the ballroom with his jaw hanging open in bafflement.

So I'd made my own pact with the Devil, I thought as I made my way to the edge of the dance floor. We desperately needed what Moran had to offer, but there was always a price to pay in the end. I tried not to dwell on what that might be.

After a few minutes of searching, I found John with the Sloane-Shermans and their odious friends, Georgia DeForest and Lulu Rhinelander Jones. They were petting him like a dog, and John didn't look as displeased as he ought to have. I tried to catch his eye but he studiously ignored me. I stood on the fringes, feeling like an idiot, as the girls shot me poisonous sidelong glances, and finally decided that I deserved a glass of punch.

I'd more than earned it, having to dance with beastly James Moran and then be shunned by my best friend for what was really an act of self-sacrifice, I thought, taking a gulp of the fruity concoction. A pleasant, loose warmth instantly spread through my chest. It's funny, because I couldn't taste any alcohol. But by the time I'd finished my first glass and started on the next, I was feeling both reckless and resentful.

I wandered aimlessly through the crowd. Several young men approached me to dance, but I turned them down. I'd had enough dancing for the night. Instead, I nibbled on pastries and played a game of scrutinizing my fellow guests. A woman with a tame white dove perched on her wrist was having a torrid affair with her footman. Another dressed as a gold-and-black wasp was blind as a bat without her glasses but too proud to wear them. A man with thick ginger whiskers had colored them so as to appear younger; traces of the die stained his left earlobe. It was all very mundane.

I stood up on my toes and peered over their babbling heads. Moran had vanished.

It was at that moment that I spotted George Kane making for the garden.

I'd kept half an eye on him all night, and he'd always been surrounded by a group of sycophantic admirers, hangers-on hoping for a bite of the Kane pie. This was the first time I'd seen him alone.

I handed my punch to a passing waiter and made an unsteady beeline for the door I'd seen him go through. Some fresh air would do me good anyway. It was stuffy in the ball-room, and my ears were buzzing from the din of drunken laughter and loud music.

I pushed through the crowd and followed the faint breeze down a long hallway to a set of open French doors. A group of men stood just outside, smoking cigars. They leered at me as I passed, despite the fact that most were old enough to be my father. A few stragglers from the party sat (or slumped) on stone benches, but as I moved deeper into the lush gardens, the sounds of revelry faded.

I wandered down a flagstone path between two tall hedges, looking for George. I thought I'd seen him come this way. But the garden was larger than it appeared, a maze of twisting lanes and dense shrubbery. Fortunately, the sky was clear and the moon bright enough to see by. I took a few steadying breaths. The scent of some night-blooming flower drifted, thick and sweet as syrup, through the air. My head began to clear.

Then I rounded a corner and nearly tripped over my prey. He was sitting on the grass next to a tinkling marble fountain, a bottle of champagne propped between his knees. His neatly combed hair had fallen into his eyes, and his cravat hung loose across his chest, like bat's wings.

"What is this wondrous vision I see before me?" George Kane declared, flashing a smarmy grin. "A naiad of the woodland forest! Or is it a dryad? I always get them confused." He shrugged and patted the ground next to him. "No matter. Come have a drink with me. Even fairies drink champagne, don't they?"

I looked down, trying to imagine this man stabbing and strangling five people. He wasn't much older than I was, and his features had the softness of someone whose idea of exertion was shooting some poor animal from the back of a horse.

But then, as John pointed out, the face our killer wore to the world would be very different from the face his victims saw in their final minutes on earth.

"Why are you out here?" I asked. "The party just got going."

George scowled. "Mother says I need to sober up a bit. So that's what I'm doing!" He held the bottle up in a toast and took a swig. "Do you happen to have a cigarette? I left mine inside."

"Sorry," I said.

"Well, don't just stand there looming over me. I'm getting a crick in my neck. Sit down or go away."

I sank to the grass across from him, on my knees, which was the only position my dress would allow.

"Who are you?" George asked. "I thought I knew all the pretty ones."

"Harrison Fearing Pell."

"Wait, Pell... as in Myrtle Fearing Pell?"

I sighed. "Yes. She's my sister."

George laughed aloud. "I remember Myrtle from school.

Quite the odd duck. We used to call her Myrtle the Misfit. Thought she was smarter than everyone else."

I decided it was time to take the wind out of Mr. George X. Kane II's sails.

"I'm not here to talk about Myrtle, actually," I said.

"Oh? What *are* you here for then?" He leaned back, a flirtatious grin on his face.

"I'm here to talk about Becky Rickard," I said.

George's grin slipped several notches.

"I don't know that name," he said.

"Oh, I think you do. I spoke to a witness who saw Thomas Sweet give her $200. They're willing to testify in court. And he's not exactly difficult to identify." I smiled. "I know that you were lovers. I know you gave her a grimoire. And I know that she tried to blackmail you, and died for it."

George's face had grown paler with each word. "Who *are* you?" He grabbed the bottle of champagne but didn't drink from it. "And I had nothing to do with her murder!"

"But—"

"You haven't got your facts straight. Becky would never have tried to blackmail me. She *loved* me, for God's sake." George put his head in his hands. "Becky was... a mistake."

"A mistake?" I couldn't keep the anger out of my voice.

"I met her through Mother," George said tonelessly. "She would come to house to hold séances. We hit it off."

"She thought you were going to marry her," I said coldly.

"I never said that, not once."

"I'm sure you implied it."

George was silent.

"Do you have any idea what you've done?"

"I told you, I didn't kill her. I don't know who did. Maybe she had another lover."

I glared at him until he looked away. "Men like you make themselves feel better thinking everyone's as rotten as they are, that's how you justify treating girls like Becky as though they're trash, but she wasn't." The gunmetal felt hot against my breasts. "The grimoire. Was it *The Black Pullet*?"

He looked up at me with an unreadable expression. "Yes. I got it from a gentleman at my club."

"Why did you give it to Becky?"

George's green eyes suddenly chilled. I felt it, as if an icy breeze had swept through the garden.

"Why the hell should I tell you that?"

"Because if you don't, I'm going straight to the police with everything I know. Your family name will be dragged through the mud. Even the Kanes can't buy their way out of a murder charge."

George considered this but said nothing. I decided to give him another little push.

"Becky wrote a letter to her sister just before she died. She names you, George."

"That little… " He swore under his breath.

"Why did you give Becky the grimoire?"

"I just wanted to test it out," he muttered. "See if it actually worked. The man who sold it to me said it was effective, but dangerous. He told me stories of what had happened to others who tried to use it. One threw himself in front of a streetcar. Another massacred his wife, children and servants and ended up in an asylum. He said I must have a medium. Performed incorrectly… well, he claimed it could open a *doorway* and there's no telling what might come through. I figured he was just trying to increase the price, but I didn't care to take a chance. So I paid Becky to try it first."

"But what do you need a fortune for anyway? Aren't you rich enough?"

George laughed mirthlessly. "My *father* is rich, Miss Pell. And he's a hard man."

"So he's threatened to cut you off, is that it?" I shook my head in disgust.

"He refused to pay my debts," George said. "I had no choice but to take matters into my own hands."

I remembered Edward saying he'd just spent the day with George at the racetrack, and wondered how vast his debts had become. But there was something wrong with his story.

"You went there, to Becky's flat, didn't you?" I said.

"What?"

"The book was never found. Someone took it."

George's eyes glazed over. His fingers loosened around the neck of the bottle. "I keep seeing things. In the mirror. *Shapes.* My God, there was so much blood. On the walls. The *ceiling.*" George looked at me, all traces of drunkenness gone. "They did it, didn't they? They let something through."

The moment stretched out, and then I heard the soft crunch of footfalls on gravel.

"What's going on here?" It was Mrs. Temple Kane. She had her son's green eyes and blonde hair, but the resemblance ended there. Temple's face was all hard planes and angles. She towered over me, and I guessed her height must have been close to six feet.

George opened his mouth but no sound came out.

"Get back inside," she said to her son in a peremptory tone.

He scrambled to his feet and grabbed the champagne.

"Mother—"

"Just do as I say."

George couldn't meet her gaze. "Yes, Mother."

He turned and stumbled down the path like a whipped dog. Mrs. Kane turned to me.

"You look tired, Miss Pell. It's been a long evening. I'm sure you wish to go home now."

I was being dismissed as surely as George, if in a somewhat more polite manner.

"Thank you for your hospitality, Mrs. Kane," I said. "It was certainly an exciting party."

She smiled, and it was one of the most frightening things I've ever seen.

"I'm so glad you thought so. Shall I fetch Mr. Weston to escort you to your carriage?"

"I can do it myself."

She inclined her head. "So independent. I suppose it runs in the family. Good evening, then, Miss Pell."

She swept up her skirts and glided away down the path.

I stood there for a moment. George had said something that tickled the back of my mind, like a maddening itch I couldn't quite reach. He'd been in Becky's flat, all right, and retrieved the book. But had he been the one to kill her? As John had noted, he could be a fluent liar. He certainly didn't seem to feel any remorse for using Becky to carry out his dirty work.

Was it true fear I saw in his eyes at the end, or simply a calculated performance?

I went back inside. John was dancing with Parthena, who clung to him like a leech. Edward had disappeared. Mrs. Kane's eyes bored into me as I crossed the ballroom, as though she could shove me out the front door through sheer force of will.

So I snagged two cherry tarts from the groaning food table and brought them out to the long line of carriages waiting at the curb. Most of the drivers were dozing in their seats. A few stood on the street, talking quietly. The mansion itself occupied the middle of the block, with a high wrought-iron fence extending around the grounds. I headed north, searching for Connor. When I reached the corner of Sixty-Seventh Street, I happened to glance back.

A slender figure lounged against the fence, smoking a cigarette. Something about the profile was wrong, distorted, like a reflection in moving water. I froze. It was Thomas Sweet. He seemed to feel my eyes on him, because he turned and grinned. Then he flicked his cigarette into the gutter and slipped through a gate into the gardens.

I watched for another minute, but he seemed to have vanished. A hound gone to heel at his master's side.

I walked quickly up the line of carriages and finally found Connor at Seventy-First Street. His eyes lit up when he saw the tarts.

"Where's the others?" he mumbled through a mouthful of crust.

"Still inside. Listen, Connor, we'll fetch them in a bit. I just need to walk, do some thinking."

"Keep out of the park," he warned.

"Naturally. I'll be back soon."

"Sure you don't want some company?" he asked.

"Thanks, but you'd best stay here."

I left him happily inflicting cherry stains on his new clothes and set off up Fifth Avenue. By Seventy-Fifth Street, the traffic had thinned. It was a perfect mid-August night. Insects chirped in the trees to my right, where the dark mass of Central Park sat behind a low stone wall.

I reviewed the facts of the case as we now knew them.

George Kane acquires *The Black Pullet* but he's afraid to

use it himself, so he gives it to his lover, Becky Rickard, along with $200 to perform the ritual. He knows she is desperate enough to accept, and indeed she does, justifying it to herself after consulting "the Spirits," which she still believes in despite the Fox sisters' fraud.

Becky recruits Robert Straker, who in turn recruits his old friend Leland Brady. For some unknown reason, she scatters sulphur on the floor of the cellar. Perhaps it is part of the ritual. Things do not go as planned, but we know that Becky is still alive after Straker and Brady leave, since she went to the owner of the building to compensate her for the mess they made.

Becky then returns to her flat, where someone comes and brutally murders her. It was someone she knew well, since she would never have opened the door in the middle of the night to a stranger. The $200 is still there, but *The Black Pullet* is not found among her belongings. Despite the savagery of the crime, the killer appears remorseful afterwards.

I say *appears* because if we are indeed dealing with a habitual and practiced liar, the scene could easily have been staged to create a particular impression aimed at throwing off the investigation.

Straker disappears the next day, after Brady reports that he acted deranged. But he leaves the only picture of his beloved mother hidden under his mattress, and cigarette ash indicates the presence of a second person in the room. His soldier's uniform is missing, and both the button found next to Raffaele's body and Mary Fletcher's account indicate that the killer dresses as a soldier. However, we have no proof that it's *Straker's* uniform.

The same day Straker disappears, Raffaele Forsizi is lured or abducted from the Third Avenue Elevated and strangled in Washington Square Park. A so-called "diabolical signature" is burned into the grass next to his body, heightening the impression that the killer is obsessed with the occult, or believes themselves possessed. This is confirmed with the death of Anne Marlowe, where another taunting message in backwards Latin is left painted on the wall in blood.

Two days later, the killer strikes again. It becomes clear he is using the elevated lines to stalk their victims, a pair this time, just hours apart. The single consistent act is to cover the faces of the dead.

That was yesterday. My steps slowed as I mulled it all over. A carriage moved past, curtains drawn tight, the *clop-clop* of the horses' hooves and soft creaking of the harness the only sounds in the still night. It was evident that the person we were dealing with was very sophisticated. Highly organized. He had managed to kill Raffaele in a relatively crowded place without being seen. He had enticed Anne Marlowe to a deserted location. He had a firm working knowledge of arcane practices, such as pacts with the Devil and the supposed dangers of using a grimoire like *The Black Pullet* to conjure wealth.

I didn't doubt that he was a lunatic. But the later victims struck me almost as afterthoughts. Part of a game that was proving too enjoyable to quit.

It all started with Becky.

I was just turning to go back to the Kane mansion when a faint but agonized scream cut through the summer night. It came from somewhere deep inside the park.

CHAPTER FIFTEEN

THE SCREAM HUNG in the air, then stopped abruptly. As though the person's air supply had been suddenly cut off.

I looked up and down the street, but there was no one else in sight. The carriage had vanished, turning the corner perhaps. Never was I so glad to have followed Myrtle's advice. I rummaged around in my bodice and retrieved the pistol. The grip was slippery with perspiration, but its metallic weight was reassuring in my hand as I took a deep breath and entered Central Park at the Seventy-Ninth Street transverse.

I ran down the winding road, trying not to trip over my skirts. I had been to the park many times with John and his brothers, but always during the daytime. We would bring a picnic lunch and they would play rugby on a large lawn called the Green, while I read a book or just lay on my back watching the clouds. I knew the Green was a bit to the south near a ladies' restaurant called the Casino. I was less familiar with this area.

Newly installed electric lamps illuminated a fork in the road. I caught a glimpse of the lake through the trees to my left, not the water itself but the red and blue lights of the hired pleasure boats. We skated there last winter, John, Connor and I, before the blizzard. When the ice was frozen solid, all the omnibuses and horse cars would fly white flags and word would spread that "the ball is up in the park!"—meaning the red ball had been hoisted on the Arsenal and it was safe to skate.

Connor wasn't living with us yet, but John had taken an immediate fancy to him. I think he enjoyed showing Connor new things, things he couldn't even have dreamt of before he tried to rob Myrtle and ended up getting a job instead. I smiled at the memory. A frosty January morning, just after New Year's. The sky was a lustrous, bottomless blue. We'd gone to one of the nearby cottages afterwards and sipped hot chocolate in front of a roaring fire. John told a ghost story, something about the restless souls of smallpox patients haunting the Gothic-style hospital on Ward's Island after its closure two years ago...

All was silent. I began to wonder if what I thought was a scream had actually been wild laughter.

I paused at the entrance to a heavily wooded area that could only be the Ramble. In the sunlight, it was reputed to be one of the most beautiful parts of the park, a rustic paradise of gurgling brooks and wildflowers. Tonight, it just looked dark and impenetrable.

"Hello?" I called, feeling idiotic. "Does anyone need help?"

Not even a cricket replied.

I was turning to leave when I heard a noise. It had a wet, *squelching* quality that made my skin crawl. With very little effort, my mind conjured up the image of a deer carcass being dressed with a sharp knife.

I switched the pistol to my left hand and wiped the sweat off my right palm. Then I returned the pistol to my right and cocked it.

"You really *are* a fool, Harry," I muttered.

I began to walk cautiously deeper into the Ramble. Trees laden with vines pressed close on both sides. The lights of the main thoroughfare faded behind me. I tried to be stealthy, but my dress rustled like a pile of autumn leaves with every step. Then the breeze died, leaving an airless void. Stinging beads of sweat popped out on my forehead and rolled into my eyes.

It was so dark that I tripped over the body.

All I knew was that my left foot caught on something in the middle of the path. I pinwheeled my arms and tried to recover, but when I looked down and saw the white flash of skin gleaming in the moonlight, I let out a shriek and went arse over teakettle, as Connor would say, into the under-growth. The pistol flew from my hand.

I lay there, gasping for breath that wouldn't come. My chest felt like a locked door with no key. My eyes still worked though. And what I saw lifted all the hair on my body straight up.

A rough stone wall crossed the path ten paces away. It was broken by a narrow archway, through which the night poured black as pitch. But something even darker stood just within the shadow of the arch. Watching me.

I groped for the pistol but my hands came away empty. Empty and wet.

I was lying in a pool of blood.

The whole scene was so surreal, my mind simply rejected it. This couldn't be happening. Not an hour ago I was dancing with John in a brightly lit ballroom filled with people. Maybe not the nicest people, but still, regular *people*.

How easy it is in New York City to tumble down the rab-bit hole. It just takes a few wrong steps. One or two poor deci-sions. The abyss is always waiting for the unwary. A hidden signal, and the trapdoor suddenly opens beneath your feet, dropping you into a lightless pit, a charnel house like the one in the Benders' cellar.

A beam of moonlight caught the glint of metal in the archway. Just a glimmer, but it was at about the height where you'd expect to see a knife if a person held it dangling point-down at their side.

I watched, breath still trapped in my throat like a wild animal clawing to get out, as the blade moved gently back and forth. A grotesque *waggling* gesture. Like some demented children's rhyme.

Round and round the mulberry bush
The monkey chased the weasel
The monkey thought it was all in fun...

My fingers scrabbled frantically through the dirt.

The blackness within the archway looked bottomless, infinite, like a hole torn in the fabric of the universe. The words Mrs. Rivers uttered at the séance, in that horrible chorus of overlapping voices, came back to me:

Abyssus abyssum invocat

Deep calls to deep

The figure shifted, moving slowly into the moonlight. I saw a pale hand, and a knife as long as my forearm, mottled heavily with some dark substance. The glint of a brass button at the cuff.

I clenched my teeth and drew a ragged stream of air into my lungs. It wasn't enough.

You're going to die here, Harry, I thought dimly. And the killings will just go on and on and on…

And then a small person leapt into the clearing, a horse-whip in his hand and fire in his eyes.

He bent over me and wrapped an arm around my shoulders, pulling me up to a sitting position. I felt my chest release and the sweet night air of the Ramble pour inside.

"You all right?" Connor asked.

"I think so. Just got my breath knocked out." I turned fearfully back toward the archway but whoever had been there was gone. Then we heard a soft moan from the figure that lay sprawled across the path. "My God, I think they're still alive," I said.

I knelt over the body. It was a woman. Her eyelids fluttered and she moaned again. I found her hand and squeezed it.

"Don't worry," I whispered. "They're gone. We'll get help."

I turned to Connor and realized our predicament. We couldn't leave her alone, but neither could just one of us stay. Whoever had attacked her might not have gone far.

"We'll have to carry her," I decided. "Although without knowing the extent of her injuries, I'm afraid—"

Salvation came in the form of a giggle, followed by a resounding slap, in one of the nearby thickets.

"Oh you devil!" A voice declared.

"But Lucy—"

"Help!" I cried. "Over here! A woman's been stabbed!"

There was silence, and then a young couple appeared, both slightly dishevelled but more than willing to come to our aid. They ran off as soon as I told them what had happened and returned minutes later with two burly policemen who had been stationed near the Boathouse.

I'd managed to find my pistol under a bush and was stuffing it back into my bodice as they came charging up the path. One had a lantern and we examined the poor woman, who was either extremely unlucky or extremely lucky, depending on how you looked at it. She was a ragpicker, as evidenced by the overladen cart parked to the side of the path. I guessed she had been sleeping in the park when she was assaulted.

I ripped several strips of cloth from my gown and one of the policemen, a man named O'Reilly, made a makeshift tourniquet while we waited for the ambulance. She'd been slashed in a dozen places and was bleeding heavily, but it seemed I'd interrupted the attack before any vital organs had been ruptured.

"Where are you taking her?" I asked as the Night Service carriage arrived.

"Bellevue, of course," O'Reilly said.

"But that's all the way downtown! She needs help immediately. Mount Sinai is just on the other side of the park."

The patrolman gave me a weary look. "Bellevue's the place that caters to her sort," he said.

"Take her to Sinai," I said firmly. "I'll pay the bill."

He looked me over and seemed to decide that I could afford it. I'd already given them my statement, including name and address. I'd told essentially the truth: that I was at the Kanes' party and had gone outside for some air. I heard a scream and entered the park, literally stumbling across her body. My driver had followed me, concerned about my safety so late at night. He startled the attacker, who ran off into the trees.

A manhunt had already commenced, although considering the park's vast size—eight-hundred and forty-three acres, with countless exits—I thought it unlikely the search would bear fruit.

"As you say, Miss Pell. Take her to Mount Sinai, boys!" he called to the white-coated attendants.

They nodded and gently lifted the woman onto a stretcher.

"You think she can identify him?" Connor asked, as the night ambulance drove away.

"I don't know. It was awfully dark." I shuddered. "I only got a glimpse of the knife. It was huge, Connor. If you hadn't come along… "

"That's twice I've pulled your fat from the fire," he said.

I gave him two kisses, one on each cheek. "My hero," I said lightly. "At this rate, we'll be engaged before Christmas."

Connor blushed.

"I don't suppose you saw anyone else leave the party?" I asked.

"No, but I was too busy trying to keep out of sight. I hopped over the wall and trailed you from inside the park. Bet you didn't hear a thing," he said proudly.

"I had no clue. Thank God you did."

We started walking back to Fifth Avenue. Groups of patrolmen moved through the trees, lanterns bobbing like huge fireflies. Central Park was the crown jewel of the city, and the authorities wouldn't take such a brazen crime lightly.

Connor fell silent, and I again went over everything George had said in the garden. I'd been on the verge of understanding something crucial when I'd been distracted by the scream. I felt sure that what nagged at me was a word, a single word.

George's demeanor had changed like quicksilver, shifting

from self-pity to cold fury and then rambling paranoia in a matter of seconds. I wondered if his mother knew everything. Was she protecting him somehow? It must be a terrible disappointment for a woman like Temple Kane to have a son like George. I wondered who had hired Thomas Sweet. Maybe it wasn't George after all.

I keep seeing things…

In the mirror.

I stopped walking.

What a fool I'd been. A blind, blind fool.

As Myrtle had put it all those years ago, *I'd looked but I didn't see.*

I thought I knew now who had killed Becky. Who had lured or coerced Raffele Forsizi and Anne Marlowe and the others to their deaths.

Who had nearly killed me in the Ramble.

The ragpicker had been bait to draw me into a deserted area of the park, I was certain of it. She wasn't taken from an elevated line, and the timing was too perfect to be a coincidence. I was getting uncomfortably close to the truth. The killer wanted me eliminated.

But could I prove it?

"What is it, Harry?" Connor asked with concern.

I realized I was standing in the middle of the street and shook myself.

"Nothing," I said, unwilling to share my theory just yet. "I'm fine. Let's go round up John and Edward. It's time to go home."

As it turned out, they were waiting at the barouche when we arrived. The hour was past three, and the party was breaking up. I let Connor tell the story, still wrapped in my own thoughts. They were appalled at my near miss, but I could see

John hadn't yet forgiven me for dancing with James Moran. He sat next to Connor on the way home, and his goodbye when we dropped him off at Gramercy Park was polite but reserved.

Mrs. Rivers helped me remove my torn, stained gown and I crawled into bed, expecting I'd never fall asleep. My mind kept returning to that narrow stone archway, and what lay beyond it, just out of reach of the silver moonlight. Fragments of images slid past. A bowl of bloody water. Billy Finn reading from a book with a black cover made of calfskin, or something even softer. The skin of another kind of animal.

Pop Goes the Weasel! played senselessly in the background, faster and faster like some manic jack-in-the-box. I knew I would never again hear that song without remembering the glimmer of a cruel blade.

But I had barely rested since Monday, and sheer exhaustion soon dragged me down into the depths of a deep and dreamless slumber.

I didn't wake for sixteen hours. The sun was already descending in its long arc when I stumbled downstairs to the kitchen. It had been eight days since Leland and Elizabeth Brady knocked on my front door. Myrtle would be home tomorrow.

The end game was at hand.

"You look like you could use a cup of coffee, Harry," Edward said cheerfully, pouring one and setting it before me.

Everyone was there. John, Connor, Nellie, Mrs. Rivers. Even my client.

"I came to tell you it wasn't Robert," he said. "The body in the river. They haven't identified it yet, but the poor fellow at the morgue was at least twenty years older and several inches shorter." Brady swallowed. "Though it had been underwater for so long the face was... unrecognizable."

"I'm relieved to hear it," I said, although I wasn't surprised. "Have you been informed of recent developments?"

"Yes, Mr. Dovington and Doctor Weston told me what happened last night. Thank God your boy came along." He looked genuinely apologetic. "I'm sorry I dragged you into this, Miss Pell. I never intended to put you in any personal danger."

"It's not your fault," I said. "But I fear that this person we seek will be enraged that they were interrupted. They will need to kill again right away. Tonight."

"Perhaps it's time we went to the police," Brady ventured. "I suppose I'll lose my job, or worse, but we can't put any more lives at risk."

"He's right," Nellie said. "You've taken it far enough, Harry. We should bring the authorities in." She smiled. "Don't worry, I'll make sure you get your fair share of credit for solving the case."

I framed my next words very carefully. I needed their help.

"We could contact the police," I said. "They would flood the elevated lines with uniformed officers. And our killer would get spooked. I don't think the murders would stop, but the pattern would change. They'd find a new way to procure victims. It's not hard, in this city. And we'd lose our one advantage. That the killer doesn't yet know that *we know the hunting ground*."

No one spoke for a moment. Then John surprised me by taking my side.

"The investigation would be back to square one," he agreed.

I cast him a grateful look, which he didn't return.

"I'm also certain that the killer has Billy Finn somewhere," I added. "There's a slim chance he could still be alive. If this lunatic goes to ground, it's as good as signing Billy's death warrant."

"So what are you proposing?" Brady asked.

I took a deep breath. "That we conduct the search ourselves. We have Connor's… associates, as well as another auxiliary force I've hired to assist. It should be enough to cover the Second, Third, Sixth, and Ninth Avenue elevated lines. We know the killer wears a soldier's uniform and I don't expect a deviation from that routine. We watch and we wait. Groups of three, I think. If they try anything, one of us will be there to stop it."

"And you really think he'll strike again so soon?" Edward asked.

"I think the killer has no choice anymore," I said. "The compulsion is too strong."

"I wish to be there, if you'll have me," Brady said quietly, pressing a hand to his forehead. "If it is Robert, I don't want any harm coming to him. He should be put in an asylum, not handed over to the hangman."

"Your presence would be welcome," I said. "So. Are we all in agreement?"

Edward, Harry, Brady and Connor nodded, Mrs. Rivers more reluctantly so. Nellie looked around and threw up her hands.

"So be it," she said. "Count me in. John Cockerill"—that was Nellie's editor at *The World*—will certainly salivate over a first-hand account of the hunt for Mr. Hyde. Though I don't have a very good feeling about this, Harry, and I'm telling you so for the record."

I looked around at the unsmiling but courageous group in the kitchen and prayed that I was making the right decision.

"Then we meet back here at nine o'clock," I said. "So far none of the murders have occurred before sundown, so that should give us adequate time to get in place. And wear your rattiest clothing, we want to blend in as much as possible. I'll draw up the assignments."

Everyone left to prepare for what promised to be another long night ahead. I realized that I couldn't even remember the last time I'd eaten, and Mrs. Rivers volunteered to whip up some pancakes and bacon, which Connor generously helped me devour.

While she washed up, I composed a short telegram. Connor was on his way out to round up the Bank Street Butchers, so I gave it to him with strict instructions to await the response. If I was right in my suspicions, the answering telegram would confirm it.

The trap had been set. Now I had only to spring it.

CHAPTER SIXTEEN

NIGHT FELL SWIFTLY as we assembled in the parlor of 40 West Tenth Street.

I had again borrowed a set of Connor's clothes and stuffed my hair into a cap, pulling the brim down low so it shadowed my eyes.

My friends had followed instructions—even Edward, although I could see it pained him to wear baggy breeches with holes at the knees and a shirt so old it was the sickly grey of New York's gutters after a rainstorm.

Nellie, whose face was the most well-known, wore a floppy bonnet, while John had somehow managed to acquire the dour vestments of a Catholic priest.

"Rupert's," he said when Edward raised an inquiring eyebrow. "Trust me, you don't even want to know what he used it for."

The Butchers found the situation highly amusing. They sprawled on the carpet looking at the pictures in Connor's penny dreadfuls and ribbing each other in some street dialect so riddled with slang I could barely understand a word. I did, however, learn their names: Clyde, Danny, Two-Toed Tom, Kid Spiegelman, Little Artie and Virgil the Goat.

They were all between the ages of six and ten. Clyde was the tallest, Danny the fastest sprinter. Tom had been run over by a carriage when he was five, or at least his left foot had. Kid Spiegelman could pick any lock ever devised in less than thirty seconds. Little Artie was blessed with wide blue eyes and a cherubic face that he used to con charitable institutions for orphans. And Virgil… he had fingers like fishhooks. Twice I'd emptied his pockets of sundry items, including mother's favorite silver salt cellar. But every time I turned my back, they started bulging again.

The Butchers had descended on the house like a pack of locusts, and Mrs. Rivers was in a lather rushing to and fro with plates of toast and jam that disappeared as fast as she could carry them from the kitchen.

"Where's Moran?" John asked, his voice tight. "It's getting late."

"He'll be here," I said. "We had a deal."

But I was starting to worry. It was ten minutes past nine.

I unfurled the telegram Connor had brought and reread it for the tenth time.

It was the final piece in the puzzle. I had showed it to no one, unwilling to tip my hand until the right moment. It was critical that the killer be confronted in the act. There was no other way.

"What line are we taking?" Brady asked. He'd dressed in plain workingman's clothes, with suspenders and a bowler hat that emphasized his unfortunate ears.

I examined the map spread on the table before us. "I'm not sure yet. I was waiting on Moran's boys, but we may as well start divvying them up. Any suggestions?"

Brady shrugged. "Downtown, the Third Avenue El, perhaps? It's the only line I'm really familiar with."

"Alright. You, John and myself will take that one. Nellie, Clyde and Little Artie can ride the Ninth Avenue Line. Edward, Virgil and Tom can cover Second Avenue, and Connor, Spiegelman and Danny can take Sixth Avenue. Remember, use your whistles to summon a patrolman if you see anything. This person is extremely dangerous. If no police are around, at least you can follow and make an identification."

"There aren't enough of us," Nellie pointed out. "Not to cover four lines."

She was right, but I was unwilling to admit it.

"We can't just give up," I said. "The killer is out there tonight. And so is the next victim."

Nellie sighed. "How will we know if one of the other teams gets lucky?"

"We won't," I said. "So we should all rendezvous back here at three a.m. We'll compare notes then."

"You really think we'll find Billy?" Kid Spiegelman asked.

The Butchers looked at each other.

"He were the best stogger we had," Artie said regretfully. "Dog-nipper too. Billy were a man of many talents."

"A right bane of the Philistines," Tom agreed.

"Ah, he's cocked his toes up," Virgil the Goat muttered.

"No he ain't!" Kid Spiegelman said. "Don't say that. I won't believe Billy's a stiff til I see it with my own gagers."

"He's not dead, and we'll get him back," I said. "I promise you."

The Butchers quieted down, but their skeptical looks made it clear that adult promises (or even teenage promises) were worth very little.

I was just rising to rally my meager troops when a knock came on the front door.

It wasn't Moran. It didn't surprise me that he wouldn't

come himself. A boy like James Moran never got his hands dirty when others could do it for him. He always kept a wide buffer between himself and his subordinates. It's why Myrtle had never been able to catch him.

But when I peered past the hard-faced young man on the doorstep, I saw two dozen others like him, slouching in attitudes of boredom across the street.

Moran had kept up his end of the bargain.

"We have four groups ready, one for each elevated line," I said, relieved that none of them appeared to be the same thugs he'd sent after me two nights before. "Yours can cover the stations. Mr. Hyde's never struck above Eighty-Ninth Street, so we can stick to the stops below that line. Focus on the east side. I think Ninth Avenue's a long shot, since the killer just struck there. We're looking for someone dressed as a soldier, or anyone who seems to take an unhealthy interest in women or boys travelling alone."

He nodded and leapt down the steps to join his companions.

I returned to the parlor. "The reinforcements have arrived," I said. "Let's go."

John, Connor, Brady and I walked across town to Ninth Street and bought tickets, two of Moran's boys shadowing us a block behind. A southbound train was just pulling in as we reached the platform. The Third Avenue Line ran every fifteen minutes all night long—they were called the Owl Cars. They weren't as fancy as the Sixth Avenue Line, which boasted conductors in braided blue uniforms and décor in the Pullman style. John kept shifting on the hard wooden seat, trying in vain to find a comfortable position.

We split up so we wouldn't attract too much attention. I sat across from John, facing him as the benches ran lengthwise. Brady took the south end of the car, and Connor leaned by the doors. The car had room for about fifty people, but was only half-occupied at this late hour. Most were headed in the other direction. It was the usual random mix of humanity: workers coming off late shifts, revellers out for a night on the town, and a few who looked like they simply had nowhere else to go.

The tracks ran level with the upper stories of apartment buildings, so you could see straight into people's flats. I caught glimpses of women sewing by candlelight, bawling babies in bassinets, and once a snoozing cat on a windowsill that seemed unperturbed by the deafening screech and clatter of the passing train.

There was no sign of our quarry.

We rode to the Chatham Square stop, and switched to the uptown side.

"I meant to ask, how *are* Parthena and Permelia?" I inquired sweetly, sidling up to John as we waited on the platform. "They seemed delighted to see you, although it's a shame poor Parthena had that red spot right on the tip of her nose. She tried to cover it with powder, but it was just too big." I peered down the tracks. "Oh well, at least it was a costume ball. The mask definitely helped."

The corner of John's mouth twitched but he kept a poker face.

"The Sloane-Shermans invited me to their country house," he said. "It's in some little hamlet called East Hampton. They say Newport has become *terribly boring*"—here he used a fluting high-pitched voice—"and swore that the Hamptons will soon be all the rage."

"Sounds charming," I said. "If you don't mind long conversations about crinoline and corgis."

"Yes, well, at least they haven't tried to kill me lately," John observed.

"That was a mistake," I said.

"I'm glad you're finally coming to your senses. How you could have—"

"I don't mean dancing with Moran," I said, unable to resist provoking him. "I mean his thugs trying to kill me."

A man in a top hat glanced over at us with a frown.

"Bless you, Father," I said hastily, trying my best to look pathetic. "I'll try St. Joseph's then. Maybe they'll have a cup of soup for a poor orphan boy."

I was spared John's response by the arrival of the uptown train. It was much more crowded. At City Hall, the car filled with newspapermen and office workers. Most were male, and the women tended to travel in pairs, but plenty were alone. Some were young, some old. Blondes, brunettes, redheads. Pretty and plain. I wondered what it was about the four victims after Becky that had drawn the killer's eye. There had to be something, some quality they shared. I didn't think they were being chosen randomly, not in an absolute sense.

I realized that I might never know. And in a sense, it was immaterial. All that mattered now was stopping the Hunter.

If we didn't do it this night, I feared we never would.

We passed the Canal, Grand and Houston Street stations. People got on and off. I caught a glimpse of one of Moran's boys standing in the shadows at Twenty-Third Street. He gave me the slightest shake of his head as the train pulled away. Nothing yet.

We rode to Eighty-Ninth Street and back down again. It was past one. The cars began to empty. At Thirty-Fourth Street,

our train stopped briefly between stations, a signal malfunc-
tion. I thought of the blizzard, and how it had so completely
paralyzed the transit system New Yorkers were so proud of.

It had begun at a little after twelve o'clock on Sunday
night. By noon on Monday, the snow had piled in drifts of fifteen to thirty feet. Some of the gusts neared eighty miles per
hour. The Great White Hurricane was upon us.

Darkness came, and still the wind blew, and the snow fell.
It seemed it would never stop. Carriages lay overturned in the
streets. Anything that wasn't nailed down—and even many
things that *were*—had been blown willy-nilly into heaps.
Power and telegraph lines, streetlamps, signs, all tossed into a
mad jumble. The city looked like a battlefield.

And still many of the elevated trains had crept along on
their ice-coated tracks. The powers-that-be hadn't planned for
it. No one thought New York would ever face a storm like
this. And by that point, the elevated was the only way to get
around. So tens of thousands of people packed into the trains.

It was absolute mayhem. Not surprisingly, many of the
trains became stuck between stations for hours on end. Some
of the more intrepid passengers attempted to walk (or by
necessity, crawl) to the next platform and it's a miracle none
were blown off the tracks by the gale force winds. Ladders
were deployed to rescue people, but they weren't tall enough,
so you had to hang down from the edge of the track and grope
around with your toes for the topmost rung. All while being
battered witless by the storm.

The disaster would surely lead to a serious rethinking of
public transit, I thought as we gave a jolt and the train began
moving again. Something less vulnerable to the elements…

"Perhaps we should give it up, check in with the others,"

Brady whispered to me. He sat a few feet away. "It's getting late, Miss Pell. This is starting to feel like a wild goose chase."

"Just a few more minutes," I whispered back, although a small doubt was starting to worm its way into my heart. Could I have misjudged so badly?

We pulled into Twenty-Third Street and the gates opened. John's head nodded sleepily at the far end of the car, Connor across from him. Only three people boarded.

Two young men whose unsteady gaits and flashy clothes signalled a long night of carousing in the Tenderloin. And a man of roughly the same age with dark, wavy hair and a mustache. A handsome man once, but whose sagging features revealed a dissolute life filled with bitterness and heartbreak.

I had seen that face many times. In a photograph taken a thousand miles away, white-capped mountains in the background

Robert Aaron Straker.

Brady started like he'd been goosed and went to rise, but I quickly laid a hand on his arm and shook my head. *Not yet.*

I turned my face down and studied my feet, silently urging Brady to follow suit. After a moment, he did, but I could see the vein pounding at his temple.

Straker looked around and took a seat midway down the car. He wore the navy uniform of a federal soldier. The third button down on the left was missing.

I tried desperately to catch Connor's eye. He finally turned and I mouthed the word *wait*, then pointed to John. Bless Connor, he understood immediately. He sauntered over to John and casually sat down next to him, whispering in his ear. John's eyes popped open in almost comical surprise.

We exchanged a long look. Then John shut his eyes and pretended to go back to sleep.

My heart pounded. I wasn't entirely sure what would happen next. There had been too many variables to foresee them all.

We stopped at Twenty-Third Street, then Fourteenth Street. Straker stayed on the train. He kept looking around, his hands writhing in his lap like snakes.

At Canal Street, a girl got on. Alone. She was just a slip of a thing, still in her teens. Auburn hair, high cheekbones, wide mouth. She looked a bit like a younger Elizabeth Brady. Her delicate face was painted, and her dress exposed an expanse of pale bosom. A working girl.

She clutched her purse and studiously avoided Straker's gaze. Something about him disturbed her. But I could see he was watching this girl. Not obviously. Not in a crude, leering fashion. But his eyes kept flicking in her direction and then away, like he couldn't help himself.

The line ended at Chatham Square. The cars emptied. The girl boarded the spur line that continued to South Ferry. Straker followed, and so did we.

Just before the gate opened, John came up behind me.

"I say we take him now," he whispered in my ear. "Between Brady and myself, I doubt he'll give us much trouble."

"Just wait," I whispered back.

"Fine, but I hope you know what you're doing," he said, and then the doors hissed shut and the train started to move.

I hadn't seen any of Moran's boys for a while. We were spread too thin. I just prayed they'd be waiting at the next stop.

Because despite John's innate confidence, I wasn't sure that ten men would be enough for what we had to do.

CHAPTER SEVENTEEN

THE GIRL GOT off at City Hall. She was eager to leave the train and the odd soldier who seemed to be watching her out of the corner of his eye. She may not have noticed how deathly pale his hands were, how the nails were caked with dirt or some other dark substance. How his eyes never stayed still. The dark circles beneath them, like half-moons carved into the gaunt flesh of his face.

She may not have noticed all those things, but she glanced back over her shoulder as she hurried down the platform stairs, and it was the look of a hare as it senses the passing shadow of a hawk. Some instinct that a predator is near.

Straker walked towards the stairs, staring straight ahead. And then a figure moved to block his way.

One of Moran's.

"Where ya goin', boy-o?" the kid asked softly, a menacing grin on his face. He had blonde hair and a pug nose, and looked like an older, much scarier Billy Flynn.

Straker didn't respond, but his fingers gave a nervous twitch.

"You like pretty little doxies, huh? Like to cut 'em up? See 'em bleed?"

Straker tried to dart around the boy, but another moved in, armed with a crowbar. They stood shoulder to shoulder in front of the stairs to the street. The platform had emptied. I heard a clock tower chime three.

Straker whirled around. When he saw the four of us arrayed in a line behind him, his face froze.

Brady pulled off his hat. "Please Robert, don't do anything foolish," he implored. "Let me help you!"

For a moment, Straker's mouth worked but no sound came out. The blood drained from his face. He raised a shaking hand and then one of Moran's thugs bowled into him, grabbing him by the arms. He did scream then, an inhuman howl that made my hackles rise. It went on and on, only stopping when the other kid slapped a hand over his mouth.

"Dear God," my client said faintly.

I kept my eyes on Straker. He'd gone limp, like an exhausted animal caught in a leg-trap.

"What do you want to do with 'im?" one of them asked me.

"We'll summon a police officer," I said. "It's City Hall. There must be one nearby."

Brady took a step forward. "You should have come to me," he said sadly. "Before this all got… out of hand. You were always too proud, Robert." His voice broke. "We were like brothers. I could have helped." He took another tentative step.

It was as though some invisible force existed between them, one that repelled rather than attracted. Because at that moment, Straker suddenly came back to life. With a wild cry, he wrenched free of his captors. It all happened very fast. I saw one of them try to seize his collar, and get swatted away as if he weighed nothing at all. Something small and white dropped from Straker's hand to the ground. In a flash, he vanished down the platform steps and into the night, Moran's boys on his heels.

Brady and John made to follow them, as Connor cursed a blue streak under his breath.

"Wait!" I cried.

They turned back impatiently.

"Let Moran's boys catch him," I said.

"But they'll beat him senseless, or worse!" Brady exclaimed. "I vowed to be there at the end, and by God, you won't stop me, Miss Pell!"

John looked at us in confusion. I took a deep breath.

"You look unwell, Mr. Brady," I said. "Have you been suffering from headaches?"

"What's that got to do with anything?"

"Bishop's Effervescing Citrate of Caffeine. It's for severe headaches. I smelled it on you earlier."

Brady frowned. "We don't have time for your little games—"

"And those half-healed abrasions on your right palm. Where did you get those, if I might ask?"

"What?"

"I think you got those when you choked Anne Marlowe with the chain. Am I right, Mr. Brady?"

His cheeks reddened. "This is preposterous!"

"Alright. Let's talk about the earth caked on your boots then. I noted a petal from a Virginia rose when you crossed your legs. They only grow in the Ramble."

John looked from Brady to me, then back to Brady, and rushed over to stand at my side.

"But all that was just icing on the cake. I realized something last night. George Kane made me think of it. You've been so clever, but you made a mistake. A mistake I'm ashamed to admit I should have seen right away."

Brady just looked at me, his features utterly impassive.

"You said that you went to Straker's flat the day after the murder. You stood behind him as he gazed into his shaving mirror and ranted about being possessed. *And yet you failed to notice the bowl of bloody water directly in front of you.* It would have to have been there. If Straker killed Becky Rickard, he would have gone straight home to wash the blood from his hands. And yet you acted as though you'd never seen it before when we all went to the flat. That got me thinking, Mr. Brady, that you've not been entirely truthful."

I bent down and picked up the crumpled piece of paper that had fallen from Straker's hand.

"So I cabled your wife earlier this evening at her parents' house in Connecticut. She confirmed that you've started suffering from recurrent nightmares. Very bad ones. That you wake up, screaming in the night. And that the night before she left, she found you standing in the garden like an automaton with no recollection of how you got there."

A shadow passed over Brady's eyes, so quick I might have imagined it.

"Then there's your position. You're a real estate agent. And what is it real estate agents do?"

"They spend most of their time travelling around the city," John said slowly.

"Exactly." I thought of the map I'd seen on his office wall. "The trains are your domain, aren't they, Mr. Brady? Here's what I think happened. I think you left Mr. Straker and returned to Becky's flat. She let you in. Why wouldn't she? I'm sure you had some excuse. Some final detail to settle. Then you stabbed her. Thirty-one times. But that wasn't enough, so you bit her. You chewed her to a pulp, Mr. Brady."

My client's features looked frozen, like the wax figures they posed in the windows of the city's finer department stores. But his pupils had contracted into empty black pinpricks.

"And then remorse struck," I said. "You covered her face so you wouldn't have to look at it. Afterwards, you went to Straker's flat, where you washed up and took his uniform. I don't know why he ran. Perhaps he suspected something. He certainly seemed terrified of you just now. You got the key from the landlord *then*, not four days later as you claimed. I should have checked that, but I didn't. You smoked a cigarette and destroyed Straker's rooms in a rage that he wasn't there. Then you returned to your office and became Dr. Jekyll again."

Brady's pale blue eyes glittered in the dim light of the station. "But why would I do such a thing, Miss Pell?"

It was the one question I had no answer for.

"And Straker?" John asked, plainly struggling to keep up. "Why was he here?"

I held up the paper I'd retrieved from the platform. "I expect this is a note to him, supposedly from Elizabeth Brady, saying she's afraid of her husband and asking Robert to meet her here in the uniform she had delivered this morning. It would be no great feat for a man to imitate his wife's handwriting. I imagine Straker was eyeing that girl simply because she bore such a strong resemblance to Elizabeth."

I handed the letter to John. He read it and looked at me with a satisfying degree of awe.

"That's exactly what it says," he muttered. "More or less."

"You didn't like the way things were going, so you decided it was time that Straker took the fall," I said to Brady, whose hands had clenched into tight fists. "You never wanted to hire me in the first place. It was Elizabeth who insisted. But you were relieved when you saw how young I am, and a woman no less. You must have thought I wouldn't get very far."

"And you was sadly mistaken," Connor chimed in.

The faint rattle of a southbound train broke the silence.

"All I want from you now is Billy Finn," I said. "You have him, or someone would have found the body. You don't seem to care much about hiding your victims. I think you used him to get to Straker. If you tell us where Billy is, there's a chance you'll escape the noose."

I felt a vibration through the soles of my boots. The headlights of the train suddenly broke around a corner and lit the platform in a blinding wash.

"*Billy*," my client said. Then he grinned and the frozen mask slid away. For the first time, I saw clearly the monster that lurked beneath. "Billy was... delicious."

I heard the screech of brakes as Brady leapt onto the tracks. He crouched for a split second, the wind of the train tearing at his blonde hair. In the harsh glare of the headlamps, the man who'd reminded me of an overgrown schoolboy when we first met now looked bestial, like some primitive ancestor of homo sapiens better left extinct.

Several hundred tons of metal bore down, the wheels sending a shower of sparks into the darkness. I had the brief thought that such an end was fitting, although I was sorry that he would evade punishment for his crimes.

At the last moment, Brady rolled out of the way, toward the opposite platform.

We looked at each other, John, Connor and I. The train was still grinding to a stop as we ran to the stairs leading down to the street. Straker seemed to have gotten away, for we didn't see him or his pursuers in the ornate station waiting room.

Connor was faster than either of us.

"Wait!" I cried, as he pelted to the nearest exit.

We burst out onto Park Row. John and Connor had stopped under the shadow of the elevated.

"These robes are *not* made for running," John panted.

"Where'd he go?" Connor panted.

"Over there!" I pointed.

It was a bizarre sight. Brady dangled by one hand from the track above, about a block down from where we stood. I was sure he'd fall, but then he swung around somehow and grabbed onto one of the latticed steel support columns. He began shimmying down it with shocking speed, like some horrible hairless ape.

I heard Elizabeth Brady's cool voice as she sat in my parlor that afternoon.

"You can just cross him off your list… the window looks down on a sheer drop and our dog has taken to sleeping directly in front of the bedroom door… She's a husky… "

The dog that didn't bark in the night.

Anne Marlowe was probably enjoying her big scene at the finale of *Mathias Sandorf* while Brady was scaling down the gutters of their house like a foul spider. Anne's friend Mary said she was so happy to finally have a speaking part.

"Harry, come *on*!" John grabbed my arm and we started running toward Brady. He saw us coming and dropped the last few feet to the street. Then he loped into City Hall Park.

The path Brady took cut straight between City Hall itself on the left, and the Italianate façade of the Tweed Courthouse on the right. Boss Tweed had embezzled millions of dollars from that construction project, though in a twist of poetic justice ended up on trial in the very building he'd used to enrich himself.

Brady was fast, but we were faster. I think he'd hurt something in the fall, for he was limping. We started closing in near the far edge of the park. The area was a lively shopping district during the day, but now the streets were deserted.

We've got you, I thought, as Brady veered south toward the post office and was momentarily hidden in the trees. His right foot looked twisted, hitting the ground at an odd angle. There was no way, even charged with adrenaline, that he could run much further.

We tore around the bend in the path into an open, grassy area bordering Broadway. I expected to find him fallen, or at best crawling.

Brady had vanished. Quite literally. The storefronts were dark and shuttered. We had a clear view of the park and both sides of the street for several blocks. He was gone.

Connor skidded to a stop and I nearly knocked him down.

"It's impossible," John muttered. "He wasn't thirty feet ahead of us!"

We spun in circles like a bunch of fools.

"Are you sure he came this way?" I asked, since I'd been lagging behind them both.

John gave me a level look. "Yes, I'm sure. He must have climbed one of the trees." John peered up at the high branches with his hands on hips. "There's no other explanation." He turned to me with some exasperation. "And you could have told us, by the way. That it was Brady."

"I'm sorry, but I couldn't take the chance that he'd suspect something," I said. "I had no proof. The only way was to find Straker, and only Brady knew where he was."

"And now Brady's gone," John pointed out. "So where has that gotten us?"

I was opening my mouth to argue the point when I felt a

faint gust of air. Just a whisper across my bare legs. It was coming from beneath my feet.

I looked down. I was standing on a rusty grate. Not a large one. Perhaps eighteen inches wide.

A memory tickled, something Myrtle had told me.

"What building is that?" I asked, pointing across the street at the corner of Warren and Broadway.

Connor trotted over and returned moments later.

"The sign says it's Devlin's clothing store," he said.

I felt mounting excitement, leavened with a healthy measure of dread as I realized the implications.

"Brady's gone under the street." I moved onto the grass. "And I think he's cornered. That's the good news."

"What's the bad news?" John asked.

"I'm willing to bet Billy Finn's down there too. Which means he doesn't have much longer. Minutes maybe."

I bent down and examined the grate. The screws had been removed and I could see fresh tool marks.

"Brady's been here before. I'd guess he's been using it as a lair," I said, as a chill shot down my spine and made its way into my stomach.

It wasn't even Brady that scared me the most, although the thought of facing him again—even injured—made me weak. No, it was the idea of going down into the grate. I've always had severe claustrophobia. Perhaps as a result of one of Myrtle's "experiments," or perhaps I was just born with it.

But I loathed small spaces. Dark ones were even worse.

I turned to Connor. "The Tombs aren't that far from here. I need you to run there as fast as you can and bring as many patrolmen and guards as possible. Tell them a boy's being held hostage by Mr. Hyde in the old Beach tunnel. That should do it."

"But—" he opened his mouth to object.

"She's right," John cut in. "We need help. And you'd beat any of us in a race, hands down."

He didn't say *we won't let you go down there, Connor, because you're eleven years old and there's a good chance none of us will come out of that hole alive.* John knew that would just make Connor dig his heels in.

"Go now," I urged. "We'll wait here. Hurry!"

Connor hesitated. Then he nodded once and ran off in the direction of Centre Street. His footfalls faded and all was quiet again.

"We aren't waiting, are we?" John asked in a resigned voice.

"No, we're not."

"Please tell me you brought Myrtle's pistol."

I patted my pocket. "Oiled and loaded. I'm not good enough to have tried it while we were chasing him, but up close… "

We looked at each other without speaking. I guessed that neither of us wanted to get within any distance of Brady that could be considered *close*, but we had to play the hand we'd been dealt.

John pulled the grate free and set it on the grass. We stared into the bottomless darkness. It was like that awful arch in the Ramble had been turned on its side and set straight into the ground. Except smaller. Much smaller. More like the trapdoor under the Bender's kitchen table. My stomach tightened in dread.

Then John flashed me his old cocky grin. It felt like years since I'd seen it.

"Ladies first!" he said.

CHAPTER EIGHTEEN

I SHOWED HIM the butt of the pistol and smiled back, although my mouth was so dry it was more of a grimace.

"No, no, I insist," I said. "After *you*."

John shrugged. "Well, I can't go in this thing, can I?" he said, pulling the heavy vestments over his head. He wore trousers and a thin nightshirt underneath. "Alright, here goes."

John sat at the edge of the grate and slowly lowered himself down, until he hung by his fingertips.

"I can't see anything," he called to me, his voice muffled as though it was coming from the bottom of a well. "I'm just going to let go."

"Be careful," I said, but he was already gone.

I got on my knees and peered into the square hole.

"John! Answer me!"

Silence.

My heart stopped beating.

"John!"

"I'm here," he called up. "It's not that far. I'll help you down."

I took a breath and shifted so my feet dangled into the grate.

"What's it like down there?" I asked, trying to postpone the inevitable.

Now that it was actually happening, I could feel a full-blown panic attack brewing. The sudden shortness of breath. The racing pulse. A spreading dimness at the edges of my eyes.

Tunnel vision. How perfect.

I let out an awful laugh and dropped into darkness.

John caught me around the waist and set me gently on the ground.

"You smell nice," he said.

"Don't get cheeky," I answered, knowing he was just trying to distract me. John knew well how claustrophobic I was.

We stood in a space about four feet wide. Enough light filtered in from above to see the many layers of grime coating the walls and floor. John pointed to the only exit—a narrow metal tube that made every cell in my body recoil. It had been covered with a hatch that now lay propped against the wall. He took my hands in his and held them firmly.

"Listen, Harry. It's not long. I already checked. I can see light at the other end. Maybe twenty feet."

"Twenty feet," I echoed tonelessly.

"Twenty feet. That's the distance from the downstairs parlor to the kitchen at Tenth Street. You've walked that a thousand times."

"Walked," I said. "Not *crawled.*"

"You can give me the gun," he said. "I'm a decent shot. I'll understand if you can't do it."

And he would. John would never hold it against me. But I would know.

That I sent him in there alone.

"No," I said, steeling myself. "But I think I'd rather go first this time. So I can see the light."

I kept my eyes fixed on the small circle ahead of me as I eased my head and shoulders into the tube. It was even tighter than I expected. Forget crawling. I'd have to *wiggle*.

I knew at that moment that I couldn't go through with it.

I was starting to pull back when some trick of acoustics carried a faint sound through the tube. Not close by, but clearly audible.

It was the whimper of a small boy.

Cold fury surged through my veins, scouring me clean of any other emotion. Leland Brady would not take another innocent. I refused to let him. And if he got Billy... Well that *would* be on my head, every bit of it. I squeezed my eyes shut and thrust myself into the tube so violently I heard a button pop off my shirt and tinkle on the ground. Once my torso was inside, John helped push my legs in the rest of the way.

Then I started to wiggle.

My breath rasped harshly. How I hated the sound of it. It was too *loud*, too *close*.

I didn't hear Billy again, but then I didn't hear much except for the blood pounding in my ears and the *swish* of my clothing sliding along the smooth metal of the tube. I kept waiting for the circle of light to snuff out, for Brady's leering rictus to take its place. But then I hit the halfway mark. It lit a wavering spark of confidence. I wiggled harder. Fifteen feet, eighteen feet...

When I got within arm's length of the end, I grabbed the lip and hauled myself out, dropping awkwardly to hands and knees on a tiled floor. John popped out moments later, like a cork from a champagne bottle.

We got to our feet and looked around.

"What is this place?" John said wonderingly.

We stood in a large rectangular room. Thick cobwebs hung

from three crystal chandeliers like the cocoons of enormous caterpillars, and a heavy layer of dust coated velvet chairs and marble statuary. Frescoes adorned the walls, their vivid colors undiminished in this sunless space. A dry fountain sat in the middle of the room. Myrtle had said it held goldfish once, to amuse visitors while they waited for the train.

I could see traces of a doorway but it had been bricked up.

"I can't believe it's all still here," I whispered.

"*What's* still here?" John demanded. "You're doing it again, Harry."

I sighed. "Sorry. Twenty years ago, a man named Alfred Ely Beach got a contract from the city to build pneumatic tubes that would move mail under Broadway."

"Nooma what?" John asked, as we crept through the room, alert for any sign of movement.

"Pneumatic," I whispered. "It's when you use pressurized air to suck something through a vacuum." Myrtle had explained it to me when she was in one of her talkative moods. My sister would be monosyllabic for weeks on end. Then, like a new weather front blowing in, she'd become full of manic energy and you could hardly shut her up.

"Anyway, instead of two tubes, as he'd shown officials in the blueprints, Mr. Beach secretly built one bigger tube. He spent $350,000 of his own money on it. He was a visionary. He didn't just want to move letters, you see. He wanted to move *people*."

"So what's down there?" John asked, looking at the far end of the room.

"It's called the Beach Pneumatic Transit Tunnel. There was a single demonstration car. You paid to ride it to Murray Street and back."

"What happened?"

"Tweed and his cronies in Albany shut it down. The entrance in the sub-basement of Devlin's was sealed eight years ago. But *this* is the station. They left it perfectly intact. And Brady found it. He must have run across the plans somehow through his job."

"Spooky," John said, lightly running his fingers across the keys of a grand piano.

"Very. I figure we came in through the ventilation system."

The light we'd seen was cast by a lantern at the opposite end from the sealed entrance. It had been set there, next to a door leading to a platform. Two bronze effigies of Mercury stood alongside the entrance. A placard bore the words, "Pneumatic / 1870 / Transit."

We crept to the edge and peered into a round tunnel, perhaps three hundred feet long and eight feet wide, which curved into inky darkness.

"How convenient," John said, lifting the lantern. Dust motes drifted like plankton in its yellow glow.

I cocked the pistol. "He knows we're here."

"I'd say that's a fair assessment," John agreed. "Do you think he's armed?"

"Yes."

"So what's the plan?"

"I hoped you had one."

John shut his eyes. "Why do I let you talk me into these things?"

A sob cut through the air. John's face hardened.

"There's no time," he said. "If you see him, just shoot."

We clasped hands and leapt down to the tracks.

"What's at the other end of this?" John whispered.

Even the slightest sounds had a way of carrying.

"I'm not entirely sure. There was a carriage. It formed

a nearly air-tight seal with the walls. A steam-powered fan would push or pull the carriage along the rails depending on which way you were going."

The air in the tunnel was warm and dry. We stuck to the left-hand side so we could better see anything coming around the curve but the lantern only illuminated about ten feet ahead. Beyond that lurked a darkness so thick it was like being at the bottom of the sea. It had weight—*texture*, that darkness. My claustrophobia began creeping back and I nearly shot my own foot off when a rat scampered across it.

"Easy, Harry," John whispered.

About fifty feet in, we started seeing things on the tunnel walls.

Words, gouged deep into the brick. The same two, over and over.

Pervadunt oculus.

They come through the eyes.

That's what Brady claimed Straker had told him. But it wasn't Straker who believed he'd been possessed by demons.

It was Brady.

He'd written it hundreds of times, in letters almost too tiny to read and others several feet high. I imagined him standing with that long knife for hours on end, mindlessly scratching at the tunnel wall like some rabid animal.

But Brady wasn't an animal. It was an unfair comparison. The thing he'd become was far worse.

John reached into his shirt and pulled out a large gold crucifix on a chain. He seemed to be muttering the Lord's Prayer under his breath.

I didn't say anything, but frankly, I was more than happy with Myrtle's pistol.

We approached the place where the tunnel curved out of

sight. John held the lantern low. I knew we were nearing the end of the line.

"He must be waiting in the dark," John whispered. "So he can see us but we can't see him."

He had to be. Ours was the only visible light.

"What's that?" John said suddenly.

"What's what?"

"I thought I heard something. Behind us."

We stood stock still, listening.

"I don't hear anything," I said.

"Rats maybe," John said, but there was a note of doubt in his voice.

"There was no place to hide back there," I pointed out. "He has to be ahead of us."

At that moment, Billy screamed, a cry of sheer terror.

Without thinking beyond the next few seconds, I ran forward, tearing around the bend in the tunnel.

"Harry!" John yelled.

The carriage was there. In the dim light, I could see a small figure inside tied up like a hog for slaughter. I smelled something rotten, the sickly sweet odor of spoiled meat. Billy writhed against his bonds, eyes wide with shock. He stared at something over my shoulder.

I spun around. That's when I saw Brady.

He was clinging to the roof of the tunnel like a lizard. I'd just passed directly beneath him.

John raised the lantern high. I pointed the pistol and fired, but I was panicky and the shot went wild. Shards of brick flew from the tunnel wall.

Brady dropped down, landing on all fours. He grinned at me.

I took a deep breath and steadied myself, using two hands this time like Myrtle had taught me.

Brady sprung.

I aimed the pistol at his forehead and squeezed the trigger.

I missed again. Worse than missed.

The bullet ricocheted off the tracks and hit John in the chest.

That moment is still frozen in my memory like a bug trapped in amber. John crumpling to the ground, a red stain spreading across his shirt. Billy's screams. My own ears ringing from the deafening retort in the confined tunnel. The weight of the pistol as it was knocked away.

And then Brady's hot breath on my cheek as he pinned me underneath him and raised his knife.

The edge was pitted and scarred from his scratchings. But it was the point he planned to use.

Some part of me had known all along that we were going to die down here. I only prayed it would be quick, but from the excited light in his eyes, I feared he intended to take his time. He placed the point of the knife against my cheek.

Then I heard the click of a hammer being cocked.

"Don't move a muscle," an ice-cold voice whispered in Brady's ear. "Don't you even twitch."

Brady froze.

"Easy does it." The barrel of a revolver jammed against Brady's temple, pushing him away.

I coughed and rolled over. I felt unclean where he had touched me. John lay in a pool of blood, his eyes closed. I ran to him and gathered his limp body in my arms.

"Get against the wall," the voice commanded.

Brady complied. His demeanor had changed dramatically.

The Hunter had retreated, leaving the fearful schoolboy in his place.

I pressed a shaking hand to John's neck and nearly wept in relief. He still had a pulse. I examined the bullet wound. It had lodged in his shoulder. I pressed down, trying to staunch the flow.

"Hang on, Billy!" I called out. "I'll come for you in a minute."

It was quiet. Then I heard a hoarse but somewhat calmer boy call back, "Thankth, Mith Pell!"

My savior picked up the lantern from where John had dropped it. He was one of the dandies from the train. I remembered his purple cravat, tied in a looping bow. Then I caught his dark eyes and felt like a perfect fool. It was James Moran. I'd been too focused on Straker to pay them much attention.

"I followed you, Miss Pell. If you're anything like your sister, I expected you'd be playing a double game." He aimed the pistol at Brady, cowering just a few feet away. Then he shot Brady in the leg. My former client shrieked. Shards of white bone jutted out of his thigh and my stomach churned.

"It's too bad we don't have more time," Moran said lazily. "I could do this all day. But I think I'd better just put you out of your misery."

Brady sobbed. I felt no pity for him, not a shred, but this was wrong somehow.

I let go of John and jumped between them. Moran looked up at the ceiling and sighed in annoyance.

"The police are on their way," I said. "Do you really want to be here when they arrive? He'll hang for what he did. It's a worse end in many ways."

Moran considered this.

"But that's no fun," he said at last.

"Then you'll have to shoot me too."

Moran regarded me with an unreadable expression. "What makes you think I won't?"

"Because that's no fun," I said.

His lips quirked in an almost-smile.

"I suppose it's not, at that." He lowered the gun a fraction. "Tell me something, Miss Pell. How did you know? About the quill? And the piano?"

"Much can be learned about a man from his hands, Mr. Moran. The overlapping stains on your right forefinger, for example. The half-healed welts at your wrist where the strings keep snapping because you apply too much pressure. It's quite a distinctive injury, if one knows what to look for. Elementary, really."

Moran gazed at me for a long moment. Then he laughed. "As if one wasn't bad enough," he muttered cryptically.

"If you want to do something useful, go cut his bonds," I said, pointing to Billy.

He put the gun away. "I'll leave that to you. I've played the hero enough tonight. It doesn't really suit me."

He turned to Brady, who was mumbling to himself. Moran said something too soft for me to hear but Brady shut up immediately. He seemed paralyzed with dread. It occurred to me that on some unpleasant level, Moran and Brady understood each other. They were kindred spirits.

"Fine." I turned my back on them both and picked up Brady's knife. Then I used it to free Billy Finn. Nasty bruises marked his wrists and ankles. I guessed he'd had no decent food for days, though Brady had thrown him some rotten scraps. But Billy had served a different purpose than the other victims, and was otherwise unharmed.

By the time I looked back, Moran was gone.

I ran over to check on John. The bleeding had slowed, but he needed a doctor. I could see he was slipping away.

"We have to carry him," I said to Billy. How we'd ever get John through that horrible tube I hadn't a clue.

"I thought they were nightmares at first," Brady whispered from where he lay slumped against the wall. "Just nightmares. But then I realized the truth… after I woke up standing there. I didn't mean to hurt them." His pale blue eyes fixed on me. "It's inside me. Something." His voice took on a whining tone. "It *made* me. I sent Elizabeth away. I did that. *I* did that!"

"He's barmy," Billy said, retreating a safe distance away from his captor.

"Yes, he is," I agreed. "John!" I leaned over my best friend. "Wake up! You have to wake up."

He moaned.

"That's it," I urged. "We're getting you out of here."

There was so much blood. We were both covered in it. I looked down the long, dark tunnel, hoping to see the glow of lanterns. But there was nothing.

"He don't look so good," Billy said, his poor thin face scrunched up in worry.

Brady turned at the sound of Billy's voice. His eyes narrowed in a kind of low cunning.

"Come over here, boy," he whispered. "I have something to show you."

Billy edged backwards. "Mith Pell?" he said uncertainly.

And then a hollow boom rang out. Puffs of dust showered from the ceiling. Billy shrank against me and I gathered him up in my arms.

It came again and again. A large crack appeared in the brickwork about twenty feet down. I heard faint shouts.

"In here!" I screamed. "We're here!"

The booming redoubled in intensity. Moments later the head of a sledgehammer broke through the wall of the tunnel and a beam of pure, sweet electric light pierced the darkness.

I didn't dare leave John, but Billy dashed down the tracks and started to help, pulling the loose bricks away as the hole slowly grew bigger. As soon as it was a few feet wide, uniformed patrolmen began pouring through.

I pointed to Brady. "He's been shot in the leg," I said. "But he can wait. This one needs a doctor right away. His name's John Weston."

"We need a stretcher down here!" one of the policemen shouted through the hole. He looked at Brady. "That's Mr. Hyde, is it?"

"Yes. His real name is Leland Brady."

The officer stared at him with contempt. "Ain't much, is he?"

And he wasn't, not anymore. Brady seemed *shrunken*, like a piece of fruit left in the sun.

The tunnel rapidly filled with people. Several medics arrived. I squeezed John's hand while they loaded him onto the stretcher.

"We'll need your statement outside," a sergeant said to me calmly. He looked very interested as to what that might be.

"Of course."

One of the medics was crouching over Brady. He seemed oblivious to his surroundings now, staring into space with a vacant look, a strand of drool dangling from his chin.

"You should tell that man to be careful," I said. "He's still—"

Without moving his head an inch, Brady's left hand whipped out and seized the medic by his neck. His right slithered into the open black doctor's bag. It all happened almost too fast to follow. But then I saw the flash of a scalpel.

In one hard motion, Brady slit his own throat.

He fell back gurgling. The medic shouted in horror, struggling to free himself as Brady clung on with a death grip.

"Get him off, get him off!"

A wall of blue uniforms surged around the thrashing pair, shutting off my view of Brady's last gruesome moments.

And then the sergeant took me firmly by the arm and dragged me to the hole, which had been widened into a rough arch. "Get her out of here," he said to the officers stationed in the basement storeroom beyond. They nodded and walked me up several flights of stairs to the street.

Police wagons jammed the corner of Broadway and Warren. I stood there for a moment in a daze. The moon hung low in the sky, but it was only half full now. Not a Hunter's moon anymore. Then someone called my name.

I turned just as Connor came hurtling into me. We clung to each other, his face pressed tight against my shirt.

"They wouldn't let me go down there," he mumbled. "Billy?"

"Billy's fine," I said, trying hard not to cry. "I just hope John will be too. Have you seen him? They brought him up a minute ago."

We caught the ambulance as it was about to pull away. It looked like Brady's body was being taken out of the tunnel, for the police milling around on the street all started gawking at a white-sheeted form on a stretcher.

"Please, let me ride with him," I begged the driver. "I'm his... sister."

"Get in then," he said brusquely. "He's lost a lot of blood."

I jumped into the back, where John lay pale and still.

"Hey! Connor!" Billy waved at us from the curb.

"You go," I said. "It's all right."

Connor ran off, a glad smile on his face, and we raced through the night to New York Hospital.

"I'm sorry I shot you," I whispered to John. "But you can't go punishing me by dying. It's not fair." The tears did come then, hot and wracking. I was wiping them away when John's eyes opened.

"Did they get him?" he asked weakly.

"Yes. They got him."

John closed his eyes again. I thought he'd passed out but then he spoke.

"You shot me."

"I know. I didn't mean to."

"That means you owe me."

"Actually, we both owe James Moran. He saved us from Brady." It was a debt I didn't care to contemplate.

"Moran?" He gave a goofy smile and I wondered if they'd given him a shot of morphine. "I don't think I want a kiss from James Moran. I'm not fond of beard stubble."

I stared down at him, shaking my head. Even at death's door, John couldn't manage to be serious.

"Come on, Harry." He puckered his lips, eyes still shut. "Let's have it."

I leaned over and gave him a kiss on the forehead, right between the eyebrows.

"How's that?"

"I suppose it'll have to do," he sighed.

Then he did pass out.

Dawn was breaking when we finally arrived at the hospital. The attendants whisked John inside and left me in the waiting room, where a pair of irate policemen found me a few minutes later. They took my statement right there. I told the truth, except for the bit about Moran. I said I was the one who'd shot Brady. One good turn deserved another.

They questioned me for nearly an hour, but in the end, they seemed satisfied. A single gun—Myrtle's—was found at the scene. Brady was dead, and I had a feeling no one particularly cared to make sure the bullets matched. The main thing is that Mr. Hyde would no longer terrorize New York City. And the Police Department had carried out a heroic rescue of three potential victims. The newspapers would love it.

I slumped down in my seat as Judge Weston, Mrs. Weston and the rest of John's tribe came rushing into the waiting room, grim-faced and peppering me with questions until John's mother could see I was on the verge of tears. She swept me into her arms and sharply ordered them to be quiet.

"Can't you see the poor thing is dead on her feet?" she said.

Mrs. Weston had John's brown eyes, although her hair was strawberry blonde, like Rupert.

"I'm the one who shot him," I confessed in a hollow voice. "It's all my fault."

Mrs. Weston held me tighter, although she was crying a little too. "Well, it wasn't on purpose." She paused. "Was it?"

"No! I was aiming for Brady."

"That's the man who committed all those terrible killings?"

"Yes."

She shook her head and muttered something about foolish children, but she kept her arms around me and stroked my hair. The judge had gone off to harangue the nurses for an update on John's condition. His four brothers—Paul, Andy, Rupert and Bill—silently paced up and down. It was the first time I had seen them together without laughter or arguing or general mayhem. The minutes ticked by.

Then the surgeon came out and told us that the bullet had

been extracted. It missed John's heart by two inches, his left lung by one. They'd decided to opt for a risky procedure called a transfusion, but it appeared to have worked. John's pulse and blood pressure were no longer falling. It had been a very close thing. But he was young and fit. They expected him to recover.

I wanted to see him. They told me I had to come back tomorrow, that visiting hours began at ten a.m. and only immediate family would be permitted in his room. I said I'd wait. But then Edward arrived and ordered me to go home.

"I'll stay here, Harry," he said stoutly. "If anything changes, I'll get you straightaway. But you're no good to anyone in this state. Go eat something." He eyed me up and down. "You might want to put on clean clothes as well."

"Alright," I said, not moving.

He scooted over on the bench and put an arm around my shoulders. "You stopped him," he said. "That's what matters. Although I still can't believe it was Mr. Brady! My money was definitely on George." Edward seemed slightly disappointed. Then his face brightened. "Though I must thank you for introducing me to Virgil the Goat. The boy is extraordinary! He taught me how to palm a card so discreetly I don't think even John Chamberlain's dealers would detect it. I'm considering taking him into my employment. Just for parties, of course."

Edward walked me to the front doors and shooed me out.

"I'll see you in a few hours," he said. "And congratulations, Harry."

It was over.

Sort of.

The hospital was on Fifteenth Street and Fifth Avenue, so I declined Edward's offer of a ride and walked the few blocks home. It was the peak of the morning rush hour. I looked such an absolute fright that even my fellow New Yorkers, who made a habit of being unfazed by anything the great metropolis threw at them, gave me a wide berth.

I hardly noticed. My brain swam with conflicting emotions—horror, guilt, relief, triumph. As I turned the corner on Tenth Street, I thought about this city. How all the bustle and money and flash and bright new electric lights hid other secret places. Dark places that were just a rabbit hole away. The poor souls who'd tumbled down there, never to emerge again.

We'd closed one of those holes, sealed it tight, but others would open in its place.

Mrs. Rivers threw the front door open and hugged me hard. Then she stepped back.

"You can tell me all about it later," she said. "Good luck, Harry."

I looked at the table next to the door. A small black hat with a blue ribbon had been tossed carelessly on top of yesterday's mail.

I went slowly into the kitchen.

A severe-looking young woman sat in one of the ladder-back chairs. She had long raven hair and grey eyes that seemed to look right through you.

"Hello, Myrtle," I said.

My sister just examined me in her entomologist way. As though she were deciding whether to pin me to her board or release me into the wild.

I got ready to run.

And then…

Then Myrtle began to laugh.

CHAPTER NINETEEN

Saturday, October 20th

COLD RAIN PELTED the windows of the parlor. Autumn had arrived with a vengeance, as it tended to do this time of year. October in New York often debuted with the feel of an Indian summer, but as Halloween approached, the temperature would suddenly drop and blustery winds would sweep in from the north, creating little tornadoes that sent newspapers flying and filled your mouth with grit if you got caught in one.

The rain started two days ago and hadn't let up since. I didn't really mind. It was cozy in the upstairs parlor. Mrs. Rivers had baked a batch of oatmeal cookies, of which only a plate of crumbs remained. The steady downpour drummed against the panes as I wiggled my toes under an afghan.

John sat in his usual place, perusing a nasty textbook on skin diseases. His left arm was still in a sling, but he'd learned to manage well enough with his right and the doctors promised it would be off within the month. Connor lay by the fire, chin propped in his hands. John seemed to be inspiring the boy to greater things, although his choice of reading material wasn't exactly scientific: something called *Risen from the Dead: Episode One, The Medical Student.*

I was busy putting the final touches on my report to the S.P.R. Uncle Arthur had promised to submit it for me, and I was almost done.

We'd learned a few things since the events in the Beach Pneumatic Transit Tunnel. A watchman at Brady's Maiden Lane office saw him leave on the nights of the murders (all save Anne Marlowe's, when he crept out of his own home). Despite the heat, Brady wore a long overcoat which the man thought strange. He was also seen lighting a cigarette, although he had never smoked before. The coat no doubt covered the soldier's uniform he had taken from Straker's flat. Detective Mallory confirmed that Brady's boots matched a set of prints found next to Anne's body at the grain elevator.

Brady had sent his wife to her parents' house so he would have free rein to roam the city.

We would never know what he told his victims, but I think he used the uniform to gain a degree of trust that allowed him to cull them from the herd. To get them alone.

I also learned from Rose Mason that the manager of the Grand Hotel in Cassadaga Lake had been arrested about three weeks after our visit for adding a mild hallucinogen to the food of his patrons. It seems the man believed it would enhance the Spiritualist reputation of the place and bring in customers. I immediately thought of the picnic lunch we'd eaten on the shores of the lake just before the séance.

Upon hearing this news, Mrs. Rivers confessed that she *might* have been a tad influenced by Connor's confiscated magazines, one of which was about a journey into the fires of hell. She *might* have pushed the planchette just a bit. She couldn't really be sure.

I saw James Moran once. On the campus of Columbia, where I'd gone to have lunch with John. He tipped his hat to me from across the street. I knew he'd never forget that I owed him one, but I figured that between me and Myrtle, one of us would put him behind bars one day. I'd told my sister everything except for the part Moran played. Only John and I knew about that. I had a strong feeling it would push Myrtle—who'd thus far been remarkably tolerant of our escapades—right over the edge.

As for the *Black Pullet* grimoire… Well, on September third, I'd received an invitation for tea with Mrs. Temple Kane. It was not a pleasant experience. She informed me that the book had been burned—which I had to take her word for, of course—and more or less threatened the entire Fearing Pell clan with financial and social ruin if I ever came near George again. I told her that I wanted nothing to do with her loathsome offspring, which was the truth, although I did privately wonder what gentleman at his club he'd obtained it from. And exactly when and how George had gotten the grimoire back from Becky. From his talk of "all that blood," I could only assume he had seen the crime scene. He must have visited her later that night or the next day to find out how his "experiment" had gone, and discovered her body.

George Kane didn't even have the decency to notify the authorities. He just left his former lover there to rot, until a neighbor smelled her.

I said those exact words to Mrs. Kane, at which point our interview ended abruptly.

What else? Connor and the Butchers finally tracked down the stock broker who had lost Straker's money. His name was Gerald Forrest and he'd been serving time at Auburn prison for fraud for the last five months.

As for the elusive Robert Aaron Straker himself...

I sat up at a knock on the parlor door.

"Come in," I called.

He was leaning on a cane, Elizabeth Brady holding his good arm. Moran's thugs had broken his leg and would have done worse if four members of a rival gang hadn't come along and been outraged that their turf was being invaded. A melee had ensued, allowing Straker to hobble away unnoticed. He'd ended up in Bellevue, where detectives found him a day later, raving and incoherent.

"Miss Pell," he said softly. He turned to John. "You must be Doctor Weston. And... "

"Connor," Connor said. "I'm a free-lance consultant."

Straker smiled. He was still handsome, although his eyes were lined and white streaked the dark hair at his temples.

"I'm glad you could come," I said warmly. "Please sit down."

"They let me go this morning," Straker said, taking a chair by the fire and resting his cane against the mantel. "We won't stay long. We're catching a train to Hastings in an hour."

Elizabeth hovered protectively behind him. She too had lost weight, although her fingernails were no longer chewed to the quick.

I knew that Elizabeth had paid for the private sanatorium Straker had been recovering in for the last two months.

"You look well," I said.

"Yes." Straker laughed awkwardly. "They say it was a case of nervous prostration. After the things I saw... " He trailed off.

"I was hoping you might be able to tell us a bit about that," I said. "If you're able."

"It's all right. I've done it enough before, with the doctors and the police. It gets easier. In fact, they say it's good for me. To talk about it."

"Did you actually witness… ?" John ventured.

"Brady killing her?" Straker finished. "Not the act itself, no. But I had a bad feeling when Leland left me. A premonition of danger. We were both shaken up after Becky sacrificed that rooster, but Leland more so. He looked strange, pale and ill. I couldn't sleep so I walked the streets for a bit. Then I thought that I'd go to the Bottle Alley Saloon for a quick drink." He grimaced. "I was drinking quite a lot then. It was the only thing that gave me solace from my miserable existence. I was about to go down the stairs when I saw that Becky's light was still on. I had the sudden thought that she might join me. I didn't care to be alone. So I entered her building. Fat Kitty owns the whole place and sometimes forgets to lock the front door. Pickles usually watches things for her." He stopped and took a deep breath. "I knew something was wrong the moment I got to Becky's flat on the second floor. Her door was ajar. And I heard noises coming from inside. A wet, slurping sound."

Connor's eyes had grown wide as saucers. I regretted letting him stay, but I knew he wouldn't leave now if the house was on fire.

"My chest tightened with a kind of nameless dread. I peeked through the crack. Leland… well, he was on all fours. It took me a moment to realize that it was Becky lying there next to him. She was… suffice to say, she didn't look human anymore. But neither did Leland. He'd removed his clothing and he was… well, he was lapping at her blood like a cat with a dish of milk. I think my mind fractured at that moment. I felt I couldn't move. Couldn't breathe. The doctors say I'd already been under a mental strain and the sight of it just…

broke me. I must have made a small noise, because Leland turned. He looked me right in the eye. And he smiled. An awful scarlet grin. So I did the only thing I was capable of at that moment. I ran."

"Anyone would have," Elizabeth said quietly.

"No!" Straker said forcefully. "I was weak. A coward. If I'd just confronted him then, I could have prevented him from killing all those others."

"If you'd confronted him then, he would have killed you too," Elizabeth said.

"I could still have gone to the police with what I knew," Straker said. "But I wasn't thinking. I was so frightened of him. His eyes, when he saw me through the crack. They looked *black*. I know now that it was a trick of my fevered mind, that's what the doctors say, but after the séance, all that talk of demons… I feared that Robert had been possessed somehow. I only wanted to hide from him."

"He described a foul wind," John said. "That he closed his eyes against it."

"I don't recall that," Straker said, frowning. "But the rest was bad enough. Anyway, I staggered into a flophouse on the Bowery and stayed there until a boy found me several days later."

"Billy Finn," I said. "I sent him to look for you."

This part I knew from Billy himself.

"Yes, I saw him watching me and grabbed him. I feared he had been sent by Leland. He confessed that he'd been offered a reward if he revealed my whereabouts. I begged him to keep it a secret, but I had no money to offer. I finally told him what I'd seen. I gave him Brady's name and asked him to relay it to you, Miss Pell."

"Yes. Well, it seems Billy had other grand plans," I said,

still aggravated with the boy. "He decided that my reward was a paltry sum compared to the money he could make if he blackmailed Mr. Brady. So he found out where his office was and confronted him outside. Not surprisingly, it didn't go as Billy had planned. Instead of getting rich, he nearly got himself killed."

"Billy always did have gumption," Connor said, laying another log on the fire.

"I don't know that I'd call it gumption," I said. "More like sheer idiocy. Brady was delighted to discover where you were hiding. He forced Billy into the Beach tunnel and kept him a hostage there, in case he needed him to send a message. But in the end, he decided that he couldn't trust Billy not to run at the first chance he got. So he left it for you himself, along with the uniform, once he'd ascertained that we'd be conducting a search for the Hunter that night. Brady was very clever. He timed it perfectly so we'd encounter you on the Third Avenue Elevated at the appointed hour."

"It's why she let him choose the line," John said. "She knew what he was up to. Though she could have mentioned that fact to the rest of us."

This was still a sore point.

"I truly believed the note was from Elizabeth," Straker said. "I'd thought of her so many times. Once I even took a train up to Hastings to tell her everything and bring her someplace safe, but she was already gone to her parents. When I saw that letter, saying she was afraid… Well, despite my own terror of Leland, nothing could have stopped me from meeting her."

Elizabeth laid a hand on his shoulder and it was evident they cared for each other as deeply as a brother and sister. I hoped that after all they had been through, they might find happiness one day, someplace far from New York City.

"I think that explains everything," I said. "I'm very grateful that you both came today."

"Well, not *everything*," John interjected. "There's still the question of *why*. Why a perfectly ordinary man would suddenly start killing people, even if he did suffer from multiple personality disorder. It makes no sense. Unless he was ... "

"Possessed?" Elizabeth said sadly. "That's apparently what my husband believed. I found a letter from him a few days ago. He'd placed it in the pocket of a coat I only wear when the weather turns, which I didn't have occasion to do until this storm blew in. The police must have overlooked it when they searched the house."

She took out a single sheet of paper. "I don't wish to read it again now, Miss Pell, but I'll give it to you. Maybe it will help you understand him better. I don't want to keep it." She set it on the mantle. "He was quite mad. I keep wondering how I could have missed the signs. I'll admit I was disturbed when I found him in the garden that night. It was just after I came to see you, Miss Pell, when you'd asked me if Robert had suffered from lost time. I found Leland missing from our bed so I searched the house, but he wasn't there. Then I happened to glance out the window. He was standing in the rain, his eyes wide and staring at nothing. But even then I didn't believe... *couldn't* believe. After all the nightmares, I assumed he'd been sleepwalking. I spoke to him firmly and took his hand and he seemed to come back to himself." Elizabeth's face tightened in pain, as though she'd been struck a physical blow. "When I read your cable, I couldn't deceive myself anymore. I felt so sickened. To think that we lived under the same roof while… " She shook her head. "It's over now, and I'm trying to put the past behind me."

"Actually, I just received something that I think sheds light on *why*," I said. "Your husband's autopsy report. I saw a copy this morning."

Nellie had brought it over. She was in a frenzy of logistical planning, having just read Jules Verne's *Around the World in Eighty Days* and hit on the crazy idea that she could beat Phileas Fogg's record. Her editors at *The World* agreed to bankroll the trip. I'd never seen her so excited. But dear Nellie had taken the time to stop by Tenth Street, knowing I'd be eager for the results.

I could tell from John's expression that he was irritated I'd kept this tidbit to myself, but I thought Elizabeth should be told first.

"I didn't know… " Her face was pale. "What does it say?"

"Your husband had a brain tumor," I said. "I doubt he was aware of it. It wasn't large, but it pressed on his frontal lobe. There are several case histories of tumors that caused psychosis and extreme aggression. It's rare, but well-documented. I might have guessed it. The last time he came to see me, he said he smelled burning rubber."

"That's a classic sign," John agreed.

"Thank you for telling me, Miss Pell," Elizabeth said slowly. "It does explain things. Would it… would it have been fatal?"

"In the end, yes, most likely," I said, reaching into the pocket of my dress. "And I believe this is yours, Mr. Straker. I thought you'd very much like to have it back."

I handed him the cameo. Straker opened it and looked at the picture of his mother. His eyes grew damp.

"Thank you," he said. "I can't express what this means to me."

Elizabeth helped Straker to his feet and they moved slowly to the door. Then she turned back.

"I nearly forgot. There's still the matter of your fee."

"Yes, as to that… " I squirmed a bit on the couch and John smiled. My punishment for withholding the autopsy results, I supposed.

Thanks to Nellie, my name had been kept out of the papers in relation to the Jekyll and Hyde case. Mulberry Street was more than happy to let the police take all the credit. So my remaining client had no clue that she'd been jigged, as Billy might say.

"I have a bit of a confession to make myself," I said in a rush. "I'm not Myrtle Fearing Pell. She's my older sister. I'm terribly sorry I lied to you. It's just… " How to explain? "It was an impulsive decision," I finished lamely. "So please don't worry about the fee."

Elizabeth looked startled at this revelation, quite understandably, and took a minute to mull it over.

"I do feel foolish," she said at last. "But I don't suppose your motives were ill-intentioned. You found Robert and you stopped Leland, which is pretty impressive in my books. So I think I'd like to pay your fee anyway."

"Oh." I hadn't expected that. "Thank you."

"We can settle it later," she said briskly. "Send a cable."

"I will."

We shook hands and her hazel eyes twinkled. "I'm pleased to have been your first client, Miss Pell. What *is* your first name then?"

"Harry," I said, feeling as though an enormous weight had been lifted.

"Well, I'm pleased to have been your first client, Harry. Try to stay out of trouble."

I heard them laughing softly as they went down the stairs.

"A brain tumor, eh?" John said. "I'd like to see those results myself, if you don't mind."

"Absolutely," I replied with no small degree of satisfaction. "But let's have a look at that letter first. I'll need to add it to my report."

John retrieved it from the mantle and we all gathered round. There was no date.

My dearest Elizabeth, it said. *By the time you read this, I will be gone as I have resolved to take my own life rather than exist with the thing I have become. The thing that lives in me. Always whispering, urging. It says terrible things, my darling. Awful things. I don't wish to speak of them, not to you, but I grow weary of fighting. The struggle is constant now.*

I have made a will, leaving you everything. Our attorney has a copy and he'll see to its execution. It's not much, I know, but I hope it is enough to keep you for a little while.

I don't expect your forgiveness, but I pray you will remember me as I used to be and not the nauseating creature I am now.

It was signed *"From Hell."*

"Too bad he didn't go through with it earlier," John muttered in disgust. "Would have saved us the trouble... Connor? Are you all right?"

Connor stared at us. He looked agitated. "Ain't you seen the papers?" he asked.

"Not in a few days," John said. "I've been studying for an exam, and Harry's had her nose buried in that report. Why?"

"Well, I suppose you've at least heard of the Ripper case in London," Connor demanded.

"Of course," I said.

The news was everywhere. First they'd called him Leather Apron, but now they were calling him Jack. He'd killed four women, horribly, and sent taunting letters to the police. I knew Connor had been following the case, but I personally couldn't stomach thinking about another maniac at the moment so I'd absorbed only the basic details.

"George Lusk, he's the chairman of the Whitechapel Vigilance Committee," Connor said. "He got a letter too. Four days ago. It came with a box that had half a human kidney inside. Look, they reprinted it."

Connor grabbed a copy of *The Tribune* and held it out.

It said:

Mr Lusk

Sor

I send you half the

Kidne I took from one women

prasarved it for you tother pirce

I fried and ate it was very nise I

may send you the bloody knif that

took it out if you only wate a whil

longer.

signed

Catch me when

you Can

Mishter Lusk.

At the very top of the letter were two words. *From Hell.*

I tossed the paper aside.

"And your point is?" I asked briskly.

"Brady wrote his letter back in early August. Before the Ripper struck. Don't you think it's strange?" Connor asked.

"A coincidence," I said with a shrug.

"I thought you didn't believe in coincidences," John said.

"I do when there's literally no other explanation. When all else is eliminated… you know what Myrtle says."

"But there *is* another explanation," he insisted. "Don't you remember what Father Bruno told us? That some demons can leave their hosts and enter another body?"

I threw my hands up. "Not that again. Really, John."

"What if whatever was inside Brady knew he was going to die? What if it jumped into someone else?"

"Like who?" Connor asked breathlessly.

"Like that police doctor whose scalpel Brady used to kill himself." He looked at me. "Didn't you say that Brady was holding onto him, that he wouldn't let go, even with his throat slashed ear to ear?"

"I'm finishing my report," I said, returning to the toasty afghan. "You two can hash out your lunatic theories all day if you like."

"I'll do better!" John jumped to his feet. "Come on, Connor. We'll conduct our own investigation."

"You're actually going out in that?" I pointed to the window, where horizontal sheets of rain battered the glass.

"You're wrong, Harry." John gave me his serious look,

the one he usually reserved for church and funerals. "And we're going to prove it."

"Good luck," I murmured, picking up my fountain pen.

John was like a dog with a bone sometimes. His shoulder...

"And you're supposed to be convalescing!" I yelled as they pelted down the stairs.

It was several hours before they returned. I was just writing up the bit about the supposed fingerprints burned into Anne Marlowe's throat (which I'll admit troubled me, since no such brand was ever found in the tunnel or at Brady's home) when John and Connor burst through the door.

"You're dripping on me, get away!" I complained.

"His name is Dr. William Clarence," John said. He was soaked through but didn't seem to notice it.

"Did you ask him if he's possessed by the ghost of Leland Brady? Or wait, it's not ghosts, it's demons, is that the correct terminology?"

"I couldn't ask him," John said. "He quit his post the day after Brady's suicide and took a ship to England. I found Sergeant Mallory. He told me."

"Dr. Clarence was probably upset by what he'd witnessed," I said. "So he went on holiday."

"Look at the timeline, Harry! Brady died on Thursday, August 16th. You figure ten or so days for the Transatlantic crossing. That places him in London just before the first Ripper murder on August 31st. It all fits."

I sighed. "What do you want me to do, John?"

"I want you to put it in your report."

"This is insane."

"Please. Just put it in the report."

So I did. Three lines, at the end.

*In an odd and doubtless insignificant coincidence,
Leland Brady used the very same expression (From
Hell) as that contained in a letter to Mr. George Lusk
of the Whitechapel Vigilance Committee, unsigned but
assumed by Scotland Yard to be from the Ripper. The
only (extremely tenuous) connection between the Hyde
and Ripper cases appears to be that the doctor who
attempted to treat Mr. Brady for his gunshot wound
travelled to London in late August. For the record, his
name is William Clarence.*

Yours,

Harrison Fearing Pell

EPILOGUE

I SENT OFF my report to Uncle Arthur. Two weeks later, he cabled acknowledging receipt and congratulating me on the case. I waited anxiously for more. Some response from the S.P.R. There was none. The days shortened. I grew listless, depressed. Myrtle was gone again, hunting a jewel thief in Paris. I watched her pack her little black beret and felt like setting fire to something.

Elizabeth Brady sent me a generous check, which I used to pay the hospital bill of the woman Brady had attacked in the park. I had just enough left over to treat Nellie, John and Edward to dinner at the Hotel Windsor.

Nellie had written a long, impassioned story about the poor woman and the plight of the city's ragpickers, who eked out a living sorting through rubbish for bits of glass or cloth to sell to the mills. She'd convinced Pulitzer to start a fund and donations poured in from kind-hearted readers. Not to be outdone, *The Tribune* made an appeal for the Forsizi family, and *The Sun* and *New York Times* joined in to raise money for the relatives of Brady's last two victims. Not surprisingly, it quickly became a cutthroat competition among the city's presses, with new tallies printed daily.

Rose Mason sent me a brief note of thanks. She and Samuel were the proud parents of an infant girl. They had named her Rebecca.

There was one final Ripper killing, on November 9th. Then he seemed to stop. No one knew why.

It was now Christmas Eve. John always spent it with his family. My parents had hoped to be home for the holidays, but a winter storm trapped them in the Canary Islands. I missed them very much.

Connor, Billy, Mrs. Rivers and I were having a vicious game of whist in the kitchen when a knock came on the front door. My housekeeper went to rise but I knew her rheumatism got bad with the winter weather.

"I'll get it," I said, wondering who could be visiting so late.

It was a messenger boy.

"Miss Pell?" he asked, shivering a bit in the cold.

"Myrtle's not home," I said automatically. "You'll have to track her down in Paris."

He glanced at the envelope in his hands. "I'm looking for Harrison Fearing Pell," he said.

"Oh. Oh! That's me!" I grabbed the letter. "Do you want to come in and warm up for a minute?"

"Sure!" His young face brightened.

We came into the kitchen and Mrs. Rivers poured him a cup of hot chocolate.

"What's it say?" Connor asked, coming to look over my shoulder.

I read the letter aloud with mounting excitement.

It was written on rich creamy stationery, embossed with the words *Society for Psychical Research, North American Division, 253 Pearl Street, New York, New York.*

Dear Miss Pell,

Your report on the Hyde case was recently forwarded to my attention. Our colleagues in London wish me to inform you that the subject you mentioned has been located and no longer poses a threat. I also wish to personally commend you for a most thorough and admirable investigation. You appear to have a keen mind, even if your professional training is somewhat lacking.

Let me get to the point. One of our best agents just transferred to another division and a matter has arisen that requires immediate action. It has certain inexplicable elements of interest to our organization, and perhaps of interest to you. If you are available to discuss this matter at our offices tomorrow morning, I would be most obliged. You may send your answer with my messenger.

Yours,

Mr. Harland Kaylock

Vice President, S.P.R.

"Tomorrow's Christmas!" Mrs. Rivers said. "What sort of person works on Christmas?"

"I don't know," I said, dancing gleefully around the kitchen as the messenger boy looked at me like I'd lost my mind. "But I plan to find out!"

I composed a quick response saying I would come at nine with my associate, Mr. John Weston, who had played an indispensable role in the Hyde investigation and had extensive knowledge of the occult.

And so it was that on the morning of December 25th, 1888, John and I stood on the corner of Pearl and Fulton Streets. A light snow had fallen overnight. It made the cobblestones slippery for walking, but I always liked how clean the city looked clad in fresh snow—for the first hour at least, before all the carriage wheels churned it into a brown, mushy mess.

As it was Christmas Day, the streets were empty.

"I told you he was the Ripper," John said again. He'd been insufferable ever since I'd shown him the letter. "*The subject you mentioned has been located.* What else could it mean?"

"I've no idea," I said. "But you're jumping to conclusions. As usual."

He smiled magnanimously. "Why don't we just agree that we were *both* right? You figured out that it was Brady, and I figured out that Dr. Clarence was a homicidal killer."

"No."

"Yes, I think so. Didn't Edward say that medium you went to... what was his name?"

"Mr. Dawbarn," I said stonily.

"Mr. Dawbarn! Didn't he say something *unclean* had touched Straker's cameo? Well, guess who else you handed it to at the flat? Oh right, that was *Brady*."

I scooped up a handful of snow and threw it at him.

John ducked away, laughing. "You just can't stand the fact that I figured out something you didn't."

"I think you might benefit from a few weeks at that sanatorium Straker stayed at," I said.

John rubbed his hands together, breath puffing white in the crisp air.

"Where is number 253 anyway?" he said, looking around.

In front of us sat the Pearl Street power station. Edison had purchased adjoining buildings at 255 and 257 for his great experiment. They were four-story brick structures with three tall smokestacks. I was surprised at how quiet the engines and whirring dynamos inside were.

We walked down the block to a decrepit looking tenement just next door.

"This must be it," John said dubiously.

There was no plaque, nothing to signify that we were in the right place, except for the crooked number on the front door.

I knocked. We heard the slow shuffle of feet, the click of numerous locks tumbling open, and an ancient man in a butler's uniform poked his head out.

"Um, Merry Christmas," John said. "Sorry to trouble you. We have an appointment—"

"This way, sir," the man intoned. "Mr. Kaylock is expecting you."

We stepped inside. John and I exchanged a startled look. The building's drab exterior gave no hint of the lavish furnishings and fine art that decorated the inside. A fire roared in an enormous hearth, and the space seemed much *larger* than the structure should be able to accommodate, like its dimensions had expanded somehow.

"Please follow me," the butler croaked.

We went up two flights of stairs and down a long hallway, to the fourth door on the left. John and I followed him into a panelled study, our boots sinking into overlapping Persian carpets.

"Shall I bring coffee, sir?"

This was directed at a tall, gaunt man sitting behind a mahogany desk.

"No, just leave us, Joseph," he said brusquely.

"Very good, sir."

Joseph retreated, breath wheezing with each ponderous step.

We sized each other up.

Mr. Harland Kaylock looked much as I remembered him from that day I'd shadowed him around. He had a sharp beak of a nose and thin lips that he held drawn into a straight line. His attire was dark and formal. The only undisciplined thing about him was his hair, which he wore in a wavy tangle that swept back from his pale forehead.

Mr. Kaylock gestured to a pair of wing chairs in front of the desk with long, fluttery fingers.

"Please sit," he said.

We did. A clock ticked. It was very loud. I started to feel a bit like the jittery narrator of Poe's *Tell-Tale Heart*.

My eyes wandered to a pair of tall glass cabinets flanking the windows, and the array of strange objects displayed inside. A milky eye floated in goo, of average size but sporting three golden irises. On the shelf above it perched a shrunken head, the tiny horns serrated like shark's teeth...

"Well then, Merry Christmas!" John ventured, flashing his dimples.

Mr. Kaylock eyed him in distaste. "I don't celebrate holidays. They're an excuse to be lazy. Now. I presume you are Mr. Weston and *you*—" he looked at me with keen eyes—"are Miss Harrison Fearing Pell."

I nodded. Don't mess this up, Harry, I thought. He's an odd one all right, but you didn't really expect different. Just play along.

"I'm sure you're familiar with the London S.P.R., so you know that their primary focus is psychical phenomena," Mr. Kaylock said. "Spiritualism, ghosts, that sort of thing. The

American branch… well, our interests are more wide-ranging, one might say. But before we go any further, I'll have to ask you to sign some documents. This is an extremely sensitive matter and I can't have you running off and blabbing about it. Is that acceptable?"

"I wasn't planning to *blab* about it," I said, trying to keep my temper in check. "But I suppose it's fine."

Mr. Kaylock slid a thick sheaf of papers towards us. I took them and started scanning the tiny print.

… both during and after contact with the Organization, Agent will not disclose or deliver to anyone, whether employed by the Organization or not, except as authorized by the Organization, or use in any way other than in the Organization's business, any information or material… There is a risk of danger, bodily harm, injury, emotional distress, or death… there is the potential for risks and dangers that may not be obvious or reasonably foreseeable at this time… I do not have any medical ailments, physical limitations, or mental afflictions that will affect my ability to… Organization undertakes no direct legal or financial responsibility for my personal safety or well being when I am participating in… I assume the risks, including, but not limited to, those outlined in Section 3 of this agreement… In the event that any one or more of the provisions of this agreement shall be held to be invalid, illegal, unenforceable or in conflict with the law according to the jurisdiction of the state of New York, the remaining portions will not be invalidated, and shall remain in full force and effect…

Mr. Kaylock gave us a thin smile and slid a fountain pen across the desk.

"Perfectly standard," he said.

"And if we don't sign it?" John asked.

"Then I wish you a pleasant morning," Mr. Kaylock said.

I let out a sigh and signed it. John shot me his *Oh, Harry, what are you getting us into now?* look, but he took the pen and scrawled his name next to mine at the bottom.

"Excellent!" Mr. Kaylock said, snatching up the papers and shoving them into a drawer, which he locked.

"Don't we get a copy?" I asked.

"Of course," he said smoothly. "I'll send it over with my messenger boy." He steepled his long fingers. "Now, we get to the heart of the matter. Perhaps you've heard of the Egypt Exploration Society?"

"Vaguely." In fact, I hadn't a clue, but wasn't about to admit it to my new employer.

"It's been around for about six years now," he said. "Bunch of archaeologists based in London. In any event, they were recently involved in a joint expedition with the American Museum of Natural History. A dig in Alexandria. It turned up several quite valuable items that were acquired by the museum."

"Like what?" John asked politely, stifling a yawn with the back of his hand.

"I'm sorry, am I boring you, Mr. Weston?"

"Not at all." John sat up a little straighter.

"Please go on," I said.

"The find included items believed to belong to Claudius Ptolemy."

"The mathematician?"

"Precisely. An armillary sphere as described in the *Syntaxis*, for example."

"That must be quite a coup for the museum," I said.

"Indeed. The expedition returned almost five months ago, but it took time to properly catalogue the new acquisitions.

Therefore, the gala to celebrate the opening of the special collection only took place last night."

We nodded, waiting for him to explain why the S.P.R.
was interested.

"Dr. Julius Sabilline led the expedition to Alexandria.
Educated at Harvard and Oxford, degrees in art history, lin-
guistics and archaeology, et cetera. One of the museum's
brightest lights."

"Was this light... snuffed out?" I guessed from his fune-
real tone.

Mr. Kaylock gave me an appraising look. Then he
unlocked his desk and removed two sheets of paper, sliding
them across to us. "A copy of the police report. It was just after
midnight and the party had wound down. Only a few guests
remained. Dr. Sabelline excused himself and went to his office
to fetch something."

I took the pages and scanned them, then gave them to
John. "Stabbed in the neck?"

"Yes, but with a murder weapon no one has seen before."

"In *New York*?" John raised an eyebrow.

"Apparently so." I thought I detected a glint of humor
in Mr. Kaylock's dark eyes but his face remained stern as a
schoolmaster. "That is not the most inexplicable thing about
the death, however. The door was locked from the inside."

"Windows?"

"There are none." Mr. Kaylock tapped his fingers on the
desk. "And here's the best part. Dr. Sabelline staggered across
the room, bleeding profusely. He collapsed near a bookcase.
There are footprints approaching and entering the pool of
blood, but not leaving it."

"That's odd," John ventured.

"It's more than odd," Mr. Kaylock said.

"Suicide has been ruled out?" I asked.

"Definitively."

"What do *you* think?"

"That we have rather a mystery on our hands." He gazed at me blandly. Whatever private theories he held, Mr. Kaylock had no intention of sharing them, at least not yet. "Our involvement has been requested. Informally, but at the highest levels. Rumors are already circulating that the objects taken from Alexandria are cursed."

John snickered.

It had to be another killer, didn't it? I thought glumly. *Couldn't be a nice haunting, or vampires, or even a good old-fashioned sewer beast.*

And then I realized that Kaylock hadn't mentioned Myrtle's name. Not once. I decided that I liked him, even if his manner was off-putting.

"Is something the matter, Mr. Weston?"

"No, I'm fine, it's just that Harry here—"

"Would be delighted to take the case," I said, smiling.

Want to find out what happens next? The next book in the Dominion Mysteries series, The Thirteenth Gate, will be released in early 2017. Sign up for my mailing list to be the first to know when it's out! You can scan the QR code below with your smartphone, or visit www.katrossbooks.com.

UPCOMING BOOKS BY KAT ROSS

QUEEN OF CHAOS
FOURTH ELEMENT SERIES #3

Persepolae has fallen.
Karnopolis has burned.

AS THE DARK forces of the Undead sweep across what remains of the empire, Nazafareen must obey the summons of a demon queen to save Darius's father, Victor. Burdened with a power she doesn't understand and can barely control, Nazafareen embarks on a perilous journey through the shadowlands to the House-Behind-the-Veil. But what awaits her there is worse than she ever imagined…

A thousand leagues away, Tijah leads a group of children on a desperate mission to rescue the prisoners at Gorgon-e Gaz, the stronghold where the oldest daēvas are kept. To get there, they must cross the Great Salt Plain, a parched ruin occupied by the armies of the night. A chance encounter adds a ghost from the past to their number. But will they arrive in time to avert a massacre?

And in the House-Behind-the-Veil, Balthazar and the

Prophet Zarathustra discover that they have more in common than meets the eye. But is it enough to redeem the necromancer's bloodstained soul and thwart his mistress's plans?

As a final showdown looms with Queen Neblis, the truth of the daēvas' origins is revealed and three worlds collide in this thrilling conclusion to the Fourth Element series.

http://katrossbooks.com/books.html

Release date: December 2016

THE
THIRTEENTH GATE
(SEQUEL TO THE DAEMONIAC)

WINTER 1888. AT a private asylum in the English countryside, a man suspected of being Jack the Ripper kills an orderly
and flees into the rain-soaked night. His distraught keepers
summon the Lady Vivienne Cumberland—who's interviewed
their patient and isn't so sure he's a man at all. An enigmatic
woman who guards her own secrets closely, Lady Vivienne
knows a high-level demon when she sees one. And this particular creature is the most dangerous she's ever encountered.

As Jack rampages through London, this time targeting
rare book collectors, Lady Vivienne begins to suspect what
he's looking for. And if he finds it, locked doors won't mean
a thing…

Across the Atlantic, an archaeologist is brutally murdered
after a Christmas Eve gala at the American Museum of Natural History. Certain peculiar aspects of the crime attract the
interest of the Society for Psychical Research and its newest
investigator, Harrison Fearing Pell. Is Dr. Julius Sabelline's
death related to his recent dig in Alexandria? Or is the motive
something darker? There's no shortage of suspects: a venal

wife, indifferent son, jealous colleague, conniving boss, and very odd patron named Lord Balthazar, who Harry's certain is not what he seems.

As Harry uncovers troubling connections to a case she thought was definitively solved, two mysteries converge amid the grit and glamor of Gilded Age New York. Harry and Lady Vivienne must join forces to stop an ancient evil. The key is something called the Thirteenth Gate. But where is it? And more importantly, who will find it first?

http://katrossbooks.com/books.html

ABOUT THE AUTHOR

Kat Ross worked as a journalist at the United Nations for ten years before happily falling back into what she likes best: making stuff up. She now lives in Westchester, a quick train ride north of New York City, with her kid and a few sleepy cats. Kat's been a huge fan of Arthur Conan Doyle since she was little, and likes to think he would have a soft spot for Harry.

ALSO BY KAT ROSS

THE MIDNIGHT SEA
FOURTH ELEMENT SERIES #1

They are the light against the darkness.
The steel against the necromancy of the Druj.
And they use demons to hunt demons...

NAZAFAREEN LIVES FOR revenge. A girl of the isolated Four-Legs Clan, all she knows about the King's elite Water Dogs is that they leash wicked creatures called daēvas to protect the empire from the Undead. But when scouts arrive to recruit young people with the gift, she leaps at the chance to join their ranks. To hunt the monsters that killed her sister.

Scarred by grief, she's willing to pay any price, even if it requires linking with a daēva named Darius. Human in body, he's possessed of a terrifying power, one that Nazafareen controls. But the golden cuffs that join them have an unwanted side effect. Each experiences the other's emotions, and human and daēva start to grow dangerously close.

As they pursue a deadly foe across the arid waste of the Great Salt Plain to the glittering capital of Persepolae, unearthing the secrets of Darius's past along the way, Nazafareen is forced to question his slavery—and her own loyalty to the empire. But with an ancient evil stirring in the north, and a young conqueror sweeping in from the west, the fate of an entire civilization may be at stake…

Buy links here: http://katrossbooks.com/books.html

BLOOD OF THE PROPHET

FOURTH ELEMENT SERIES #2

Visionary. Alchemist. Savior. Saint.

THE PROPHET ZARATHUSTRA has been called many things. Now he spends his time drawing pictures of weird-looking goats. That's what happens when you've been stuck in a prison cell for two hundred years. But the man who might be mad, and is definitely supposed to be dead, has suddenly become very valuable again…

It's only been a few weeks since Nazafareen escaped the King's dungeons with her daēva, Darius. She hoped never to set foot in the empire again, but the search for the Prophet has led them to the ancient city of Karnopolis. They have to find him before Alexander of Macydon burns Persepolae, and Darius's mother with it. But they're not the only ones looking.

The necromancer Balthazar has his own plans for the Prophet, and so does the sinister spymaster of the Numerators. As Nazafareen is drawn in to a dangerous game of cat and mouse, her newfound powers take a decidedly dark turn. Only the Prophet understands the secret of her gift, but the price of that knowledge may turn out to be more than Nazafareen is willing to pay...

Buy links here: http://katrossbooks.com/books.html

SOME FINE DAY

A GENERATION AGO, continent-sized storms called hypercanes caused the Earth to flood. The survivors were forced to retreat deep underground and build a new society.

This is the story that sixteen-year-old Jansin Nordqvist has heard all of her life.

Jansin grew up in a civilization far below the Earth's surface. She's spent the last eight years in military intelligence training. So when her parents surprise her with a coveted yet treacherous trip above ground, she's prepared for anything. She's especially thrilled to feel the fresh air, see the sun, and view the wide-open skies and the ocean for herself.

But when raiders attack Jansin's camp and take her prisoner, she is forced to question everything she's been taught. What do her captors want? How will she get back underground? And if she ever does, will she want to stay after learning the truth?

Buy links here: http://katrossbooks.com/books.html

ACKNOWLEDGEMENTS

Special thanks to Jessica Therrien, Simon Wilcox, Eva Thaddeus, Deirdre Stapp, the design team at Damonza and all the wonderful folks at Acorn Publishing. Also to James D. McCabe, Jr. for *Lights and Shadows of New York Life*, which was indispensable to researching this book.